Full shock registered inside her brain as she realized where she'd seen this man. Her body started to quake, and she clutched her hands to her chest.

"No, th...this *cannot be*," she choked out. "Tell me who you are. I demand to know your name!"

Are all the fae so dumb *and* beautiful, he thought. "Ye ken who I am." Stephen's head caught a glimpse of the fae, as she started to take a few hesitant steps backwards. What the bloody hell was wrong with her? She was standing too close to the edge. If she was not careful, she would slip on over.

Why did he care? She could just vanish, right? Stephen rubbed his face, the remnants of a headache still behind his eyes. Sweet Bridget! Now the fae was yelling at him.

She waved her hands, all the time shaking her lovely head. "You are *not* him!"

He had to put a stop to this, or she would fall. Perhaps, she was a *daft* fae. He certainly did not know their ways, nor did he want to find out. However, this creature was becoming more agitated, and for some unfathomable reason, he did not want her to come to any harm.

"Och, fae healer, stop your babbling," he dismounted with a groan.

"No, no, no!" Pointing a finger at him, she continued to walk backwards. Stumbling, her foot twisted among some tree roots, causing her to lose her balance.

Stephen swore as he lunged for her, grasping her arm and crushing her against his chest. "Are ye truly daft?"

Praise for Mary Morgan

"Powerful, intense, romantic.. all great words to describe this fabulous book. I seriously can't wait for the next book!!"

~Tea and Book

~*~

"I am so happy to have read this book and have a new author to add to my list. Watch out for this lady and keep updated on her books. It is so worth it. I mean Dragons, Druids, Fae and Highlanders all in one book. How can you go wrong."

~Kimi's Medieval Blog

~*~

"The author has created a fantastic fantasy world with her own special spin on ancient legends and myth that spins a web and ensnares the reader. The story has some surprising twists and lots of charming characters and takes the reader on a journey to historical Scotland."

~Literary Addicts

Dragon Knight's Medallion

by

Mary Morgan

Order of the Dragon Knights Series
Book 2

Dragon Knight's Medallion

COPYRIGHT © 2014 by Mary Morgan

Cover Art by *Debbie Taylor*

The Wild Rose Press, Inc.
PO Box 708
Adams Basin, NY 14410-0708
Visit us at www.thewildrosepress.com

Publishing History
First Faery Rose Edition, 2014
Print ISBN 978-1-62830-644-6
Digital ISBN 978-1-62830-645-3

Order of the Dragon Knights Series, Book 2
Published in the United States of America

Dedication

For my mother,
who taught me how to fly over the rainbow.

Acknowledgements

I poured my heart and soul into this book (and the first one), which I could not have done without the support of so many people.

Thanks to my children, Noelle, Amanda, and Nicholas. Your words and support mean the world to me. I love you all "to the moon and back"! You kept the faith when I faltered.

A big round of hugs to my "Borders Romance Readers Group." Your excitement, tears of joy and love keep me going. You are my first street team!

Many thanks with love to my sisters, Mimi and Vici, and my big brother, Randy. You have inspired me to become a better person. I may be the oldest, but it doesn't mean I'm the wisest of souls.

Finally, a big thank you to my husband—for listening to my endless story plots, and for showing me how to use Google Earth! Now, I can take a trip to Urquhart and sit at the entrance for inspiration. It's the little things I love about you that make my life complete.

Prologue

They were an ancient order, descended from the great Tuatha De Danann, the Sidhe, or in simpler terms, *the fae*. Half human and half fae, each one blessed with mystical powers. Each warrior given Holy Relics from the Tuatha De Danann and guardianship over their Dragons.

They were known as *Dragon Knights*.

With the dawn of Christianity, the Dragons were systematically hunted down and slain, leaving only one. She was taken from Ireland to a land across the sea, settling in the Great Glen near Urquhart with the MacKay Clan, descendents from the MacAoidh.

Yet, there were those who believed the Order had too much power, and they tried to possess it for themselves. They were evil and twisted, and their plan succeeded one fateful night.

The brothers of the Clan MacKay—*Dragon Knights*, fought a battle. Blood spilled onto holy ground, bringing forth the wrath of the fae. Their relics were taken, the Order banished, and their names stricken from the Hallowed Halls of the fae.

However, not all was lost. For the fae loved these men.

Therefore, a quest for redemption was given to each. Duncan MacKay, the first brother fulfilled his. Now it was time for another sibling to step forward.

This brother will renounce his own heritage, seeking solace behind the walls of an abbey.

Nonetheless, peace will elude him—for danger lurks within the shadows.

In order to confront his future, he must accept his past.

And for Stephen MacKay, the light of redemption and love will come from the very source he seeks to escape.

Chapter One

Arbroath Abbey, Scotland—Spring Equinox 1206

"Lugh's balls!" he roared. The pain seared into his head like a burning spear. Shards of blazing torment pounded in his ears, the agony so intense, he collapsed at the river's edge. Beads of sweat trickled down from his temple as he gasped for air knowing that if he did not regain control, he would black out from the excruciating pain. He realized what would follow, and with every ounce of his being, he tried to block the force attacking him. Another shard of pain lanced through his mind, causing a guttural cry to escape his throat. The power was too strong. His mind screamed at him to let it in, and with a moan of defeat, he did.

The vision slammed into him with a formidable energy, angry that it had been denied access. Layers of colors and images flew across his mind's eye and try as he might, he could not control their flight. Warriors with swords clashed in battle, screams filled his ears. The vision peaked, and he could see himself standing in the center—drenched in blood with the bodies of his fellow monks slain at his feet.

"Nae!" His fists pounded into the riverbank, as he shook with the violence he had witnessed.

Laughter, vile and evil, echoed somewhere in the realm of his vision, and when the last wave of the revelation blurred from his sight, he retched violently onto the ground.

Taking deep gulps of air into his lungs, he slowly returned to his surroundings. He needed to heal quickly, and reached out a trembling hand toward the water. Allowing his instinct to guide him, he drew the water to him. It gently caressed his outstretched hand, and he formed a cup with his fist. Bringing his unsteady hand up to his head, he relished the cool liquid as it washed over him, feeling its healing power descend over and through his body. He understood he took a great risk if anyone came upon him, but if he did not, the consequences would be dire.

As expected, the water helped soothe the raging pain still centered behind his eyes. He waited patiently, until the last wisps of the vision left. Taking another deep cleansing breath, he noticed his heart had regained its normal beating. Slowly he opened his eyes. He thanked God for the gray, misty morning. Without it, the sun's light would hurt his sight.

The sound of water lapping gently at the edge of the stream carried a gentle healing power. Bending low, he cupped both hands within the water and lifting them out, watched as the water turned to ice. Taking it, he placed it on the back of his neck to help with the pain.

Sitting back on his haunches, he heard his horse snicker and then nudged him slightly. "Aye, my friend...I'm still among the living," his voice sounding hoarse.

After the last remnants of the ice melted, Stephen MacKay stood on shaky limbs, and his gaze wandered out toward the trees. This vision had nearly destroyed him, and he cursed the power that sent them.

When he and his brothers had been doomed, and their relics stripped that Samhain night, his relic—a stone he wore around his neck—was the only item able to control his visions. He could care less about the pagan item, but it was a powerful tool that worked with his power of sight and water. Without it, the visions had become more intense, almost blinding. Once when he had lost consciousness, he woke lying in his own vomit. If only the Guardian had removed his powers along with his stone. Instead, he was reminded each day his blood flowed with that of the fae.

Bile rose within him. He fought it and taking another cleansing breath of the brisk air, he turned to see Grian, his great warhorse eyeing him warily.

Stephen reached out a hand, and Grian trotted forward. "What would I do without ye?" He heaved a great sigh, and giving a scratch behind the horse's ear, took one last look around before mounting, and then slowly making his way back through the thicket of trees.

As they made their way through pine and oak, Stephen tried to push aside the vision. It was one that foretold the future—a bloody sign for his fellow monks. What did it mean? Why was he the only one left standing? Could he have slain his fellow brothers? He fisted his hands on the pommel. "Nae, it cannae be!" he growled.

Grian reared up at the sound of approaching footsteps. Stephen went for his sword, more on instinct, until he saw it was only Brother Osgar. "God's teeth! Ye ken better than to walk right up to Grian," he bellowed.

"Truly?" Osgar stood out from the large oak, arms

crossed and tucked into his monk's gray robe.

If Stephen did not know better, he would have taken him for a passing druid. He could not fathom wearing the long robes, thinking them too constrictive in movements. No, he favored his leather trews and tunic, which he belted at times with leather.

"Aye, ye ken this horse does not welcome ye, or any of the monks."

"Humph! Pray tell me *why* said beast then accepts the apples I give him?" Osgar cocked his head to the side, eyes narrowed more at Grian than Stephen.

Stephen snorted. "Perhaps he only favors ye, then. Why are ye on this path so early? Did ye sneak out of prayers again?"

The monk chuckled softly. "I could say the same of ye, Stephen, but I ken a part of your soul is tied to another faith, one that is present on the first day of spring."

"Ye ken naught!" The silence between them stretched out. Only a slight breeze flitted past, and dead leaves whirled past Osgar. Even Grian stood motionless, as if waiting for something or someone to break the tension.

Casting his gaze to the sky, Stephen let out a deep sigh, and dismounted. Raking a hand through his hair, he turned his sight back to his friend. "I am...*sorry*, Osgar." He winced as the pain in his temple throbbed. It would be a long day, one now filled with headaches.

"Ye had a vision?" Osgar asked softly.

Stephen's shoulders slumped. He had hoped to keep it from him. "Aye."

"Do ye remember it?"

Brushing past him, Stephen went to sit by an old

oak, taking solace against its vast trunk. "Nae," he muttered. For the first time ever, he lied to his friend. He was not going to divulge the vision until he could study it himself. "Pray tell me ye have food in your pack."

"Dinnae I always?" Osgar stepped over a fallen branch and sat on a small boulder next to Stephen. Placing his pack down, he proceeded to pull out bread, hard cheese, and an ale skin. Grian trotted over to him and nudged his head against Osgar's back, causing a bark of laughter to come forth from the monk.

"Aye, there's something for ye too, my friend." He retrieved an apple out of his pack and pulled forth a dirk from his boot.

Stephen arched a brow and muttered, "Traitor beast."

"A fine one, too," smirked the monk. He tore off a large portion of the bread, handing it to Stephen along with some cheese.

"Since when do ye carry a dirk? I ken none of the other monks carry weapons, so why do ye?" he questioned, taking a bite from the cheese and bread.

Osgar shrugged and removed the stopper from the ale skin, presenting it to Stephen first, who waved it off with his hand. Taking a swig, Osgar wiped his mouth with the back of his hand before answering. "I like to gather herbs for the kitchen, ye ken this. Besides, one can never take for granted what animal they might come upon."

"Ye are indeed the strangest monk I have ever come upon. Ye are not like the others." Stephen reached for the ale skin and drank deeply, relishing the cool liquid.

"Ye are correct my brother, but nor are ye."

He noticed the wary look in Osgar's eyes and briefly closed his. "Nae, I am not like the others," his voice pitched low. When he reopened them, he saw the monk had flinched. No doubt from the shift in the color of his eyes.

"Then we are in accord," said Osgar.

"Humph!"

They broke the rest of their fast in communal silence, allowing the food and drink to nourish and feed their bodies, more so for Stephen who still felt a bit weak.

Once upon a time early mornings were his favorite, and Stephen relished being the first to welcome the first rays of light. Especially on holy days such as this, but those days were gone. He'd tossed them aside when he awoke the day after that bloody night. Not only did he disregard his heritage, but also anything to do with the old ways. He had wandered for months with no clear direction. Then one day he came upon Osgar foraging for herbs. The monk persuaded him to come to the abbey—to take shelter, rest, and nourishment. Osgar also spoke with the other monks, convincing them it would be best if Stephen stay on with them, for however long he needed.

When the first vision came upon him, it was Osgar who stayed at his side, waiting until it passed. With the loss of his relic, the visions had become more violent. He had tried to keep to himself, but Osgar was ever watchful, keeping a keen eye on him and shielding him from the others. Once, a traveler recognized him, spewing vile comments about not only Stephen, but also his brothers, calling them heathens and murderers.

Osgar swayed the others, explaining all were under God's protection, not just a select few. Did not the druids believe in the one God, he had questioned. Stephen smiled inwardly remembering that day. In the end the monks agreed, and welcomed him fully into their community. He would be forever indebted to the wise old man—one who seemed to be more druid than monk. Perhaps he was in his other life.

A blackbird swooped down from a nearby branch, landing close to them. It eyed the men with its black eyes, tilting its head.

"Good morn, my small feathered friend," laughed Osgar. "Looking for some meager crumbs, I suspect." He tossed bits of bread and cheese to the bird, who immediately lunged for the feast.

Standing, he shook out his robes, and more crumbs fell to the ground. "It is time I made my way back to the abbey." He placed a gentle hand on Stephen's shoulder. "Stay, enjoy the morning's light. Besides, the bells of the abbey might not be good for one's head." He tapped his finger lightly on Stephen's skull.

Stephen let out a groan. "Aye, Osgar, ye are correct."

"Seek me out when ye return. I'll mix a brew for your head."

He nodded, watching as the old man wandered off through the trees. Then he glanced back at the blackbird. "I ken why ye are here, and I will only say this once. I am no longer a Knight, nor do I honor the gods and goddesses. This may be the first day of spring, but nothing more. Go tend to a druid and leave me!"

Chapter Two

"When the dragon unfurled its wings, she presented them with acorns, dandelion, dogwood, honeysuckle, jasmine, rose, tansy, and violet, the herbs of spring."

Stephen awoke suddenly, the bitter coldness of the afternoon touching his face. He had fallen into a deep sleep after Osgar departed. Whenever he suffered from a vision, he required rest, and this time was no different. Slowly he eased his eyes open. The sky still held a gray overcast, but now the smell of snow and the sea filled his senses. Though it might be the first day of spring, winter still held a firm grasp on the land.

Rubbing a hand over his slightly bearded face, he stood and nodded silently to Grian. Reaching for his fur cloak, Stephen paused. For a brief moment he longed for his plaid. Why he thought of it now, he could not answer. He had not worn it since he entered the abbey. It lay folded at the bottom of the chest in his room.

A reminder of his past and a life he wanted no part of ever again.

"Time to go my friend, before it snows." He quickly mounted Grian, before pausing to glance back at the river. This vision troubled him greatly, and he would have to ponder its meaning later. The monks were now his family, and he would do everything in his power to protect them. What disturbed him greatly more was the fact he held the bloody sword, as if he had slain them all. Shaking his head to rid the horrific thoughts free, he gave a nudge and mumbled a click for Grian to set out.

Stephen entered the village near the abbey's gates, and into the midst of a great commotion between one of the monks and the young lad, Ian. Brother Timmons was scolding Ian for something to do with a basket, which lay upon the ground. Usually, he stayed far away from the villagers, considering his past and pagan heritage. Yet, when Brother Timmons raised his hand dangerously close to Ian, causing the lad to flinch, he steered Grian over to the ruckus.

"A good day to ye, Brother Timmons and Ian," greeted Stephen, keeping a stern look on Timmons.

"Stephen," replied Brother Timmons, folding his hands within his robe. "Is there something I can do for ye?"

"Nae. I was just passing through and thought I could lend a hand." He kept his expression neutral, but noticed the lad shaking a bit. "Are ye having trouble with your basket, Ian?"

"The basket may be his, but the contents belong to the abbey," hissed the monk.

In one swift move, Stephen dismounted causing Ian to jump backwards. Perhaps his heritage and size frightened the boy. "Step forward, lad. Show me what ye have."

Ian trudged toward the basket and pulled out an apple, presenting it to Stephen. He swallowed before placing it in his outstretched hand. Stephen knelt beside the basket and glanced inside. Tossing the apple into the air, he peered over his shoulder at Brother

Timmons, who now stood hands clenched at his sides. Stephen took a bite, and smiled. "Hmmm, indeed."

"I say ye do not have nearly enough. Let's say we go and fetch some more." He stood and ruffled the lad's hair.

Ian's eyes grew wide, and he glanced quickly to Brother Timmons then back at Stephen. His hands fidgeted, and Stephen understood the lad was probably torn between picking up the basket, gathering more apples, *or* running away.

"Those apples belong to the abbey, and ye have no right letting the boy take them. He stole them from the abbey and not only should he return them, but he should be punished, too," demanded Brother Timmons.

Stephen narrowed his eyes at the man, and then turned back to the lad. "Tell me, Ian, where did ye find these apples?"

"Oh sir, I did not steal them from the abbey. They were lying on the ground by the walls!" he exclaimed.

"All the same, they belong to the abbey, and he and his family are heathens," spat out Brother Timmons.

Stephen held up his hand to silence the monk. "Truly, there is no harm with apples picked from the ground *outside* the abbey? They would have shortly rotted if left there. Do not ye think it best for a family, regardless of their religious beliefs, to benefit from these rather than they rot?"

The monk's face contorted with suppressed fury, and he pointed a finger first at Ian then at Stephen before he stormed off.

"Well, that went verra well." He rubbed his jaw.

The lad stood with a shocked look across his features. Finally, he nodded and lunged at Stephen, embracing him in a big hug. Stunned, he could only return the hug. The simple act of the lad's compassion was too much for him, and a wave of sadness engulfed him.

He missed his family.

"The next time ye need any apples, or anything else, come seek me out. My name is Stephen," he croaked.

The boy stepped back from the embrace, a smile upon his face. "I ken who ye are."

Stephen crossed his arms over his chest and asked, "Truly?"

"Oh sir, ye are the great Dragon Knight. We all ken that," he boasted.

Letting out a big sigh, he bent to retrieve the basket full of apples, handing it over to Ian. Placing a hand on his small shoulder, he shook his head. "Nae, I am just Stephen, lad. I am no longer a Dragon Knight."

Ian just shrugged his shoulders then added, "Once a Dragon Knight, always a Dragon Knight. It is what my father says." Turning, he sauntered away, then halted, and turned. "Thank ye kindly, Sir Stephen. I will always remember this day."

Stephen stood still. Ian's words touched a part of him that had been sealed off for many moons. "God be with ye, young Ian," he whispered.

Upon entering the abbey walls, Stephen went immediately to seek out Brother Osgar. His headache had subsided, but he still felt queasy. The strength of the vision had sapped much from him this time. He gave a nod to several passing brothers, understanding this was their time of silence. Living among them had brought a sense of peace, not that he wanted to join their order, but it allowed him to heal. In the process, he repaid their kindness by helping with the continual building of the abbey. Some of the brothers formed the red sandstone, and the villagers lent their talent, too. He was content to lift and move the stone, for it allowed his body the manual labor he sought.

Then there were times when he would escape the confinement of the abbey walls, sword in hand, to search out a desolate place to wield it in practice. After such days, he would mourn not being in the lists with his brothers.

Walking through the cloisters, he proceeded to stroll through a back gate, which led him down another path. Pushing aside a heavy wooden door, Stephen stepped through to a massive garden, one filled with many herbs and vegetables.

"Ah, Stephen, I have just finished preparing your healing brew," greeted Osgar, as he brushed dirt off his robe. "Spring is here. Just look at the wee flower buds on the lavender."

"Ye could have fooled me with the smell of snow in the air," muttered Stephen.

Osgar tilted his head and smiled. "Aye, but she will come forth."

He narrowed his eyes at the old man, "Osgar, if I did not ken better, I would say ye were a druid."

"Perhaps ye are correct, my son," stated Osgar, giving him a wry smile.

"Nae," Stephen spoke in a shocked whisper.

The monk sighed deeply, and then turned toward his workshop at the back of the garden. Waving his hand for Stephen to follow, he ambled along slowly.

"Bloody hell, Osgar!" Stephen was at his side in

two strides, pulling him around to face him. "I've been here these past ten moons, and ye are just sharing this wisdom about yourself? Ye do realize how I feel about them and their kind!"

Osgar slowly glanced down at where Stephen had his arm in a tight grip. "Please do tell me, Stephen, since ye yourself are one of their *kind*."

He released his hold of Osgar as if his hand was on fire. "I no longer keep company with them," he snapped.

"Aye. Yet, ye are one of them." Osgar eyed him cautiously. The monk moved into the work space and Stephen followed.

Slamming his palm onto a workbench, he fixed his friend with a glare. "There is naught I can do about the blood which flows within my body, but I do have a choice on the path I have chosen."

Osgar picked up a mortar and pestle and gathered some herbs. Placing them within the bowl, he proceeded to grind them. "True, your blood does flow with that of the fae, but tell me this, what is the path ye are on?"

"Humph!" Stephen pushed away from the table. He stood by the small arched window, gazing out at the darkening sky. Did he really know himself? Would he always be doomed to wander the land, unsure of his next step? When he came to the abbey, he prayed for answers to the questions he sought, but with each passing month, uneasiness slipped its fingers within him.

The grinding continued, and then Osgar moved to a small hearth where a pot hung over a fire. Dipping a ladle in, he withdrew some liquid, pouring it into two mugs. Then he tossed in the ground herbs and stirred the contents. Stepping over to Stephen, he held one out. "Drink this. It will help with the aftereffects of your pain."

"This is my fate. To live with the pain." Stephen's gaze returned to Osgar.

Osgar grimaced. "Now ye are playing the martyr, and it does not bode well for ye."

He cocked a brow in response and with a sigh took the mug from Osgar. Swirling the contents, he asked, "Tell me, why would a druid want to join the Tironensian order? Do the other brothers ken who ye are?"

The druid turned monk did not reply immediately. Instead, he sipped slowly from his mug. Turning away, he moved over to the bench and sat down. He sighed deeply, placing his hands on the workbench. His words came forth softly. "I came to the abbey seeking the truth about the one God of the new religion. They say he spoke of love and all were part of his flock."

Intrigued, Stephen came over and sat down across from him. "Aye, I've heard this, too."

"As a druid, we are always learning, and this is why I am here. It remains to be seen if I choose to stay within the fold." He shrugged. "Now, do the others ken?" He chuckled softly, saying, "Aye, some do and accept. There are others like myself here. However, there are a few who do not want us to stay."

"Why dinnae ye say something?" Stephen asked, shocked there were other druids besides his friend.

"Would ye have been accepting of them? Nae, I think ye would have never stayed, and your path led ye here to this abbey for a purpose. A place ye ken is near a huge body of water." Osgar took another sip from his mug.

Stephen's fists clenched as the words resonated. "Then ye understand all of me and my powers? Ye ken of the order of which I was once a part?"

"Aye, and ye are still a part of the order."

"Nae!" he roared.

The water in the pot burst forth, splashing its contents everywhere, and in the process extinguishing the fire.

Stephen unclenched his fists, and rubbed a hand across his face. "Forgive me, Osgar. I let my temper control me." He rose slowly. "It might be time to take my leave."

Osgar just shook his head, rising up as well. "Nae, my son. All are welcomed, and the search for one's soul or fate is always a journey. Sometimes the journey may be dark, but ye are never alone." He placed a hand on his shoulder. "Ye were led here for a reason, Stephen. I believe ye are on a quest—one that may take ye to Hell, but it is one ye must seek out."

"I am cursed."

"I do not believe so. Why would ye still receive visions? Why would ye still possess great powers?" Shrugging slightly, he continued, "Ye have a destiny to fulfill, and ye must not give up on the gods and goddesses, too."

Stephen narrowed his eyes at the last, stepping back from Osgar's grip. "They are *naught* to me. How can ye speak thus, knowing what ye do?" he spat out.

"I believe the Lord is the greatest druid of all, and I still believe in the others. That has not changed."

Stephen picked up his mug and finished its

contents. Placing it back down on the table, he moved toward the door. "The truth I have learned here today will stay within these walls, for I fear not all the brothers will welcome ye and your kind. I would guard yourself against Brother Timmons."

"Yes, I did hear what happened in the village earlier."

"Sour news travels fast within the abbey," Stephen remarked.

The monk nodded in agreement, saying, "Aye, but what ye did for young Ian will travel the winds far more quickly than in these walls."

Stephen frowned and crossed his arms across his chest. "How so?"

Tapping a finger to his mouth as if debating whether to say anything further, Osgar walked over to Stephen. "Our young Ian MacDuff is destined for great things. He will be the next Master Druid and will sit on the council."

"*Ian*? How do ye ken this? He is but a small lad."

"It is not for me to say, but it has been foretold and the vision confirmed. Ye must pray for his safety, for I fear for him and his family. If the news should reach the wrong men, it would prove fatal. There are those who seek to eliminate all druids. The current manner is burning at the stake."

Stephen waved his hands. "The brothers, here?"

"Likely a few, but Rome would seek it. I do ken they are sending a council in the next few months to view our progress here at Arbroath."

Stephen let out a long held breath and started to pace the room. Stopping before the spilled water, he grimaced. "I may be battling my own demons with the druids, but I would never want harm to come to them or to ye, Osgar." He raked a hand through his hair, contemplating his next thought. "If Ian is destined to be the next Master Druid, then he will require a guard. One may never ken if he is to become a druid, or bishop, no?" The thought of anyone burning a small child, simply because of religious beliefs, was too horrific for him to fathom.

"True," smiled Osgar.

"Thank ye for the drink." He gave a curt nod, and strode toward the door, realizing for the first time in over a year, he felt some purpose to his life. Yes, he thought, what better way than to serve one who is destined for greatness. His life was now meant to serve.

Opening the door, he welcomed the icy blast of air. It revived his spirit, and he walked proudly out into the afternoon.

Osgar stood still, slowly watching the Dragon Knight amble off through the garden. Lifting his head upwards, he spoke the ancient language, giving thanks to the Goddess, and one to Saint Michael, too. Stephen's quest had been prophesied along with Ian's. The Knight was destined for greatness, but first he must meet his fate.

"Brother Osgar!" shouted Brother James, running into the workroom.

Osgar held up his hand to still the impatient man, watching as he tried to regain his breath. "What is so urgent that has ye in a flux?"

"We have news, Brother Osgar. The council from Rome will be here in the next few weeks."

He folded his arms within his robe, and nodded slowly. "Yes, although their arrival will be earlier than expected, it is good news, Brother James."

"We have much to do, and a meeting is planned after prayers!" exclaimed Brother James.

"I shall be along shortly."

Brother James nodded, before quickly turning and making haste back through the garden.

A deep sigh escaped Osgar's lips as he stepped out into the garden. Casting his gaze up at the sky, he whispered, "So it begins."

Chapter Three

Present day—Boston, Massachusetts

"A Dragon's tail has been known to span many centuries, so that one may travel its length."

Laughter bubbled forth from Aileen as she jumped into the air to grasp the wispy floating dandelion. "Gotcha!" Holding it gently in the palm of her hand, she closed her eyes and made a silent wish. Upon opening them, she blew softly, and watched the gossamer plant head hover for a brief moment before a gust of wind took possession. She stood mesmerized as it drifted away from her sight.

"I see you're still making faery wishes," chuckled her Aunt Lily.

Aileen stepped toward her aunt and linked arms. "Of course! As I recall it was you who taught me them." Then she gave her a gentle squeeze.

Nodding her head in agreement, she replied, "Yes, I do, and you would always listen spellbound."

"Don't forget the endless list of questions, too," smiled Aileen.

"Yes, but that is how one learns." Her aunt returned the pat.

The cool breeze touched Aileen's cheek and she inhaled deeply. "I love this time of year, Aunt Lily, when life springs forth from the ground, starting the cycle all over again." She absently touched her pendant. In the center rested a moonstone surrounded by Celtic spirals. Rubbing it in contemplation, she brought her thoughts back to the present. "Spring is a chance to do it all over again."

"Are you speaking of nature, or yourself?"

"Both," she sighed.

Aunt Lily halted, turning to look up at her niece. "Now you hear me, Aileen, you are not to blame for the failure of your relationship. Jim had another agenda, one that did not include you in his life. To put it bluntly, he used you to better himself in the community."

"I know, Aunt Lily, but how could I have been so wrong about him?"

"Because you were looking at the outside, and he kept you from seeing what was inside of him." Tapping a finger over Aileen's heart, she added, "It was his heart that was ugly."

"Do you think he put a glamour spell on me?"

Her aunt put her hands on her hips and glared at Aileen. "Glamour spell? You? I think you are stronger than you think. You fell for a man that was tall, taller than you, and devastatingly handsome. If you want to know the truth, we all fell for him in the beginning."

"You did?"

"Yes, and don't go telling the others I told you, either," commanded her aunt.

Aileen nodded slowly. "Yes, he was taller than me. It's difficult to always find someone taller than I am. I don't know many females who are six feet three inches, do you?"

"No. The only one I knew to be as tall as you are

was your mother, bless her, and she stood well over six feet. She and your father were extremely tall. Now, take a look at me." She gestured with her arms. "I'm short."

Aileen stepped over to a large oak tree and sat down against its trunk. She brushed her hand casually along its rough bark. "I miss her so much at times," she whispered.

Her aunt dropped down next to her and grasped her hands. "There isn't a day that goes by I don't think of her, too. She was too young to be taken from this life." She brushed aside a strand of hair from Aileen's face. "Yet, I see her every day in you."

"Except I have my father's eyes."

"Of that there is no doubt, though I do believe yours have more of a violet hue than his."

"Which can be a curse when others see me, too," she muttered.

"Stop that!" Giving Aileen a sharp smack on her leg, Aunt Lily added, "It just means you are very special. Since when did you become so critical? And, don't tell me it's because of Jim, or I'll smack you again." She said the last with a smirk.

Putting up her hands in surrender, Aileen just shook her head. "I stand corrected. I had a momentary lapse."

"Now..." Aunt Lily stood, reaching for Aileen's hand. "I think you should consider your father's offer."

Aileen got up, brushing off the leaves and dirt from her cotton dress. "Really? Fly to Scotland and what? Watch him on one of his archeological digs? He's so immersed in his work he really doesn't have time for me to hover nearby. No, I think he was just being kind. And I *believe* someone called him." She crossed her arms across her chest and narrowed her gaze at her aunt.

"*Moi?*" Aunt Lily gave her a look of mock indignation.

She bent near her aunt's face. "Yes, you."

"Honestly, Aileen, I don't understand what you're talking about. I speak with your father quite often and—" Before she could finish, they heard Cara yelling and running through the clearing toward them.

She waved her hands frantically at them. "Aileen, Lily! I have great news!"

Cara came bounding across the ground, braids whipping around her face. Coming to a halt, she held up her palm to stop their questions. Bending over and clasping her knees, she fought to control her breath. "Whew! I need to exercise more!"

"Humph!" Aileen blew out the word, casting her eyes to the sky. "Cara, out of our entire group, you are the only one in fantastic shape. Now spit it out."

"Why, thank you, Aileen," sassed Cara. "You'll never guess where we, the Society of the Thistle, have been invited to visit?"

"Where?" asked Aunt Lily.

"Shall we play charades, or shall I hum a tune?" Cara asked, all the while looking like an imp with a bit of valuable knowledge.

"Cara, for the love of—" scolded Aileen.

"All right, ahem...the Society of the Thistle has been invited to Scotland to assist in doing research at Arbroath Abbey."

Aileen flinched and grabbed Cara's hand. "Let me guess, an Aidan Kerrigan sent the request?"

Cara reached for Aileen's other hand, eyes alight

with glee. "Yes! Oh, Aileen, isn't this *great* news."

She extracted her hands and started to pace. "Why would my *father* want the Society of the Thistle, one that deals only in the history and preservation of historical herbs and plants, to come to Scotland?" Aileen stopped pacing, but kept her gaze on her aunt.

Her aunt just shrugged her shoulders in response. "Don't look at me. I know absolutely nothing."

"I don't have all of the details now, but when Maeve got off the phone with him, she blurted out that we were all invited to Scotland. She said he required our assistance, and he would pay our expenses," replied Cara. She stepped over to Aileen, touching her lightly on the arm. "Are you not excited about this? It has been over a year since you've seen your father. I thought you would have been over the moon with this news."

She saw the disappointment in her friend's face, and couldn't blame her for her own insecurities. When her mother had died of cancer several years ago, Aileen and her father retreated to their own separate worlds, hers here in Boston, and his back in Scotland. Their grief so vast neither could stand to be in each other's company. Instead of seeking solace and comfort together, they turned to work. Yet, on occasion, she would get a call or email from her father. The details were always the same, wondering how she was, and what he was presently working on and where.

Strange, he'd only asked her a week ago to come visit him at Arbroath Abbey, and now this bit of news.

She gave her a weak smile. "I'm sorry, Cara. It just seems peculiar, especially of my father."

"Let's go find Maeve and find out the rest of the details, shall we?" Aunt Lily asked. "You must admit this sounds intriguing. Your father is paying for all of us to fly to Scotland."

Aileen nodded slowly. "Yes, Mr. Penny Pincher must need us something fierce to send for all of us."

Her aunt only snorted and muttered something else under her breath, as she and Cara made their way back to their home, which also served as the business location for the order.

"Whatever are you up to, Dad?" she mumbled out loud, before reaching for another dandelion head and blowing it into the wind.

Chapter Four

"She gathered the fragrant cluster of meadowsweet, and made a poppet for her wedding day."

When Aileen approached her home, or what was now officially called the Society of the Thistle, she stood in front of the three-story house. Tilting her head to the side, she let her gaze drift upward, staring at the window with the beveled glass on the third floor. Sunlight glinted off the pane turning it into an ethereal scene. Her mother's bedroom. The very one where she uttered her last breath. How her mother had loved the view from that room. You could see the clearing through the oak trees, and she often would say the faeries used to play on Beltaine, dancing and singing. In spring, it was a glorious sight, when the flowers emerged from their sleep and spread their petals in all directions.

A month after Aileen's mother had died, her father left for England on an archeological dig. Over a week later she received a packet, explaining he had transferred the deed to the house over to her. It was then she realized he would never return to the States. Her Aunt Lily moved in soon thereafter, and within six months, they moved the Society into her 200-year-old home.

The Society preserved the history and lore of plants

in historical settings. Theirs was an ancient society based on the beliefs of the druids and nature. Each of the members had a unique gift, be it psychic, or healing. They all held firm in their pagan beliefs, and honored their treasured past.

There were presently seven in the Society—herself, Aunt Lily, Maeve, Maeve's daughter Teresa, Sally, Cara, and Gwen. All were descendants from the original order, which originated in Scotland almost eight hundred years ago.

Aileen's thoughts returned to her mom. She chewed on her bottom lip, as a lump swelled within her chest. How could she leave here? Her mother's spirit still lived within, and to take a trip across an ocean would be like severing a limb. What could possibly be in Scotland that was more important than her work here? Perhaps they all didn't need to go. If she still couldn't handle her own pain, how could she manage her father's grief? A cool breeze touched her neck, and her hand absently strayed to the spot. "*Mom*?" she whispered.

Shaking her head slowly, she entered her home, where she was immediately assaulted with sounds of yelling mixed with laughter. Of course, Teresa's voice could be heard over all the others. Aileen placed the flowers she had gathered on the front entry table. The commotion emanated from the kitchen. She could hear Teresa yelling for Sally and Cara to make sure their passports were current.

She passed Cara and Sally on her way to the kitchen, and Sally clasped her hands in jubilation. "Isn't this wonderful, Aileen?" she gushed. "Scotland! Land of magic and mists."

"And don't forget the men, too, Sally," Cara blurted out.

Sally placed her hands over her heart and swayed. "Big brawny Scots with husky burrs...*oh my*. How could I forget?" They both erupted into fits of laughter, as Aileen gave them both a wry smile before walking away.

Upon entering the kitchen, she spied her aunt and Maeve, heads together, talking in low voices, and taking notes. Teresa had a large map of Scotland at one end of the table, and she looked to be circling places with a highlighter. Gwen kneaded bread, but she nodded for Aileen to come over.

"Do you think you could toss in the rosemary for me?"

Aileen gathered up the herbs in the mortar and pitched them into the large bowl. "Rosemary garlic bread?"

"Yes, and creamy tomato soup."

She watched as Gwen continued the slow process of kneading the bread, and folding it just so, repeatedly. Out of all of them, she knew her friend would understand her dilemma. Casting a glance over her shoulder at her aunt and Maeve, she let out a deep breath. "I don't want to go."

"Hmmmm," replied Gwen. "I thought you would feel that way. How much more time does it say on the timer?"

Aileen peeked. "One minute."

"It's done." Giving it one last pat, Gwen removed the round loaf and placed it into a large greased bowl. Taking a nearby towel, she draped it over the top and put it inside the oven to proof. Dusting her hands off on her apron, she flipped her long auburn braid back over her shoulder. "Let's go take a walk in the garden. Besides, I think it's a tad noisy at the moment."

"You think?"

Leaving the other women at the table, they silently made their way out to the large herb garden right outside the kitchen. Gwen meandered over to the lavender bushes, which were just in the beginning stages of sprouting their buds. Aileen watched as she gently brushed her hand over the leaves. "I just love spring, don't you, Aileen?"

"Yes, you know I do." She smiled.

Gwen then drifted over to the peppermint, snipping off some leaves with her fingers. When she had gathered a handful, she placed them into the pocket of her apron. "I thought we would have some tea afterwards. I also made some cranberry orange scones."

"Thanks, Gwen. You know those are my favorite." Aileen sat down next to her friend. "I thought I was up early, but you must have been up before dawn."

Gwen chuckled softly. "Oh yes, giving blessings to the Goddess, then straight into the kitchen." She lifted her head up to the sunlight. There was still a brisk chill in the air, but the warmth of the sun was a welcoming balm. Aileen closed her eyes, too. They sat in contented silence for a bit. Bumblebees hovered nearby, and birds chirped in a melody, as if announcing spring had finally arrived.

"She wants you to go to Scotland."

Aileen flinched, her eyes snapping open. "What are you saying?"

Opening her eyes, she placed her hand on Aileen's, "I'm saying your mother wants you to go to Scotland."

Aileen snapped her hand away and leapt off the bench. "Sweet Bridget! How do you know this? Have you seen her?"

"Oh, Aileen," she sighed. "You know very well I speak to the spirits." Holding her hand out to ward off any further questions, she continued, "And no, I have not had any communication with her prior to this morning."

Her mouth snapped shut. Although bundled in her fur-lined jacket and boots, the chill creeping down her spine gave Aileen tremors. Hugging her arms tightly around herself, she walked away from Gwen. Oh, how she'd begged Gwen to contact her mother after she passed, but she had received no messages. Once, she had even doubted her friend's abilities. So why was this morning diffcrent?

"What exactly did she say?"

Gwen let out a sigh. "You realize it doesn't work that way."

"Then explain it to me." She waved her hands in the air.

"I had a vision before I woke this morning. She told me your destiny is in Scotland. When I opened my eyes, I could smell her scent."

"Honeysuckle?" whispered a stunned Aileen.

Gwen nodded. "Yes."

Tears pricked her eyes, and she glanced away. "Why would she tell you my destiny lies in Scotland? Could she not come to me?"

"Would you have listened to her? No, I think understanding you, your dream would have been only that...*a dream*, and not a vision." Gwen blew out a soft sigh.

Aileen bit her lower lip to stop the retort. Yet, she knew in her heart, her friend was correct. Gwen had the gift of vision and sight. Her mother had chosen Gwen to deliver this message, for she realized that only from Gwen would she truly believe.

"Would you like those tea and scones, now?"

Aileen responded with a weak smile and a nod.

"Good. Come in when you're ready." Gwen turned away to leave.

"Thank you, Gwen."

"You're welcome, my friend."

She watched her walk out of the garden and her mind began to swirl with questions. Why would her destiny be in Scotland? This was her home. Did her mother want her to reconcile with her father? Nevertheless, why would she say *destiny*? Her parents had always told her that her destiny was forever changing, and one's path should not be forced. She felt as if she was being pulled to a place she did not want to go.

Yet, why was she fighting this?

"Because I have to face my father," she snorted.

A sharp breeze whipped past her, and a hummingbird hovered briefly in front of her. She remained still, watching as it flitted out of sight. Then, Aileen caught the sweet scent of honeysuckle.

"Oh Mom," Aileen uttered, before a sob caught in her throat.

In that moment, her decision was made. She would travel to Scotland and meet her destiny.

Chapter Five

"The druid filled the bowl full of poppies and moonstones, so the dragon could dream sweet dreams."

"What a glorious sight for sore eyes," whispered Aunt Lily. She leaned against Aileen, who had stirred awake to hear her aunt's voice.

"And that would be what?" she murmured. Slowly opening her eyes, she attempted to stifle a yawn. It was only a five-hour flight, but with the constant chatter of her friends, it seemed longer. Stretching her long legs out as far as she could, she glanced to see what her aunt was gazing at.

"Home, Aileen. I've come back home." Her voice carried a note of melancholy, and Aileen understood her meaning.

Her mom and aunt had spoken numerous times of coming back to Scotland. They both had been born here, but their parents had uprooted their tiny family for Boston in order to take over the Society of the Thistle. Her mother was only two and Aunt Lily four, but they vowed one day they would come back. Her mother did make the trip, and there she met her father.

Sadly, her aunt never made the trip, until now.

Aileen grasped her aunt's hand and gave it a gentle squeeze. "You've come home for her, too." Her aunt merely nodded, keeping her focus on the land.

33

It was then Aileen noticed what her aunt gazed upon. The clouds had dispersed from earlier, and now the sight of so much green did more than beckon. It actually touched a place within her soul, and she gasped. The water of the sea gently caressed the land, calling her to come forth. Her senses swam, and she fisted her hand to her chest. "I have...*returned*."

Aunt Lily twisted slowly to look at Aileen with a look of alarm spreading across her features. "What did you say?"

She shook her head to clear her senses, blinking several times. "I...I don't know." She shrugged. "It's a feeling of déjà vu."

"Perhaps."

They both sat staring at the landscape below, watching as the city of Aberdeen came into view. It was a clear day, but for a few clouds drifting by. Maeve tapped Lily on her arm interrupting their silence.

"Will Aidan be meeting us at the airport?"

"I don't think so, Maeve, seeing how busy he's been lately. He might be sending someone else," her aunt responded.

"Humph!" Aileen bristled.

"Aw, dear, don't fault your father for what he does," chided Maeve.

Aileen blanched. "I'm not, Maeve, but he could at least meet us there."

Maeve narrowed her eyes at Aileen, and whispered low, "This from one who didn't want to come, because of *said father*?" She gave her a sharp jab on the arm before reclining back in her seat.

Aileen closed her eyes and prepared for the landing, but most of all for seeing her father. She had to get her emotions into check, or they would surely tumble forth when she saw him. To come from a family of healers who possessed great skills of empathy was at times a curse. Her parents had the gift of empathy and passed it down to her. It had been a battle most of her life to build the walls strong against the gift, since not only could she feel other's emotions, she could actually heal with her own. However, since her failed relationship a few months ago, combined with the death of her mother, it had left her weak and unable to be around others for any length of time.

Gwen had been the one to pull her back from the brink of total seclusion. She worked with her every day, helping her with her mental exercises, and mixing teas with healing herbs. Her father certainly did not want to help. He had abandoned her for Scotland, and there was the rub. The one and only person who could help to rebuild her shields chose to leave her helpless and adrift.

Rubbing her hands across her legs, she drew forth from her well of strength and surrounded herself with her mental armor. Taking long, deep cleansing breaths, she focused so hard, that when the plane touched down on the tarmac, Aileen did not feel the jolt.

"Well, Dad, let's see who is the stronger one," she muttered softly.

****

To say the airport in Aberdeen was bustling would be putting it mildly. A mass of people filled the terminal. If this had been six months ago, Aileen would have never been able to make the flight. She started to feel a bit unsteady, but she blamed it on the food they served on the plane. What she craved was a cup of hot

35

tea.

They made their way to the baggage carousel, and again the same strange sensation of déjà vu washed over her. She tried shrugging it off, believing it was tied to something she read in a Scottish magazine, but then her vision blurred, and her heart started to pound erratically against her chest. Feelings of anxiety clawed at her, threatening to take her down into the abyss of darkness.

"Shields up, Aileen." Gwen's soothing voice pierced through the veil.

Those simple words centered Aileen. Nodding slowly to her friend, she kept her gaze steady. Gwen might have thought she was overwhelmed by so many people's emotions, but it was something else entirely. She would have to talk to her friend about it later.

Sally, Cara, and Teresa were as giddy as they had been before they left. It was a wonder Aileen did not have a headache from their constant chatter. Nonetheless, their chatter helped to soothe her nerves.

"Do you know where you're going, Lily?" asked Gwen.

"Yes, he said he would meet us at the end of the baggage—"

"He's here," interrupted Aileen, coming to a halt. She did not see him, but rather felt the wave of his emotions prick her outer conscience.

No one questioned Aileen, they just all froze as one, until Aunt Lily saw him emerge from the crowd some distance away.

If anyone had remarked that Aidan Kerrigan was tall, it would have been a huge understatement. The man loomed over others at six foot, seven inches, and when he would pass by others noticed. At fifty-five, her dad could easily pass for someone of forty. However, she did notice a slight graying at the temples, but it only added character to his rugged features.

Aileen thought back to a conversation she'd witnessed between her mom and aunt. Aunt Lily teased her mom, saying Aidan must have been chiseled from a dark Irish God with his looks, and large indigo eyes. Her mom had winked. "If you only knew."

Her dad strode past her aunt and the others, giving her a quick nod before he stood in front of Aileen. He reached out and gently touched her hair. "So like your mother's," he murmured softly.

"Oh Dad," Aileen choked out, stepping into his loving embrace. He held her, stroking her head and soothing her in words of Gaelic, which made her sob even more.

Aileen was the first to break contact. Looking up into his eyes, she saw his pain mirrored hers. It was then she realized they both needed each other so they could heal. If it meant she had to be the stronger one, so be it.

"I've missed you so much, Dad," she muttered into his chest.

"Aye, as have I missed you. I'm glad you are here." He pulled back and cupped her face with his hands. "This is the home of your mother and yours, too."

She nodded slowly, sensing he wanted to say more, but kept silent.

They both could hear everyone sniffling behind them, and her dad turned toward Aunt Lily, reaching for her hand. He gave her a gentle squeeze. "I'm glad you brought her to me."

"It was long overdue, Aidan," replied her aunt.

He scanned the rest of the group, and they all made a lunge for him ending in one big group hug.

"Ladies, please..." He chuckled. "It's been eons since I've had so much attention."

Aileen stepped back to give the others some room, marveling at how much she'd truly missed her father. He was a giant in the mass of her friends, but she saw the shadows that haunted him, and worried.

He angled his head at her, giving her a wink.

Yes, it was good to be here...*back home*.

Chapter Six

"Dogwood leaves, flowers, and wood can be used as a protective charm. The four petals symbolize the elements of Earth, Air, Fire, and Water."

"This is where you live?" A shocked Aileen stood on the path in front of her father's home, and scanned the massive architecture he called home.

"Do you like it?"

"It's a castle! What's not to *like*?"

"Aye, that it is, named Balleycove." He gave her a wide grin.

"How long have you had this?" Aileen asked, still stunned by the vision in front of her.

Her dad remained quiet, as if deciding what to say. "Let's just say it's been in my family for a while."

She shot him a look filled with confusion. "Excuse me? And why did I not know about this?"

He stepped away from her, keeping his hands tucked behind his back. Taking a deep breath, he cast a look over his shoulders as if sizing up some great decision. "Your mother and I thought it best not to say anything."

Aileen walked over to her father and placed her hand on his arm, watching as he looked down to where she touched him. "Dad, what is it you're *not* saying?"

Grasping her hand with such fierceness that Aileen

stiffened, his voice remained low. "Before you were born, your mother had a vision of your destiny taking you to Scotland, and it would end here. We decided long ago we would never tell you of your home here, for fear that you would visit, and your life would end."

"Then why in the blazes did you send for me now?"

His eyes bore into hers, and for a brief moment, she swore they changed color.

"Because I believe it's time you came home. Even your mother's vision was not clear about your path here. She had prayed over the years she would get more, but none came."

"I wish she would have told me, Dad. She tried...you both tried to protect me too much, without realizing that perhaps I'm supposed to be here."

"Yes, that's what I'm thinking, especially since I've come across something which leads to that conclusion." He rubbed a hand across his jaw. "My colleague found a book in the diggings. At first it depicted drawings of plants and herbs, along with some medicinal advice."

"Oh Dad, what a find!" she exclaimed. "Is it something the Society can help research?"

He held up his hand to silence her. "I would prefer they don't hear about the book, just yet."

Aileen frowned. "Then why send for us? I don't understand."

He stepped in front of her, placed his hands on her shoulders, and looked directly into her eyes. "On one of the pages your name is inscribed, and underneath is a picture of your pendant."

The ground beneath felt as if it had opened up and

swallowed her whole. She tried to speak, but words failed her. The air was too warm even as a cool breeze skittered across her face. At the moment, *impossible* was her only thought.

"I've got you, honey." Her dad tucked her close. "Believe me when I saw it, it felt as if I had been punched in the gut, too."

She grasped her pendant, as if it was her lifeline. Finally, when words could be fully formed, she muttered, "You must be mistaken. It's probably just an ancestor."

"Nae, Aileen. The pendant is yours. Your mother had it made after she had the vision. She used to hang it on the mobile in your crib for protection. It is your distinct moonstone pendant, complete with the Celtic spirals."

"No, Dad, you must be wrong. I would like to see this book." Pushing him aside, she gave an unladylike snort and walked toward the castle.

Her father had gone from a grief-stricken man to one who lost his mind. If she understood his meaning, she would have had to be transported back in time when the book was written. "Poppycock!" Glancing back at her father, she just shook her head.

She passed her aunt on her way inside, who gave her a questionable look.

"Aileen, are you okay?"

Aileen waved to her. "Sure, only my father has lost his mind. I think coming to Scotland was not in our best interest." Then she paused in thought. "But you know what? I think we should stay and take advantage of my father's hospitality. Just take a look around. It seems as if he's some grand laird, and I'm just finding out about it."

"*Aileen*." Aunt Lily cautiously moved toward her.

Aileen pointed a finger at her aunt. "Did you know about this castle?"

She watched as the truth splayed out across her aunt's features. "I can explain," her aunt said slowly.

"Don't bother. I've already heard enough, and at the moment I don't really know what to believe." Aileen stormed off to the sounds of the others. At least she would feel safe and normal being around them.

****

Aileen spent the rest of the afternoon in the company of Cara, Sally, and Gwen exploring parts of the castle. Maeve and Teresa went to tour the garden with the caretaker. She did not say a word to them, yet realized Gwen knew something was bothering her, and waited until they were alone to mention anything.

"I wish you would tell me what's crawled up your ass, Aileen," snapped Gwen.

"Is it that obvious?"

Gwen tapped her finger on her chin. "Well, let's see, first you started to compare your father to one of the lost boys who should be with Peter Pan. Then you said you were going to place a call for the wagon and have the men in white jackets cart him away. Hmmmm, I would say something is definitely wrong with you." She narrowed her eyes at her. "You might have had the others in fits of laughter, but I for one, found it disturbing."

Aileen cringed and walked over to an alcove where a huge bench sat. The sky was turning to dusk, and red and gold streaked the horizon. She sat and gazed out the large bay window that overlooked a town and the sea beyond. Seagulls cawed in the distance, and she pressed her head against the glass. "It's so beautiful here, isn't it?"

Her friend walked over and sat down next to her. "Yes, it is. A land filled with magic, that's for sure. Your father said Arbroath Abbey is south of here, and his dig is nearby."

She frowned. "Yes, magic with gateways to other realms through stone circles. Could it truly be possible?"

Gwen grabbed Aileen's hand and said in a hushed tone, "How could you not believe? You of all people comprehend that magic is real. Look around you, Aileen. Your blood, my blood, is part of this land. Did you not feel it when we arrived?"

"I did the moment I saw the land from the plane," whispered Aileen.

"Then what's bothering you?" Gwen squeezed her hand.

Aileen stood retracting her hand from Gwen's. "I can't talk about it at the moment. However, when I solve this riddle, you'll be the first to know. Now, let's see if we can go find the others. I think Maeve mentioned dinner is at eight, and I'm starving."

Gwen narrowed her eyes at Aileen, but only nodded. "I'll be the first you tell?"

Aileen laughed loudly. "Yes, Gwen, I swear!"

****

Dinner was a lavish scene—filled with many different delicacies to tempt them all. A chicken broth with vegetables and dumplings started them out, followed by venison filled with sage, almonds, and apples. Then there was salmon with dill sauce, roasted asparagus, and fingerling potatoes. A spinach and bacon salad with a warm balsamic dressing, and freshly baked bread, too. Dessert consisted of a warm apple tart and a cheese platter. Wine flowed freely across the massive oak table, along with the conversation and laughter.

Aileen sat next to Gwen and Teresa. Her father sat at the head of the table next to Maeve and her aunt. Every so often, he would attempt to send a question her way, but her answer was a shrug, for she did not wish to engage in any conversation with him.

Glancing around where they sat, she could only think of it as the great hall. A huge stone fireplace rose at the far end. All along the walls were richly woven tapestries depicting life in medieval times. She was sipping her wine, when one of the tapestries caught her attention. Placing her glass down, she excused herself, walking over to the wall where it hung.

The tapestry was magnificent in its colors. Rich in golds, greens, browns and reds, it was divided into four panels. Each of the panels held a man standing alone, half facing away. In the center of the four panels was a dragon, and beside the dragon was a young woman. She had long dark locks and wore a crown of silver. In her lap, a book rested, with one of her hands across the top of the leather as if bestowing a caress. Her eyes held sadness, and Aileen actually felt sorry for her. Yet, it was not the woman she was drawn to, but the Highlander in the bottom left panel. Dressed in a long plaid and boots, with his dark, short-cropped hair, he stood out from the rest. Then she noticed the medallion around his neck. The stone was green, but curved around it was a dragon. All of the embroidered men were striking. Yet, this one called to her. He stood proud, arms crossed over his massive chest. Aileen started to reach out and touch him, when a husky burr spoke quietly behind her.

"I see you've taken an interest in our *Knight*."

She spun around coming face to face with a devastatingly handsome man. She thought her father was tall, but this one was taller with an amazing pair of sky blue eyes. His dark auburn hair was tied back in a leather thong. Her mouth dropped opened, and then she snapped it shut. She quickly turned her focus back to the tapestry to hide the heat spreading across her face. "Knight?"

"Aye. They are all Knights." He moved to peer at the tapestry, a frown marring his features.

Aileen glanced at him sideways. "They don't really look like knights, except for that one on the top left side. He's the only one wearing armor."

"And yet they were," he responded. "They were of an ancient order, descended from Ireland. Part man, part fae, each gifted with an elemental power. They ruled for over a millennium, until the death of their sister."

"How sad," gasped Aileen. "What happened?"

"She was killed on sacred ground defending the man she loved." He turned to look at Aileen. "One of her brothers took his sword preparing to slay her lover, when she stepped in front of the blade, ending her life."

"How tragic, but only legend, right?"

"Nae, lass."

"What tales have you been telling my daughter, Liam?" Her dad's voice startled her. So involved in the tapestry scene, she didn't realized he'd followed her.

"Why, only the most important one of all, the Order of the Dragon Knights." The handsome stranger flashed a smile at Aileen. "I'm sorry, but we have not been introduced. I am Liam MacGregor, a colleague and old friend of your father's." He took hold of Aileen's hand and placed a gentle kiss across the top.

Something skittered through her senses, and a ripple of energy washed through her body. She trembled slightly and slowly removed her hand from his. Narrowing her eyes at him and then at her father she said, "Well, you must have known him from birth, since you seem to be about my age."

Liam burst out laughing and slapped her dad on the back. "Oh, she's an intuitive one."

"Aye, she is."

Aileen eyed them both suspiciously.

"I've known Liam all of his life. He knew your mother, too."

"I am sorry to hear of her passing," Liam said solemnly. "She was a beautiful spirit, and her light extinguished far too soon."

"You knew my mother?"

Liam nodded.

She turned back toward the tapestry, her eyes brimming with tears.

"Yes, she was too young to leave us." Aileen brushed away a drop that had slipped down her cheek, "As with this young woman, too."

Letting her gaze travel back to the knight with the medallion, she asked, "What is his name, Liam?"

It wasn't Liam who answered her, but her father's gruff voice. "Stephen MacKay."

When she looked back over her shoulder, there was

a look of anger etched on her father's face—not for her, but it startled Aileen. His anger seemed to be directed at the image of Stephen.

"Enough of legends!" he snapped. With a gentler tone, he added, "Get some rest, Aileen. We can talk in the morning." Pressing a kiss on her forehead, he turned and walked away.

Aileen watched as her father left the great hall, and then directed her gaze at Liam. He too watched Aidan's exit intently. "Perhaps, you can tell me who my father is, Liam, since I truly don't know who the man is anymore. Also, where is this book that he spoke of, which has a picture of my pendant?"

Liam slowly let his gaze travel back to Aileen, then to the tapestry behind her. He angled his head to the side as if studying the picture before him. Drawing in a long breath and releasing it, he shot her a glance. "The ancient text does depict your pendant and your name. The author of said document is none other than this man." Liam pointed to the man in the tapestry. "Stephen MacKay."

Chapter Seven

Arbroath, Scotland—April 1206

"When the Warrior went into battle, he had the Dragon prepare him a draught of goat's thorn, basil, hops, and horseradish."

Although the ship was not a huge one, its cargo and the men standing on board spoke of riches. Their long brightly colored robes announced to all that they were from Rome. The water slapped against the wooden hull, causing it to sway back and forth. The men did not seem to be frightened nor did they make any movement to grasp the iron rail. No, these men did not fear the sea, for their leader was one who had once walked on water. They cast their gaze out toward the villagers, who had come to see their new visitors.

Some were in awe, and others frightened by what they brought. Fear of their old ways...*pagan* ways held dear to them, or so Stephen thought.

He stood on the hill above the dock and surveyed the ship with its passengers. They had traveled across the channel from France. He knew the bishops had first visited the monks at Tiron Abbey and pondered what they would make of the progress of the one here. With the help of most of the monks, they had been able to set a pace of continual building of the abbey, which would make even his brothers proud. Why he thought of them now, he could not fathom. An ache formed every so often when his thoughts returned to them and that ill-fated night.

He rubbed absently with the heel of his palm to his chest. Try as he might to soothe the dull pain, it would always be there reminding him of what once was.

"Will ye not greet them, Sir Stephen?" asked Ian.

Stephen should have realized the young lad was with him. He seemed to follow him wherever he went. In truth, he did not care, for he was mindful of his duty to serve the young druid. Some days his conscience would pull at him when he was in prayers—prayers that would take him back to his own beliefs. So similar in many ways.

He looked down at the young lad whose gaze was cast toward the scene below. "Nae. I shall not be greeting them, and for the love of God, please just call me Stephen."

Ian smirked. "Ye cannae expect a butterfly to fly without its wings. How can ye be who ye are without your name?"

"Argh," groaned Stephen. The lad was always talking in nonsense...druid babble. He reminded him of another druid he'd known long ago. "Why do I fret," he muttered.

"Humph!" Ian snorted.

He allowed his focus to drift back to the ship, where the men had now disembarked and were walking with Brothers Timmons, Charles, Thomas, Seamus, James, and Patrick. He smiled knowing Osgar would not be there to greet them. As much as he was a part of the Tironensian Order, he would always be a druid at heart, and like Stephen, Osgar felt there was more to their visit than just an inspection of the abbey.

Ian stepped away from the edge of the hill and picked up a leather bound journal. A set of quills in a wooden box lay next to it. He brushed his hand over the top. "Did ye draw today?"

"Nae." Stephen walked away from the harbor view and to his horse. Drawing forth a water skin, he opened it and drank fully. Wiping his mouth with the back of his hand, he handed it to Ian who took it and sipped slowly.

"Thank ye, Sir Stephen." The lad glanced back down at the journal and box, then crossed his arms across his chest in thought, his eyes taking a far off look. "I ken ye have not found your fire." He moved over and gently touched Stephen's arm.

"Ye shall, and verra soon," Ian said with the eyes of a much wiser and older man.

He shook his head. The lad may be only ten winters, but in the few weeks Stephen had been in his company, he'd shone a spirit of one who inhabited an old soul. "I will pay heed to your good judgment."

Ian gave Stephen a broad smile. "Good."

The bells started to chime in the distance, and Ian closed his eyes. His look was one of joy, and Stephen knew the lad enjoyed hearing them, as if he understood their secret melodic tune. He also knew Ian would sneak into the abbey to be closer to their musical sound. With the arrival of the bishops, he would have to keep him out of harm's way.

Still keeping his eyes closed, Ian spoke. "Brother Cesan is at the ropes."

"How can ye tell?"

"The chimes are slower," he replied opening his eyes with an authority of one who knew what he was talking about.

Rubbing a hand over his face, Stephen picked up Ian and placed him atop his horse. "It would be best if ye stayed away from the abbey until the bishops from Rome depart."

The youngster tilted his head to the side. "Dinnae worry, Sir Stephen. No harm will come to me, for I have ye."

"Just obey me this once." Stephen's look was firm as he mounted Grian.

"Aye," sighed Ian reluctantly.

Taking care not to journey through the village, Stephen made his way up through the hills away from the abbey. This path took longer to reach Ian's home, but he did not want to chance a meeting with the village's new visitors. He would have to rely on Osgar to keep him informed as to their happenings. He was not privileged to sit with them, as he was not one of the brothers. Nevertheless, he was curious. His warrior instincts had gone on alert the moment he heard of their impending arrival.

Thank the God he had no more visions. The last one left him uneasy, and unable to grasp its meaning.

"Och, there ye are, Ian!" Betha, Ian's mother, shouted. She placed her hands on her hips and glared at her son.

"Good day to ye, Betha." Stephen nodded, as he swung down from Grian. Taking a hold of Ian, he placed him on the ground in front of his mother and laid a firm hand on the lad's shoulder. "I'm sorry, but we should have told ye we went to see the advent of the bishops."

Ian stiffened, and Stephen said a silent prayer the lad remained silent, unless he wanted his mother to conclude it was a lie.

Betha's face softened, and she drew Ian into her embrace. "The next time I will not be so forgiving," then placed a kiss on his head. "Go see your father. He needs help at the anvil."

"Aye," said a blushing Ian. He turned toward Stephen, angling his head to gaze up at him. "Thank ye for our morning, and I will keep my word about the abbey."

Stephen arched a brow. "I will hold ye to your word." Ian nodded and ran off toward the back of the cottage where his father had his forge.

"I ken Ian followed ye out on your journey this morning," remarked Betha, turning her focus to him.

"Aye, I thought as much," Stephen acknowledged. "I have ordered him to stay away from the abbey, while the bishops from Rome are here." He had no intention of frightening Betha, but he deemed it was warranted she should know about the bishops.

She drew in a sharp breath. "So it has begun?"

His brows drew together in a frown, not comprehending her meaning. "What has begun?"

"Oh, Sir Stephen, we ken who our son is, and his path," she spoke softly. "His father and I thought ye understood this, too."

"I ken he will be the next Master Druid. In truth, that is where my insight ends," he interjected, folding his arms across his chest.

Betha moved closer, the wind whipping at her wrap. She gently placed her hand on his. "Have ye not heard of the great cleansing here at Arbroath? The one foretold by the druids?"

Stephen shifted uncomfortably under her touch. "Nae," he muttered.

She frowned. "Hmmmm."

A bird cawed in the distance and Stephen followed its direction. "I have been...*away* from druids for some time." His feeling of guilt left him unsettled. He had sworn off their kind and should not have to give an explanation to anyone.

Betha pulled her wrap more tightly around her and followed his sight to where the bird had now flown out toward the sea. Inhaling deeply, she said, "The cleansing at Arbroath will begin with the arrival of visitors from a distant shore, and end in the burning of several druids."

Stephen reeled from her words. Would he be the instrument of destruction against the brothers of the abbey? There was only one way to stop this cleansing.

Taking a hold of her arm, he looked deep into her eyes when he spoke, "Then you must take Ian from Arbroath, as well as any druid who dwells here."

She shook her head slowly. "We cannot escape our destiny, and ye are our destiny."

"I will not kill for ye!" A flash of anger stirred his blood, and he spoke more harshly than he intended.

"That is not what is prophesied, Sir Stephen," Betha responded in a shocked voice.

He arched a brow. "Then pray tell me."

She glanced away, tugging at her wrap and Stephen understood she knew more than she was willing to reveal.

Nodding her head slightly, she responded, "It has

been foretold."

"Enough!" Stephen interrupted with a wave of his hand. "In *your* words."

Betha placed her hands on her hips and glared at him. "Ye will lead the druids and Ian from Arbroath and take them to the Great Glen near Urquhart. There, now ye have all of it."

"Me?" Stephen recoiled. "Who has prophesied this?"

The wind thrashed wildly around them now, and Stephen had an uncanny feeling it was being stirred by something not all the way human. It was similar to what his brother, Duncan could do. Betha was poised a few feet away, but she stood still within the swirling mass, as if she controlled the wind. A slight smile formed on her face, as if reading his thoughts.

"I, Betha MacDuff, niece to the great druid Cathal, have seen the vision." She bowed her head slightly, then turned and walked away.

Stephen could not move, nor breathe. The wind stopped as suddenly as it started. He stared at the woman strolling back to her cottage, a woman who was niece to one of the most powerful druids. Cathal was not only powerful, but he was once the druid elder for his clan. Did he realize his niece was living so close to the abbey? Why would she choose to do so?

"I've made a fresh pot of stew, and ye are welcome to join us. Unless you care to stand there and wrestle with your list of questions for me," Betha called out over her shoulder.

He responded with a grunt and stepped forward. "I would be honored to sit at your table."

"Whist!" Betha waved at him. "It is I, who am

honored to have ye in my home and for the care ye have shown our son. We understood his path, but never fathomed a Dragon Knight would be his protector." She walked into the cottage leaving Stephen once again speechless.

Upon entering Ian's home, he removed his cloak. Betha gestured for him to sit, and ladled some stew into a bowl. "Shall we not wait for Donal and Ian?" he asked.

"Nae. I want this time alone to answer any questions ye may have. It is best Ian not hear this." She paused in thought, then continued, "I believe he is unaware of his destiny, and for the moment I would like to keep it as such." Pouring some ale into a mug, she passed it to him.

Stephen nodded in understanding. Then taking the mug, he drank deeply. "Why are ye here, Betha? The forest would provide a haven for ye."

"This is our home, Sir Stephen. Donal was born in Arbroath, and I would not ask him to leave. Still, he does worry we are too close to the abbey and the new religion." She tore off a piece of bread and ate in silence.

"Have ye not considered the new religion?" he asked between bites of the stew.

Betha gave him an incredulous look. "Truly? Do ye even have to ask?" Sighing she remarked, "I am of the old ways. It flows in my blood and spirit with each breath I take." Reaching out, she placed her hand on his arm saying, "It is *who* I am."

A wave of uneasiness crept over him. It was who he was, too, and he wanted nothing to do with it anymore. Yet, each time he tried to rid himself of the old ways they slithered back in. He wanted to curse his fae blood, but it would require him to cast out his brothers, too. Stephen feared that if he looked deeply into his soul, it would reveal that he still longed for the old ways. He placed his hands down on the table and considered his next question.

"I have only seen the death of the druids and not of any of the order at the abbey."

He flashed her a look of surprise. "Is it part of your gift to read thoughts?"

"Nae," she chuckled. "I just thought ye should know."

Moving from the table, she took his bowl. "Would ye care for more stew?"

Shaking his head, he asked, "Do ye ken when this will happen? If it has begun, as ye have stated, then what is next?"

She frowned and sat back down on the bench. "Ye understand it does not work that way. What have ye seen, Sir Stephen?"

"Humph!" he growled.

She folded her arms across her chest and scrutinized him. "Ye are a *Dragon Knight*, and the one who holds the gift of visions. Plying me with your questions will not answer your own. I have passed along my wisdom, and now it is up to ye to follow your fate." Betha stood and came over to him, placing both hands on his face. "If ye continue to fight the path ye are on, it will *destroy* ye."

Stephen shrugged out of her grasp. He rose and went over to the window, noticing Donal and Ian were approaching.

Her voice was low when next she spoke. "Ye will

ken the time, Sir Stephen. Do not forsake us."

Turning, he saw the look of concern in her eyes. He had put himself as protector of Ian. Now, he was making another decision that did not bode well with him.

Walking over to her, he laid a gentle hand on her shoulder. "I give ye my word I will protect not only Ian, but the other druids as well."

"Swear by the oath of a Dragon Knight," she commanded.

His blood boiled with anger, and he was certain his eyes changed color, but Betha did not flinch.

"My word as a Dragon Knight, on my honor," he reluctantly ground out.

Betha smiled. "Then it is done."

Instantly, Ian came bounding into the cottage, Donal following closely behind him. Ian's father nodded in greeting.

"Sir Stephen, are ye joining us?" asked Ian.

"He has already eaten, Ian. Go and wash." Betha shooed him away.

Stephen paused at the door, one more question still burning to be asked, "Do ye ken where Cathal is?"

She hesitated briefly. "Aye. He is journeying to Burrow Cove to meet the druid elders. If the snows have melted he should reach it by Beltaine."

"Snows? Where is he traveling from?"

"Why from Glen Urquhart," Betha declared.

Stephen felt the blood leave his face. Could Cathal have knowledge of his brothers?

Giving her a curt nod, he strode from the cottage with more questions than when he entered.

Chapter Eight

"The smell of evil is comparable to the corpse flower, which has a stench of rotting meat."

"How dare you question me!" bellowed Bishop Augustus. "We are here from Rome on Holy orders to view the design of the abbey and to witness the work you have done among the people. You have failed to inform the Holy Father that pagan heretics still reside in the village. As of this date, you have not converted them."

Osgar winced. Though the words were not directed at him, he felt the stirrings of something sinister.

"If I may present," replied Brother Patrick, as he waited for permission to speak.

His face a mask of crimson, Bishop Augustus gave him a curt nod.

"Many have converted, and those which have not are few. I do believe they have fled north."

Bishop Augustus gave a sardonic smile, as he tilted his head to the side to glare at Patrick. "That is *not* what my messengers have told me."

Spies, Osgar thought. Rome had sent spies, or perhaps they were already among them in the abbey.

"Then what have your messengers told you?" asked Brother Colin. He had stood within the shadows, but now stepped forward.

The bishop slowly turned his focus to Colin. "Not only is the village beset with pagan worshipers, but one is kin to a druid."

Osgar willed his face to remain impassive, yet his hands clenched within the folds of his robe. He himself had been a druid, along with Colin and Cesan. Only the three of them knew about Betha. He would trust these brothers with his life, knowing they would each give of themselves to keep her and Ian safe.

"I can assure—"

"Enough!" Bishop Augustus silenced Colin with a flick of his wrist. "It is time Rome dealt with these sinful heathens."

Osgar and Cesan glanced at one another in an unspoken thought. If the bishop knew about Betha, could they also have knowledge of Sir Stephen? What of Ian?

Bishop Augustus stood. "This meeting has ended. I wish to discuss a more private matter with Brothers Timmons and Charles. The rest of you may leave." He made the sign of the cross as the others got up and left the hall.

Colin marched over to Osgar and Cesan ready to burst, when Osgar held up his hand in warning. "Not here. Meet me at my work room in one hour." Colin nodded and stormed off.

When they were outside away from prying eyes and ears, Osgar turned to Cesan. "Find Sir Stephen, and have him meet me in the healing garden after prayers have started."

"Aye," muttered Cesan, then strode away through the cloisters.

Osgar dipped his head to a passing brother. He let

the sound of the ocean soothe his taut nerves, as he gathered his thoughts. Stepping out of the cloisters and walking through an archway, he watched as the waves rolled back and forth, the white foam glistening on the shore.

Bishop Augustus had stunned them with his announcement. His awareness of the druids, particularly Betha, was unexpected. And it troubled him. How much more had he or Rome discerned?

They needed to warn the others. Osgar did something he had not done in many moons. He said a silent prayer across the breeze to the Mother Danu, asking her to protect and watch over her children.

****

The dark hooded figure stayed hidden within the recess of the walls, watching. He recognized these three were once mighty druids. His lips twisted in disgust to think they would betray their own kind to join an order of sniveling men.

"Weak men who should burn," Lachlan hissed quietly.

Oh yes, he thought, he would gladly see their bodies burn, and who better to do it than the believers of the one God. He would bide his time, until the moment of revelation. First, he would make sure one man's identity would be exposed. He had failed with his brother, Duncan, but he would not fail this time.

"I will see you burn at the stake, Stephen MacKay, and I will be the first to take up the torch and set your body ablaze." His hands dug into his arms through the folds of his robe, and he drew forth blood, reveling in the pain. "But first, you will lead me to your stone."

Stepping away from the stall, he walked quickly

away.

****

Stephen wandered through the back nave of the abbey on his way to the south end where Osgar maintained a huge section of the garden. The heady scent of lavender prickled his nose, and he followed it until he was in the medicinal part of the gardens. His warrior instincts kicked in the moment he saw Osgar with a weapon in his hand—a druid sickle.

He cocked an eyebrow.

"It is not what you think, Stephen," scoffed Osgar.

Stephen folded his arms across his chest. "Then tell me why a brother is using a druid's sickle in the garden...in the gloaming?"

"I find it shears plants more cleanly. Besides, we have more pressing problems than to worry about my sickle." He gathered the comfrey and cowslip, placing it in the basket on the ground. "Come, let us withdraw to the back of the garden."

Stephen followed him past the healing and vegetable garden. They went through a hedge and into a clearing, that looked out toward the sea. It was breathtaking to watch as the sun slipped beyond the horizon. The light splintered across the water like colorful fingers reaching out before receding into the darkness. He turned to see Osgar sitting on a stone bench against an old oak. The man looked worried.

"What troubles ye, Osgar?" Stephen asked, settling down next to him.

"The bishops from Rome ken Betha is kin to Cathal."

"How can this be?"

"It seems they have spies, or as Brother Augustus

stated, *messengers*."

"Judas's balls!" Stephen snapped. "Do ye ken these spies?"

The monk's shoulders slumped. "Nae. I fear it could be any of the brothers, except for two."

Stephen fisted his hands on his thighs, knowing whom he meant by the other two. "Who are the other druids?"

"Brothers Colin and Cesan." He angled his head at Stephen. "Does this distress ye?"

He uttered something unintelligible under his breath and got up from the bench. He ran his hands through his hair in frustration. He had tried hard to forget the past. To bury who he was and the old religion. With the dawning of spring, the door opened back up, beckoning him to reenter.

The wind whipped his cloak around him as he considered what next to say. He watched the waves dip, and without thought, he pushed them back with his power.

"Careful, lest ye return back home," replied Osgar.

Stephen could not help himself and let out a bark of laughter. "Did I ever leave?" he asked over his shoulder.

Osgar smiled. "Only ye can answer that one, my friend."

Nodding his head in agreement, he strode back to Osgar. "So, the bishop has spies, but we do, too. There are only the four of us who can be found steadfast. I say we watch and listen. When the time is right, I will take Ian and Betha to the hills, or farther if need be."

"Ye would guide them from this place? These druids?" he asked frowning.

Stephen rubbed the back of his neck as he rose to lean against the tree. He felt its strength infuse him with warmth. It had been so long. He crossed his arms over his chest and gazed down at Osgar. "Aye, I would and any who would need my protection. I may be at war with the old and new, but I will not have to stand by and watch as others slay innocents."

His friend nodded slowly. "Can ye not tell me your latest vision?"

"Ye realize my visions are just a small sight of possible conclusions." He bent and picked up a small stone tossing it out far over the cliff and watching it crash below against the rocks.

"Aye, but yours are *different*."

"I ken who I am. Ye do not have to tell me!" Fury rode his frame as he stormed away from Osgar.

Placing his hands on his hips, he glanced back at Osgar. "I was standing on a hill and at my feet were some of my brothers, slain. And in my hand, I held a bloody sword." He cocked his head to the side, "Feel free to clarify its significance."

Osgar stood, walking over to Stephen. He tapped a finger against his mouth in thought. "Who were they?"

"I did not see their faces, only their robes," he whispered.

"Ahhh, then ye ken what ye must do?"

"Aye, druid!" snapped Stephen, frustrated with his unwanted duty. "I must open myself to the visions and let them become a part of me, *again*."

"Ye cannot fight who ye are." Anger infused Osgar's words. He threw his hands out toward the sea. "Your journey led ye here, and now ye must make peace with it. Take up the mantle of who ye are!"

"How can ye honor both?" Stephen hissed.

"Why not?" replied Osgar.

Before Stephen could utter a retort, Colin came running toward them with a look that sent a wave of uneasiness through him.

"We have trouble," gasped Colin.

He lurched forward grasping the man's arm. "Ian?"

"Nae, Betha. The bishop's guards took her." Colin wiped a hand over his face. "Donal sought me out. They held a sword at Ian to get her to come with them."

"Bloody hell!" Stephen roared, releasing his grip on Colin. "Where are Donal and Ian?"

"Cesan has taken them to the hills. Betha had already started to pack their belongings when the guards stormed into their home."

He grimaced. "Why would Betha be packing? She told me they were not leaving."

Colin shrugged.

"She had a vision," Osgar interrupted. "It would be the only reason she would flee." He turned toward Stephen, a look of worry creased his forehead.

His jaw clenched, and he realized what he had to do. The ocean roared behind him, giving him strength—infusing him with a power he had not felt in over a year. "I will free Betha and bring her to safety. Are there any others in the village that would be in danger?"

Osgar let out a deep sigh. "Aye. There are a few families who still honor the old ways."

Stephen pointed a finger at Colin. "Go to these families. Tell them to be ready an hour before dawn's first light." He glanced back at Osgar. "Do ye ken where they might take her for questioning?"

Osgar blanched. "The abbey is a holy place. There is nowhere..." He paused in thought before his eyes lit up. "Aye, there might be."

"I shall return when the families are safe," said Colin.

Stephen shook his head. "Nae. Until the threat is removed, no one is safe. I fear whoever this spy is will have ye already on their list, and that includes ye, Osgar. Ye should go to the hills."

"This is...my ho...home, Stephen," stammered Osgar.

Placing a gentle hand on the man's shoulder, Stephen tried to comfort him. "And it shall be once again. But heed me on this, *druid*." Stephen said the last with reverence.

"Aye," whispered Osgar. He bowed his head to Colin. "Go with God, and our Lady."

"And the same with ye, Osgar."

They watched as Colin descended away from the abbey and down the hill to the village.

"I would feel honored if ye would bless me before I take my leave, Osgar."

Osgar gave a weak smile, "It is I who would be honored, *Dragon Knight*."

Stephen knelt in front of the man, feeling the last ray of light fall over his shoulders.

The druid placed his hands on Stephen's shoulders and cast his eyes up toward the sky in an invocation.

"Bless this Knight, our Lord, and light his path. Give him the strength of your sword arm, St. Michael. Let the hounds of Cuchulainn be his guards. In the blessing of the Old Ones, and the New One, keep him safe on his journey."

Osgar lowered his arms and stepped back from Stephen in awe, as the sun's last ray of light cast a glow about the man, illuminating the fae within.

Chapter Nine

Arbroath, Scotland—April, Present day

"From his lips, he spoke the truth. Yet, the nettle's sting prevented her from understanding its meaning."

How green the land seemed, so vast and luscious. The hills behind her fell in soft mounds decked in blossoming heather. The air was pungent with sea salt, and the rhythmic sound of the ocean soothed her senses. The winds swept over and around her causing her hair to fly wildly about, yet, she didn't care.

Taking a deep breath, Aileen surveyed the climb up the hills. It would be so tempting to just walk away. She had spent the night with deep dreams haunting her. Liam's words resonated in them, and she found herself running away.

"There has to be an explanation," she murmured.

Her gaze caught sight of a seagull, and she longed to take flight. Nothing made sense. Neither her father nor Liam. Castle Balleycove. The book. She rubbed her pendant, more confused than ever. "Oh Mom, show me a sign." Sighing, she stepped on the mossy path leading downward and back to the castle.

Aileen entered through the back entrance, which led directly into the kitchens. Her head was pounding, and before she sought out her father, she needed a strong cup of coffee.

The smell of fresh baked bread and laughter spilled forth, and she smiled.

"Well, there you are. If we had known you were going to take a walk this early, we would have joined you," said Maeve, smiling back.

She didn't want to worry her friends with her sleepless night. "I was up early. And considering how everyone drank last night"—pausing to wink at Sally and Cara—"I wanted to take a look at the grounds of the castle."

"Then I hope you've worked up an appetite, because between Gwen and your father's cook, Susan, we're in for a treat." Maeve moved to sit down at the kitchen table.

"Good morning, Aileen," said Aunt Lily walking into the kitchen. "Did you sleep well?" Peering over her shoulder, she tried to see what all the commotion was about.

Ignoring her aunt's question, Aileen whispered, nodding in the direction of the two women. "Both of the chefs are apparently cooking for us this morning. This should be a feast. I should have waited to take my walk after I ate."

"How early have they been at it?"

Overhearing Aunt Lily's question, Teresa replied, "Since five this morning." She moved past Aileen placing a basket of freshly baked scones on the table.

"Sheesh! I thought I was the only one up," muttered Aileen. Noticing a pot on the table, she grabbed a mug and prayed it was coffee. The rich aroma filled her senses, and she poured until the liquid reached the brim. Holding the mug and inhaling, she sipped it slowly, before taking a seat beside Cara. Her friend had one too many last night and gave her a brief smile as she nursed her cup, too.

Closing her eyes, she allowed the hot brew to do its magic and clear the cobwebs from her brain.

"Good morning, Aileen."

She opened her eyes to find her father standing next to her. He had a smile for her, but a shadow of sadness creased his features. Her heart lurched.

Giving him a warm smile, she replied, "Good morning, Dad."

He glanced at the women talking and preparing the food in a frenzy of words and movement, and chuckled. "I knew Gwen would immediately fall in love with the kitchens and Susan."

"Yes, it looks like she's found nirvana," chortled Aileen, sipping more of her coffee. "Have you eaten?"

Her dad turned back to her. "Aye. I thought I would come and let you know I will be in the library. Come see me after you're done here." Before he took his leave, he placed a kiss on her brow.

Nodding, she gave him another smile.

Instantly, Gwen and Susan started bringing forth steaming dishes and more baskets containing breads. Aileen definitely made a mental note to take another long walk after her meeting with her father. This time she would roam the hills to work off all the food she was going to consume.

****

Several hours later, and feeling refreshed from the warmth of food, friends, and abundant mugs of coffee, Aileen made her way down the corridor to the library. She paused every once in a while to admire another tapestry, richly woven with scenes of medieval life.

Again, questions as to why her parents kept this knowledge from her made no sense. She just could not fathom that, because of a vision her mother had, both her parents withheld part of her heritage for her safety. Knowing her mother, she would have shared her vision preparing her for whatever lay ahead, not shielded her. But her dad may have asked her to wait since he didn't seem as sure of the vision.

Pausing outside the library's huge oak doors, she took a deep fortifying breath and pushed them open. To say the room was large would be an understatement. The word immense suited its description better. The only wall which wasn't adorned in rich, dark paneled shelves filled with books held a fireplace dead center in the room. Several ladders were on either end, and Aileen itched to climb up and view the books on the top shelves.

Her father stood next to Liam, their backs to her, and she could hear them arguing. They were looking at some kind of document on a table at the far end of the room. Liam had his fists clenched on the table shaking his head back and forth.

Aileen really wanted to look at this book, the one with her name in it, yet, she did not want to get in the middle of their heated conversation. Deciding she had waited long enough, she stepped forward.

"Should I come back another time?" Her voice tinged with just a bit of sarcasm.

Both men snapped their heads up at the sound of her voice.

"Nae!" her father barked out. He quickly folded up the document and slid it into the desk.

"I'll keep you informed of the progress."

He gave Liam a curt nod in response.

Liam gathered up a scroll off the chair and strolled over to her. "Listen with an open heart," he said, placing a gentle squeeze on her arm.

Anger simmered within her, but she swallowed back the harsh retort. Nodding slowly, Aileen let her gaze travel to a gaze that bore into hers behind Liam's back.

Liam released his hold, taking his leave.

She crossed the room to stand before her father. "I would very much like to see this book, since you seem to be so concerned about its contents. Perhaps, I can shed some light on its mysterious drawing."

Her father arched a brow and folded his arms across his chest. "Perhaps..."

"Well?"

He let out a sigh, and stepped away to walk over to a paneled bookcase. Easing his hand along the upper ledge of one of the shelves, he released a latch, and the entire bookcase opened to reveal a passageway. He then proceeded to disappear from her sight.

Aileen snapped her mouth shut and scurried after him. The moment she passed into the dark tunnel, she heard the bookcase close behind her; a cloak of darkness descended over her.

"Dad," she squeaked.

"Keep walking, Aileen. I'm lighting the torches."

Light filtered and bounced off the stone walls, and she took a deep sigh of relief. The air cold and musty caressed her shoulders as she took careful steps forward. Keeping her pace steady, she gingerly followed the lit torches along the curves. Where in the blazes was her father taking her?

"Not much further," he uttered. "How are you doing?"

"Just peachy, Dad!" she replied sarcastically.

Her dad chuckled, and she wanted to smack him. He was just full of surprises.

She halted before some stone steps that spiraled downward. They were incredibly narrow and considering how damp the air was, Aileen hesitated before taking a cautious foot forward.

"I'm right here, Aileen. Take my hand."

She looked down into his eyes, and for a moment, something flashed within them.

"Aileen." His voice soothed her senses.

She reached out to grab his hand and slowly made her way down the steps. In truth, there were only a few, but fear fed her nerves.

"Here we are." Taking a large key, her dad unlocked a large medieval bolt in the wooden door. When he opened it, light flooded the area.

"Oh my..." she murmured.

He smiled as he led her inside the massive room. "Only electricity will do inside here." He moved away from her and strolled down the aisle of artifacts that were neatly organized on tables and shelves.

Aileen scanned the area, slowly making her way toward her father. There were swords displayed against one wall, and metal armor on another. Scrolls rolled neatly and tucked into slots framed one wall, with books shelved next to them. Pottery adorned tables, as if someone was cataloguing the pieces, and she marveled at their craftsmanship. She let her fingers glide reverently over a bowl with dragons painted on its sides.

"Beautiful artwork, isn't it? Liam believes it's from the ninth century."

Aileen gasped, snatching her hand away from the bowl and onto her chest. "The ninth century? My God, Dad! This is like some sort of treasure cave." She shivered more from the artifacts, than the bitter coldness of the room.

"Aye." He took a coat from a nearby chair, and draped it around her. "There's no heat in this room. It would destroy most of the items, especially the scrolls."

"Is this where you work most of the time?" she questioned as she made her way to a table.

Her dad followed her gaze before he answered. "At the moment we are focused on a particular dig near the abbey, but I find solace in being down here."

Aileen knew without asking her father that the leather bound book lying on the table was the one he wanted to show her. Its coloring was dark and simply made, and she reached out a trembling hand to touch it. A warm rush of heat filled her senses, and she pulled her hand back, as if she had been burnt. Her sight blurred, and she leaned against the table for support.

"This is the book," she whispered.

Her father's arms went around her shoulders, "Aye, Aileen. This is the journal of Stephen MacKay. He was a Dragon Knight who came to live at the abbey for some months in the thirteenth century. Most of the pages contain the daily progress of the building of the abbey, which is a boon for us. Then on others, there are partial drawings." He released his hold and rubbed a hand along the back of his neck. "He would start a drawing and then cross it out, as if he was not content with what he had drawn."

"I want to see the picture of my pendant." Reaching out to open the journal, the contact sent heat throughout her body. The pages were so thin, and she trembled with each turn. Why did she feel this way?

"On the last."

She gently folded back the pages to the last one. There in all its glory, was a drawing of her pendant, every nuance of hers mirrored on this page. However, what truly had her gasping was not just the drawing, but also her name...her full name, *Aileen Rose Kerrigan*.

"It's…it's impossible," she stammered. She looked up into her father's face—a face filled with certainty that this was indeed real. "How can this be?"

His brows furrowed. "Anything is possible, Aileen." He sighed and moved away from her to lean against the table.

Laughter bubbled forth and burst free. She hugged the journal against her chest and let the mirth subside.

"Honestly, Dad? I may believe in magic and healing, but what you are suggesting is preposterous! It's not possible for me to travel to the—" She waved her hand in frustration.

"Thirteenth century," interjected her dad.

"Right," she said, pointing a finger at him.

Then a thought occurred to Aileen. Her dad had connected the drawing within the journal with her mother's vision. She was astounded that a man of his intelligence would come to this kind of conclusion. There had to be a rational explanation—not this insane one.

"You cannot believe it, Dad."

"Believe what, Aileen? That it's *real*?"

Exasperation filled her and stepping in front of him, she held the book up. "You can't possibly think this journal and mom's vision are connected. It would only mean one possible theory."

Arching a brow, he countered, "That your mother's vision of your life ending here in Scotland, and the journal of Stephen MacKay could only mean you will indeed travel back to the thirteenth century?"

The look in her father's eyes frightened her.

Standing to his full height, he placed his hand upon her cheek. "Aye, my dear daughter, it is *precisely* what I mean."

Chapter Ten

"The Dragon mixed together henbane, belladonna, hemlock, and aconite to deaden the pain, yet she was helpless without the angel of Death."

Aileen fled the room with the journal still in her clutches. Fear and nausea clamped a hold on her body with its icy fingers around her heart. She heard her father yelling her name, but she refused to listen any further. It was not that his words had frightened her; no, it was his unfathomable belief it was indeed a possibility. A belief backed up with evidence, now held firmly against her chest.

Her breath came out in small gasps, and she found herself staring at the large tapestry in the great hall. It was the one that had drawn her toward *him* last night. The set of his chin suggested a stubborn streak. One she understood well herself. Instinctively, she reached out and grazed her finger along his chin, as if she could awaken him from his unearthly gaze with her touch.

"Talk to me, Sir Stephen. Tell me this cannot be."

The salty tang of the sea drifted past her, and she longed for the water's soothing comfort. Not waiting for an answer from her Knight, Aileen left the great hall seeking the solace of the ocean. A force unknown, each step bringing her closer to the water, drove her. Aileen could not get there fast enough, and her walk shifted to a full out run. She stumbled once, but kept the pace until the foam of the sea lapped at her boots.

She watched as the waves rocked back and forth to a timeless rhythm all their own. Their gentle cadence working their magic, Aileen felt her heart fall into tune with the sound. Her fingers were still tightly woven around the journal, and with strength from the water and something else she could not explain, Aileen opened to the first page of the journal.

Journal of Stephen Malcolm MacKay
January, in the year of our Lord, 1205...
Cold...so verra cold.

Then below the words was a drawing of a snowy landscape, partially done. Without thought, Aileen started to move down the sandy beach turning each page carefully. Pictures of the foliage jumped out at her, their Latin names coming to life before her eyes. Sometimes they would be followed by a personal observation, others just a passing scribble.

Her footsteps brought her to a small cave. Looking up, Aileen noticed she had wandered far from the castle. The sun streamed down near the entrance beckoning her to come forward. Closing the journal, she stood in front of the opening, hesitant to enter. The darkness was not her friend, yet something winked at her within its depths.

She blinked several times, thinking it nothing but a trick of light, but there it was again, a flash of something inside. "By the Goddess, get a grip, Aileen," she muttered. Walking carefully over the rocks, she glimpsed an object just inside the moss-covered opening. Stepping gingerly past a sand crab, she made her way inside the cave.

The briny smell assaulted her senses as she bent to look at what had caught her eye. It was a dazzling green stone lodged between the crevices of a boulder and the sand. Reaching out, she gradually eased it away from the confines of the wall. The stone warmed in the palm of her hand.

"Holy crap!" Aileen stumbled out from the cave and into the sunlight. The green stone was just not any green stone, but a medallion. The heavy chain attached was stunning in its craftsmanship. She blew across the top to remove some of the sand particles, and then her heart froze. Recognition flared in her mind, realizing where she had seen this.

Aileen was trying hard not to shake. However, in her trembling left hand, she held the journal of Stephen MacKay, and in her right hand...his *medallion*.

"No! Impossible. Isn't it?" She swallowed the bile coming forth, glancing at her hands in disbelief.

"I need help," she uttered looking around in desperation.

Clutching both items against her, she walked as quickly as her feet could carry her across the beach and back home.

When Aileen pushed through the front door, she was still running, and in an effort not to collide with her aunt, they both succeeded in tripping past the entry table, spilling the contents in Aileen's hands across the entryway.

Aunt Lily was the first to start laughing. "What the hell! Are you okay?"

"Physically or mentally? At the moment...I don't know," she exclaimed in frustration.

Her troubled remark put a stop to her aunt's

laughter, and she looked at the items strewn along the floor. Bending, she picked up the journal and medallion. "What are these?"

Aileen backed up slowly, pressing herself against the wall. "In your hands is the journal and medallion of Sir Stephen MacKay."

"Aileen, *where* did you find these?" Lily said in a hushed tone.

Now it was Aileen's turn to laugh. "Well, you see, the journal was in my father's possession, but I came upon the medallion down by the ocean this morning." Pushing away from the wall, she took the items from her aunt. A shadow of something passed over her aunt's face.

She rubbed the medallion's cool surface infusing her with strength, her gaze directed at her aunt. "Tell me something...have you always known about the vision my mother had of me coming to Scotland, and meeting some untimely ending?"

Aunt Lily's shoulders slumped, which told Aileen all she needed to know.

"So your father's finally told you." She reached out a hand, but Aileen took a step backwards. "You don't understand, dear." Her hand fisted. "I made your mother a solemn vow—a promise not to say anything to you."

"There are so many secrets locked into each of you that it makes me wonder whose truth is real." Turning away, she headed back outside. She needed distance...distance from everyone.

"Aileen?"

She paused, refusing to meet her aunt's gaze. Aileen had enough of her own emotions without seeing the anguish in Aunt Lily's.

Her aunt's voice carried an edge of steel when she spoke. "You are descended from magical people, Aileen, and magic is at the core of who you are. There is still so much you need to comprehend *and* learn." Her tone took a more ominous turn. "Do not close yourself off to the possibilities of it all. To do so will only bring you destruction."

Aileen drew in a long breath and held it, holding back a terse retort. She would not give her the satisfaction of an acknowledgement. Holding her chin high, she deftly walked away from her aunt, seeking consolation away from the people who had called themselves *family*.

****

Aileen had traveled far, her steps leading her to their own destination. She didn't care where they went or what they were in search of. Peace and solitude was what she sought, and she kept moving. Something skittered past her, and she came to an abrupt stop, glancing around at her surroundings.

The ruins of Arbroath Abbey loomed in front of her.

They were majestic with the sunlight dancing off the red sandstone. She cast her gaze to the distinctive round high window at the south end. Thoughts of long ago pierced her thoughts wondering what it would have looked liked lit at night. Aileen knew this window was used as a beacon for mariners, and known locally as the *Round O*.

Seagulls cawed in the distance, and she moved toward the ruins. She felt empowered with the sea behind her. Marveling at the foliage of various plants,

Aileen stopped and touched them, mentally cataloguing each for a later time. As she stepped through the arch's entrance, it was as if time stopped and a hushed silence descended.

"Is this where you once stood, Sir Stephen?" Her gaze touched on the medallion—expecting him to appear and answer her.

She continued to stroll slowly across the damp ground, and choosing a sunny location, sat down with her back against one of the walls. The warmth of the stones infused her body. Her hand rested over the top of the journal, hesitant to open it again.

Taking the medallion, she shoved it into her coat, and opened the book. "Tell me who you are."

Her first thought was to turn to the last page again, yet, she wanted to know more of the man who had written her name on the page. There were copious notes on the daily building and repairs of the abbey. Then on some pages, there would be a mixture of plants drawn along the borders. At times, she could tell when he was frustrated. His notes would be curt and scribbled, and sections of drawings were scratched out, or partially completed. On one of the pages, Aileen saw a detailed account of a tisane. From the combination of the herbs, she could only deduce their mixture as one used for treating headaches.

"Eight hundred years has passed, and we still haven't deviated much from the treatment of headaches."

The sound of voices brought Aileen out of her thoughts and the journal. How dare someone invade her peacefulness? Standing, she brushed off bits of leaf and pebbles, and moved silently toward their conversation.

The voices sounded terse and low, as if arguing.

She crept up against the wall, but recognized instantly one of the speakers. Her father was here. Then she recognized the other one more clearly and realized it was Liam.

Blast! Why did they have to be here? She looked around trying to figure out an escape plan without either noticing her.

Until...

"I order you not to utter one word about her involvement with the MacKay," her father hissed. "If anyone is going through the veil, it will be me!"

Aileen moved closer until she could see their faces.

Liam gave him a skeptical glance. "Really? Remember, you are no longer a Fenian Warrior of the Sidhe. How do you propose to cross over?"

"I may have given up my powers, but not my *heritage*," Aidan said in a guttural voice.

"Aye, that may be, but you cannot travel the veil without me, and I won't let you go."

Aidan's eyes blazed with fury. "You will not take my daughter through! Do you hear me, Liam?"

"Bloody Hell, Aidan! It is her destiny!"

Aileen felt as if all the air from her lungs had been sucked from her body. Her legs trembled as she emerged from her hiding place.

"Wh...*what are you*?"

Her father and Liam both turned at the sound of her voice.

The former was the first to speak as he stepped toward her. "Aileen?"

"Stay back," she ordered with a wave of her hand.

He froze. Raking a hand through his hair, he

nodded to Liam. "I think I would like to be alone with my daughter."

Liam gave him a curt shrug, yet before he could move away, they heard someone yelling in the distance.

Both men turned away from her, their focus elsewhere.

Aileen had to escape—*now*. She did not want to be alone with this stranger from God knows where. Taking a few steps back, she crept along slowly until she felt the side wall, silently disappearing from her father and Liam.

Lily was running hard, waving at them frantically.

Something was wrong. Aidan could see it in her eyes.

"Has Aileen been to see you?"

"Aye, she's here, but—"

"She's gone," uttered Liam.

Lily grabbed Aidan's arm. "Aidan, she has Stephen's medallion."

Panic seized him. "By the hounds—nae! Aileen!" he roared.

"Damn!" Liam hissed out, before taking off through the abbey.

"My God, Aidan," sobbed Lily. "If she has the medallion here within the walls..." Her voice trailed off.

"Then I will kill Liam with my bare hands, if she crosses the veil of time without him."

****

The more she ran, the deeper Aileen went within the abbey. She gave no thought as to her direction, and at times, she could have sworn she heard Liam yelling her name. "Like hell I'm going to stop and talk to you." She cringed, slinking quickly along the walls.

Then Aileen had a thought. Perhaps if she stayed hidden in one of the smaller buildings they would think she went back to Balleycove. Casting a furtive glance behind her, she took note of her surroundings. Off to one side was dense shrubbery. After pushing through it, she found a wooden door built into the wall. Silently thanking the Goddess, she gently lifted the latch and opened it slowly.

She let out a groan. "It would have to be shrouded in darkness."

Hearing Liam call out her name again was all the incentive Aileen needed. Gathering her courage, she stepped inside and closed the door behind her.

The first odor to assault her senses was musty and metallic. Wisps of light from the door filtered around her, but she could barely see a few feet in front of her.

"Aileen, where are you?" Liam's shout had her moving rapidly away from the door. "It's now or never," she mumbled.

Touching her pendant for strength, she took a few shaky steps forward. Aileen moved along the wall, bracing herself against its surface for support, absently touching the medallion inside her coat. With each step she took, a piece of her fear seeped away. Her breathing became steady.

A gentle breeze flitted past her, its warmth caressing her face. She moved away from the wall propelled by some force. It was as if something or someone needed her desperately.

A tingling sensation wrapped around her skin and prickled her senses. Bright lights danced before her eyes. She blinked once, then twice, and stopped. Heat cascaded from the top of her head to the tips of her toes.

Aileen felt empowered and within seconds, everything exploded in an array of brilliant colors and her body seemed to fly apart.

Chapter Eleven

"Do not sing to me of your praises, nor accolades. Give to me a song bejeweled in violets."

Stephen kept within the dark corridors of the cloister—waiting. He would bide his time until he saw the one man who could lead him to Betha. Osgar had told him about an old cellar, no longer used for storage. It was the only place he could think of that they could hide someone from the prying eyes of the others. Stephen's frustration at not being able to locate the cellar grew each hour that passed.

Time was his enemy.

He could not fathom what means of questioning they would inflict on Betha. His instincts did not bode well when it came to this particular man from Rome. Nae—they screamed at him. As a warrior, Stephen relied on his gut, and it was churning at the possibilities. Betha had referred to a cleansing. Was she the first?

Low voices emanated along the north side, and Stephen pressed himself further back within the darkness. They were low, but he recognized the one instantly as Brother Timmons.

"Can we not give her some ale?" asked Timmons.

"No!" snapped Bishop Augustus. "I can see you have no belly for this. I do have a man who will oversee her questioning. Do you think you can handle the brothers? Will they stand with us? By the right hand of God?"

"Of course! We will do all in our power to wipe the heathens from Arbroath."

"Good. Now go and discuss this with the other brothers. We shall all meet in the morning after prayers."

Stephen crept out from the shadows, and saw Bishop Augustus scratch his chin in thought. *Bloody hell! Would the man not move?* He touched the cold steel of his sword for strength, wishing as an afterthought, it could have been his stone.

Finally, Bishop Augustus turned and made his way out. Stephen followed him. The air hummed with energy, and he looked about. It prickled along his senses, but he had no time to search out its meaning. Keeping his focus steady, he made his way along the corridors at a stealthy pace.

Why was the bishop heading for the nave? He waited then slipped inside. Peering around, he spied the man going to the front. He watched and waited. His prey was removing a rug, and lifting a latch.

"God's blood," he rasped low. No wonder none of the others knew about this. The cellar was below the nave. Moving quickly, he descended down through the spiral stairway after the bishop.

The air reeked of death.

A second wave of energy crashed into him, and Stephen had to steady himself. Something was not right. Yet, this was not the time to dwell. He paused letting the shift of power ease, and then continued forward.

Voices talking low carried along the dank walls. He froze, trying to determine where they were coming from. Slipping inside the corner against the wall, he saw a light from a torch coming forward. He held still as two cloaked figures ambled along. One of the men paused briefly, then continued onward.

Stephen emerged slowly, casting a glance back at the departing men. Making his way around the corner, he came upon a door, partially ajar.

"So you refuse to tell us of the other druids? Hmmm...Perhaps I should ask Lachlan to serve you more penance?"

Lachlan? Stephen reeled. He knew the name, and yet...it was impossible! The man was dead. Why would a druid who was supposedly dead be consulting with the bishop? It could not be.

As he peered into the room, he could see Betha's breathing was labored, but she would not relent. She held her bloody chin high, her eyes blazing at her captor. "I will *never* tell ye anything," she rasped out. "Ye can question and torture me, but by the Goddess I will not tell ye what ye seek."

The bishop smacked her hard. "Your heathen ways are at an end, and—"

Stephen silenced him with a blow to the head.

A sob erupted from Betha, "Sweet Mother Danu!"

"Can ye stand?" he asked, hesitant to touch her. Blood stained most of her dress and pooled around her feet.

"If she cannae, then I will carry her," replied Donal from behind.

Stephen lunged without thought, sword poised at his friend. "Bloody hell! I could have run ye through."

"Donal," gasped Betha.

He was at her side in two strides. Lightly touching her injured face, he said, "When Osgar told me that ye might be kept hidden in another cellar, I realized Sir Stephen would need my help."

"How, Donal?" Stephen interjected. "Osgar did not ken this place."

"Aye, but this was the original place where we kept the wine." He gave a wink to Stephen. "Ye ken I helped to build this."

Tears streamed down Betha's face. "Get me out of here."

Donal swiftly cut her bonds and lifted her from the chair. "Can ye walk?" Then he noticed her foot was badly misshapen. "What have they done?"

"My punishment for not talking...among other things." She silenced his further questions with a kiss.

Stephen approached the door, keeping watch for anyone. He had shoved the bishop to the side, and bound his hands.

He heard Donal say, "Shall I kill him for ye, Betha?"

Betha shook her head. "Nae. We have bigger fears than this depraved creature."

Stephen cast a glance back at her. "Lachlan?"

"Aye." Her eyes were wide with fear.

"We'll talk more when we get ye safely out of here."

After what seemed like an eternity, they made it safely outside the abbey walls. Darkness had descended, which gave them much needed cover for their escape. Donal gently placed Betha on his horse.

"Your horse, Sir Stephen?"

"By the old abbot's cottage. I will take the passage under Osgar's work room. Ye ken where it will lead?"

Donal nodded. "Then we shall leave ye. The others are in the caves, and some have gone deeper into the hills. We shall await your arrival."

"Go with the God and Goddess, Sir Stephen," whispered Betha.

Stephen gave her a sad smile. Taking her hand, he placed a gentle kiss on it. "I believe they are no longer walking with me, but I thank ye."

He watched until they were no longer in his sight before setting out to retrieve Grian. Stephen had prepared quickly and secured his horse earlier. Now, he had to delve back within the abbey grounds. It was only a matter of time before they found Bishop Augustus.

Darting quietly along the corridors, he was relieved not to encounter any of the brothers. Slipping out the side door, he crept through the gardens. The crescent moon was lifting her face in the night sky, and he cast a passing glance.

A feeling of something he was not prepared for trickled down his neck. Leaning against the door leading to the tunnel, he took in some deep calming breaths. "Nae," he muttered, knowing he had to get to the tunnels soon. A vision was starting, and for the first time in many moons, Stephen would welcome it. The possibility of making some sense of recent happenings was now prominent.

He stumbled inside and bolted the door. Pinpricks of light swam before his eyes as he fought for control. He only required a few more moments. Pushing aside the heavy panel, he heaved himself inside cloaking himself in darkness. Making sure he was sealed in,

Stephen groped his way along the stone walls.

"By the hounds! Not...yet," he growled out through clenched teeth. Slamming a fist against the wall, he tried to focus on moving forward. Pain seared into his temples, and he tripped. He fell to his knees and try as he might, there would be no standing. The entrance was so very close, but he would not make to its safety.

This time the vision succeeded in its forced entry.

The smell of burning flesh filled his nostrils. Images of people, their screams clawed at him. Horror and chaos covered the burning hill. One man stood out before the blaze, mocking them with glee. Someone called out his name, and the man turned around.

Pointing his staff at Stephen, he roared, "I ken who ye are!"

The vision left him as suddenly as it came, leaving him with blinding pain. Stephen retched on the ground, and blacked out.

Chapter Twelve

"The path to her lover was not scented with flowers, but with distrust and disbelief."

The steady rhythm of her heart was all Aileen could hear for the moment. She knew she had fainted. Her thoughts were scrambled, and she rubbed at her temples with shaky fingers. Opening her eyes a fraction, she tried to make out her surroundings. Faint light fractured off the wall, and she breathed a sigh of relief.

Then her memories unfolded in her mind. Her dad, a Fenian Warrior? Liam? Tears stung her eyes. "You do have a lot of explaining, Dad," she muttered.

The journal! She glanced around and noticed it was missing. Standing slowly, she took a few wary steps back to try to locate it. Yet, the further she went, the more the darkness enveloped her.

"Sweet Bridget," she hissed. Peering back toward the light, she heaved a sigh. Somehow, the journal must have gotten lost within the tunnel. Determined to come back with a flashlight, Aileen moved along to the entrance.

A low moan snapped her from her goal. "Who's there," she asked, hugging her arms around herself.

Silence greeted her.

Swallowing her fear, she stepped cautiously ahead.

Then she heard it again. It sounded like someone in pain. Her steps quickening, she rounded the corner almost colliding with someone sprawled out on the ground.

"Oh my...*who, what*," Aileen stammered for words, as she stood before the great hulking form of a half dressed man.

Again, the man groaned.

She stooped down looking for some type of injury. There was no sign of blood around him, only his...*sword*?

"What the hell?" She jumped back quickly. "Is there a Renaissance faire nearby? Excuse me, can I help you? Where is the pain?" Leaning forward again, she reached out, and gently touched his shoulder.

"Nae," he mumbled, rolling over.

Aileen gasped. Never in all of her life had she seen such a man. His pewter gray eyes seared into hers, stealing her breath. She was locked in their mesmerizing hold, wanting to spend forever in them. A frown skittered across his features, and she wanted to smooth it away with her hand. Taking her fingers, she brushed them across his forehead. Instantly, the contact sent shivers up her arm.

She licked her lips trying to regain her composure. "I am a healer. Tell me where is your pain?"

In one swift move, he clasped her wrist, trapping it within his iron fingers. The mere contact sent more heat to her already warm face. Slowly, he rubbed his thumb across the vein in her wrist, and Aileen glanced down, enthralled by his touch. Desire flared swiftly, and she reached out with her other hand.

"Nae," he growled, pushing her away from him.

"Do not touch me, *fae* healer."

She drew back, shocked and embarrassed. What just happened? She was so close to placing her lips on his hand. Strong, big hands. Wait, did he just call her a fae, as in *faery*? The man surely must have taken a blow to the head. She had to get him to the hospital. Tampering down her strange feelings, she watched as he stood to an imposing height.

"Holy Lugh..." she muttered, clutching her hand to her breast. This man was taller than her father.

"Leave me, fae." The burr of his voice, deep and sensual, sent a ripple of awareness though her.

Snapping out of her trance, Aileen glared at him. "Excuse me for trying to help, but you were moaning in pain. I would suggest you seek a doctor for treatment, since you obviously had some sort of head trauma." There was something about him that niggled at the back of her mind. She had seen him somewhere before. Perhaps it was with her father.

He raised his eyebrow mockingly at her. "Humph!" Then bending to retrieve his sword, he walked away.

Aileen watched as he stormed from the tunnel. He was so devastatingly handsome, as if carved from the Gods themselves. Finally realizing she was now alone she proceeded to follow him out of the tunnel into blazing sunlight. Coming to a halt outside, she could see the ocean down below.

Yet, that wasn't what was bothering her.

How in the blazes could it be morning sunlight? When she was running from Liam, it was early afternoon. Did she pass out the entire night? "Everyone must be frantic." The need to get back home took precedence over her demented Highlander.

She surveyed the surrounding area, and couldn't make out where she was. "The tunnel isn't so long I would have become lost," she muttered to herself. Stepping past some pines and other foliage, she emerged out along the edge of a cliff.

Hearing a horse snicker, she saw the man greeting his horse. Seeing him in the sunlight, she gawked at him. He really was into whatever role he was playing. Aileen marveled at the detail of his boots and belted tartan. She hollered, "Hey, I don't think you should be riding him. You really need to see a doctor." He ignored her warning as he mounted his horse. "Well, don't say I didn't warn you."

He gave her a heated look, before casting a glance to the side.

"Goodbye..." Her words froze on her lips, unable to continue. Full shock registered inside her brain as she realized where she'd seen this man. Her body started to quake, and she clutched her hands to her chest.

"No, th...this *cannot be*," she choked out. "Tell me who you are. I demand to know your name!"

Are all the fae so dumb *and* beautiful, he thought. "Ye ken who I am." Stephen's head caught a glimpse of the fae, as she started to take a few hesitant steps backwards. What the bloody hell was wrong with her? She was standing too close to the edge. If she was not careful, she would slip on over.

Why did he care? She could just vanish, right? Stephen rubbed his face, the remnants of a headache still behind his eyes. Sweet Bridget! Now the fae was yelling at him.

She waved her hands, all the time shaking her lovely head. "You are *not* him!"

He had to put a stop to this, or she would fall. Perhaps, she was a *daft* fae. He certainly did not know their ways, nor did he want to find out. However, this creature was becoming more agitated, and for some unfathomable reason, he did not want her to come to any harm.

"Och, fae healer, stop your babbling." He dismounted with a groan.

"No, no, no!" Pointing a finger at him, she continued to walk backwards. Stumbling, her foot twisted among some tree roots, causing her to lose her balance.

Stephen swore as he lunged for her, grasping her arm and crushing her against his chest. "Are ye truly daft?"

She shook her head. "No," she whispered. "I want to know your name."

"By the saints, fae. Ye ken it is Stephen MacKay."

Her eyes went wide. "*Dragon Knight?*"

"Nae, no longer," he retorted with a scowl becoming furious with her list of questions.

Her voice was barely a whisper, as he could see the color draining from her face. "The year?"

He eyed her warily. "It is the year of our Lord, twelve hundred six."

Instantly, the fae's eyes closed, and she slumped to the ground.

Chapter Thirteen

"For their path was strewn with roses, but within their beauty lies the thorn of disbelief."

There was one thing Stephen would not do, and that was leave a foolish fae wandering the abbey walls. They would snatch her up the moment they laid eyes upon her.

He inhaled deeply.

The salty scent of the sea helped to soothe his senses as he held the limp body of the fae in his arms. A hard lump had settled in his chest realizing she was on the brink of going over the edge. His fingers trembled as he swept a lock of hair from her face, the color of the moon. The light danced off her skin, causing it to sparkle with radiance, which surely led him to believe she was one of the fae. He traced the curve of her cheek and along her jaw willing her to open those eyes—eyes that immediately told him all he needed to know. No one had eyes such as hers. They reminded him of lavender reeds on a warm sunny day.

As if she heard him, Aileen opened her eyes and their gazes locked as one.

Stephen swept her up in his arms and carried her to his horse. He set her atop Grian's back and mounted behind her.

Giving Grian a nudge, they moved onward.

His hand brushed against her thigh, and she trembled under his touch. "Why do ye choose to wear this type of clothing, fae?" he asked hoarsely.

She eyed him askance. "It is what we wear in my time." *Why does he keep calling me fae?*

"Humph!" Grumbling something else under his breath.

"Oh my..." She tried twisting around to marvel at her surroundings.

"Is there a problem?"

She waved a hand about. "No...it's just that the landscape is vastly different. The trees are more lush and green."

Aileen did something she rarely did without permission. Letting the gentle rhythm of the horse soothe her senses, she closed her eyes and let go. Breathing deeply, she let her power sweep out and inside the man behind her.

It only took a moment for the first wave of emotions to sweep into her. Searing pain... Distrust... Wariness... Emptiness... Lust. *Lust?*

Her eyes flew open. Lust for who? *Her?*

Stephen brought the horse to an abrupt halt. "I ken what ye are, and if ye ever try that again, I'll give ye a demonstration of the last one."

She cringed. "How do you know?"

His breath was hot against her ear. "Part fae, remember?"

She gave him a terse nod.

With a click to his horse, they resumed their ascent into the hills, moving along the edge of the trees and stream over the crest of the hill. Gently maneuvering down the path, Stephen dismounted. Grabbing an ale skin from his pouch, he went down to the water's edge.

A shocked Aileen watched in mortified silence as he walked away. How could she have forgotten he was part fae? "Damn, damn," she sputtered out. It was one thing to probe another's emotions, but to have one aware of it..."Blast it all!"

She chewed on her bottom lip in frustration. How could this have happened? Is this what Liam meant by the *veil of time*? Of all the magical beliefs in her world, she never envisioned this one. Why was she here?

She looked down at her garments and blew out a long breath. "At least I'm wearing a dress that goes to my knees and my long coat. What would you have thought if I was in shorts, and a tank, Stephen MacKay?"

Her gaze traveled back to watch as he splashed water on his face. His muscles seem to ripple with the water he sprayed himself with. She pondered what he would look like without any clothes. Heat dotted her skin, and her palms tingled. Primal thoughts invaded her senses, and for one split second, she was sorely tempted to find out for herself.

Shaking her head, she muttered, "Not in this lifetime." Sealing off her emotions, she watched as Stephen stood back up and returned.

"Here, drink this." His words were as clear and cool as ice, squashing the last tendrils of her emotions.

Taking the skin, Aileen nodded her thanks and took a swig. "Holy crap!" she gasped, spitting out the foul tasting liquid. "What the hell is this?"

"'Tis ale," he replied incredulously.

She shoved the ale skin back at him. "Well, no thank you. That's just nasty. I think I'll go get some water."

Before she could even get down, he was holding out another skin. "This one is water, though I ken no other who would choose water over ale."

"Well, I do, and I think I'm going to need more than what's in this," she stated.

Stephen shook his head slowly. "Water over ale? We were always told the fae loved their amber liquid...in *any* form."

Aileen gave him a queer look. "Do they? I haven't asked them lately."

She saw something flash in his eyes, but only briefly.

"I will fetch ye some more."

Watching as he went back down to the water, Aileen stared up at the sky. "Oh Goddess, how am I going to get away from this place and gorgeous man?"

****

Osgar stood still, eyes closed...searching. Stephen had not returned after two days, and the air hummed with uneasiness. The men had already started discussing who would venture back to the abbey to search for him. Donal and Fergus were by far the strongest, yet their strength was required here in the hills. He could hear the voices of the women, countering what some of the men were saying. As always, Betha's voice carried over the rest.

He opened his eyes, and took in the last rays of light descending over the trees, saying a small blessing of thanks for their continued safety.

"Stephen is a trained warrior. We should only send one man," said Osgar, moving toward the small enclosure.

Betha's gaze grew troubled. "What about Lachlan? Is Stephen strong enough to face a powerful druid?"

Her question was greeted with grunts and nods, and Osgar held up his hand to silence them. "True, Lachlan is among them; however, we must all remember *Sir* Stephen is on a quest. I ken that it is all part of his journey. We must trust in the gods and goddesses."

"We trust in your wisdom, Osgar," uttered a small voice in the back of the crowd.

Osgar tilted his head, as the people parted to see who had spoken. "Thank you, Ian."

Ian smiled back at him and closed his eyes. "He comes and he is not alone." Snapping his eyes back open, he glanced at his mother. "May I go and greet Sir Stephen and his lady?"

"He brings another?" asked an astounded Betha. She looked around in disbelief at the others. "I thought we were all here?"

Cesan stepped forward. "We are. None were left behind."

"Ian?" Betha waiting for him to explain.

Ian just shrugged. "His lady is not from this land. It is all I ken. May I go now?"

"Aye, but only to the ridge," sighed his mother.

Osgar watched the lad run off, then caught Betha's gaze. "He will need guidance and soon. Will ye be taking him to the council gathering?"

Betha's focus was on her departing son. "My heart cannot answer that question, Osgar. Ian's wisdom is growing every day. There is no more I can teach him. In truth, he is now teaching me."

Donal quietly stepped forward and put his arm around her shoulder. "But we ken what is best for the lad."

"Aye, we will be taking him to the gathering. There, we will put him in the care of the druid council," she uttered softly, tears misting her eyes.

Osgar only nodded. "Donal, I believe Betha has stood far too long. Ye may want to take her back to the fires for some rest."

"Do not start to tell my man what to do with me." Her eyes blazed with fury.

"Your foot is still swollen, and our journey has just begun," said Osgar, grateful he was able to focus her back to the present and not on her son.

"Humph!" She smacked Donal's hand away when he tried to attempt to help her.

****

Ian tried waiting patiently on the ridge, tapping one foot then another. Something crept silently across his path and stopped in front of him. "Greetings, my friend. Are ye here to welcome Sir Stephen, too?" Silence ensued between Ian and the red fox.

"Well, if ye are not here for him, ye are welcome to join me."

The fox angled his head at Ian as if he understood his words. He padded over to him and sat down. "Aye, I thought as much."

They both sat still. The first stars winked at them in the early gloaming. Trees rustled with the arrival of the nocturnal creatures.

Ian bolted upright. "They're here."

The red fox sniffed the air, prancing twice around Ian before dashing off through the pine trees.

"Over here, Sir Stephen," waved Ian.

"Hold, Grian." Stephen dismounted quickly, and

grasped Ian. "Greetings, young Ian. Are ye out here alone?"

"Aye. Dinnae worry, I had protection. May I see your lady?" his voice thrummed with anticipation.

Stephen went pale for a moment. Turning to help the fae down from his horse, he nearly collided with her. She glared at him, but managed to give a smile to the lad.

"Hello."

Ian's smile was wide. "Greetings, my lady." He held out his hand to her. "May I?"

"Of course," she replied eyeing him warily.

He grasped her hand firmly, noting a slight frown on her face. "Ye feel it, too? I ken who ye are, my lady." Giving her a slight bow. "My name is Ian."

She managed another smile, although weaker than the first. "Please just call me Aileen."

Tugging her gently along the trees, he maneuvered them through the thick pines. Hearing a slight gasp, he looked over his shoulder. "It is all right, my lady. I will not let ye fall. And Sir Stephen is behind ye."

When he made it to the small clearing, he released her hand. "Ye can rest by the fires and take shelter in one of the caves."

"They are a warm beacon in the night," she uttered softly.

A gasp came forth from a woman sitting on a boulder near the fire. "Sweet Danu!"

All activity ceased, and the people just stared at her. Ian saw her hugging her cloak more protectively around her.

"This is Sir Stephen's lady," pronounced Ian.

Betha stood with the help of a staff and Donal.

"Does the *lady* have a name, Ian?"

"Yes. My name is Aileen," she interjected.

"And I am called Betha. This is my husband, Donal."

"Beautiful fae," murmured someone in the crowd. They all started to come forth and greet Aileen, with a bow or nod.

Stephen snorted and moved away from the gathering.

Ian ambled over to Osgar who was standing in the back away from the group. "So the Guardian has sent us a fae."

Osgar smiled slowly. Lifting his head to the mass of stars, he said softly, "We are honored and blessed, though, I ken Stephen will not see the light of your plan. In time, yes, *in time*."

Chapter Fourteen

"The faeries spread a wreath of foxgloves, roses, and jasmine on their path, but they were blinded by their stench of nonbelief."

The evening was spent in constant chatter about what else but *her*. Aileen try as she might, there was no avoiding the persistent questions. They asked about her land, why her speech was strange, and her clothing. They wanted to know if all the women wore such flimsy material. One of the children tugged at her hand and asked if there were any fae children.

Then there was the vast amount of food they kept trying to get her to eat. When she insisted she was full, they would sit back and wait, until she would nibble a piece of bread, cake, or fruits. Afterwards, they would take it away only to catch one of the small children actually burying her half-finished oatcake. Suppressing a giggle in her hand, Aileen shook her head.

"I believe I have something for ye, Aileen," said Betha.

She held up her hand to wave off any more food. "Thank you, but I don't think I can eat another bite."

"Nae, not food," she chuckled, moving from the boulder. "I have a gown that might fit, though it will not be long enough to cover. Ye may find the *Cailleach* still has her iron grip here in the hills, and the nights are cold."

"Yes. I'm grateful that I had my coat when..." She let the last trail off, remembering that Betha didn't know where she came from.

Betha disappeared deep into the cave. In a moment or two, she returned and handed it to Aileen. "'Tis a beautiful chemise ye have on, but this will keep ye warmer."

Aileen smiled. "Thank you, Betha. It's lovely."

"I'll leave ye to change. Then come and sit with me by the fire."

"More questions of my land?" she asked twirling the material between her fingers.

Betha squeezed her hand. "Nae, only the one that has not been asked." Turning aside, she ducked and left Aileen wondering what question it would be.

Quickly changing and putting on the gown, she felt instantly warmer. Moving outside, she found Betha and sat down next to her.

"Here, drink this."

Aileen took the cup hesitantly. "What is it?" She sniffed the contents and then smiled. In her time they would have called it peppermint tea, but now, "Mint brew with other herbs?"

"Aye. I noticed ye are not drinking the ale, and Sir Stephen mentioned that ye prefer water. It is one of my own mixtures."

Aileen let the warm liquid permeate her body, and watched the flames dance within the fire. "So, what is your question?"

Betha angled her head to the side, as if studying her. "How did ye meet Sir Stephen?"

"That's it?" she blurted out. She saw the look of

alarm on Betha's face and reached out a hand. "I'm sorry, it's just everyone keeps asking me about my land, the colors of everything, how long I'm staying, that I expected something else."

"'Tis a simple question, I thought."

She only nodded. "I found *Sir* Stephen in a tunnel near the abbey. He appeared to be unconscious and in pain."

"He must have had a vision. Why were ye in the passage?"

"Passage?" Aileen frowned. "Oh, the tunnel or burrow?"

"Aye," said Betha shifting slightly.

How much to reveal, Aileen thought. "I was trying to get away from someone. I had overheard some disturbing news and got lost within the abbey tunnels." There, at least that wasn't a lie.

"Did he speak of the vision with ye?"

Aileen snorted. "Heavens, no! He told me to go away, after I tried to help him. I told him I was a healer, but he refused my touch."

Betha's eyes went wide. "A healer? Now I grasp why ye were sent."

Before Aileen could respond, she could sense him standing behind her. His power swept over and through her. She started to tremble, and clenched her hands in the folds of her gown.

"Then pray tell us all, Betha." His tone held a challenge.

She eyed him narrowly. "Ye ken Aileen is a healer. She might have been sent to help ye with your visions."

"No *fae healer* will be touching me. I will seek out Osgar if I require healing," he snapped.

Aileen's mouth dropped open, and all she could do was stare at the retreating beast. How dare he! "Of all the idiotic beings I've encountered in my life," she hissed out. Standing, she looked down at Betha. "Thank you for the kindness you've shown me, but I think I'd like to rest for the night. Is there anywhere I can lie down?"

"Aye. Ye may share the cave with us and some of the other women. Donal, my husband, will be sleeping near the fires with the other men. Just grab one of the wraps inside."

Rubbing her temples, she handed her cup to Betha. "Good night."

"Sleep well, Lady Aileen," whispered Betha.

****

The sound of light chanting brought Aileen out of a deep sleep. Soft snores emanated from the side of the cave, and she blinked trying to adjust to the dimness inside. Smiling, she saw a mother and daughter curled up together. Quietly, she made her way outside, tugging on her coat.

Sunlight sprinkled the sky with its first golden rays of light, and she welcomed them by stretching outward. "Good morning, Lord and Lady, light and love." She yawned lazily, letting whoever was chanting lift her spirits.

Looking about, there were those tending to the cooking, and some greeted her with a nod and smile. Aileen marveled at this small group of people, which she had numbered to be about fifty. Why were they in the hills and not in the village, she wondered. None of them had spoken about the abbey or where they were traveling. Perhaps they were on a pilgrimage. A question for Betha later today.

Then there was her dilemma of how she was going to return home. Her shoulders slumped. What did her aunt and the others think of her disappearance? They must all be worried. Yes, even her father. "Oh, Dad, why didn't you ever tell me?"

"Are ye talking to the faeries?" asked a small voice.

Aileen looked down to find a small girl gazing up inquisitively at her. "No, just random thoughts, spoken out loud."

The small girl let out a sigh. "Oh." Then her face lit up. "May I touch your hair?"

Aileen started to laugh, but held back. "Sure, sweetheart." She bent down to her level, and the girl reached out gingerly to pull blonde strands between her fingers.

"Verra lovely," she murmured.

"What is your name?"

"Caitlin, my lady," she gushed.

Aileen tried not to frown, but she was getting tired of being called *lady*. They could call Stephen whatever, but she couldn't fathom why they attached such nobility to her.

She touched Caitlin's hand lightly. "Just call me Aileen."

Caitlin shook her head. "Nae, 'tis not right."

"Why not?"

"The fae are to be respected and shown honor." She cupped her tiny hand to Aileen's cheek. "Your eyes are lovely, too." With a big smile and hug, she scampered off, leaving a stunned Aileen still kneeling on the ground.

"Did ye lose something, Lady Aileen?" asked Ian, approaching from behind.

Snapping out of her thoughts, she shook her head and stood. "Good morning, Ian."

"Greetings to ye, too. Have ye broken your fast?"

"No, I haven't."

Grabbing her hand, he pulled her toward one of the fires. "Good, then ye can eat with me."

They ate and shared small bits of conversation. For some reason, Ian chose not to probe her with any questions. The food was filling, though what she could use was a strong cup of coffee.

"Have ye met Brother Osgar?" he asked between a mouthful of bread and cheese.

Picking up a small bite of cheese, she replied, "No, Ian. Is this Brother Osgar taking everyone on a pilgrimage? Is that why you're here in the hills?"

He frowned. "Pil...pilgrimage?"

"Yes, a pilgrimage to a holy shrine. Isn't Brother Osgar from the abbey?"

"Aye," he said slowly. "A shrine like the one to Brigid or the Mother Danu? We call them *turas*."

Aileen popped the cheese into her mouth, and enjoyed its taste, before answering, "Well, I guess you could say that would be one type of shrine, but I don't think Brother Osgar would take you to one of those. He might take you to the one of St. George, or—"

Ian gasped and grabbed her hand firmly. "Nae, not the dragon slayer! And Brother Osgar was and still is a verra powerful druid."

A deep voice rumbled behind her, "They are here because they believe in the old religion, and enemies have arrived from Rome to destroy them."

110

"How horrible," Aileen sputtered out turning around to face Stephen. "Where are they going? What can be done?"

"We speak tonight at the council," Ian interrupted.

Aileen was shocked. It only confirmed that she needed his help. She certainly did not want to venture any further away from the abbey. It was her only place back to her time.

At least it's what she prayed for.

Standing, she looked into eyes swimming with so many emotions. "I need for you to take me back to the abbey tunnel, Sir Stephen."

"*The abbey*? Nae, fae. If ye want to return, just whisk yourself back. My place is here protecting these people."

"What is *wrong* with you? I cannot just whisk myself back. And stop calling me fae!" snapped Aileen.

Stephen raked a hand across his face, and then leaned closer to her. "Ye *are* a fae, and I will call ye such until ye take your leave of me." Stepping aside, he made his way to leave.

Fury blazed within her; hot and searing. She fisted her hands on her hips. "Damn you, Stephen MacKay!" she bellowed.

Stephen froze, and glanced over his shoulder. Arching an eyebrow, he drawled, "Cursing at me, *fae*?"

"I am not a fae! My mother's name is Rose MacLaren, and my father's name is Aidan Kerrigan," she hissed out. Marching over to where he stood, she jabbed a finger into his chest. "And my name is Aileen Kerrigan, so the next time you want to call me something, remember it well." She saw something flash in his eyes, but she didn't care. Her head was pounding, and she was tired of him treating her like some leper. Her only thought was to flee this group and the man who made her insides melt with fire.

Stephen standing with Osgar heard Ian approach but was still in shock from her words. Watching her storm away from his view, he rubbed the back of his neck in frustration.

"Aileen does not ken who she is, Sir Stephen."

Placing a gentle arm on Ian, Osgar asked quietly, "What were the Gods thinking?"

"How could she not know she is the daughter of one of the most revered Fenian Warriors of all time?" Stephen scoffed.

"Maybe they chose not to tell her," sighed Ian.

Stephen whirled around to Osgar and Ian, his words like daggers. "Then how can she be of any help?"

Ian just shrugged.

"Perhaps, she is here for your help, Stephen."

Stephen shook his head. "Nae, Osgar, not me...not me." He silenced them further with a curt wave of his hand before stalking off in the opposite direction of where Aileen went.

"Aileen's not going to be verra happy when she returns."

Osgar eyed him questionably. "Why is that, Ian?"

"Well, if she did not like us calling her fae, what is she going to do when everyone bows each time she comes into our sight?"

"Ye are correct, my young druid," sighed Osgar.

"Who will tell her?"

Osgar squeezed his shoulder lightly. "I believe our Sir Stephen should be the one."

"Oh, that's a reckoning I would verra much like to witness," chuckled Ian.

Chapter Fifteen

"Come sit with me on the dew-covered grass, and I will weave you a gown of marigolds. Then you shall open your eyes to the truth and your destiny."

Stephen sat lazily atop a boulder allowing his gaze to travel over the vision sitting among the foxgloves. She brushed her hand casually through their petals, and his breath caught. Did she not know how she stirred his blood? Try as he might, whenever she came near, his lustful beast roared. He wanted to strip her there surrounded by all those flowers and take her.

He had blamed it on her fae blood, using it as an excuse to shun her. Yet, she didn't even know where she came from. How *did* she come to be here? The questions seemed to be mounting with no answers.

He would not be led astray by her or her lovely violet eyes.

She rolled over onto her back placing an arm across her face. His cock surged forth, and he cursed silently. There were more important matters to deal with than satisfying his needs. Rising from his place, he watched a hawk circle above. Its languid movement in the sky told him all was well. No travelers in the distance.

As he stepped down, he thought he heard her crying. Glancing over his shoulder, her shudders could be seen from his perch. What would cause her to weep? Did someone hurt her?

"By the hounds!" he muttered. If anyone attempted to bring her harm, they would answer to him.

His shadow covered her form as he watched the tears mar her lovely face.

Resting on her elbows, she asked, "Is there something I can do for you?"

She had no idea the power of those simple words. He almost stripped aside his wrap to show her just what she could do with that luscious mouth of hers. "Why were ye weeping?" he asked hoarsely.

Aileen cringed. "I'm sorry. I didn't think anyone was around." She sat up hastily, brushing out the folds of her gown, and dabbing at her eyes.

Stephen knelt before her. "Did someone hurt ye?"

"No...just tired, and I have a headache."

Sheer annoyance crossed his face. "Ye weep for that?"

"I also have a lot on my mind," she snapped. "If you must know, I could use a good cup of black coffee. I'm having caffeine withdrawal. And it was an exceedingly *long* day on an animal that I'm not accustomed to, and I'm exhausted." She waved a hand at him. "Now if you don't mind, I would prefer to sulk in quiet melancholy."

He knew he shouldn't, but his hand reached out gently brushing the last tear away from her cheek, not fully fathoming her words. "Then tell me." His voice low.

She blinked. "How can I explain, when I don't understand myself? I've just found out I never truly knew my parents." She pounded her fist against her breast. "Everyone knew, but *me*."

His jaw clenched. Why would they keep this wisdom from her?

She rolled over and stood up. "Forget it. Please leave me alone."

At that moment, he made the decision to tell her a story...a story about the great Aidan Kerrigan. "Nae," he growled, tugging at her hand to stay her departure.

Stephen couldn't move. His hand devoured hers within his, and the heat sent flames of desire to parts that were already swollen. He caressed his thumb over her wrist in small circles, and then dropped it as quickly as he took it. Looking into her eyes, he noticed the desire as well. *Do not be led astray.*

"Do ye ken who your father is?" he asked taking a step back to lead her toward a boulder.

Aileen looked at him skeptically, before sitting down. "Well...I thought I knew who he was, but as of yesterday? No."

"We all ken the story of the warrior, Aidan Kerrigan."

"What?" Aileen jumped up. "How? That's impossible."

Stephen took in a deep breath. "Aidan Kerrigan was a Fenian Warrior who gave up his powers and immortality for the woman he loved. His story is told in bardic tales to this day."

Aileen slumped back down in shock. "What is a Fenian Warrior? And when you say his story is still told, how far back are you talking about?"

"The Fenian Warriors protect the realm of the faery world and this one. There are some who are known to travel the veil of time."

"Stop!" Aileen put her hand up. "I overheard my father talking about the veil of time. He didn't want me to go." She rubbed at her temples. "He was a warrior for the *faery*?"

"Aye," said Stephen slowly.

Aileen closed her eyes. *I will not faint.* When she opened them, she cast her gaze out toward the green hills. "No wonder he is lost. He gave it all up, only to have her for a brief time," she choked out.

Stephen frowned. "She is no longer with him?"

Aileen sadly looked up at him. "No, she died last year."

"I am sorry for your loss." His tone soft. "He was the only one to ever defy the fae."

"All for the love of a woman," Aileen interjected.

Stephen nodded solemnly. "Your father, Aileen, was one of the oldest warriors of the Fenian branch. No one kens his beginning."

She gave a weak smile. "I want, no *need* to go back, Stephen, to my father. This isn't my time."

He shook his head slowly. "Nae. It is too dangerous. I must get these people to the gathering. But I give you my word, Lady Aileen, I will escort you back to the abbey after I see to their safety."

She swallowed, trying desperately not to look into his eyes. "Please do not call me Lady Aileen, just *Aileen* will do."

"Ye have two choices. I can call ye fae"—he noticed the look of utter disbelief on her face—"*or* ye can allow me to call ye Lady Aileen. Whether ye choose to believe it or not, part of your blood flows with the blood of the fae."

"I suppose there's no compromise with you," she

retorted.

Stephen crossed his arms over his chest. "Nae. And I might add everyone did hear ye loudly proclaim your heritage. Do not be so harsh when they *bow* before ye."

"Blast," she muttered. "I might as well get this over with." Shaking her head, she continued her rant as she trudged down through the trees. Before she stepped completely away from Stephen, she tossed out, "Well, if my father is old by your standards, he's actually ancient by mine. For you see, my time is the year two thousand fourteen."

"Bloody hell!"

His eyes narrowed when he heard her chuckle.

She jabbed a finger in his direction. "I'm not going to be the only one in shock this afternoon, Stephen MacKay."

He watched as she moved steadily away through the pines still talking about *her* century.

Fisting his hands on his hips, he glared at the woman who had shocked him by her words. "Gods teeth!" Why would the fae send her back through the veil without her knowledge? He was in awe of her strength at hearing the news about her parents. Yet, she was part fae. It was evident the moment he laid eyes on her exquisite face.

He was still pondering the situation when Colin approached. "Lovely fae. Do ye ken why she is here?"

"Nae." He shook his head. "I need to seek the counsel of Osgar, or perhaps Cathal."

Colin shifted uneasily. "We have another problem."

He whipped his head around. "What?"

"They have started the cleansing. Seamus brought

news of the first. A young villager by the name of Garret was burned in the abbey square."

"And they call us heathens?" hissed Stephen. His hand cut through the air, adding, "Is Seamus safe among them?"

Colin nodded. "Aye. He will ken the time to leave, but for now, he has chosen to remain. He will seek out others like us or gather information."

Stephen grasped the man's shoulder, his voice one of steel, "I give ye my pledge no one here will come to harm. We will discuss this after the council tonight without the women."

"It won't sit well with Betha," he grumbled.

"Aye, and it can be my head she'll take," stated Stephen before walking away.

****

The aroma of the stew she was stirring smelled heavenly to Aileen. She had prodded and begged one of the women to let her help with *anything*. Finally, Betha came to her defense, saying the meal would be twice as delicious with a fae adding its power.

Earlier when she descended from the ridge, all conversation had ceased. One by one, they all came forth and bowed. Some of the children even brought her flowers. She had to swallow a retort when one inquired about the mighty Aidan Kerrigan. All she could tell him was he was doing well. Now, her jaw ached after an hour of constantly smiling.

Stephen trekked through only giving her a cautionary glance before heading in the opposite direction where Osgar was talking to Cesan and the other men. Her heart skipped a beat whenever he was near, and she cursed her body for its betrayal. She was just another burden to him. Yet earlier, for a brief moment, she thought she saw a flash of desire within those stunning eyes.

"Not in this lifetime," she uttered softly, noting this was the second time she told herself. The only comfort she would take was his promise that he would return her to the abbey. If she came through, then she could certainly go back.

"What troubles ye, Lady Aileen?" asked Ian, placing a gentle hand on her shoulder.

"Hmmm...where do I begin?" She shook her head in dismay.

Eyes full of wisdom for one so young, he peered down at her. "It is always best to start at the beginning," he said matter of factly.

She squeezed his hand gently. "Yes, you are correct. I think for now it might be best to sort it out in my mind, first."

"Let the words settle in your heart. There ye will find the answers you seek." Giving her a broad smile, he reached into the pot, and quickly pulled out a chunk of potato, plopping it into his mouth. Licking his fingers with glee, he gave her a quick hug and scampered off.

Bemused and humbled by his words, Aileen stared after him. "You are destined for great things, Ian."

Chapter Sixteen

"For the Dragon carved out their path from the roots of the Oaks, and the dew from the thistle."

If looks could kill, Stephen was sure that those Betha aimed at him and Donal were lethal. She stood, hands on her hips, giving them both an earful. How she learned Seamus would not only be joining them, but someone had been burnt at the stake, was not something he could fathom. People scattered like ants to get away from her wrath. He clenched his jaw hoping she was almost through with her tirade.

"Men! Ye think ye ken everything?" she shouted. "Dinnae keep anything from us again. We have a right to know."

Donal tried to take her into his arms. "Whist, love."

"Nae!" She batted his arms away. "Dinnae whist love, me!" She stormed off, leaving both men feeling like two scolded boys.

Stephen rubbed the back of his neck to relieve some of the tension. "Now would not be the time to tell me I was wrong, Donal."

"Ye ken she has the sight. We should have told her." Donal narrowed his eyes at Stephen. "Now my bed will be cold tonight, no thanks to ye."

Stephen grimaced as Donal followed in his wife's path, still muttering under his breath. He observed

Aileen standing back against a pine and raised a dark brow questionably. "Would ye also like to add your words of wisdom?" He crossed his arms across his chest in an attempt to scare her off.

Stepping over to him, Aileen looked at him directly. "No words from me," she said smiling. "I believe Betha said all that was needed. Now, I think I'll go and see what needs to be done before we leave."

Aileen had gone only two steps when she heard him mutter, "Brazen fae." Halting in her steps, she turned and asked, "What did you call me?"

The smirk on his face told her all. Storming up to him, she glared up at him. "Why is it so difficult to say my name?"

He stood there staring at her.

Aileen saw the look of lustful invitation all over his face. Taking a few steps back, she felt her face flush. "Forget it."

"Lugh's balls," he hissed, while watching her lovely backside saunter quickly away. One moment more and he would have taken her into his arms to feast on those delectable lips.

"Trouble with the lass?" asked Osgar who had silently meandered over to him.

"Humph! All women are trouble this day."

Osgar chuckled softly.

Stephen eyed him narrowly. "I find no humor in this."

"Nae, I expect ye would not."

"Why would the fae send the daughter of Aidan Kerrigan through the veil?"

Osgar took a deep breath. "*Aileen* is here for some purpose—one she seems to be unaware of at the moment." He tapped his finger to his chin in thought. "When we arrive in Finlow, I pray Cathal will shed some insight, if he is there.

"Aye. 'Tis best we get moving. It will be several days till we reach Finlow."

****

The extraordinary clean air and the warm sun on her back brought a smile to Aileen. Birds chirped, singing their song of spring. Once, she spied a hawk circling close by as if part of their band of travelers.

To take her mind off *him*, she let herself soak in her surroundings. Her horse ambled along, and it was just fine by her. Everyone else could saddle up to the almighty Stephen MacKay. He brought forth emotions that had a mind of their own. Hurtling without thought, they filled her body and mind. She was good at building a protective wall around herself. Yet, when he was near, it was as if someone else inhabited her being. Staying far, far away was the best solution.

"Oh look!" she exclaimed in child-like delight. The small rust-colored animal stood still as if watching the riders.

"It is my friend, Lady Aileen," replied Ian. "He has been with us for the past few days."

She eyed him in shock. "Like a dog?"

"Aye," he chuckled.

"But he's a fox, Ian. What if he attacks you?"

"Nae, he will not harm me. He will only be with us until we reach Finlow."

"Hmmm...then where is he off to?" she asked skeptically.

He shrugged. "Did not tell me."

Okay, she thought to herself. Now the boy

communicates with animals. "What's in Finlow, Ian?"

"Other travelers and the druids. They gather for the feast of Beltaine."

Aileen's eyes went wide. She would be with others to celebrate the May Day. How could she have forgotten? Singing, dancing, bonfires, and so much more. "I'm going to observe the day with druids," she said softly, her gaze drifting back to the man who stirred something primal in her.

Stephen felt Aileen's gaze although she rode some distance back.

He slowed Grian, twisting around and meeting her violet eyes across the path of the others.

"Trouble?" Donal asked.

He swallowed, clenching his fists. "Nae."

"Would ye like me to go fetch the lass?"

"Which lass?" he barked out.

"The one ye cannot take your eyes off of."

He glared at him. "See to it that one of the men is at the rear. There are women and children."

"Anyone ye would like to handle it?"

Stephen shrugged and then noticed Donal smiling at him. "What?"

Donal held up his hands in surrender. "I'll send Brian," and turning he made to leave.

"*Brian*? Nae! Are ye trying my patience? Everyone can see Brian is smitten with the fae."

"And how is that a problem?"

Stephen wanted to wipe the smirk off Donal's face. "I'll go myself, *nae*—ye go, Donal."

"Scared of the fae, are ye, Stephen?" His laughter rang out as he quickly departed before Stephen could utter a retort.

****

Aileen decided to eat her evening meal with a young new mother. She had noticed earlier the woman was traveling without a husband, and made up her mind to keep her company. When she saw Stephen eating with Betha, Ian, and Donal, she quickly gathered her items heading in the opposite direction.

"Have you eaten, Mara?"

"Nae, Lady Aileen." Carefully she brushed a finger across the baby's face, as he suckled softly from his mother's breast.

"I believe I have enough for both of us. May I share your meal?"

Mara's eyes went wide. "Och, ye would want to share with me?"

Aileen gave her a huge smile. "Why of course. There is plenty, and you do need to keep your strength for your baby." She nodded toward the contented infant. "What is his name?"

Tears glistened in Mara's eyes when she spoke, "His name is Robert, for his father." Mara looked up at Aileen and noticed the confusion. "My Robbie died over the winter. Sickness in his chest." Casting her gaze back to her infant, she added, "He never knew he had a son."

Aileen knelt beside her. Placing a gentle hand on her shoulder, she said, "I truly believe he knows."

"Aye, that's what Osgar says."

They shared a meal and conversation well into the evening, with the waxing moon dusting them with its luster of light. Aileen was cradling Robert when Betha approached with a mug clasped within her hands.

"I've brought ye a brew of nettles mixed with

honey, Mara." She brushed her hand across the top of the now sleeping bairn. "How does he fare?"

"He's a ravenous one," she said through sips of the tea. "Thank ye, Betha."

"Aye, that is good. He seems to be content with ye, Lady Aileen."

"Och, she is a natural. He took right to her," Mara replied.

Aileen gave her a slight shrug. It felt good to hold him, reminding her of possibilities. His little hand stretched out seeking hers, the tiny fingers grasping hold of her one. Watching in awe, she desired to have one herself. Sadness engulfed her realizing if she didn't return to her own time, none of this would ever happen.

"Ye may return whenever ye wish. Stephen has left to seek out Osgar."

Betha's words jolted her from her thoughts. "I think I'll stay here for the night," she muttered, her face burning with heat.

"Then I'll send Ian with an extra wrap. Sleep well."

She glanced up watching Betha stride away, wanting to say something more, but the words strangled in her throat.

****

Lachlan watched as the man paced furiously spouting angry words. His jaw ached from clenching it so hard. They were all fools, he thought. Stephen and his band of followers had silently crept away, leaving a hushed stillness within the village. He was not to blame—nae, it was their inability to see through their own beliefs, and act swiftly. They were a pathetic group of men, and he forced down the bile of being in their midst.

How much longer would this tirade continue? He could end this now with one quick snap of the neck. However, he still needed the bishop, and there were too many witnesses present.

"If I may interrupt, Bishop Augustus?" asked Brother Patrick.

Lachlan turned toward the brave man standing in the back. Foolish, he thought for one to step forward when the bishop was talking.

"Do you have any valuable information that would require you to speak?" spat out the Bishop.

Brother Patrick's face turned crimson from the harsh remark. He moved away from the wall and tried to compose himself. "I would think that since the heathens have left, we could dispense from any further actions." He scanned his surrounding brothers to try to judge their reaction. A few were nodding in agreement.

The bishop's nostrils flared in anger. "You would want these heathen people spreading their beliefs deeper into your country?" He advanced slowly toward him. "Why, I would think you would want to squash this uprising, considering that some of them lived among you here in the abbey."

Brother Patrick would not back down. "We are peaceful men." He cast his gaze to his remaining brothers. "To seek out these people to cause harm, is not what our Lord taught us."

The slap came hard and swiftly. "How dare you tell *me* of our Lord's teachings! I believe some time in solitude will remind you what your true mission is here, *and* to respect those in authority within the church."

Brother Patrick clenched his fists, and with a curt bow left the room. No one said a word, stunned by the outburst of both men.

"Would anyone care to add further their unease over the church's teachings?"

Lachlan arched a brow at the bishop. If only this man was a druid. He would have been a great ally.

"Will you be ready at dawn, Lachlan?" asked Bishop Augustus.

Lachlan nodded affirmative.

"Good. You will take ten of my guards with you. You do understand you must return these heathens," his tone harsh and demanding.

"Aye." This was not part of his plan, and he had to act quickly. "In truth, your Holiness, if there is resistance from the men?"

The bishop folded his arms behind himself as he paced in thought. "What would you do, Lachlan?"

"Burn them all," he answered.

"Then let it be done." Giving the sign of the cross over Lachlan, he took his leave.

Chapter Seventeen

"The meadow was filled with the scent of the Mother awakening, and her children were the flowers who spread their petals over her gown of green."

"When will we get there?" asked one of the children.

"Yes, when?" chimed in a few of the others.

Aileen was beginning to wonder herself, and almost shouted out the question also.

"Soon, children," chided Agnes.

They were giving the horses a rest, and had been walking for what seemed like hours. Aileen stopped to rub the knot that had formed in her back. It didn't help much that she was sleeping on the ground, too.

One little girl plunked down rubbing her calve. "My leg hurts."

"Whist," said Agnes in a gentle tone.

"Here, let me see if I can help." Aileen stooped down beside the girl. "What's your name?"

"Cora," she whimpered.

She gave her a smile taking the young girl's leg into her hands. Drawing in long, deep breaths to slow her heart, Aileen let the energy of healing start to flow out from her hands, and into the leg. Massaging the muscle, she concentrated on the silvery light she always saw when the healing process would begin.

"Oh, Lady Aileen, that feels verra warm."

Keeping her eyes closed, Aileen nodded slowly, letting the last of the energy surge through. Gradually, she opened her eyes, patting the leg gently. "There now. I think you'll be feeling much better. Why don't you stand and walk."

"Oh thank ye," she beamed, throwing her arms around Aileen in a hug.

Agnes's eyes were wide when she exclaimed, "Your eyes, Lady Aileen!" She gently touched Aileen's face, whispering, "They are so pale."

"They'll be fine." She gave her a reassuring smile as she stepped aside.

Moving swiftly past the chattering children, Aileen tried to distance herself for a moment. Even though the healing was minor, it still left her drained. Stirrings of something skittered across her senses, and looking up she saw the source.

Her heart started beating faster. She hadn't seen Stephen for several days, which was just fine by her. He made her *feel* emotions she could not explain.

Yet, there he stood watching her—he the hunter, and she his prey.

And this prey wanted to be captured.

She couldn't take her gaze from his. He stepped forth from the shadow of the tree, his horse following closely. *By the Gods!* He wore only his plaid wrapped around his waist and over his shoulder. Tattoos adorned his upper arms.

Aileen wasn't aware of her feet moving, until she stood directly in front of him. Now, she noticed the tail of a dragon wrapped around his left forearm, and on his right rested the head of the dragon. Her fingers itched to trace their path.

He reminded her of Adonis and Aengus Og, Gods of love, strength, *desire*...

"Thank ye, for taking care of the wee lass," he said hoarsely.

"Huh? Oh, it was nothing," she murmured, snapping her gaze from his gorgeous forearms to his face.

Then he smiled fully at her, showing his dimples. She wanted to take her lips and taste them. Reaching out with her hand, she was inches from his face, when he grasped it.

In one swift move, he lowered his mouth across her fingers, while keeping his eyes level with hers. She could feel his soft warm lips, mixed with the stubble of his beard. Waves of pleasure shot through her body, and to her very core. Instantly, he dropped her hand leaving her wanting so much more.

Aileen's mouth dropped, as he sauntered away still smiling. Trembling, she clutched her hand against her chest.

Confusion and desire both raged a war within her.

****

By the hounds! What was he thinking? Nae, that was the problem, he *wasn't* thinking.

He had observed her healing of the young lass, ready to turn away. Then, she came walking over to him. He became beguiled with her tresses that caught the sunlight, and eyes that even from a distance, shimmered. Her skin tasted of wildflowers and the sea. And Stephen wanted more. He brushed his hand lightly over his mouth savoring her taste.

Something nudged him from behind, and he let out

a long sigh.

"I give ye this time to rest, and ye are following me like some doe-eyed lass."

Grian gave a loud snort.

Grabbing his muzzle, he gave him a firm pat. "Do not complain later." Climbing atop, Stephen glanced about at the small band of travelers. With any luck, they would reach Finlow by evening.

Donal came quickly riding up to him. "We have a visitor. Cannot tell who it is."

"Get the women and children behind that set of rocks. I'll wait here."

Ian came running forth, skidding to a halt before them.

"Bloody hell, Ian! Where have ye been?" barked Stephen.

"I was on the boulder with Brian as lookout," the lad blurted out and then added, "The rider is Seamus."

Stephen's jaw clenched. Damn the lad was defiant.

"Did I not ask ye to stay with the other children?" It was the first time since he had encountered the lad that his shoulders slumped.

"Answer Sir Stephen," said a stern Donal.

"Aye, ye did," he muttered grudgingly.

"If ye are to become a druid and a *warrior*"—Ian's head snapped up—"then ye must learn to follow orders," said Stephen.

Ian's eyes shone brightly. "Thank ye, Sir Stephen, for reminding me of my quest."

Again, he was taken aback at Ian's words—the druid, warrior, and young lad all battling for control in one body.

"Go see to the others," scolded Donal.

Seamus came in riding hard, and the look on his face told Stephen all he needed to know. Trouble rode not far behind.

"We need to press forward," grunted Seamus, dismounting from his horse.

Stephen frowned. "Aye, we'll be at Finlow by night." Grabbing his shoulder, he asked, "What is it? More burnings?"

"Nae, worse."

What could possibly be worse? "Tell us."

"The bishop has sent Lachlan and a group of men to bring back the villagers."

"How many?" demanded Donal.

"Ten of the bishop's guards."

Stephen laughed. "We can take on ten guards." He noticed Seamus shaking his head. "More?"

"Aye, Lachlan has men following his group. I do not believe they know they are being followed."

"Lugh's balls!" Donal spat out.

"Aye," said Seamus. "There's more."

"*More*?" Stephen croaked, beginning to hate the word.

"If he does not return with them, the bishop has given Lachlan permission to burn everyone."

"Who the bloody hell *is* this Lachlan?" Donal asked.

"Lachlan was once a feared and respected druid," replied Osgar, approaching from the trees.

Stephen whipped his head around. "I thought him *dead*."

Osgar shook his head in agreement. "We all did. Currently, he seems to have the ear of the bishop. Disturbing."

"Then we cannot stay long in Finlow. We must reach the gathering, and seek out Cathal." Stephen turned toward Seamus. "Where are they now?"

The messenger rubbed the back of his neck in thought. "They were riding up the coast, but when I saw Lachlan talking to one of his men, they turned toward your direction. We have two, perhaps three days on them."

Stephen turned to Donal. "When we reach Finlow, see to more horses. We will need as many as we can get for the children and women. They won't be happy, but we will have to leave on the morrow for Grenlee through the pass."

"The gathering?" asked Seamus.

Osgar chuckled. "The bonfires of Beltaine might be their undoing with so many of us."

Stephen eyed him skeptically. "Are ye planning on joining the feasting, Osgar?"

"Of course," he replied, smacking Stephen on the back.

The other two men started laughing, leaving Stephen stunned and speechless. Shaking his head, he mounted Grian.

"I'll take some food and rest, before I set back out in the morning," Seamus said.

Stephen gave him a curt nod, and with a prod to his horse, he took off. He squinted at the sun, trying to put Osgar's words out of his mind.

A long time ago, Beltaine was his favorite feast day. It brought back vivid memories of laughter and gaiety. He could see his sister gathering all her brightly colored ribbons for the maypole and his brothers fighting over the comely lasses.

His chest seized on the recollections. Trying with all of his might, he squashed back those memories. His hands clenched hard around the reins, and making a silent vow, Stephen knew he would not be among the feasting.

It was no longer a part of him.

Chapter Eighteen

"The Dragon wrapped her wings around the lovers, so they may never know pain again."

Rain showers greeted them on their second day after leaving Finlow. The air was much cooler as they ascended farther into the hills. Aileen huddled deeply into her coat, thankful it was at least fur-lined. Earlier in the morning, Betha had braided her hair, weaving it around her head.

Stephen had kept their pace steady, only stopping briefly to tend to personal needs or grab a quick bite of cheese and bread. She was amazed at how the children showed such relentless strength; not a one uttered a complaint. So when her thighs were burning by yesterday evening, she had to hold back a harsh reply to their leader when he spied her limping. He actually had the gall to ask if there was a problem.

"He probably thinks I'm a burden," she lamented in a hushed tone. "Sheesh, why do I care?"

Her horse snickered at her comments as if in understanding.

"Now Buttercup or whatever your name is, I would appreciate if you wouldn't take offense to my conversation."

"Ah, I see ye have taken a fancy to Buttertwill," said Osgar trotting up beside her.

She rolled her eyes and smiled. "So, it's Buttertwill, and here I've been calling her *Buttercup*."

"It's no wonder she has not balked, then. I believe she likes ye."

"What?"

Osgar laughed softly. "She must have found a kindred spirit, for she's a feisty, quiet lady."

Aileen gave him a sidelong glance. "I don't know if I should be flattered or insulted."

"I would never insult one of the *fae*, Lady Aileen."

Now it was her turn to laugh.

"Come seek me out by the fires tonight, and I'll give ye salve to help with the stiffness in your legs."

"Thank you, I will, Osgar, or should I call you *Brother* Osgar?"

He let out a long audible breath. "Osgar will do. I am still pondering on the fate of returning to the abbey."

"We all seem to be at the crossroads of our lives."

Osgar arched a questioning brow at her. "Aye, and ye have been speaking to our young Ian."

"His wisdom does seem to brush off when one has a conversation with him," she said, looking about to where he rode just ahead of them.

Laughter peeled forth from Ian. He had caught sight of two brown otters playing, and their splashing caused not only his outburst, but one from the rest of the children as well.

Aileen glanced at Osgar, who in turn started to laugh, easing some of her pain as well as thoughts of being in the thirteenth century.

They moved along a narrow path running parallel to the river with the water cascading downward in the opposite direction. The rain had turned to a light mist and the gray light a perfect silhouette against the drenched trees. It seemed they were headed to a grove above the water for the night.

Pine limbs slapped at her, as her horse trudged through the mud and leaves making its way upward. Each evening it was the same—find a safe location tucked away from prying eyes.

Aileen watched as the men started to dismount, helping the women and children. Not really needing any help, she slowly lowered herself from Buttertwill, when stabbing pains clutched her thighs and lower back. "Ouch!" She grimaced, collapsing onto the ground.

"Lady Aileen," gasped Osgar. "Here, let me help ye."

Waves of pain took over, and she shook her head staying him with her hand. "Let me just rest for a moment," she breathed out.

"I'll go fetch some help."

Before she could stop him, he was gone.

When she opened her eyes, all she saw were the large muscular legs of the man in front of her. Aileen didn't need to look up to know who they belonged to. *Blast Osgar*! She certainly didn't want Stephen's help.

Turning her head away, she muttered, "I'm fine, really."

Aileen gritted her teeth, and prayed he would just go away. Instead, she felt herself lifted into his massive arms. Instinctively, she wrapped her arms around his neck. Their eyes locked, and that's when she noticed his eyes scanning her face. His lips parted briefly, as his head bent down to hers. He was going to kiss her, and she was going to let him.

So very close...

"Ye can bring Lady Aileen this way. I've got some salve for her legs," interrupted Osgar.

Stephen frowned, his handsome face suddenly solemn. "Lead the way."

For some unfathomable reason, Aileen felt disheartened. She'd truly wanted him to kiss her. Peering at him from a sidelong glance, she noticed a muscle twitching in his neck. His face showed several days growth of a beard, which only added more to his already striking features. Then she wondered why in the thirteenth century he would keep his hair short?

At that moment, Aileen wanted to be bold. What was the word he called her? *Brazen*?

"Stephen?" she whispered.

He didn't even look at her when he answered, "Aye?"

Be brazen, Aileen. "Why do you keep your hair cut close to your head?"

Stephen came to an abrupt halt. The look he gave her was one of disbelief. "*My hair*?" he croaked out.

"Yep."

Placing her down gently, Stephen absently ran his hand through his short locks and eyed her skeptically.

Aileen rubbed her upper thighs, still feeling a bit shaky. She waited patiently for his answer, until she heard the sharp intake of his breath. He was watching her hands moving up and down on her legs. Heat infused her cheeks.

Brazen no more, she quickly turned and stumbled away.

He was at her side in two strides, halting her path.

"I have always kept my hair short. It is easier in battle and when I am in the water. I was often chided by my brothers for doing so."

She gave him a huge smile. "I like it."

"Och, there ye are, Lady Aileen," blurted out Osgar. "Come, I have a small fire going."

Before Aileen knew what was happening, Osgar took her elbow, and steered her away.

Stephen was stunned. By the hounds! She actually said she *liked* his hair. And what possessed him to tell her about his brothers? From the moment he took her into his arms, he wanted to flee to some remote part of the woods and ravish her entire body. He had come so close to tasting those berry lips, until they were rudely interrupted.

Clenching and unclenching his fists, he stormed off in the direction of the other men.

****

Betha gave out a small groan.

"Is there enough?" asked Aileen.

"It will do until we reach Grenlee," she answered as she pulled out the last of the dried meat, berries, bread, and a small portion of what was left of the cheese. "There will be no cooking tonight. I will save the few remaining oatcakes for the morning."

She nudged Ian. "Take this to your father, and Sir Stephen."

"Here, take the wine skin and what's left of the wine, too," added Osgar.

"You have wine?" asked Aileen.

He leaned in close to her and mischief sparkled in his eyes. "Aye, took it from the cellar before we left."

"If I had known you had some wine, I would have

140

visited you earlier," she said with a smirk.

"Is that all it would have taken?" Osgar chuckled, giving a wink to Betha.

"Do not let him fool ye, Aileen. The man has more and will be sharing it at Beltaine," she laughed, taking a seat next to her.

"Och, I think I can spare the Lady Aileen a cup. It might help to ease some of the tenderness from her body, as well."

Betha watched as he strode away to fetch the wine. "Did his salve work?" she asked.

"Yes, immensely. It has a warmth to it. Do you know what's in it?"

"Nae. It is druid based, and druids can be closed-mouthed when it comes to giving out their secrets, especially curative remedies. It seems to be doing wonders for my ankle, and here I thought I understood the healing ways."

Aileen frowned. "Yet, he is a brother at the abbey."

"Aye, but always a druid first. I ken he seeks the knowledge of the one God, and found a calling when he arrived at the abbey."

"Will we truly be safe in Grenlee?"

Betha sighed. "I reckon once we get there, we will have strength in numbers. It should be a time for great feasting, not for planning our defenses." She shook her head sadly.

Aileen's thoughts turned to events in history, and she shuddered at the memories of witch hunts across the centuries. She never thought that in her lifetime, she would be battling the same. Taking a look around at their band of travelers, her heart felt akin to their beliefs. Smiling, she realized she would stand with them, no matter what they were facing.

"So will there be a Beltaine celebration?" asked Aileen, as her eyes encountered Stephen's back.

Betha chuckled, and Aileen snapped her gaze back in questioning. "What?"

"We could not hold back the feasting as surely as the Mother awakens from her deep slumber. I see ye have felt its pull." Betha tilted her head toward Stephen.

Aileen swallowed, the much hated heat spreading across her cheeks. "I won't...you think me and...*him*? *Together*? Egads!" She stood abruptly and went to stand against a tree.

"The threads of fate are woven deeply between both of ye, Aileen," said Betha softly.

"No, no, no." She shook her head. "He will take me back to the abbey after he sees everyone to safety. I will celebrate with you but must return home."

Betha shook her head slightly.

Aileen glanced at the almost full moon, wanting to just close her eyes, say a prayer, and find that this was just a wild dream. Her eyes misted slightly. "I left my father not understanding who he was. I ran in fear of him. I was angry, hurt, and in shock. Then, the next moment, I awake in a tunnel and find Stephen."

She slid down the trunk of the tree looking up at Betha. "I have to make things right—he *needs* me now. There are so many questions I have only he can answer." She pointed at Stephen. "I don't have time for *us*."

"Be verra careful the road ye force your heart onto, Aileen." Betha's tone firm, but gentle. "Ye were sent to him—*us* for a purpose, and if I understand the *fae*, they will reunite ye with your father when the time is right."

She stood and came over to her, stooping beside her. "All will be well, *Lady* Aileen, daughter of a great Fenian Warrior, *daughter* of the fae."

Aileen slumped into her arms, sobbing softly.

"Let it go, lass," soothed Betha. "May the light of our Lady help to guide ye."

The tension from the last few days drained away while she found comfort in Betha's arms, healing the wounds. Never before had she allowed another to heal her. Somehow the older woman had slipped through her barriers, helping to banish the anguish within Aileen.

Drawing back, she looked at Betha. "Are you a healer, too?"

She smiled. "Ye could say that." Giving Aileen's hand a squeeze, she stood, wrapping her plaid more tightly around her body. Taking her staff to lean on, she paused in thought. "Do not worry about tomorrow, for it has yet to present itself."

"So true, Betha. However, I can still plan what *not* to do," she murmured watching as the woman hobbled away.

Laughter peeled forth from the trees, and Aileen narrowed her eyes, questioning who or what was Betha MacDuff.

Chapter Nineteen

"When the Maypole entered her womb, all life sprung forth, and the cycle of rebirth began anew."

The land beckoned—*come play with me*, as intoxicating smells of pine mixed with wild grasses tickled her nose. As far as the eye could see, the ground was carpeted with buds of bluebells and foxgloves all waiting to burst forth. Wildflowers already in bloom stretched their dainty petals upward to the sun. She could feel the ground beneath her, yawning and awakening from its deep slumber.

Its touch trapped Aileen in bliss.

Freeing herself from her boots and socks, she giggled when her toes encountered the warm grass. She hadn't felt so alive in such a long time.

Casting her gaze out over the hills lush with the purple hues of heather, her vision blurred from the sheer beauty of the land. Breathing in deeply, she allowed the magic of the day to infuse her body and soul.

"Beltaine eve," she murmured.

Laughter spilled out from behind her, and twisting around she saw several young girls with baskets. One of them she recognized as Caitlin, and she gave them a wave.

"Lady Aileen!" shouted Caitlin. "We are gathering

more flowers. Will ye help us?" she asked drawing in breath from running.

"Absolutely."

The young girl grabbed her hand, and they wandered where clusters of wildflowers were growing. "Oh look! Faery flowers."

"I believe those are called foxgloves."

Kneeling down on the soft grass, Caitlin whispered a small blessing before she pulled the flowers from the ground. "These will be for ye," she said beaming up at Aileen.

"For me? Why?"

"Ye are the faery lady, and these will be for your hair."

A screech sounded to their right, and two small rabbits made a dash from their hiding place. The other girls erupted into more fits of laughter.

She looked back at Caitlin, and they both burst out laughing, too.

Aileen spotted some bluebells and daisies, so taking a basket she went to gather them. She had only gone a few feet when *he* stood staring at her. They had managed to avoid one another ever since their arrival in Grenlee, five days ago. There were so many people that one could truly become lost within the crowd.

Five extremely long days.

Her heart started racing just at the sight of him. He must have bathed in the nearby stream, for his hair was wet, and he wore only his plaid. The sun glinted off his muscular body, making her mouth go dry.

He gave her a small nod. "Aileen."

Did he really speak to her? "Stephen."

"Gathering flowers?"

"Bathing in the stream?"

He laughed softly.

She knew she shouldn't ask, but she had to know. Aileen's feet propelled her to him. She couldn't stop herself. "Will you be at the bonfires tonight?"

A shadow of sadness passed over his features. "Nae. I will be on watch."

She swallowed. "Oh, I see." Biting her bottom lip, she then asked, "Perhaps at the dancing?"

His jaw clenched, and he shook his head. "I no longer honor the old ways."

Aileen flinched. "What? How can you...a *Dragon Knight*, toss your beliefs aside?"

That's when she truly saw it. His eyes went from pale pewter to shards of ice in an instant. "Great Goddess," she uttered.

He stepped so close she could feel his breath across her face. "It was by magic this evil spread," he hissed out. "At times, I've spat on the old *beliefs*."

Sadness engulfed her, and she pondered why he felt so. When she spoke, her voice was gentle. "No, Stephen, the old and the new are beautiful paths. If we cannot accept them, we both might as well spill our blood, for it is our heritage."

He just shook his head and looked away.

"In every belief, there is always an evil present, tainting and testing us." She laid a hand on his arm, adding, "Just look what is happening with the new religion." Releasing her hand, she stepped back. "This *cleansing* is part of your new religion. Yet, knowing how this new belief will grow in time, makes me believe in the good of it."

He frowned at her, and Aileen continued, "Do I

follow it? No, my heart is with the old, though the new preaches the very foundation of ours—*love*."

"Your words may hold some truth, yet, it was the old ways that destroyed my family," Stephen said hoarsely.

"What happened?"

"I failed to prevent the death of my sister."

"How?" Her voice barely a whisper.

"It is a verra long story."

She shrugged her shoulders slightly. "I have all day."

He gave her a small smile, and ever so gently, tucked a strand of her hair back behind her ear. "This is not the day. Enjoy your feasting, Lady Aileen."

She stood frozen from his touch, watching as he strode away. What was it that drew her to him? They were as different as night and day. And yet, they were bonded by blood which was as ancient as the land they stood upon.

"Maybe it's for the best you aren't at the bonfires, Stephen." Taking a deep breath, she walked slowly back to the others.

****

Stephen's mind continued to ponder the words Aileen had spoken to him. Here was another one, so bent on binding the two religions, as if they could. She spoke the same drivel as Osgar.

When he first glimpsed her barefoot and laughing, he couldn't remember a sight so tempting. By the Gods, did she understand the view she presented? His immediate response was all too evident in his manhood, and he tried in vain to tame the beast. In the end, all he could do was gaze upon her.

Shaking the vision from his mind, he saw Donal speaking with some of the newly arrived druids. Hope soared when he realized Cathal might have joined them.

"Greetings, Sir Stephen," said the elder of the two. "I am Gorlan, and this is my apprentice, Alan."

Stephen gave a short nod.

"It is an honor, Sir Stephen," stated Alan. "We had not expected to have a Dragon Knight at the gatherings."

Stephen grunted. "I see ye have much to learn, since I am no longer a Dragon Knight." He turned toward Donal. "Has Cathal arrived?"

Donal frowned at Stephen's lack of respect. "Aye, he is here." Before Stephen could depart, he halted him saying, "He is with Betha. Give them some time together—*alone*."

"Done. I shall await him at the north entrance. Any word from Seamus?"

"Nae."

Stephen departed the group, having no desire to converse with the druids. They and their kind still put him and his brothers on this vaulted pedestal, and it left him with a bitter taste in his mouth. Did they not understand they were cursed? Surely ones so high and mighty would scorn him.

When he spotted his horse, he gave a sharp whistle. The horse gave a soft snicker and followed Stephen away from the rest of the crowds.

They ambled for some time until he could no longer hear anyone.

Warm breezes flitted over him as he stood in the shadow of an oak, watching Grian drink from the stream. This is where he would wait and stay the night.

The water would soothe his soul, and being away from the others would prevent him from being tempted. Especially by the fae with lavender eyes.

He rubbed at his eyes trying to convince himself this was truly for the best. Alone. Yet, why did he feel so unsettled?

"Argh!" He pushed away from the tree, scaring the birds from the nearby branches.

"Ye seem to be troubled, Sir Stephen."

Stephen reeled back, sword unsheathed.

"I can assure ye I mean no harm."

"Cathal?" asked Stephen.

The druid nodded, smiling broadly. "It is good to see ye, my son, and that ye remember me."

"It was not recollection. Osgar told me."

Stephen did something that he would never do to another druid, he embraced the elder. "It is good to see ye, too."

"Come, let us sit by the water. If I recall, it was your desired place to be when ye were troubled."

Stephen followed Cathal and together they sat upon boulders looking out at the water, with Grian happily contented to graze along the edge.

They sat in silence for some time, until Stephen asked, "Has Betha told ye all?"

Cathal raised his chin to look at Stephen. "If what ye mean, has she told me about the bishop, the cleansing, *and* my brother Lachlan, then my answer is yes."

"Aye, and what about *me*?" he asked, sarcasm lacing his voice.

"It is not her place. 'Tis yours."

Stephen blew out a long held breath. "I am on a

road with no ending, no direction." He glanced back at Cathal. "I am driven between two worlds. And now the fae have decided to send the daughter of a Fenian Warrior back to our time. For what?" he sneered.

Cathal clasped his hands together. "So I have heard. She is the daughter of Aidan Kerrigan?"

Stephen nodded affirmative.

"Why does this bother ye? Perchance, she is here to help ye on your quest."

"*Quest*?" he roared, standing.

"Yes, Sir Stephen. A quest for *redemption*."

Stephen's laugh was almost sinister in its tone. "I will never seek redemption. I am no longer a Dragon Knight, nor do I wish to reclaim that rank." He glanced back out toward the water. "Ye may as well call a Fenian Warrior to take her back to her own time this moment, instead of me carting her back to the abbey, and through the passage from which she came."

"So all is lost?"

"All was lost the moment my sister was slain."

"Then I will let your brother know ye have forsaken your heritage."

Stephen stiffened, slowly turning around. "We have all forsaken our *heritage*," he spat out.

Cathal shook his head, saying, "One of your brothers has fulfilled his quest and has redeemed his relic."

"*Who*?"

"Duncan."

"By all that's holy!" roared Stephen. "He killed our sister, and he has been redeemed?" He pointed a finger at Cathal, adding, "Now ye have sealed my fate with this information, for if the *fae* saw fit to grant him redemption, then they are no better than the bishop and his followers."

"Sir Stephen, ye must understand—"

Stephen halted his words with his hand. "Nae, no more! Ye can see to the daughter of the Fenian Warrior. I wash my hands of her."

"Ye may wash your hands of Aileen. Nevertheless, ye cannot wash the fae blood from your body," Cathal uttered harshly. "Ye are fighting a battle ye will surely lose."

"Then so be it," he stated. Grabbing Grian's reins, Stephen headed off into the trees.

Chapter Twenty

"He drew her to the water and feasted upon her body, letting the light, and the sweet scent of flowers wash away the bitterness that had bound him in chains."

"For the love of the Goddess, dinnae move," scolded Cora, as she continued to weave flowers in Aileen's long tresses.

"How many have you already woven into my hair? I believe there must be at least a hundred," grumbled Aileen.

Cora snorted. "Nae, it is not too many. Only a few daisies, foxgloves, cowslip, lady's smock, and bluebells." She continued to pull, weave, and braid the flowers.

Betsy traipsed through with a bundle in her arms. "Oh, Lady Aileen, your hair is lovely."

"Is that the gown?" asked Cora.

Betsy took her eyes from Aileen's hair and gazed on what she was holding. "Aye, Betha thought this would bring out the color of her eyes."

Aileen started to say something, but Cora placed a hand on her head to keep it steady. "Lay it next to the others."

"I don't need another gown, Cora. This one will do," she stammered. She tried not to say anything when they first approached her with a bundle in their arms.

Little did she realize they intended to primp and fuss over her in preparation for the celebration.

She eyed them narrowly, curious if Betha had anything to do with this. "I still say that this gown I'm wearing is just fine."

"Whist! Not for the feast." Cora snatched the flowers Aileen started to twist in her hands. "There now. 'Tis ready. Let us help ye with your gown."

Aileen stood, wishing she had a mirror.

"Did ye bathe in the stream?"

She gave an unlady snort. "As best as I could. The water was freezing."

Both women gazed at her in confusion, and she realized *they* might be used to bathing in frigid water, but she certainly was not.

Aileen's mouth dropped open when she saw the gown. It was beyond what she had expected. The richly woven material was dyed a most glorious color of lavender. Gold and silver trimmed the edges of the sleeves and hem.

She let them help her put on the gown, then they belted it with a gold and silver chain, that left a portion of the chain angling down the center of the material.

But when she glanced down, she couldn't help but gasp. "I'm practically spilling out of the neckline." Aileen tried to tuck her breasts down into the gown. "It's too low."

"Nae." Cora smacked her hands away. "It is beautiful."

"Do you think so?"

"Aye," responded both women.

"Fit for a faery queen," Aileen murmured, gently fingering the chain.

"Now ye are dressed properly, my lady," Cora wiped a tear from her eye.

"Thank you...thank you all." Aileen twirled in her dress, causing an outburst of gaiety from the others.

Evening approached, and Aileen realized it was time. The others departed to change and anticipation seized her. It would be a celebration lasting until dawn. Afterwards, they would dance around the maypole with more feasting mixed with storytelling.

Aileen had tried in vain to get some rest in anticipation of the festival. But each time her mind would betray her, and Stephen would enter its depths. He told her he wasn't going to the celebration and part of her was relieved. Nevertheless...there was another part, more primal, that *wanted* him there.

She shouldn't be sad. This was a time of joyous merriment.

"May I escort ye, Lady Aileen?" asked Cathal.

"I would be honored, Cathal. I have heard much of you today."

He chuckled. "I hope it was all good."

"Of course. You are the great Cathal. One of the elder druids and counsel, I hear, to the MacKays."

He waved off her compliments. "I have been away from the MacKays...until recently."

"Oh. Have you spoken to Stephen?" she asked, as they continued onward.

"Aye," he said sadly.

They approached the unlit bonfire, and Cathal turned to face her. "We shall talk more after the feasting. I must gather with the other druids."

"Yes, I would like that."

She'd turned to leave when Cathal added, "Do not

give up on Sir Stephen."

Shocked by his remark, she replied hastily, "He doesn't want my help, and I'm not here to help him."

"Then ye are both lost within the darkness," he stated, before taking his leave.

Aileen watched him walk away. "Sweet Mother Goddess. I'm not *lost*. Why..." She sputtered for lack of words. As far as she was concerned, tomorrow she would be on her way back to Arbroath Abbey.

And then she would be free of Stephen MacKay.

Her fury went from fiery to a soft simmer once she saw Betha, Donal, and Ian. Betha gave her a warm embrace, and handed her a goblet of wine.

"From Osgar," she said smiling.

"I shall have to thank him later." Aileen took a sip, letting its sweet taste linger on her tongue. She leaned in close to Betha. "What will happen next?"

"When all have gathered here, the druids will come forth chanting and give a blessing before they light the great fire. Afterwards, there will be feasting and dancing. Ye may choose to do whatever ye wish." Betha gave a sideway glance to Donal, noticing the smirk on his face.

"What?" asked Aileen, sipping more of her wine.

Donal grabbed Betha's hand with a twinkle in his eye. "Then there are some who will go off and make their own feasting."

Betha actually giggled.

Aileen just stared at the two, somehow feeling like a third wheel. "Okay...I think I'll stay here," she muttered under her breath.

Within moments, all became still and hushed. Chanting started beyond the trees, and Aileen watched in awe as the druids arrived, singing praises to the God and Goddess. In their hands, they held the torches that would light the massive bonfire. Closer they came, their voices ringing through the air. She could only recognize some of the words, for they mostly spoke in Gaelic.

Then she saw Cathal stepping forward praising those who were here. Raising his torch high, he asked permission from the God and Goddess to bring forth the light. "We gather at this festive time, and welcome the return of our Lady. May she blossom with the fruit that was planted with the seed of the God. May the season be fruitful and rife."

He slowly lowered his torch, setting fire to the wood. Sparks shot forth, and a resounding response echoed from the crowd.

"Hail the May Lady!" they shouted.

Aileen lifted her cup, making her own prayer as well. Someone passed her a portion of the wreath cake, and she devoured it, licking the stickiness from her fingers. She slowly backed away watching as the wood took a fiery life of its own, the blaze hot against her cheeks.

Some of the men and women were already dancing around the fire. She laughed when she spied Betsy twirling around.

Betsy waved her over. "Come dance with us."

Aileen held up her hand in protest. "Oh, no...I'm fine just watching." Turning blindly, she stumbled into Brian.

"May I have this dance, Lady Aileen?" he asked.

"I really shouldn't, Brian."

He looked so dejected she decided to throw caution to the wind. "You know what? I haven't danced in ages.

I think I will take that dance."

"I would be honored," he said proudly, holding out his hand.

Aileen swallowed the last of her wine, before putting the cup on a log. Taking his hand, she gathered her dress and joined in dancing with the others.

In no time at all, she found herself being swept away with the contagious merriment. Letting her shields slip just a bit, she relished the gaiety, twirling, and singing. When Brian would gather her close, however, she would spin out. On and on, around the inferno, laughter peeling out.

She felt young and carefree.

****

Stephen was gathering some food, which Betha had prepared for him understanding he would be away all night. She and Donal had pleaded with him to join in the feasting, but he waved them off rather rudely. He wanted no part of the festivities.

Almost colliding with a couple, he swore softly. Placing the food across Grian, he shifted hesitantly. It was then he spotted...*her*.

His hand froze on the leather sack. Sweet Mother! What was she doing? And dressed like that? She was a Goddess of the flame. He watched as she was swung up into the air by none other than Brian. Then he dared to slide her down against *him*.

Dark fury burst somewhere deep inside Stephen. "I'm going to kill him," he rasped out.

The blood roared in his head, as he stormed across the open field, never hearing those who greeted him in passing—one hand held firm against his sword.

Stephen waited as any warrior would. Let the

enemy show himself, he thought.

When their dancing brought them nearer to him, he darted in front blocking their path.

They never saw him coming.

Aileen's back slammed into his chest, and his arms grasped her instantly in a firm grip. "Hey, ouch!" She tried to move, but he held her solid against his body.

Brian skidded to a halt. "Greetings, Sir Stephen." He went to grab for Aileen's hand, when Stephen let out a growl of warning.

"What is your problem? Did you just *growl*?" demanded Aileen. She tried to pry herself loose, but he continued to hold her firm.

"Mine," he snarled.

Instantly, Brian's face went white.

"Thank ye for the dance, Lady Aileen," Brian clipped out. Giving Stephen a curt nod, he stomped away.

"Bloody. God. Damn. Hell," Aileen snapped.

Stephen released her, only spinning her around to face him. Something primal within him tore loose. He tried to reason with himself that this was insanity, though his mind and body wouldn't yield. His gaze dropped to those lips—*lips* he had fantasized about for weeks.

"*Aileen*," he choked out before his mouth took hers in a plundering kiss. His lips moved over hers devouring their softness. The kiss became urgent, pleading in its need. His tongue sought hers, and the dance of desire seared their bodies. Raw passion took over his anger, and she opened fully, drawing him against her body. She took her hands and wrapped them around his head, threading her fingers in his locks and pulling him in deeper. Never in all of his life had he felt so right in someone's arms.

When he broke from the kiss, his breathing was labored. Her eyes were dark with desire for him, and he shook with such need, it frightened him.

"By the hounds," he uttered hoarsely. In one swift move, he picked her up. Carrying her to his horse, he ignored the hoots, and remarks coming from the crowd. Placing her on Grian, he swung around in back, taking off through a large group of oak trees with only one clear thought in mind.

Aileen settled back within his arms, as he uttered a groan. The tight knot in him begged for release.

"If ye keep wiggling like that, I'll stop now and plunge my cock into ye, taking ye here on my horse." His brogue so thick he could barely understand himself.

She gasped. "And I would let you."

He nuzzled her ear. "Do not tempt me."

They continued to ride in silence, the cool night air helped to simmer their blazing yearning for each other.

Stephen halted Grian near some pines, dismounted, and slid Aileen to the ground. He tugged at her hand and she followed him blindly, not caring where he was going.

He lifted her and ducked under some thick pines, emerging within a small grove. Placing her down in the center, he saw a look of awe over her face as she glanced around.

The full moon was making her ascent, its milky glow casting a magical scenery around them.

It was perfect for this night.

Stephen turned, hands clenched at his side. "This night is all I can give ye," he uttered softly. "Will ye give yourself freely, wanting only this?"

She strolled over to face him. Taking his fists, she unclenched them and weaved her fingers through his. "And I shall ask nothing more from you after this night." She looked deep into his eyes, adding, "I need you tonight, Stephen. Make love to me, here, now—*all night*," she pleaded.

"Och, Aileen, what have ye done to me?"

She lowered her head shaking it slowly. "I am just as confused as you are."

Taking her face into his hands, he traced his tongue over her already swollen lips, capturing them with his and suckling lightly. Her moans swallowed up by his mouth.

When he released her, she turned around removing the chain around her hips. Glancing over her shoulder, she gave him a seductive smile. "Undo my laces, *please*."

His hands shook with need, fearing that he would spill his seed before he had a chance to enter her. Gathering strength, he slowly willed himself to undo the laces from her gown. Slipping the last lace free near her bottom, he traced his finger down to just above the cleft between her buttocks. Then bringing it back up slowly, he slipped the gown from her shoulders. Placing kisses along the back of her neck, he turned her around to him.

Her pendant gleamed in the moonlight, and he touched it lightly.

"My mother made it for me," she whispered.

Stephen watched as she eased the gown down past her hips, where it fell in one quick swoosh onto the ground. He let out a growl as she licked her lower lip.

"Ye are so verra beautiful, *fae* Aileen," his voice thick with desire. He stroked her breasts, heavy in his hands. Taking his thumbs he flicked at their rosy nipples, all the while watching her eyes darken with yearning, and feeling her body trembling from his touch.

"Clothes off, now!" she demanded.

"Hungry for what lies beneath, are ye?"

"Yes."

"I have to taste these first." Slowly, he brought her pert nipples to his mouth, inhaling her scent. His tongue lavished the tip, right before his mouth suckled one, then the other.

She clutched at his head, her fingers capturing his locks. Pleasure built with each lick, yet, it was the graze of his beard that sent tingling pinpoints of pleasure downward. By the Gods she was on fire, and this was only the beginning.

"Now I'll remove *my* clothing," he said huskily.

Aileen watched enraptured by his hands, as he removed the dragon brooch from his plaid. He unwrapped it quickly, laying it down upon the ground for their bed. Next came his tunic, and she hissed inwardly at the Adonis standing before her. Black hair dusted his muscular chest, a trail of which led down to his large swollen member.

She instinctively reached out with one hand, but he captured it, placing a kiss in the palm. "Wait," he breathed into her hand.

Dropping her hand, he moved away and placed one booted leg upon a boulder. He slowly undid the laces on his boots, giving her a splendid side view of him. She found herself clenching her hands, aching to touch him. The erotic display of his masculinity was driving her insane.

Tossing his boots aside, he strode back to stand before her, his gaze traveling over her. With her flowers strewn throughout her hair, and the moon glistening off her pale skin, he thought her truly a Goddess of the fae.

He captured her close, taking her mouth with savage intensity, as she grasped his head urging him deeper. No longer gentle, their kisses became demanding, urgent in their need. His tongue swept inside seeking hers, and she surrendered. He then took his finger and trailed it down to her nest of curls. Stroking her already moist folds, he slid two fingers deep inside her, as he captured her moans with his mouth.

"I want to taste ye, but I cannae last much longer," he growled, placing his forehead against hers. As he released his fingers, she took his hand and placed it toward his lips. Instantly, his cock jerked against her stomach, and she drew him down to the ground. Without a word, she opened her legs fully to him.

Stephen uttered a groan, taking her mouth with such fierceness. He rubbed his cock at the entrance of her soft folds, her musky scent filling his head.

"*Pleeease*, Stephen. In me *now*," she hissed out.

He drove in with one swift thrust, gasping when she threw her leg around him driving him further within her. Pulling out slowly, he rammed back into her, his grunt of pleasure echoing hers. Stephen watched his Goddess writhe with pleasure, her rosy nipples dancing with each thrust. Their mating dance becoming more urgent.

"*Oh Stephen, I need...*"

"Come for me, *Aileen*. Let me feel your pleasure," his voice low, as he grazed his teeth along her neck.

Aileen arched wildly, screaming his name.

Stephen could no longer hold back, and with a guttural cry, he sought his own release. The wave of pleasure swept and crashed over him.

And in that quiet moment, with their bodies still quaking from bliss, they both knew in their hearts the promises they made earlier to each other had just been completely shattered.

Chapter Twenty-One

"When she removed her rose-colored glasses, the reality was far better than she imagined."

The only sounds around the lovers were those of the nocturnal creatures and the gentle sound of the pine branches moving with the night breezes.

Stephen tugged his wrap more securely over them, relishing the fullness of the woman in his arms. She was tucked against his chest, her arm wrapped around his waist. He sensed her to be awake, since every so often she would move her hand to play with his chest hairs.

Neither felt the need to say anything at the moment.

He drew in a long breath gazing up at the twinkling stars, which were overshadowed by the brilliance of the moon. Memories flooded him of the times he spent with his brothers outdoors trying to spy the different animals or beasts within the bright lights. There were many arguments on whose depiction was the best. Some nights, the heated discussions would turn to fists, with Angus threatening them with the might of his fire.

A lifetime ago.

Absently, he stroked Aileen's soft hair, still woven with flowers.

"I'm afraid it will be weeks before I can get them

all out," murmured Aileen against his warm chest.

He chuckled softly, inhaling their scent, and something else. Tipping her chin up, Stephen nuzzled her neck. Then taking his tongue, he licked from her neck to her chin. "Mmmm...ye smell like cinnamon."

"Uh-huh," she sighed, waiting for his lips to touch hers. When he didn't react, she opened her eyes to find him smiling at her. "Cinnamon? Well, it could be the cake I had earlier." She rubbed along his leg, getting the response she wanted when he let out a groan.

His mouth captured hers, smothering her lips within his. Slowly, he took his fingers and caressed up her thighs, stroking her sensitive core. She arched back with a moan, wanting his fingers deeper. He placed a kiss on her nose, and tossed off the plaid.

"Wh...*where* are you going?" she asked, still aching for more of his kisses, and tugging the plaid back around her.

"I'm hungry."

Aileen sat up on her elbow, too stunned to speak. Yet, as she watched his backside walk away, she gazed lustfully at the sight of his muscular body—a perfect male specimen—scars, tattoos, and all.

Stephen gave a short whistle. Emerging from the trees trotted his horse. "Resting well, Grian?" The horse only snorted as Stephen removed a satchel. Then giving him a smack on the rump, Grian ambled back into the trees.

"Your neck reminded me that Betha packed some of that very cake, and…" Aileen stared, as he took out a small wooden pot. "Some honey." Sitting down next to her, he opened the pot. Dipping a finger inside, he drew out some. A sensual glint appeared in his eyes.

He saw her lips parted in anticipation. Taking one breast in his hand, he blew across it. With the other hand, he smeared honey across the pert nipple. "Now, I will feast on your body." His voice low before he suckled deeply.

Aileen gave a violent shudder. "Oh, God, that feels so-o-o good, Stephen." She felt him rumble with laughter, his warm mouth continuing to lavish her breast.

With one final taste, he released her breast. "I have to have seconds." Dipping his finger back into the pot, he did the same with her other breast.

Aileen rested her elbows on the ground to watch in sheer heated lust, as he feasted on her. "More," she growled. He placed small amounts of honey on her stomach and thighs.

"Where shall I go next?" the burr of his voice sent shivers down her spine.

Tossing her head back, she pleaded, "Please end this agony."

Retrieving more honey, he leaned near her ear. "Spread your legs for me, Aileen."

Her legs were already a pile of mush, but she complied.

"I am verra hungry for *your* honey pot." His smile positively wicked.

"I would have thought you had enough honey," she rasped out.

Ever so slowly, he placed the warm honey on her most sensitive spot. His breath was hot, and Aileen clutched at the plaid as his mouth covered her nub, flicking and tasting the honey. A wave of pleasure slammed into her, and she clutched his head, arching up wildly.

When he finished his ministrations, he took her mouth in a burning kiss. She devoured his lips, smelling the honey mixed with her own scent.

Breaking from the heated kiss, she glared at him. "My turn to feast now."

Stephen eyes blazed with desire at her intent.

Aileen snatched the pot from the ground and swiftly shifted their positions.

He lay back, placing an arm under his head. Then taking his cock in his hand, he teased her by stroking it in front of her. "Take me."

"Not so fast." Dipping her finger into the pot, she tasted the sweet nectar pulling her finger out of her mouth with an exaggerated pop. "Doesn't taste good by itself."

Placing drops of honey on both his nipples, she grazed her teeth over his skin before she licked the honey from them.

Stephen let out a sharp hiss. *By the Gods, such sweet torture!* His eyes feasted as her naked body loomed over his, her silken hair trailing down his body with each succulent kiss she placed.

Sweet torture indeed, he only hoped he was prepared for what she would do next.

Aileen took the pot, and holding it high she let the amber sweetness drop slowly, covering the head of his aching cock.

"*Aileen,*" he growled in warning.

"Shhhh." She placed a finger on his lips.

He watched her eyes, hooded with raw desire, and then she gently grasped his arousal. "Spread your legs for *me*, Stephen."

167

His body quaking with need, he let her take control.

"Sweet Mother!" he roared. Her mouth was hot around him. She teased her tongue along the side of his shaft and down to his balls, before bringing it back up again. Beads of sweat broke out on his forehead. His control swiftly ebbing away.

"Must...have ye...now," he gritted out.

Aileen ignored his pleas. Never before had she wanted to taste a man. Her craving to have him consumed her. Drawing him deeper into her mouth, she suckled fiercely.

Stars burst before Stephen eyes, and he thrust madly into her mouth, as her tongue did its sensual dance. He had never experienced such ecstasy. Throwing back his head, he shattered totally within her mouth, an explosion so powerful he felt the roar of her moan within his body.

His body still humming, he drew her close with shaky limbs. Drawing the plaid around them again, he heard her say softly, "Must get some more honey from Betha."

"Aye, and a bigger pot of it," he chuckled hoarsely.

For the first time in many moons, Stephen let himself drift off, completely and totally sated. An owl hooted in the distance, and he smiled inwardly, until the darkness of sleep took over.

****

"Go away," mumbled Aileen. She was in nirvana, and something, or someone was bothering her.

There, she felt it again. This time she tried to swat at it, but her hand was stuck. "Blast it, stop," she uttered with more feeling.

Opening one eye, she spied the culprit. Stephen had one of her flowers and was brushing it over her face. Finally yanking her hand free, she swatted at him.

"Time to wake my faery queen," he drawled.

"Are you my faery king?"

A look of sadness passed briefly over his features. "Nae, just a man." He swiftly rolled her onto her back and placed a gentle kiss on her mouth.

"Your bath awaits," he said. "In case ye have not noticed, we are one mighty sticky mess."

Aileen snorted. "And where might that be?"

"In the stream, where else?"

"Absolutely not!" she exclaimed, pushing him off her. "I am *not* getting in that icy water."

His mouth twitched with amusement. "Och, it's not so bad."

"Seriously?"

Standing abruptly, he pulled her to her feet. "I will keep ye close." He gave her a playful wink.

"No!"

His eyes flashed. "Do not force me, Aileen."

"Ha! You so wish." Then regretted the dare the moment the words left her mouth.

"Have I ever told ye how much I love a challenge?"

Aileen shivered, but she wouldn't give in to his threat, or challenge. "You may go in if you wish, but I'll just clean myself when we're—"

She never finished the sentence, for he tossed her over his back.

"Blast you, Stephen! Put me down!" she yelled pounding her fists into rock hard muscles. The man didn't even flinch.

Slapping her bottom firmly, he said, "Stop your griping, woman. I just want to clean ye."

"What is it with you and water?" she breathed out, trying to push herself off his shoulder.

He shrugged. "It is my power."

Aileen froze. This was the first time he had spoken anything about himself, or who he was. "Power, as in you can control water?"

"Aye."

"Well, why don't you put me down, and I'll attempt to get in."

"Liar."

Aileen's heart beat wildly as the first cold splash of water came into contact with her legs. She squirmed with all her might. There was no way in hell she was going to submerge herself in the stream.

"Hold still or I'll throw ye in," he growled.

Her breathing came out in short bursts, as he stepped further out into the stream. The water came up to his groin, and she swallowed back a sharp retort. She kept waiting for him to lower her, but he stood extremely still.

When she was about to ask what was wrong, he released his hold, and she went sliding down his body right into the water. Sinking deep within, her feet hit the bottom, becoming completely drenched.

He was a monster!

Sputtering for air, she wiped the wet strands away from her face. "Why, you..." she stammered, until realization dawned on her.

The water was *warm*.

He stood there with his arms across his chest and a smirk on his face.

She cupped the water in her hands, letting it slip through her fingers. "Did you do this?" she asked in utter astonishment.

He nodded slowly with a slightly arrogant smile.

Her gentle laughter rippled through the air, right before she plunged back down into the water.

Chapter Twenty-Two

"As the harp began to play the lovers a song of their story, their strings of fate were snapped in two."

Stephen stood transfixed by the beauty splashing in the water before him. Laughter continued to bubble out from those divine lips each time she would burst forth from the water. One would have thought her some mystical sea-maiden. He bit back a curse watching her bum descend under the water. His gaze followed her body as it glided toward him, floating lightly on her back. Her pert nipples bobbed in the air, beckoning him.

"If I would have known that I could have my water heated, I would have asked much sooner," she said sighing, her hands gently moving with the rhythm of the water.

"Do ye like the water?" Stephen asked hoarsely.

"Always have," she replied softly, not realizing the feast she was presenting to the hunter until his arm captured her underneath.

Stephen took his mouth and suckled lazily one breast, kneading the other with his hand.

Aileen's eyes snapped open. "Stephen?" she asked, hesitantly reaching out to touch the dragon on his right arm. "It's shimmering."

He tilted his head to look at where her fingers

traced the outline of the beast. "She blazes when I use my powers," he said quietly.

"Does it hurt?"

"Nae."

"So beautiful," she whispered.

He shuddered at her words. No one had ever found the dragon beautiful—frightening, aye, but not beautiful. In that moment, some part of him fractured.

His lips pressed against hers, then gently covered her mouth in sweet tenderness. He took his time placing small kisses on her eyelids, then her nose, and capturing the sigh that escaped from her lips. She swayed in his arms, trailing her fingers along the muscles of his back.

His mouth grazed her earlobe. "Wrap your legs around me," he whispered, grabbing her bottom.

She complied, and he plunged deep into her. "Oh my—"

Resting his forehead against hers, he continued to move in a rhythmic dance of pleasure. Never had Stephen taken a woman in the water. Yet, here he was sharing the most intimate part of himself surrounded by the very gift he had fought against for so long.

His soul cracked open a fragment more.

"Open your eyes, Aileen." His voice husky, as he slowly slid in and out of her.

She tilted her head back, keeping her gaze upon the man whose eyes mirrored hers in yearning. Aileen pressed her fingers deeper into his arms. They were buoyed with the gentle lapping of the water. Each heartbeat melding into one—a fusion of souls.

Stephen tried to control his release, but just watching her desire build, and the color of her eyes change to beautiful hues of lavender was sending him faster over the abyss.

"I cannae..." he rasped, before letting go and emptying totally into her. Aileen followed with a guttural cry of his name. He shook violently and took her mouth voraciously. The vortex of bliss sweeping them away on its current joined as one.

He did not want to let her go. They stayed immersed within the soothing waters for some time letting the beating of their hearts slow. Her legs were still around his waist with her head cradled against his neck.

By the Gods! What were they going to do? What was *he* going to do? By taking her in the water, he sealed his fate, and the realization frightened Stephen more than life itself. Gently lifting her, he carried her out of the water over to the boulder against the shore. She lay back against it watching him.

Did she feel the same?

Placing a soft kiss on her lips, he stretched. "I'll go fetch my wrap."

Aileen's heart was still beating rapidly. She'd felt something shift out on the water, as if a part of her melded with him. A union of body and soul. "No, this cannot happen," she sighed, hugging her knees close to her chest.

Still contemplating their last encounter, Aileen heard what sounded like a growl. Quickly standing, she peered around. If there were any animals out there, her best place of safety would be in the water. However, Stephen was out there. She could yell his name, but then he would come running, and run into danger. Clenching her fists, she heard it again. This time, she realized it wasn't an animal.

Aileen sprinted toward the glen.

"*No*," she gasped. Kneeling down on the ground was Stephen. He was rocking back and forth, obviously in a great deal of pain.

"Stephen, what is it?" she asked lightly touching his arm.

What followed was a torrent of words she couldn't understand.

"Please, Stephen, tell me where it hurts?" She tried to turn his head, but he thrust out of her grasp.

"Damn," she hissed out. Grabbing the plaid, Aileen wrapped it around herself, and sat down to wait.

Mere moments turned to at least ten grueling minutes, before she witnessed any sign of his pain receding. He blinked open his eyes, briefly. With a groan, he vomited on the ground.

And Aileen waited.

"Water," he rasped low.

She grabbed the skin, emptying the contents of wine. As fast as she could, she ran back to the stream filling it to the brim.

When she returned, he was crawling toward an old oak.

Holding his head, she lifted the water to his lips.

"Nae," he bit out. "Here." He shook as he held out his hands to her.

Frowning, Aileen did what he requested. The water pooled in the palm of his hands, and she gasped in shock.

The water had frozen.

"Neck," he whispered.

She knew instantly what he wanted to do. Taking the ice, Aileen placed it on the back of his neck.

Understanding what he needed, she sat behind him on the plaid. Saying the healing words she knew so well, Aileen let her breathing become steady reaching for the light within. Shards of crystal colors danced before her eyes. Within moments, the healing energy of her power passed into him, soothing, and mending the burning pain that radiated inside his head. Her energy quickly melted the ice. Aileen then used her fingers. She continued to caress his neck working her way up to his temples, and through his scalp.

Simple touches, but ones that would ease the pain.

He tugged her hand within his, gently stroking her palm. "Thank ye...for your gift."

Aileen sighed, laying her head against his back, she took strength from his warmth. As always, the healing sapped her greatly.

Time passed. A hawk circled lazily above, and the air chilled.

Taking a deep breath, she stood. Reaching for her gown, she stepped into the material. There were questions she wanted to ask, but hesitant to hear the answers.

She took a sip of the water, noticing Stephen looking away, a frown marring his features.

At a loss for words, she gathered their items, scanning the area for his horse.

"I have *visions*," Stephen said softly. "They leave me with searing pain."

Moving to sit down next to him, she asked, "Have you always had these visions?"

"Aye."

My God, she thought. How could he have lived like this all his life? "I am so sorry, Stephen. Will it help to talk about the vision?"

He rubbed a hand over his face, shaking his head no. "Same vision, same ending."

"Bad?"

He snorted in disgust, while he grabbed his tunic, pulling it over his head. Standing weakly, he whistled for Grian. Instantly, the horse emerged from the trees.

Aileen wanted to inquire more, yet held back. Gathering her tangled mass of hair, she swept it to the side in an effort to braid it.

"Here, let me," he said.

She arched a brow skeptically.

"Aye, I do ken how to braid."

After he was through, he tied the laces on her gown, placing a soft kiss on the back of her neck.

"I don't understand, Stephen."

"What dinnae ye understand?"

"Why would you be given such a gift when it leaves you with such pain?"

He reeled her around to face him. "It was not always like this."

"How long then?"

Pausing, as if trying to decide how to answer her, he finally answered, "Since the night I was cursed."

"Oh," she breathed out. What more could she say? She only understood the legend in bits and pieces. Biting her lip, she was about to ask what happened when she saw him rub his forehead, as if still in pain.

She reached out to him. "I can help more with the healing."

"Nae." He shook his head slowly. "There are times when I miss my relic. With it, I was able to control the burning pain when the visions entered."

"Relic, as in medallion? Is it something you wear around your neck?" uttered a shocked Aileen.

He nodded, placing his pack onto Grian. "Aye, 'tis a stone set in silver."

"Oh my stars!" yelled Aileen. "How could I have forgotten?" She cupped a hand over her mouth in glee. "All this time."

Stephen eyed her suspiciously. "What are ye talking about?"

"Can you ever forgive me, Stephen?" she asked, smiling weakly.

He placed his hands on his hips. "What do I need to forgive ye for?"

She swallowed. "You see, Stephen, *I* have your medallion—your stone."

Chapter Twenty-Three

"The truth is better served with honey, than with lye."

"Judas's balls, woman!" roared Stephen.

Aileen cringed. "I can understand you're angry, but not this angry. I didn't realize how important the medallion was to you. You should be grateful I found the bloody thing in the first place. *And* traveled eight hundred years to deliver it!"

"Where is it?" his tone remained brisk, snapping her out her thoughts.

"In my coat."

He went to reach for her, but she backed up suddenly. "I didn't realize the gravity of the situation," she protested, pushing past him. Wanting no help from him, she mounted Grian.

Instantly, he was behind her, still grumbling beneath his breath. It was all reminiscent of when they first met. As if the past twenty-four hours never existed.

A long silence ensued as they traveled.

Stephen's mind reeled. All these weeks, she had it in her possession. By the Gods! How verra cruel to send her back through the veil with no knowledge of what she had. A deep rumble started in the pit of his stomach, and burst forth. He felt her tense, as he continued to laugh. So verra cruel, but so verra sad.

He could only laugh at the irony.

He slowed Grian somewhat before they came upon the crest of the hill. She truly didn't deserve his anger.

"I am sorry, Aileen," he uttered softly.

Her shoulders slumped, and she let out a long held breath. "I am, too." She twisted sideways to look at him. "Honestly..."

"Whist, my bonny fae." He placed a finger against her lips. "How could ye fathom?"

"But I did, Stephen. I saw it in a depiction on a tapestry, which just happens to be in my father's home."

"Truly?"

"Yes," she said smiling. "It's beautiful, one with your brothers, and sister, too," she uttered the last softly.

His gaze grew troubled. "I am honored he would think so highly of us."

Aileen touched his arm lightly. "I would like to know what happened that night." He started to object, but it was her turn to shush him with a finger to his lips. "Only when you are ready."

He gave her a terse nod, before urging Grian forward.

****

Betha was the first to eye the lovers coming over the hill. She waved Ian over, telling him to fetch his father. Smiling as they rode closer, they had no idea the entire camp spoke of the Dragon Knight and his lady joining on such a special night. It was as if hope soared with the likely pairing of the two.

"It is the easy part," muttered Betha.

Some of the men nodded, and the women blushed as they rode past them. It was the day after feasting, and most were still feeling the effects of wine, ale, and lovemaking.

"I've sent Ian to bring Cathal. 'Tis best to let Seamus rest," said Donal giving her a squeeze on her bottom.

Betha leaned against him giving him a mischievous look. "Later, my love."

He growled into her ear just as Stephen and Aileen approached.

"Sir Stephen, Lady Aileen," smiled Betha.

Aileen blushed slightly. Her appearance was enough to suggest what had happened between Stephen and her. Thank the Goddess she didn't have a mirror.

Helping her down, Stephen gave her a reassuring smile before turning his attention to the others.

"Betha, might I have a word with you?" asked Aileen.

"Of course. Have ye eaten?" she asked as they made their way along the path.

"Not much, but first, I need to get my coat."

Betha raised a brow in question, but only nodded. "Meet me over there between the two oaks. There is some stew, and a portion of a wreath cake. We can have a moment before the feasting and dancing resumes around the maypole."

At the mention of the cake, Aileen felt a searing heat on her face. All she could think of was Stephen licking the cinnamon from her chin last night and what he did afterwards. "Thank you, I'll be along shortly."

Quickly making her way toward the leather satchel one of the women had let her borrow, she dug her hand deep within the pocket of her coat. Snuggled tightly within her scarf, Aileen pulled it forth. Chills took hold of her realizing this medallion was not only linked to Stephen, but to the *fae*.

Rubbing her thumb over the green stone, warmth spread throughout her body, lifting her spirits. To be chosen to return such a valuable item caused her heart to soar. Wrapping the precious relic in her scarf, Aileen went in search of Stephen. Her stomach protested furiously. However, it could wait.

She didn't have to go far to find him, since he was making a path to her.

"Here it is."

"Sweet Mother" was all he could say, as he reached out to take his stone.

Searing pain burned his fingers the moment he touched it. "God's teeth!" Stephen bellowed.

Scared, Aileen dropped it onto the ground. They both stood over it looking as if it was some great beast.

"I just touched it moments ago," whispered a stunned Aileen.

Stephen clenched his fist still feeling its tingling effects.

"The relic must be cleansed," replied Cathal as he ambled over to them.

"Bloody hell!" barked Stephen.

"But Cathal, I can touch the medallion—stone. I just did so moments before, and it was warm to the touch, radiating a peaceful energy."

"Aye, and that is as it should be, Lady Aileen."

"Explain," Stephen said tersely.

"Lady Aileen has been chosen to return the *medallion*. Furthermore, before it can be returned to *ye*, it must be cleansed by the Great Dragon."

"By the hounds, Cathal! I do not have time for

this!"

"And why is that? The lady has brought back your relic and ye cannae ride the two-days' journey to have it cleansed?" Cathal shook his head in disbelief.

"That would be *five* days," snapped Stephen. "Besides, I have promised Aileen I would return her to Arbroath Abbey."

"Is it true?" Cathal questioned as he looked at Aileen.

Great Goddess! Stephen wanted no more to do with her. Their magical night together meant *nothing* to him. He was going to keep his promise. Again, she was the fool. Yet, what did she expect? It was what she had told him she wanted.

Sadness and confusion engulfed her.

"Aileen has requested to return to the abbey, so she may return to her own time, *and* her father," Stephen said bluntly.

"Is there no other way, Cathal?" she asked quietly.

He sighed. "Nae. The stone must be purified in the waters where the Great Dragon resides." He stepped closer and gripped her hands. "Is there anything I can say to sway your mind and make this journey?"

Aileen swallowed. If the medallion were given to her for a purpose, then she would see it through. From this moment on, she would erect as many shields around her heart and feelings.

She wouldn't be swept away, *again*.

She turned to Stephen. "Then I will make this journey, and when it is completed, you can take me back to the abbey. Now if you don't mind, I think I'll go gather my things, eat, and get some rest. I suppose you will want to leave at dawn's light." With a nod to both of them, she scooped up the medallion and quickly left before Stephen had a chance to protest.

"God's blood!" Stephen yelled in frustration. "Do ye not grasp the dangers that are upon us, Cathal?"

"I would think there are many. In truth, ye are the one with the visions. Have ye spoken with Betha, or Osgar regarding their interpretations?"

"Nae," he replied waving him off.

"Would ye care to share them with me?"

Stephen breathed in deeply watching a black falcon circle above them. He did not like to share his visions with anyone. They were his to interpret. After they left him, he would draw his thoughts in an effort to better understand their meaning.

Perhaps if he had chosen to share his visions, his sister might still be alive.

He glanced back at Cathal. "The visions are of battles yet to be fought. Each one ending in death."

"Whose death?"

"Some of the brothers from the abbey." Stephen knew what his next question was and answered, "Nae, I did not see their faces to know which ones." He went over to lean against a pine for support. "Then there was the burning, or as Betha has stated, the cleansing."

"Aye, she has told me of her vision."

Stephen nodded in understanding. "I had one this morning." He pursed his lips before adding, "It was a vision of Aileen, dying. Now ye realize why I must return her to her own time and father."

Cathal stroked his beard in thought. "How accurate are your visions, Stephen?"

He frowned. "Accurate? Visions a portent of the future, or as close as they can be. There have been times when a single event can change their course, but even I am not that powerful to prevent what will happen."

"If I may ask, who was more bonded to the fae? Margaret, or ye?"

Stephen's jaw clenched. "We both were. They used my visions to speak to me, and Mar...Meggie spoke directly to them. Why?"

"Have ye not heard their messages to ye, then?" he asked, signaling to the black falcon.

"I told ye I no longer honor those ways," he ground out.

Stephen watched as the black falcon landed on Cathal's outstretched arm.

"Perhaps if ye had listened to them, ye would have a better understanding."

"Why would they have anything to do with me? After that night, I would think they would have turned their backs on us completely."

"Sorcha, this here is Stephen MacKay, brother of Duncan. He, too, thought all was lost." Cathal tilted his head to the side. "Until he wove all the pieces of not only that night, but of the ones that came before."

"What the bloody hell do ye mean, Cathal?" he asked in warning.

Cathal looked directly at Stephen. "There was evil magic that night, and *none* of it was from the Dragon Knights."

Stephen's jaw dropped, and then snapped shut. Was there something he missed? Who would want to do this to his family? "*Who*?" he rasped out.

"Let us gather some food and drink. We can talk more away from the feasting." Cathal saw him hesitate.

"Unless ye would rather join in?"

Stephen rubbed a hand over his face remembering the feasting he had of one lovely lady. "I could do with some food and ale."

"Good." Releasing Sorcha, they watched as she flew off ahead of them.

Stephen's mind reeled from Cathal's revelation. He needed to find out more about this evil person or persons. In the meantime, he had to deal with coming face to face with the Great Dragon and asking for her forgiveness.

He let out a long breath. How could he possibly ask for absolution, when he could not fathom forgiving himself?

Chapter Twenty-Four

"When a Knight strides into battle, he often leaves behind his heart."

After much food and ale, Stephen stretched out along the back of an elm tree. He had probed Cathal relentlessly about this evil. Strange, how the druid would try to weave his brother, Duncan, into the telling. There was no way he was going to listen to how Duncan redeemed himself. Of all the brothers, he could not grasp why he would be the first.

Taking another sip of ale, he asked, "Ye are certain Lachlan is at the core of all of this?" Stephen suspected there was more to the story than what Cathal was sharing.

"I can most assuredly say that he is," replied Cathal taking the ale skin back from Stephen.

"How did ye come upon this wisdom?"

"Have ye thought much on the days leading to that fateful night?"

"Humph!" Stephen grumbled, taking his hand over his unshaven face.

Cathal sighed. "This is where ye must begin your journey, so ye can understand what it is ye are facing."

Before Stephen could reply, he noticed Donal and Seamus approaching on foot.

"Think on my words, Stephen." His voice stern.

He gave him a curt nod, standing to greet the two men. "What news, Seamus?"

"They are scattered and confused," he said with a smirk. "I ken some of the guards from the abbey desire to return. Yet, it is the one called Lachlan who refuses and keeps them onward."

"He will never give up," interjected Cathal. "His focus is entirely on obtaining the relics, and let me warn ye, he only needs one to control all of your powers."

"What?" Stephen asked incredulously. "How is that possible?"

Cathal let out a long sigh. "His power is based in evil, one that has grown since the day he fought off death. I have just recently consulted with the Elders, and we are all in agreement."

"What of Angus and Alastair? Can they not be warned?"

"Their journey has yet to begin. This is your time, not theirs."

Donal and Seamus glanced at one another. It was Donal who spoke. "I hear ye are taking the Lady Aileen to the waters near the Great Glen."

"Aye. She has found my relic."

"Praise the Gods!" exclaimed a shocked Donal.

Seamus stepped forward. "Then I would be honored to accompany a Dragon Knight and his lady safely to the Great Glen."

"I thank ye, Seamus, but this journey we must make ourselves."

"Sir Stephen, do ye not think it is best to have protection now that ye see the threat?"

Cathal laid a hand on Seamus's arm. "Nae. They must make this journey on their own. I believe ye are needed here."

"Then I will rest and depart on the morrow to keep watch on this foul person. It will be my pledge to ye."

"May the God and Goddess keep ye safe, Seamus."

Seamus gave a nod, leaving for much needed rest.

"I shall go see to your provisions," said Donal. Before leaving he added, "It is good ye have regained your stone."

"If that were only true." He turned toward Cathal after Donal was out of sight. "Tell me why someone has not ended the life of Lachlan?"

Cathal just shrugged. "Trust me when I say I, too, wish it so." Shaking his head, his sight took him beyond the hills. "When did Lachlan's heart falter, and when did he abruptly choose the path of evil?" He released a shuddering breath. "It is beyond my comprehension. I will continue to work with the Elders in hope of finding a weakness in the evil that my brother has spread."

Stephen placed a hand upon his shoulder, understanding the sadness in the druid. "I ken he is your brother, but this can end no other way."

"He was lost to me the moment he walked the dark path of evil. When his death comes, I will ask for his heart," he uttered solemnly.

Cathal grasped Stephen's hand firmly. "May the God and Goddess light your path."

Stephen tried to draw back, but the druid held firm.

"Remember..." said Cathal, as he tapped Stephen's forehead with his finger.

Releasing him, he strode away leaving Stephen stunned and speechless. He absently rubbed the spot where Cathal had touched him. "Remember *what*?"

Shaking his head slowly he took off in the opposite

direction. "Druids and their riddles," he muttered.

****

Aileen sat in silence while Betha braided her hair. Laughter and music spilled forth from the distance as the feasting continued in full force. She nibbled on some bread and cheese after eating a bowl of soup full of wild mushrooms.

Trying to stay focused, her mind continued back to Stephen's words. He was so eager to see her back to the abbey that her stomach clenched at the thought of spending four days alone with the infuriating man.

An extremely sinfully gorgeous, man.

"So, what is it ye wanted to speak to me about?" asked Betha, as she wove a ribbon through her braid.

Aileen blinked. "Huh?"

"Is your mind confused, or is it your heart?"

How could she possibly know? "I'm sorry, is it so obvious?"

"Oh, aye," said Betha smiling.

Aileen threw the last of her bread to a nearby bird, frustration clawing at her. "He…he makes me so mad!" She shot Betha a sideways glance. "But that's not what I wanted to talk to you about." She stood and leaned against a tree.

"What happened the night Stephen and his brothers were cursed?"

Betha let out a long sigh. "They fought and their sister was killed on hallowed ground."

Aileen waved her hand in the air. "I know that. I want to understand how she died, *and why*? Stephen says he is cursed, but what does it mean?"

"The MacKays—*Dragon Knights*, had been at odds with the MacFhearguis clan for years. The

MacFhearguis claimed they were the rightful heirs to the sacred relics."

"Are they?"

"Nae. 'Tis always been the MacKays. On the night of the battle, Margaret MacKay went to meet her lover at the stones. There they were to be handfasted, running off together to start a new life." Betha's eyes misted when she continued, "For ye see her lover was Adam MacFhearguis, and they both understood their families would never accept their troth."

"Feuding clans, Romeo and Juliet," whispered Aileen.

"Who?"

"Nothing, just another similar story told by a bard." Betha nodded in understanding.

"Yet, her brother, Duncan, I believe, killed her."

"Margaret stepped in front of Adam, and took the blow that was meant for him. She died that night. The Guardian of the fae descended to level the curse—*a curse* which removed not only their relics, but fouled their names."

Aileen tried to digest all of this. Then another thought caused her to frown. "If they are cursed, then why did I find Stephen's medallion and travel back here?"

Betha smiled slowly. "It is an answer only Stephen can give ye, Aileen. I believe that the fae have not truly forsaken them. Each has been given a journey back to that night."

"A chance for redemption?" interjected Aileen.

"Aye, and only Stephen kens what he has to do. He must remember the words of the Guardian. In truth, I fear he has chosen to forget that night."

"The Great Dragon..." whispered Aileen.

"Seek the wisdom of the Great Dragon. She will help ye to guide your heart," Betha said softly.

"I don't need wisdom for my heart. I will cleanse the medallion, give it to Stephen, and go home."

"Ye cannae fool me, Aileen."

"It doesn't matter. He doesn't want me, and I have to return to my father. Case closed."

"Hmmm...then ye had better build a stronger fortress for your heart, for I fear it will shatter if ye do not face your true feelings."

Aileen's jaw tightened, and she refused to say any more on that subject. She would encase her feelings for Stephen in a box of steel under lock and key forever. Her meal took a sour turn within her stomach, and she hugged her arms tightly around her. Wanting to talk about something other than her and Stephen, she asked, "Will you be safe here?"

Betha frowned. "I ken we will eventually travel north, deeper into the Great Glen. 'Tis not what Donal and I want to do. Though, it would be safer for us until this madness passes." She brushed the crumbs off her gown and stood. "We will await your return before heading north."

"Five days," sighed Aileen, as she watched Ian come running through the grasses.

"Lady Aileen." He waved. "Ye promised to dance with me and the other children."

"I believe Lady Aileen must rest, since she and Sir Stephen will be making a journey to see the Great Dragon."

Ian eyes went wide. "Truly?"

Aileen tried to smile at the boy. "Yes, it is. Have

you met this *dragon*?"

"Nae. But I have heard she is wise and gentle." Ian took her hands in his. "Do not fear her."

"Her?"

Betha bobbed her head in acknowledgment.

"Aye. They say she is verra lovely. She will help ye seek the answers to your questions, too."

"I didn't know I had any," Aileen muttered under her breath. "I think I'll take that one dance with you and the others. Go fetch them, and I'll meet up with you in a few moments."

Ian gave a shout of joy before dashing off.

"Tsk, tsk, Lady Aileen, soon he will have ye listening to the bardic tales at dusk."

"He does tend to sway me in my decisions," she replied in a lighter tone.

"Mayhap, he can help your heart." Betha gave her arm a gentle squeeze. "Try to get some rest. If I ken Sir Stephen, he will be starting out *before* dawn's first light."

Aileen's shoulders stiffened. How could she have known such bliss only yesterday, and then today feel as if it was only one sided? Her face flushed as the memories of all they had done came tumbling forth once again.

Perhaps a few hours with the children and listening to stories would put her in a better frame of mind.

"Would you like me to make you a comfrey wrap before I leave?" Aileen asked, pushing away from the tree.

"Nae," answered Betha, waving her off. "Donal is returning shortly and can help me."

"What do ye need tending to, wife?" Donal

interrupted, placing his arms around her. "Is there something special I can help ye with?" he asked, brushing a kiss along her upturned face.

Aileen couldn't help but notice the mirth in Betha's eyes as she moved into him. Understanding instantly what Betha had meant about Donal taking care of her *needs*, she rolled her eyes, and strolled away.

It seemed Beltaine had infected everyone with lustfulness.

Chapter Twenty-Five

"For no one saw the shadow pass over the land until the beast struck out at them with its mighty claw."

Lachlan watched in greed as they carved into the deer they had slain, blood oozing from its neck and belly. So much blood, he pondered. His nostrils filled with the coppery scent and licking his lips, he clenched his hands in frustration at the loss. The ground was stained with it, and the magic called to him to drink.

At least he could request a portion of the animal. They had wandered aimlessly for weeks searching for the villagers, and his anger had only intensified. He was limited to the amount of magic he could use, and without a blood sacrifice, his vision was clouded.

Motioning to one of his most trusted followers, he waited until the man was close enough, so no one else could hear. "See to the heart and bring it to me immediately."

The man nodded, slowly removing his dirk.

"Manus...take heed, and let no others see ye do this unless it is one of ours."

"Understood," replied Manus.

Lachlan turned from the site to prepare for what he hoped would be some insight as to where the people had fled. He was using the bishop's men for his own purpose, yet, as soon as he found what he was looking for, they would all be slaughtered like lambs to their one God.

Passing his other two followers, Seth and Gavin, he nodded silently to them. They did not have to be told, for they understood when the time presented itself, Lachlan would require time alone to use his magic.

With the killing of the deer, it worked twofold for everyone: fresh meat to fuel the body and fresh blood to kindle the magic.

Earlier, Lachlan had noticed a small cave tucked behind some bushes, which had been searched earlier. Now, it would serve a much better purpose. He ducked within and stripped down. Instantly the damp cold seeped through his skin, when he seated himself against the back wall.

He removed his sickle and waited.

Time slowed, but Lachlan knew Manus would not fail him. A sinister smile formed when he heard footsteps approaching.

"Lachlan?"

"Bring it forth, Manus."

The man stooped to enter, halting within a few steps.

"Leave it there on the ground. Go eat with the others. Be my ears and eyes for any knowledge. I fear they are getting restless to return to the abbey."

"Aye, my lord."

He waited until Manus left. The scent of blood immediately called out to him. The man was wise in leaving some blood on the heart. Yet, it would not be enough.

Taking his sickle, he stood, and sliced it across his palm. The blood seeped forth, and he clenched his hand into a fist causing it to flow freely. Walking in a tight circle around the heart, he let the blood drip onto the ground. Finishing the circle with himself inside, Lachlan picked up the heart with his wounded hand, letting the blood of the deer mingle with his own.

Chanting the words softly, he raised his hand above his lips and ever so slowly took the heart into his mouth. The only sound emanating within the cave was the deep suckling, and gorging noises he made.

Dark magic demanded the blood.

The tremors started to course through his body. Threads of blinding light pierced his thoughts, and he fought to control the demon of sight. It was always such. He knew better, but still the druid reached out with his power to take over.

In the end, the demon won out, demanding more of his humanity. And each time, Lachlan gave away a bit more of himself. He feared there would come a time when there would be nothing left of himself. But the power called to him.

Did it matter if he was man or demon as long as he had the power of the Gods?

It whispered inside his head, "*What do you seek?*"

"Where are the travelers?" Lachlan knew it could seek out the knowledge within him. However the demon always forced him to utter his request.

Black mists swirled like snakes in his mind, and laughter dark and malicious peeled forth. "*Are you sure there is not someone else you seek?*"

The demon had never questioned him before. Why now? Unless... "Show me the Dragon Knight," he hissed.

The blackness dissolved, and the mists opened up

to a glen tucked against the hills. People were dancing to music, celebrating the feast day. Lachlan growled in frustration searching for the man. He was as invisible as the wind as he passed among the people searching for the man. His fury built as the demon kindled it within his mind.

At last, he spied him in the distance. Stephen MacKay! The man had been assisting the villagers all this time. Where were they?

"*Will you burn them all in my name?*" demanded the demon.

"Yes, anything," Lachlan rasped out.

"*Anything? I shall require an additional sacrifice at the time of my choosing.*"

His heart pounded furiously against his chest, and he feared his decision today would haunt him in the future. Did it matter? Druids were always known to travel unknown paths, and this was no different.

"You need only ask, and it shall be given," he answered.

"*Done!*"

It was then Lachlan heard someone praise the kind people of Grenlee. His face turned to triumph right as the demon released its hold. His vision clouded over, but not before Lachlan noticed a woman watching the Dragon Knight. Her hair glistened in the sunlight like those of the...*fae*!

Gasping for breath, he slumped down upon the ground. He realized the price for seeing this vision was great. It would probably take his soul, and he no longer cared.

Violent laughter shook his body. "Ye sent one of your own to help the Dragon Knight?" he sputtered out.

Gathering what little strength he had, Lachlan stumbled out of the cave. Manus had left water outside understanding he would require cleansing. With shaking hands, he wiped the blood from his face and hand. It still oozed blood, but he would bandage it.

Wiping his mouth with the back of his hand, he snarled. "*Now*, I ken where to find them all."

Lachlan dressed quickly, making his way back to the camp with the smell of meat drifting past him. He walked toward the guards from the abbey, giving a passing nod to his own men. "After much prayer, the Lord has shown me another path where these heathens have traveled."

The guards never thought to question him, since he had the confidence of the bishop. Yet, one stepped forward.

"Our Lord has spoken to you?" asked the leader of the guards.

Lachlan tempered his fury at his impudence. "Yes, through prayer and fasting, he has shown me a place I once visited. The place is called Grenlee. It is northeast of where we have been searching."

The guard stood his ground for a moment longer, then relented. "Then we travel hard to this Grenlee at dawn's light."

Lachlan gritted his teeth, making a solemn vow that if this guard gave him any trouble, he would be the first to die. For the moment, all must go according to his new plan.

Grenlee was only five days away.

Chapter Twenty-Six

"They made a lover's potion mixed with roses, honeysuckle, jasmine, and gardenias, but both refused to drink from the vessel of love."

Stephen tilted his head up to gaze at the last dwindling of stars. Dawn was spreading its cloak of light in the east. A few birds chirped in the distance as the land awoke from its slumber.

He loved this time of morning.

Glancing back, he detected Aileen's stiffness as she rode Buttertwill. He could sense her thoughts, and knew her to be angry with him. Hell! He was angry too. To finally find his stone, and then be told it had to be cleansed by another—yes, they were both angry.

In truth, he could not deny what he had felt out there in the water. His cock surged forth just recalling her sweet body as he took her in the stream. He could still taste her on his lips, and absently, he placed his hand over his cock and squeezed.

A flicker of movement caught his attention, and he came to a halt.

Bloody hell! How was he going to make it through these next five days, when he could not even survive a few hours without his body betraying him?

"What is it?" Aileen asked quietly coming up beside him.

Stephen briefly looked at her, noting how her hair shimmered like moonlight in the early dawn. Taking a deep breath, he cast his eyes at the falcon perched in a nearby tree. Its beady eyes narrowed at them.

He nodded to Aileen. "We have a follower."

Aileen glanced toward the direction of the falcon. "I've seen that one before."

"Aye. Indeed we have. It seems Cathal has his eyes everywhere," he drawled.

Recognition dawned on her face. "That's Sorcha! Does he think there will be problems? Is this why he sent her?"

Stephen choked on a laugh. "Druids don't *think*—they meddle."

"It is comforting to know that if we need help, she can send a message to him," Aileen said smiling. "She is rather beautiful."

He just sat there staring at her. "And ye think I cannot protect us?" He gave a nudge to Grian, taking off down the path, mumbling about interfering druids.

Aileen grumbled, "I can see it's already going to be a long day." Though, as she watched him, old yearnings surged forth. Her hands clenched the reins tightly, causing Buttertwill to give a loud snort of displeasure.

"Sorry, my friend," she muttered softly. "Let's get going, but if you don't mind, I think we'll keep some distance between Stephen and us."

Aileen kept her gaze focused on Stephen who was riding ahead of them. If he kept them at this pace for the entire day, she feared her legs would never be able to move again. Grateful for the salve that Betha had given her to ease the pain, she allowed her mind to tease her with memories.

She tried with all her might to lock Stephen out, but it was as if they had created a bond that night, which could not be broken. Sealing her heart with chains didn't help, either. For each time she gazed at him, they dissolved, leaving her open and reeling.

"Oh, Goddess, help me," she pleaded softly.

Instantly a cool breeze gently touched her face, bringing peacefulness to her spirit. It was then Aileen reached out to the beauty of the land. She had been traveling without seeing what passed before her eyes. Heather and foxglove dotted the scenery. Wild poppies jumped out waving their petals at her. Mists hugged the giant mountain ridges, beckoning her. The air was cooler, yet, the scent of spring filled her head.

Rabbits skittered past and for a brief moment, she thought she saw a fox. Could Ian's friend be following them, too? She had no doubt it was possible, especially since he would be the Master Druid one day.

She heard the ripple of a nearby stream, and smiled. The beauty of Scotland was all around her.

Feeling renewed, she let the vision feed her soul, tapping into the greatest source of energy—*Mother Earth*.

****

The rest of the day passed quickly. Stephen stopped several times to let her tend to her "personal time," as he often said. They had shared a light fare of honeyed bread, and berries, but ate without looking at one another.

Only once did Stephen see a rider in the distance, and he quickly led them away. He knew this part of the land. They were on Fraser soil, and he prayed Robert Fraser was still the laird. Being an old friend of his father, he remembered the times he had visited. Joyful, boisterous times.

Wiping a hand across his face, he slowed Grian. Thoughts of his family had been weaving their way into his mind daily. Again, he thought of his brothers...one in particular, Duncan.

Was he at Urquhart? Were his other brothers there as well?

Without hearing her, Aileen moved up beside him, shaking him out of his reflections. She was flushed from the day's ride with her hair coming loose from the braid. He snapped his attention to a place in the distance.

"We shall spend the night at the base of that ridge." He shifted slightly. "This is Fraser land. So I hope the current laird is still alive."

Aileen's eyes grew large. "Are you afraid someone will find us?"

"Nae. Frasers were our friends and allies, except it has been several years. We will have to do without any fire, for I cannot take the risk."

Aileen nodded, following his lead as he led them higher up to the ridge. They had to dismount halfway up, then it leveled out. The trees virtually blocked the view from below.

After tending to the horses, Stephen placed several plaids on the ground, close to two trees. "Are ye hungry?" he asked stiffly.

She just stood there...frozen.

Stephen frowned. "Aileen?" He saw her wince.

"My legs. I don't think I can sit down on the ground," she replied.

Stephen tried hard to swallow the laughter, instead

coughing into his fist. "Och, Aileen." He reached for her hand, but she swatted it away.

"Don't you dare laugh at me!" she snapped. "This is your fault! I'm still not used to riding long periods of time and at the speed you pushed us."

"*My fault*?" he asked in mocked offense.

Her eyes narrowed to slits. "Get out of my way. I think I'll take a walk to stretch them out." She pushed past him as he started to choke on his own laughter.

"Men! Only you would make fun of my predicament," she grumbled with each painful step.

Grabbing the salve Betha had given her, she proceeded to move past the horses until she was out of sight.

Stephen followed her a moment later. His lust surged forth when he found her applying the sweet-smelling ointment. He had only intended to offer her an apology. However, the sight of her dress hitched up to her upper thighs took all of his control not to snatch the pot and apply it to those milky legs. His mind drifted to where those legs were recently wrapped around him, urging him deeper within her.

His hands clenched; his cock swelled, and Aileen noticed.

"I am fine," she said softly, dropping the folds of her dress, and turning her back on him.

"Good," he clipped out, leaving as silently as he had approached.

"By the hounds," Stephen gritted out, pounding his fist against the pine. And this was only the first day. Rubbing his face, he moved away from the trees.

Seeing her approach, he gathered some food. "I'll return shortly. I want to make sure we cannot be seen."

He pointed to the plaids. "There is food and drink."

Aileen gave him a passing glance, slowly and gently lowering herself to the ground. She let out a hiss, but placed her hand out to stay Stephen's help.

"Rest, Aileen."

She didn't even look at him, waiting until he was out of sight to let out the long-held breath. Her heart was pounding. For one brief moment, she almost handed him the pot just to have his hands on her. Hands that were big and strong, knowing just where to send her spiraling.

"Goddess, why can't I block him out?"

Sorcha cawed, and Aileen thought it sounded like laughter.

"Thanks." Shaking her head, she guzzled deeply from the ale skin—grateful it was water.

"One day down, four more to go."

Sorcha cawed again.

Chapter Twenty-Seven

"For once you've kindled the fires of passion, you have two choices: step into the abyss of love, or rip out your heart, and toss it into the sea."

Aileen was aching and grumpy. It was unlike her to wake feeling so sour, but just casting a glance at the cause made her insides churn even more. She couldn't even see the first rays of dawn as she chewed on her oatcake. Stephen had awoken her with a slight nudge, and then proceeded to pack their few items.

She was downright cranky over the fitful night of restless sleep. When she would drift off, dreams of *him* would invade her mind. His lips on hers, caressing her body. At one point, she knew she actually moaned.

Sweet Bridget! What she wouldn't give for a good cup of strong black coffee.

"Time to go, Aileen," Stephen said, interrupting her thoughts.

"Coming," she muttered low.

Taking deep calming breaths and stretching, she slowly let Stephen help her onto Buttertwill. She didn't even bother to thank him. All she could think of was soon it would be light, then afternoon, and then evening, and another day would pass.

Slowly ticking them off until they were back at Grenlee.

Stephen kept them at a steady pace for most of the day. Yet, by early afternoon, Aileen's body matched her mood. *Foul*. And if he glanced back at her one more time, she was going to scream.

The look on his face told her all she needed to know. He was impatient, irritated, and frustrated.

Could his mood match hers? "I doubt it," she snorted.

"Hold, Grian." Then turning him around, Stephen waited for Aileen to catch up.

"What ails ye?" he asked, his tone more curt.

Aileen took a moment to catch her breath. "Nothing. I'm *fine*."

Stephen shifted closer. "Nae. Your face tells me ye are in discomfort." He reached out for Buttertwill's reins, but she smacked his hand away.

"I might be sore, but I can assure you I can continue," she snapped.

"Humph! Stubborn fae," he quipped.

"So now you're back to calling me *fae*?"

Rubbing a hand over the growth of beard on his face, he took a deep breath in and out. "*Aileen*, I am merely trying to help. I do not want ye in pain. We will reach the lower valley of the Great Glen tomorrow. I have no wish to carry ye to the Great Dragon."

Hot fury boiled forth from Aileen. "Don't worry, Stephen MacKay, if I have to crawl to the Great Dragon, I will do so without your help. You will never have to touch me again, much less carry me." Giving a nudge to her horse, she took off away from him.

"Cold-hearted man!" Tears stung her eyes and choked her voice. He already found her so distasteful, he couldn't bear the thought of touching her. Sharp pain stabbed at her heart. Why did she care? Why, why, *why*?

The scenery blurred, until she heard the thunder of hoofs approaching from behind. Grasping tighter to Buttertwill, she urged the horse faster. Tufts of dirt and grass flew past as they raced onward. A pine limb smacked against her face, and she ignored its sting.

Aileen felt no fear. At one point, she heard Stephen yell her name. Exhilaration and pain fueled her desire to get further away. She was being carried away along with the winds. If only they could take her back home.

When the path became narrow, she started to hold back. Feeling refreshed, Aileen led Buttertwill on a small gallop. She spotted the river weaving its way ahead, calling out to her. This time she would take charge, instead of waiting for him to make the decisions.

"I think we deserve a break, don't you Buttertwill?" Taking shelter in a small grove of pines, she quickly dismounted. She gave a grunt from the pain within her thighs.

Stretching them out, Aileen gasped when strong arms reeled her around.

"God's blood, woman!" Stephen roared, as his lips came crushing down on hers.

His kiss was not gentle, but she welcomed the harsh invasion. His tongue swept within, seeking. He took and plundered, and she surrendered. She moved harder against him, taking her hands and wrapping them around his neck, bringing him deeper.

Their breaths mingled, and the kiss became more urgent, demanding, as if their world would dissolve into thin air.

Stephen growled low, gripping her bottom against his raging erection. And she responded by wrapping one leg around him.

Slowly, he pulled back from the kiss. However, he kept his hands around her, and she could feel them shaking. "Does that tell ye how much I *want* to touch your body?" he rasped out. "Each hour that passes makes it increasingly difficult to be around ye."

Aileen couldn't reply, for she felt dizzy and unfulfilled.

Stephen took his thumb and grazed it along her swollen bottom lip. "I crave your body *constantly*," his voice thick with emotion. "Yet, ye are not of this time."

Turning, he walked down to the river, his fists clenched by his sides.

Emotions swam before Aileen as she watched him walk away. He *did* want her as badly as she wanted him. However, he was a Knight—one who would see her safely back to the abbey, so she could return home.

Confusion waged a war within her. For she truly didn't know where *home* was anymore.

****

Castle Leomhann—Home of the MacFhearguis Clan

"It reeks of horse muck!" snarled Michael MacFhearguis, reaching for the pitcher of ale. Pouring a hefty amount, he guzzled deeply. Wiping the back of his hand against his mouth, he let out a belch.

Alex glared at him. "Duncan is not our enemy. It is the bloody druid, Lachlan," he hissed.

"I tell ye, he's up to no good." Michael lashed out. Pointing a finger at Alex, he added, "Has he come to our aid in search of Adam?"

All was quiet.

Michael gave a smirk. "It is foolish Lachlan would travel south. I can tell ye he favors the north, for there he will find many more followers. To even mention the druid's name leaves a bitter taste in my mouth. Black traitor," he spat out going for the pitcher again.

Michael eyed his other brother over the rim of his cup. "What say ye, Patrick?"

What could he say, Patrick mused. That his brother was an ass? He had let his rage for the MacKays cloud his vision, and in doing so, Lachlan had taken control. Adam had been missing for over a year, and inwardly he sensed his brother, the laird, had wasted precious time listening to the druid.

Patrick pushed away from the wall to stand before Michael. It took every ounce of strength not to throw his cup at his brother. "I realize ye have no love for the MacKays, nor do I. In truth, there is no reason why Duncan would betray us. He wants Lachlan's head as much as we do." He kept his gaze steady with his brother. "I will take some men, and meet with Duncan at Hollow Ridge."

Alex stepped forward. "I shall go with ye."

Michael's eyes narrowed. "Nae, Alex. Patrick will go alone." He turned to Patrick, adding, "Ye can take Sean and Arland."

"Christ's blood!" yelled Alex. "And what would ye have me do?"

Michael cocked his head to the side. "Why with Duncan away from Urquhart, we shall pay a visit," he replied.

Patrick stiffened. Was his brother insane? To be caught on MacKay land could mean an all-out war.

Alex was stunned into silence.

"You cannot be serious, Michael?" Patrick asked incredulously.

Michael clapped the back of Patrick's shoulder. "Oh, but I am. We will wait a few days until the MacKay is away from his land."

Stepping aside, he bellowed for a guard.

Patrick and Alex just eyed one another in a silent understanding. Their brother was on dangerous ground, and one slip would mean a battle neither was willing to fight.

One of the guards entered, and Michael started issuing orders.

Stepping around Alex, Patrick grabbed the pitcher of ale with his back facing Michael. "It will be up to ye to restrain him," his voice low, pouring the liquid slowly into his cup.

Alex gave a snort. "He'll most likely slay me first."

"Still, it will be up to ye to keep him away from Urquhart Castle." Patrick swirled the contents of his mug before swallowing.

"Aye," he hissed. "Have ye heard any word on the other MacKays?"

"Nae."

At that moment, one of the serving lasses came into the hall. She moved passed Michael, but not before he gave her a wink.

"How long do ye think ye will be gone?" asked Alex as he kept his eyes on his brother.

Patrick shrugged, watching as Michael now flirted outright with the serving lass. "It all depends on how far south Duncan wants to travel. His courier gave no mention of what news of Lachlan, only that he had traveled south." He glanced back over his shoulder at the outburst. Michael had now pulled her into an alcove, while his hand roamed over her breasts.

Alex just rolled his eyes.

"Guard him well, Alex," said Patrick finishing the last of his ale. "I do not relish the idea of returning, and finding ye as laird of Leomhann."

"Ye think we cannot hold our own against the MacKay, or the few men he has at Urquhart?" scoffed Alex.

Patrick crossed his arms over his chest. "Aye, I ken that ye probably can. My concern and *yours*...should be when and if his brothers return." He grabbed a strong hold of his brother's arm. "They have magic and the druids on their side, and I for one, do not want to be on the receiving end of their wrath."

Alex's shoulders slumped. "Ye are correct, Patrick. We cannot win against the MacKays." He raked a hand across his face trying to ease some of the frustration. "Perchance I can persuade him to bring some women folk, for it seems to distract him."

Patrick gave him a smirk as soft moans echoed from the alcove.

"Judas's balls! Could he not wait to take the woman until we had left?" growled Alex.

"I have faith in ye, Alex. Do what you must, be it..." He waved to where Michael sat. "...providing him with women, or persuading him to *not* take up arms against the MacKays."

"Ye should be the one riding with him, not me. Ye have more patience," muttered Alex, frowning. He went to retrieve his sword, but not before he added, "I may have to knock him out, if he chooses not to listen to me."

"Whatever it takes, brother. Just do not kill him."

Alex cursed softly under his breath as they both left the hall. Neither had looked Michael's way when they passed, realizing their brother was deep into pleasuring himself just by the grunts emanating forth.

Chapter Twenty-Eight

*"When the Knight skipped the stone across the water,
the Lady appeared dressed in shimmering seashells."*

A light drizzle greeted Stephen and Aileen the next morning—the air smelling of clean pine, and fresh earth. Both nodded in greeting upon awakening as Stephen fetched her long coat to ward off the morning chill, placing it gently across her shoulders.

They remained quiet while they broke their fast with dried berries and oatcakes. Neither felt the need, nor desire to speak. Words could no longer soothe away the ache they both felt somewhere in the recesses of their hearts.

Their journey this morning would take them through Caedons Pass, and from there they would be at the lower valley of Urquhart. Stephen pondered what Aileen's reaction would be to the Great Dragon. He sensed her to be unafraid. However, he would rather wait until they were at the water before he told her how to approach the Great One.

As they rode, the drizzle turned to showers, matching their mood, solemn and pensive. Sorcha was still their ever-faithful companion, camping down with them at night, and arising before dawn's light. Stephen only grunted when Aileen remarked on her beauty. Yet, watching her take flight again as she swept through the rain drenched sky, he took in her ebony features.

"Perhaps ye are correct, Aileen," he remarked softly.

Sorcha let out a screech as if she had heard him. Before she disappeared over the pass, she circled in an arc around them.

Stephen slowed Grian, waiting for Aileen. They had reached Caedons Pass, climbing up over the ridge. The rain had finally ceased, and the sun broke through.

"Caedons Pass?" Aileen asked, giving Buttertwill a light pat.

"Aye," he answered, noting the dark circles beneath her eyes. Stephen knew she had not slept much, making the journey more wearisome.

Taking a deep breath, he looked across the valley and to the loch below where a swirl of mist crept along the edge. It was breathtaking. The water shimmered with hues of blue and green, beckoning one to come forth. On the far bank stood a red stag, his stance proud, more in welcome than fear. He stood watching, his gaze never wavering.

"Are you anxious?" she asked.

He turned from her to look out at the valley again. How long had it been? His heart lurched at the memories, not realizing how much he ached to see the land—*his home*.

"I am," he answered solemnly, giving Grian a nudge to continue onward.

Buttertwill gave a soft whinny, and Aileen leaned forward. "You feel it, too, my friend." Her voice a low murmur. "Shall we?" Giving a light scratch behind the horse's ear, they slowly descended down into the valley.

Stephen dismounted, leading Grian to a wild patch of grass away from the water's edge. He waited patiently for Aileen to come forth. Grabbing her waist, he swept her off her horse. Giving Buttertwill a pat on the rump, he watched as the horse meandered toward Grian.

"Are ye ready, Aileen?" he asked, tilting his head to the side.

She smiled up at him. "Yes, Stephen. I am ready to meet the Great Dragon."

"Stone?"

Opening her hand, she pulled it forth. Rubbing her thumb across it, Aileen marveled at its color. "Is it my imagination, or has the color of the stone changed?"

"Nae, not your imagination. The stone kens it is close to home, and the color shifts. At times, it can be a bright green."

"It's beautiful," she breathed out.

Stephen nodded. "Aye, the Stone of Ages."

Aileen's head snapped up. "What did you say?"

"Stone of Ages," he repeated, shifting around her.

"Stephen…" Aileen clutched at her pendant with her other hand, eyes wide. "My mother called *my* pendant, the Stone of Ages, too."

Frowning, he slowly turned back around. His hand reached out hesitantly to touch the moonstone, afraid his fingers would encounter fire. Yet, the stone remained cool. "Strange," he murmured, his fingers trailing across her neck, and he felt her shiver from his touch.

"Your stone might have come from the *Tuatha De Danann*, as well," he said half-aloud.

"Well considering what I've just found out about

my heritage recently, I wouldn't doubt it," she said with a chuckle. Then in a more somber voice, she added, "My mother made it for me. She called it my amulet of protection." Aileen shook her head. "So much to learn."

"It is lovely," he whispered, meaning more than just the pendant. His eyes roamed the light in her eyes, and for a brief moment, he wanted to take her mouth with his. She drew him forth like a bee to honey— *lavender honey.*

Clenching his fists, he took a step back.

"What now?" she asked, turning her gaze out to the loch.

His brow furrowed. "I call forth the Great Dragon."

Aileen lightly touched his arm. "Are you worried?"

Stephen kept his focus on the water. "Nae. She was the one who helped me with my power of water when I was a young lad." He rubbed a hand over the shadow of his beard. "When she comes forth, she may speak to ye inside your head."

"I am ready, Stephen." She squeezed his arm, gently.

Placing his hand over hers, he took deep calming breaths, and walked close to the water's edge.

Stripping off his boots, he tossed them aside, and then stepped into the icy water. The contact flooded his senses making him sway. The water spoke to him on some ancient level, searching for the man who was hidden in the recess of his soul. A part of him wanted to let go and open fully, but the anger held fast onto his spirit.

Stephen closed his eyes, letting the rhythm of his power ripple out across the loch. Raising his hands upward, he spoke the words to call forth the Dragon.

"Hail the North, I call upon thee, from the Mother who will set us free."

"Hail the East, there are those I seek who will help with the peace."

"Hail the South, the fire that will forge the bond."

"Hail the West, where all will journey to the next Realm."

"From the four quarters, I, Stephen Malcolm MacKay, call upon the One who came from the stars with the Tuatha De Danann. Come forth, Great One."

The wind shifted, and the mists thickened. Aileen watched in utter amazement as the valley took on an ethereal glow, shimmering as if it was lighted with a thousand candles of various colors.

The air whispered to her of...*magic*.

She reached out with her senses, gasping at the serenity of the place they were now standing on. It wasn't long before they were engulfed within the mists, a cocoon of warmth.

She became lightheaded. A slow, warm thrill of euphoria coiled through her body. She wanted to jump into the water and play. Suddenly, she saw movement in the middle of the loch. Her eyes went wide as the mists parted.

They say in the legends that you should fear dragons. Run...scream...hide, so she had been told. Yet, here she stood before the most benevolent creature she would probably ever encounter. Pure love radiated from the dragon, bobbing gently in the water. There was absolutely no way she could tell how huge it was, for she only saw its head and long neck.

Eyes the color of many-faceted crystals blinked at her—*waiting*.

She swallowed, not knowing what to say. Thank the stars Stephen stepped forward, for she felt like a fool just staring at the dragon.

"Great One," Stephen said with a small bow, "I ken it has been far too long since my last visit, and I beg forgiveness. I have brought with me the Stone of Ages to ask a favor. I humbly request to have it cleansed by ye." He motioned for Aileen to present the relic.

The air shifted slightly. The dragon had not even looked at Stephen when he spoke. Was it confused? Upset? Aileen glanced his way.

"I would be most grateful..."

In a blink of an eye, the dragon whipped her head around to him. "Your words are not allowed here, Knight, especially from one who no longer *believes*. Look within to find the source of your anger, Knight, and you will discover it has naught to do with magic. You betrayed yourself."

Aileen gasped.

With a deep sigh, Stephen grabbed Aileen's elbow. "Let us leave this hallowed place. We are not welcome."

She looked confused. "Why? What happened?"

"Greetings, Aileen, daughter of Rose MacLaren and Aidan Kerrigan, Fenian Warrior to the fae. *You* are most welcome." Her words were like a melody of song within Aileen's mind.

She snapped her head around to look up at the dragon. Instantly, warmth and love touched her heart. She turned back toward Stephen, lightly touching his face. "I will be fine. She wants me to stay."

Stephen hesitated, and then gave her a curt nod. With one last look upon the dragon who had been his friend and mentor, he strode from the water's edge. Picking up his boots along the way, he knew without looking that the mists had now shrouded Aileen and the dragon from his view.

With each step he took, his heart splintered a bit more.

Aileen swallowed the lump in her throat. She could no longer see him, and turning, she greeted the Great Dragon with a small nod of her head.

"Hello, Great One."

"I have awaited the daughter of the great Fenian Warrior for some time." The tone of her speech danced across Aileen's senses like strings on a harp—soothing and harmonious.

"I thought you were angry my father defied you?" uttered a shocked Aileen.

"Aidan Kerrigan *defied* the Tuatha De Danann, not I." The Great Dragon bobbed gently within the waters. "The Fenian Warrior chose to seek me out for my wisdom and advice. He was given a choice, and he chose wisely."

"My mother," whispered Aileen.

"*Love,*" replied the Great Dragon.

"My mother passed away last year." Her eyes misted with unshed tears.

"Her passing rippled across the veil."

"Really?"

"Do not be sad, daughter of Aidan and Rose Kerrigan, for she is in the land of forever—the *Summerland.*"

Aileen wanted to ask so many more questions. Who was her father? Why didn't he and her mother ever tell her about her heritage? Why *was* she sent here? For Stephen? Herself? Her mind seemed to burn for the answers.

The medallion's stone was cool in her palm, and with a heavy sigh, Aileen held up the medallion in front of the dragon. "I understand I might not have any right to ask, but I really would like you to consider helping Stephen. I found this in my own time, and came through the veil to give it back to him." She let out a short bark of laughter. "Not that I had a choice, but since I am here, it would mean so much to me if you could do this."

Aileen stepped closer to the dragon, letting the water lap gently at her feet. "He truly is a good man."

The Great Dragon was silent for a moment. "Do you love the Knight?"

"Lo...*love*?" she blurted out. Flustered, Aileen rubbed her forehead. "I really don't know. Perhaps?"

"Hmmmm," sighed, the Great Dragon.

"It's complicated," stammered Aileen. "Stephen has a duty here, and I have to return to my father. It is my duty to be with him." There, she answered truthfully.

Moments passed. The mists grew thicker, and Aileen pondered if she should just leave.

"Duty is not a *lorica*," spoke the Great Dragon. "You and the Knight wear this around your hearts."

Aileen stiffened. "What is a *lorica*?"

"A breastplate for the soul."

"The soul and heart are two separate entities. You said that we wear this around our hearts," she replied mystified.

"Are they not bonded?"

"Well, I suppose they could be," she muttered low.

221

Glancing back to where Stephen had disappeared, Aileen's love for him was real, regardless of the duty to her father. Try as she might, to deny it would be futile.

Taking a deep breath in and out, she peered up into the dragon's eyes. "I'm asking you to do this for the love I have for him. For the love that *you* have for him. Help him, please."

Aileen waited, clutching the medallion tightly in her fist. The only sound was of the water gently caressing against the shore.

"Remove your pendant and weave its chain around the Knight's relic," said the dragon.

Unsure, Aileen ran her trembling fingers over the moonstone.

"Trust me," said the dragon in such a way, that Aileen's thoughts went directly to her mother's voice. She often would chide her for the same. *Trust me*...said her mother.

With a broad smile, she removed her pendant, twining the chains together. One soft and fine, the other heavy and solid.

"Now what?" she asked, tilting her head to the side.

"Place it on the water's edge."

Aileen bit her lip as she gently placed the two pieces into the water. Only they didn't sink, but floated. The water's current taking them out to the dragon.

Aileen watched in awe.

The colors around the dragon intensified, while swirls of mists circled the water. The dragon grew before Aileen's eyes, making them tear up from the brilliance. She clenched her arms around her waist and waited.

A song of a thousand voices filled the sky, filling her soul with their love. It was too much for Aileen to take in, slowly sinking down on the wet ground. In a flash of dazzling colors, the two pendants exploded in the air. Shielding her eyes from the array, Aileen shook not from fear, but from an overwhelming mix of emotions.

After several moments, she slowly opened her eyes. "Great Goddess," she choked out. With trembling fingers, she touched the two pendants lying in front of her. Except now, they were *different*.

"What did you do?" asked a stunned Aileen.

"Bound by blood...bound by stone. From the land before yours, the two shall be as one."

Aileen swallowed. She didn't know how, but her pendant had bits of green in it, and Stephen's had moonstone in his. "They're beautiful."

Standing, Aileen asked, "But why did you join them?"

"You and the Knight have a destiny to fulfill."

"I still don't understand, why..." Aileen froze as the air shimmered brightly again.

"Blessings of light and love, Aileen Rose Kerrigan." The dragon's voice but a light whisper on the winds, and then she was gone, taking the mists and colors away.

A bird chirped in the distance, an otter darted across the water's edge, and Aileen's stomach clenched. How was she going to explain to Stephen that his pendant and hers were joined, when she couldn't comprehend its meaning?

Chapter Twenty-Nine

"Beware the breath of the Dragon, for her song of air will infuse you with magic."

Searing pain lashed through Stephen's heart. He was crouched against the back of a pine tree with his hands clasped on either side of his head, rocking back and forth.

The dragon's words were like knives, and he understood. It hit him with such force it blinded him. How could he stand in her presence when he had renounced his own heritage? He was asking for magic, when *magic* was what he was rejecting. Foolish and heartsick, Stephen realized the stone was no longer his. He might as well have Aileen toss it into the loch.

"Sweet Brigid! I'm here, Stephen," she blurted out trying to catch her breath. "Here, take your medallion," placing her hand on his shoulder.

Eyes that mirrored a stormy day looked into hers. "I cannae."

"Why? Did you not have a vision?" she asked, slumping down next to him.

"Nae. It is no longer mine." He rubbed a hand over his jaw, leaning his head against the rough bark. "I have been proud believing *she* would help me. I had no right to ask."

Aileen smiled. "I *believe* she still loves you,

Stephen, or she wouldn't have done this." Taking his hand, she turned it over, placing the medallion in his palm.

Stephen flinched, waiting for the pain, yet, there was none. He snapped his gaze up to Aileen, then back to his medallion. It was then that he saw the Stone of Ages was different.

"Bloody hell! What did she do?" he asked incredulously.

Aileen held her pendant up. "It would seem she has combined *both* of the stones. I have pieces of yours..." She let out a breath before adding, "...and you have pieces of moonstone in yours."

Stephen frowned. "Why?"

"Oh, how I hoped you wouldn't ask that question so soon." She lowered her eyes, adding, "Something about us fulfilling a destiny."

Silence greeted her and she glanced back up. The beginning of a smile tipped the corners of his mouth.

"Och, Aileen, I have kenned that for some time." He reached out and tucked a stray strand of hair behind her ear. "Here, let me put your pendant on."

Swallowing, she nodded. Twisting around, Aileen swept her braid off her back. As his fingers touched her neck, she gave an involuntary shiver.

"I thank ye for what ye did today." His breath hot against her ear.

"It was nothing." Her voice barely a whisper.

"Aye, it is."

Tipping her head around to meet his, he captured her lips in a drawn-out kiss. Her lips were warm and gentle, as she surrendered to him. Breaking slowly away, Stephen drew her back to cradle against his chest. His arms wrapped around her waist.

Time stood still. What had happened earlier on the loch, mere echoes in the distance.

"It is my fault she died." His words spoken low. Instantly, he could feel her stiffen, and Stephen feared she would not want to hear any more.

"How?" she asked, softly.

Drawing her in closer, Stephen leaned his head against the tree, letting the memories spill free from their prison within his mind.

"Several days before her death..." He drew in a sharp breath, then slowly released it, struggling with the words. "I had a vision—one where the MacFhearguis was slain."

Aileen frowned. "But he wasn't."

"Nae."

He kept silent for a moment, trying to release the tension in his body.

"I *wanted* him to die," he rasped out. "To cut him out of her life. I should have understood the visions are only a warning of what can happen. But I refused to believe in any other conclusion. I held the knowledge back from her and the others."

"If you had shared this knowledge, perhaps your sister would still be alive today." Her voice barely a whisper.

He pulled his arms tighter around her. There was no need for words. His sister was gone—*dead*. He could only move forward, instead of running away.

His medallion bit into his arm, and she reached out to take it out of his hand. "Here, let me." Turning around, she placed it over his head letting it rest against his chest. Her fingers touched the black hair peeking out of his tunic.

"I love ye, fae Aileen." His voice hoarse.

Tears washed her eyes, and her lips quivered.

"Do my words offend ye?"

"*My Stephen*," she choked out. Placing her hands on either side of his face, she kissed him as tender and light as the summer breeze. "I believed I would never hear you say those words. I love you, too."

He growled low, taking her swiftly and passionately into his arms. Taking her mouth with savage intensity, he thrust his tongue deep within.

Aileen returned his kiss with reckless abandon, and he took it all. Her body arched toward him, and he craved her touch on his bare skin.

His fingers untied her laces, and he pulled the gown off her shoulders causing her to shudder. He smiled sensing it was his touch and not the cool air brushing against her skin. "Must taste ye," his voice sounded thick with desire.

Aileen quickly slipped her arms out of her gown. She no sooner had them out, when he cupped her breasts, his mouth suckling deeply. A low moan erupted from within her.

Noticing her gazing at him, he asked, "Do ye like to watch?"

"*Yes.*"

Stephen slid one hand down her waist to her thigh, seeking the soft flesh under her gown. "What does my Aileen want?" he asked as his fingers rubbed gently between her sweet folds.

Her eyes mirrored his with raw passion. "Touch me, Stephen, or take me," she growled out.

His smile washed over her, wicked with need. "So

ye want me to touch ye...*here*?" Stroking his thumb over her sensitive bud, his eyes flashed. "Or...*here*?" he taunted and drove two fingers inside her.

Her breath came in heavy pants. "Stop...tormenting me."

Stephen chuckled low, removing his hand. An outcry of protest no sooner escaped her lips, then his descended over hers silencing the cry.

Quickly lowering them to the ground, Stephen shoved aside his plaid, his cock thick with need. He rasped into her ear, "Ride me, Aileen."

Aileen hitched up her gown, bunching the fabric behind her, letting him guide the tip to her entrance. With leisurely and taunting movements, she inched down until he was fully seated inside her, straddling her legs on either side of his.

"*Aileen*..." A guttural growl followed.

"Is this how you want me to *touch* you?" She rode him slowly up and down.

Stephen grabbed her hips, a wild look seared across his features. "I will take ye now!" he roared.

He could not hold back, for his need to come in her was fierce. He wanted to claim and mark her. Her beauty undid him. With unbridled strength, Stephen forced her hips to move faster.

"Come with me, *leannan*," he gritted out. Her nipples teased him as they danced before him.

Yelling her name, Stephen broke free. Waves of ecstasy crashed over and through him. His soul burst forth, hearing Aileen's cry of release. They were as one, soaring over the hills and water. Each melded into the other, and the world tilted.

He caressed Aileen's back, fingers gently

loosening her braid. She lay against his chest, while he remained inside her. His cock still thrummed with desire and partially hard, he knew he could take her again. However, he had other plans that included water.

For the first time in his life, Stephen would sell his soul, and fight any man or fae to keep the woman he loved by his side.

There was only one who could defeat him. *Aileen.*

Somehow...someway, he had to persuade her to stay here with him, forever.

"Mmmm, you feel good," she murmured against his chest, rocking gently against him. His cock swelled even more.

His hand found her soft breast, and he teased the nipple to hardness. "I ken a better place to make ye feel even better."

"Ohhh, but I'm liking this," she sighed, finding a more steady rhythm.

"If I do not stop, we will never make it to the water, and my plans involve much more play time." He swiftly lifted her off his member, releasing a cry of protest from her.

Rolling out from under her, he stood, stripping off his tunic and boots. "Would ye like to play in the water?" He held out his hand to her, enticing her not only with his body, but his warm smile.

Aileen gave a throaty laugh, reaching for his hand. "Will you do magical things to me in the water?" she asked with a teasing smile.

"Magic?" he drawled, placing tender kisses along her neck and shoulder.

"Yes, for magic is everywhere, Stephen. It's even in a kiss." He smothered her last words with his lips.

****

Aileen's skin resembled shriveled prunes. Stephen had literally kept her in the water for several hours. Not that she was complaining, oh no. Just remembering all he did to her body caused her to shiver anew.

The man was insatiable.

At the moment, he was hunched over a fire cooking their meal of salmon with wild garlic. Her stomach grumbled loudly.

"Hungry again, *leannan*?" Stephen asked, giving her a wink.

By the Gods, he was scrumptious when he smiled. "I need real food," she scoffed, trying to keep the smile off *her* face.

"Gosh, that smells so good." She crouched down next to him, breathing in the aroma of their meal. Watching the sun slip silently over the ridge of the mountains, she yearned to stay here forever.

"Open your mouth, Aileen," Stephen urged, shaking her out of her thoughts.

The first taste assaulted her senses, sweet and delicate. She licked her lips catching each morsel. "It is delicious," she moaned.

Stephen licked his fingers, before pulling more fish off of the twig. Placing it gently into her mouth, he let out a hiss when her tongue teased across his fingers.

"It is good, aye?"

"Mmmmm, yes. I never realized how good fish could taste."

Stephen laughed. "Well, considering our fare lately, this is a feast."

Her heart split seeing the mirth on his face. Why did life have to be so complicated? And when did she fall so helplessly in love with him?

She took a swig of ale, letting her sight take her across the loch.

"What happens now, Stephen?" Her question barely a whisper on the breeze.

He exhaled deeply, fearing this conversation. *Would she stay with him, here in his time? Could she give up all she knew in her time?*

Taking her chin, he placed a feather light kiss on her lips. "I do not have the answer." Swallowing the dread in his throat, he asked, "Do ye want me to take ye back to the abbey? I will honor my vow, if that is what ye truly want."

Aileen was hesitant, twisting his tartan within her fingers. "No, but I am torn in my feelings."

Drawing her closer to him, he looked directly into her eyes. "Then I shall help ye with those *feelings*."

They both sat in silence, watching as the first stars dotted the evening sky. Their thoughts were a reflection of the other, embarking on a new destination.

Chapter Thirty

"If the sun is shining, the birds are singing, and all is right with the land, that's when the storm comes with a vengeance."

The first rays of dawn barely had a chance to spread out across the sky when Stephen came to wake Aileen. A feeling of unease had swept through him during the night. He almost longed for a vision to show him something. *Anything.*

"Time to go," he whispered in her ear.

She stretched like a cat, spreading her arms and legs out in invitation. Rubbing a hand through his rough beard, he quickly removed himself from the sensual haze. Not a moment too soon, for her breast peeked out of his tunic she was wearing, her rosy pert nipple teasing him.

Grabbing his *sgian dubh* and soap, he walked down to the water's edge to shave. The splash of cold water on his skin sent the last vestiges of lust away as he continued with his shave.

"Did you know I like the roughness of your beard on my skin?" Aileen asked quietly.

"Ye do?" Wiping the last of soap and hair off his blade, Stephen faced her. "Do not worry, *leannan*, it will grow back by nightfall."

Aileen wrapped her arms around his neck and

pulled his head down to kiss her, trailing kisses along his clean-shaven chin. "I love the sensation when you rub your rough face against my breasts."

He cupped her bottom and squeezed.

"You taste of the sea, soap, and male. A heady combination."

Stephen groaned in her ear.

"Want you." Her voice rasped, husky with need.

Crushing her in his embrace, he was on the verge of lifting her and taking her against the nearest tree, when he heard footsteps.

Two men approached from the trees.

"Hold verra still, Aileen," he said low into her ear. "We have guests."

He cursed himself for not being more alert. All he had was his *sgian dubh*, and that was on the ground. Thank the Gods he was at least near the water, though he would rather have his sword.

One of the men moved forward, his face a mask of rage. The other man stood back. Something about him rippled along Stephen's senses. Had they met before?

"Remove your hands from her, *now*!" growled the man, as he unsheathed his sword. A sharp hiss of steel, sliced through the air.

In one swift move, Aileen twisted out of Stephen's embrace. "*Dad*?" she squeaked.

Stephen looked at Aileen as if she had sprouted horns. He pointed a finger at Aidan Kerrigan. "He is your *father*?"

"Aye," interjected her dad. He kept his sword level with Stephen, showing no mercy.

Aileen ran to her father, tears misting her eyes. "How...*why* are you here?"

He kept his blade level with Stephen, giving Aileen a gentle kiss along her temple, while holding her firm with one arm. "I will answer your questions in a moment, but for now go stand next to Liam. I have unfinished business with this man."

Confusion marred her features. "Dad, this is Stephen MacKay."

"I know who he is. However, it doesn't explain why he is with my daughter and the both of you half naked."

"Now just one minute..." Her voice rose.

His eyes didn't waver from Stephen. "Liam, please take my daughter away to put on some clothes."

"I will *not* be treated like this," she gritted out, squirming in her father's strong embrace.

Liam quietly moved to take Aileen from her dad.

"How dare you!" She slapped at Liam.

Stephen's eyes flashed with anger, his fists clenching. "Take your hands off of her." He didn't dare move, the blunt of the sword now level with his chest.

"I will let you fight for my daughter, *Knight*. Fetch your sword," demanded her father.

Stephen shook his head, slowly. "It would be foolish to fight ye, Fenian Warrior."

"Scared I'll win?"

A feral look passed over Stephen's features, and he stomped over, retrieving his sword.

The challenge had been tossed out.

"You're insane!" yelled Aileen, trying to twist free from Liam's strong grasp.

The first clang of steel upon steel grated along her nerves, and her stomach clenched. This could not be happening, her mind screamed. She would *never* forgive her father for this.

Her dad swung his blade, drawing first blood along Stephen's arm.

"Nooooo!" she screamed. "If you kill him, I will never speak to you again!"

Neither man heard her words, each caught up in the moment of their fighting. Her dad took a blow to the jaw, but not before he nicked Stephen's shoulder.

"Hold still, Aileen," demanded Liam. "Your father won't kill him. He just wants to test his mettle to see if he is worthy of you."

"He's a barbarian," she hissed.

"No, he's an *ancient* Fenian Warrior, trying to defend his daughter's honor."

"Really?" Her tone dripped with sarcasm.

When her father backed toward the loch, Stephen took swift advantage. Calling forth the water, it rushed forth. Unaware and off balance, her dad slipped. Sliding back, he landed with a thud in mud and water.

Chest heaving, Stephen pointed his sword at the warrior's chest. "Have I proven myself?"

"No fair, you cheated with your powers," responded her dad with a smirk.

At that remark, Stephen roared with laughter and extended his hand to help the man stand.

Aileen tasted copper in her mouth from where she had bit her lip earlier. Now *both* idiots were laughing and clapping each other on the back.

Liam started chuckling, his grip loosening. Aileen took advantage, breaking free. She turned and with all of her might, slugged him square in the face.

"Shit!" he bellowed.

Aileen shook out her hand, not giving him the

satisfaction that her actions pained her, too. Instead, she stormed off to where her items lay. Grabbing her gown and other articles, she went for the trees.

"Aileen," said Stephen.

"Sweetheart," said her father.

"Go to hell...both of you!" Her fury rising with each step she took.

****

The misty gray light of the morning matched all of their moods.

Her dad snapped at Liam.

Stephen sent a curse flying at Liam, with a promise they had unfinished business, as well.

Liam flipped off her father and Stephen, storming off through the trees.

And Aileen remained silent, nestled against Buttertwill. Idiot men, she thought to herself, watching the bickering continue between all three.

She was still furious. To think her father traveled back over eight hundred years to start behaving like some medieval, domineering father, just set her teeth on edge.

"Humph!" Almost choking on the dried oatcake, she took a long swallow from the water skin.

Come to think of it, why was he here? Smacking her thigh with her good hand, she made up her mind to take control of the situation. Questions that had troubled her for weeks needed answers. Answers only one man could give her.

Dusting off the last remaining crumbs from her gown, she held her head high, taking off toward the grumbling group of men. If she wasn't so angry with Stephen, she would have asked him to make a block of ice for her hand. At least she hadn't broken it on Liam's face of granite.

Aileen stopped abruptly in front of her father. "You are long overdue in explaining who and what you are." She folded her arms across her chest, giving no room for him to back out.

Stephen stepped hesitantly toward her, but she held up her hand to stay his movement. "We'll talk later."

He only nodded and then made his way to the horses.

Her dad motioned for her to sit beside him on a log. "Ask your questions, Aileen."

There were so many in her mind, all fighting to be first. In the end, there was only one. "*Why?*"

His shoulders slumped, and Aileen saw the weariness in her father's face. He would never recover from the loss of her mother, and he couldn't always be there to protect her.

"I am no longer a little girl, but a grown woman." She kept her voice gentle.

He closed his eyes and let out a groan. When he opened them, he said, "Your mother and I made a difficult decision many years ago based on her vision. We truly felt in our hearts that keeping the truth from you would keep you from harm." He let out another deep sigh. "I now understand it was wrong, for the fates are always telling us that our destiny is one of our choosing."

He took both of her hands in his, giving a gentle squeeze. "We were so very wrong in keeping you from your path. We were just trying to protect you."

Aileen squeezed his hands back. "You and mom were always telling me to go and *find* my destiny, and

Mary Morgan

yet, you held it back from me."

He looked in her eyes, eyes that mirrored his own. "One day when you have children, Aileen, you will understand the fierce loyalty called *protection*."

"We all live, and we all will die, Dad."

"Aye, now you're quoting me?" he replied with a grin.

"You held back so much. Did you know I met the Great Dragon?"

His eyes went wide. "By the Gods, truly?"

Aileen had to choke back the mirth that was at the back of her throat. Ever since her father had appeared, he had slipped back into some medieval warrior, including the use of language.

"Yes. She is the most wondrous being ever. I felt as if I never wanted to leave her presence."

"Och, aye. She is a beauty."

"She told me about how you came to her for advice. Also, that you defied the Tuatha De Danann to be with Mom." Aileen paused, waiting for his reaction.

He kissed her hands, and stood, clasping his hands behind him. His eyes scanned the loch, bringing forth memories suppressed over the past few years. "I am a Fenian Warrior to the faery. I was part of an elite group of guardians who protected the realm of fae and human. There are many different echelons, but I was part of the high command."

At that moment, Aileen didn't see her father standing before her, but a proud *warrior*.

He continued, "As an elite guard, some can time travel, which we call the *veil of time*. I am one of the oldest warriors. However, on the day I met your mother, something shifted." His voice took on a far off tone. "I was returning from a task, when I literally ran into her on the streets of Glasgow." He glanced briefly at Aileen. "She was studying at the university, and on her way to the pub to meet some friends. I turned to slip down the alley and back through the veil, when she tripped landing into my arms. She had the most glorious scent of any human I had ever encountered."

Her eyes filled with tears. "I take it Fenian Warriors are not allowed to fall in love with humans?"

"Nae," he answered quietly. "I stayed that day, and every day thereafter. She never made it to see her friends that evening. Instead, she spent it with me. We talked into the wee hours of the morning, and I walked her home. I gave her my soul that night, and in turn brought down the wrath of the faery."

"What happened?" asked a stunned Aileen.

"Fenian Warriors have never taken a...*human* as a soul mate. It is not permitted."

"It sounds like an archaic rule."

He arched a brow. "Do you have any idea how old I am, Aileen?"

"Well, I have heard the villagers and Stephen say you were ancient. One of the oldest."

Her dad's laughter rang out across the loch, frightening a pair of geese on the other side. "Dearest, I am older than your Mother Earth."

Chapter Thirty-One

"Do not follow the path of a rainbow, for it will not lead you to riches, but to the realm of faery."

Aileen's eyes felt as wide as saucers. How could this man in front of her—*her father* be older than this planet? His blood flowed within her veins, and she hugged herself with the realization she may never fully understand her own heritage.

"Whe...where are you from?" she spit out.

He waved his hand in the air. "A place among your stars. My home is called Taralyn, your home, too. There is so much I need to tell you, but that discussion is for another day."

"Tara? The hill of Tara in Ireland? Is that..." She never finished her sentence.

"Yes, where the Tuatha De Danann first arrived," he paused. "In truth, I don't want to overwhelm you."

"You're not. Besides, I need to hear this."

Aileen stood on shaky legs, needing to feel the strength of him. Looping her arm around his, she asked, "Did Mom know?"

"Yes. You see she is...*was* exceptionally gifted. She recognized the moment we touched." He hesitated briefly, letting the memories of long ago wash over him. "Of course there was my *aura*, too."

Sorcha cawed above them, and they watched in

silence as she drifted over the water.

"You gave it all up...your immortality, powers, *everything* for her," she said, tightening her grip.

His smile was broad when he nodded in agreement. "I would do it again, even knowing that we had only these short years together. Besides, look at the life we created." He tilted her chin up to meet his gaze.

Aileen's heart lurched. It was then she truly saw him. Her father *and* a Fenian Warrior. She pulled her pendant out. "This is what the Great Dragon did to mine and Stephen's."

He reached out, brushing a thumb across its smooth surface. "Great Goddess! She melded the stones," he uttered incredulously.

"She told me we had a destiny to fulfill." Swallowing, Aileen laid her hand across his. "I love him, Dad," she said softly.

"Does he love you, too?" he asked, his tone stern.

"Yes." Realization dawned bright and illuminating and Aileen started to laugh.

"I fail to see the humor in this."

"I'm just happy you both held me back, now."

"You are? Why the sudden change of heart?"

"Oh Dad," she beamed. "If you had told me everything, I may never have met Stephen, or been able to find his medallion." She gave a slight push against his arm. "This *is* my destiny—all of it." Standing on tiptoe, she brushed a kiss on his cheek. "I love you."

The next moment Aileen was crushed against his chest. "What a fool I've been to lock you out of my life for the past year. I have wasted precious time. But as you've just stated, your course was already set in motion, regardless of what I have done."

She hugged him tight. "I think I need to go and speak to Stephen."

Muttering a soft curse, he released her.

Narrowing her eyes, she added, "But don't think we are done talking. I want to know all about my people. We've only started."

He rolled his eyes. "I suppose there will be no rest tonight."

"Nope." Turning to leave, Aileen paused. "Dad, why are you and Liam here?"

He hesitated for a moment. "We're here to help you with your journey. Also, I needed to see you were safe."

Her throat thick with emotion, she only nodded.

Hastily making her way over to Stephen, Aileen felt a wave of uneasiness pass over her. Was there more to what her father was telling? Could it have anything to do with the bishop and his men? Or for that matter, did they know who the druid Lachlan was?

The whisper of the loch called to her, and she saw Stephen crouched along the bank, Grian nudging him. Her smile was immediate. How could she stay angry with him? Whispers of anxiety floated off of him, and for a brief moment, she thought to read his emotions.

Taking the last few steps at a run, she nearly tripped. Stephen turned at the last moment, catching her in his arms.

"Trying to take flight, *fae*?" His eyes were alight with humor.

"Oh hush, and just hold me," she retorted.

Moments passed before either spoke. Thunder rolled in the distance, while a flock of geese flew over the loch. It was Grian who snorted, breaking the peaceful silence, pressing his nose against Aileen's back.

She pushed him away. "Go bother someone else. He's mine at the moment."

"He likes ye," said Stephen, drawing her closer. He gently tipped her chin up. "Ye realize I will fight for ye, including your father."

Her eyes narrowed, briefly. "So medieval."

Stephen let out a roar of laughter.

Aileen stared at him in amazement. The man was positively stunning, and he should laugh more often. She reached out to touch the rugged line of his jaw, his skin a warm caress for her hand.

In an instant, he captured her fingers, taking them into his mouth. Her sudden intake of breath made him instantly hard, and she wished there were no others around.

"Ye sorely tempt me to take ye." His eyes alight with desire.

"What's stopping you?" Her pulse quickened at the possibility.

Stephen squirmed. "Well, your father for one."

Aileen sighed deeply. "I can't comprehend what the next few days will hold for us. I only know that at this moment, standing in your arms, I want *you*." Her hand brushed down his arm, clasping his hand.

"I love you, Stephen. My father will just have to accept the idea I'm here to stay."

Her words and her smile were his undoing.

Capturing her mouth, he let out a groan swallowing her breath within his. His mind swirled, reveling in her touch as she placed her palms under his tunic onto his skin.

Breaking free from her succulent lips, he quickly scanned the area. "This way," he uttered hoarsely.

Aileen gripped his hand tightly, blindly following him with no concern for the others. Her body ached with a fierce need to have him in her. She licked her lips, tasting him.

Twigs snapped, leaves rustled, as they rushed further into the trees oblivious to all, except their burning passion for each other. Deeper into the dense foliage they traveled. Gray light sliced through every now and then, so thick was their passage. More thunder sounded, making its way toward them. It would only be a matter of time before the rain descended.

She trusted him as she ducked beneath the branch he held aloft for her. No sooner did she slip under and out from its reach then he drew her to him.

"I need ye fierce, Aileen." His eyes were but shards of gray—almost glowing in their intensity.

"No more fiercely than I need you," she stated. Taking his hand, she placed it on her breast. "Take me now, hard, Stephen."

In one swift move, he hitched up her gown, and shoved two fingers across her womanly folds, moist and ready for him.

"I see ye are ready for me." His breath waxed hot against her neck, before he grazed his teeth down the side of her throat.

Aileen didn't want his fingers. She wanted him inside her, now! When his fingers left her, she took advantage and reached for his erection, easily slipping her hand beneath the folds of his plaid, and squeezed.

"Lugh's balls, woman," he groaned.

With her other hand, she brushed them gently over

his balls, saying, "No, I believe these are yours." A delightful shiver of wanting ran through her, and when she gave another gentle touch, she saw a tremor roll through him.

"Hold your gown up."

His eyes flashed and his voice so hoarse, Aileen could barely understand him. Releasing her grip, Aileen slowly raised up her gown to her thighs.

Grabbing her around the waist, he growled low, "Put your legs around me."

She did as he commanded, and he backed her against the tree. Not giving her time for thought, he entered her in one thrust, her heat searing him.

She shuddered, clinging to his body.

His grunt was the only response she got. There was no room for gently kisses or wooing. She nipped at his neck tasting sweat and his own intoxicating scent. He rode her faster, plundering her mouth with his tongue. An assault she gladly surrendered to.

Her pleasure broke swiftly. As lightning flashed across the sky, Aileen screamed his name.

Stephen let out a cry as he pumped his seed deep within her. So violent was his release, he thought the ground shook.

Bringing them both slowly to the ground, he cradled her onto his lap, and held her still quaking body. Draping the plaid around them, he laid his head back against the solid bark for support.

If an enemy had come upon them, Stephen knew he would be helpless to defend them, so depleted was his energy. He pressed her close to his heart as if his *life* depended on her very existence.

In that moment—within his heart, Stephen realized

what he had to do.

There was only one problem he could foresee. Aileen's father had to give his permission. That thought alone, caused his stomach to clench. Her father would most likely take a sword to him...*again.*

He closed his eyes, reveling in her warmth. She moved slightly on his lap.

"Marry me, Aileen."

She slowly turned with a look of pure astonishment etched across her face. "Stephen?"

Thunder clapped loudly above them, causing a squirrel to jump out of the nearby tree, twittering madly as it scampered off. Within seconds, the clouds opened up, unleashing a downpour.

Quickly standing, Stephen tossed his plaid over her shoulders before shoving her out from under their love tryst. By the time they managed their way through a few trees, both were drenched. Stephen looked the worse for wear, with only his tunic on, and boots covered in mud and leaves.

The instant they stepped onto the banks of the loch, Stephen was greeted with the edge of Aidan's sword. He realized what their appearance looked like, and rather than try to defend himself, he smiled bravely and said, "Aidan Kerrigan, I ask consent to wed your daughter, Aileen."

Aidan's answer was a fist to Stephen's jaw.

Chapter Thirty-Two

"Sometimes the storm is an omen of danger, and sometimes it washes away the grime of battle."

"Really, Dad?" Aileen shoved past her father to tend to Stephen's face.

"I do not need tending, *leannan*." Stephen gave her a weak smile, trying to move his jaw around.

"*Leannan*, my ass," her father spat out. "And my answer is no!"

"Why?" asked Aileen, hugging the plaid around her in an attempt to keep warm as the wind turned to a biting fury.

"I suggest we seek some shelter before we are thoroughly drenched," interrupted Liam.

"There's a cave behind the trees up beyond the horses," replied Stephen, standing.

Her dad stormed off in the direction of the cave, and Liam turned to Stephen. "If you wish, I can help to ease the pain."

Stephen snorted in disgust.

"I think I've got it covered, Liam." Aileen's tone was cool.

Wrapping his arm around Aileen, they made their way up to the horses, and led them up the hill. Rain pounded the ground with brutal intensity, making the climb difficult. Thunder clapped right above them, causing Buttertwill to give a start.

"Shhhh...my friend," soothed Aileen as she stroked her wet mane.

Stephen slipped on a patch of mud, biting back a curse.

"This storm seems to have a mind of its own," shouted Aileen over the howling wind.

"Aye, it's..." Stephen halted, his gaze looking back down to where they came from. Nae, it couldn't be. He continued to scan the area, his breathing a bit labored. Was this Duncan's doing?

Liam had continued upward, standing next to Aidan at the entrance of the cave.

"Stephen?" Aileen paused.

Lightning splintered across the loch as if the Gods were throwing spears of light. The air sizzled with energy.

A quick glance at Aileen, told Stephen she felt it, too.

He took quick strides to reach her. "We need to get out of this storm." Taking the reins from Buttertwill, he motioned for her to continue climbing.

"This storm is fierce," muttered Aidan, as they stepped inside. "At least the cave is large enough to accommodate us."

Liam had gathered brush from the entrance to help build a small fire. It was a cozy scene, if only the atmosphere of those present were a match.

"Here, Aileen, take this dry plaid," stated Aidan, removing the wet one from around her shoulders, and tossing it to Stephen.

"Is there another for him?"

"Nae."

Aileen looked at Liam. "Really?"

Liam's body tensed, then he nodded his head toward the back wall.

To Aileen, it seemed they came prepared by the lump of tartans against the wall. Striding over, she seized one. Giving her father a glare, Aileen handed it to Stephen.

"Traitor," hissed her dad.

Liam grimaced, but continued to kindle the fire without looking up.

Aileen stomped her foot. "Stop this, right now!" She marched over to her father, jabbing a finger at his chest. "Quit treating my future husband as some kind of barbarian."

"I told him, no," he retorted with a scowl.

"Future husband?"

Aileen turned around, giving her *future husband* a huge smile. "Yes. My answer is yes, and it's all you need."

"Humph!" replied her father, and then went to sit next to Liam.

She practically threw herself into Stephen's arms. "When this is all over with, I will be your wife. For now...be content with my promise."

He delicately touched the stray wet lock of hair against her cheek, pushing it aside. "My heart is yours," he said softly and gave her a gentle kiss, not wanting her father to take up his sword, again.

Thunder rumbled again, making its way across the Highlands. Stephen tilted his head to the side, as if listening.

"What is it?" Aileen asked, her brow furrowing.

"This storm feels like the verra ones my brother,

Duncan, would pitch around when angry."

Confusion marred her features. "Your brother? Why would you think that?"

"Duncan's power is the command of the sky. One does not want to be around him when he unleashes his fury. His storms are the ones of legends."

Aileen arched a brow. "Could he be nearby?"

Stephen just shrugged, but he cast a glance at Liam who was spreading out some food.

"What say ye, Fenian? Do ye sense Duncan?" asked Stephen.

Liam hesitated, rubbing a hand across his neck as if deciding how best to answer. "I don't know, since I've sealed myself off from my powers."

"Cursed fae! A Fenian Warrior hiding from the fae. What good are ye to us, then?" protested Stephen.

In a blink of an eye, Liam was on Stephen, pressing him against the stone wall, dirk at his throat. "Do not fear, the *warrior* is still here."

"Are we doing this again?" snapped Aileen.

Stephen's eyes narrowed to shards of gray, fists clenched. "Ye ever pull a blade on me again, I'll bury it in ye." His tone deadly.

Aidan sat quietly against the wall, arms across his chest with a look of smug satisfaction.

"Enough!" shouted Aileen. "I'm tired, cold, hungry, and worn out from all this testosterone." Pointing a finger at her father, she added, "Wipe that smirk off your face, and get used to the fact I am marrying this man."

She turned and faced Liam. "I sure hope you brought enough food, because I'm famished. And please don't tell me all you have is oatcakes, since I'm pretty sure I can't eat another dried one."

"Bread, cheese, dried beef, apples, and some nuts," replied Liam, backing away from Stephen.

Aileen almost swooned. "Thank you!"

Saving the last for Stephen, she pleaded, "Don't even *ask* about that word, testosterone. I'll tell you later. And for the love of God, will you put on some dry clothes."

Stephen didn't hesitate, removing the wet item off his body. Quickly retrieving the dry plaid, he wrapped it around his waist.

"Happy now?" he asked, his smile as intimate as a kiss.

She just stood there, mouth gaping open in shock. Heat prickled along her spine at the recent memories of them together, and she shook her head to rid the lusty thoughts away.

"Beast!" she teased.

"Shall we eat?" Giving her a wink, Stephen placed his wet tunic across a small boulder near the fire.

The only sounds now within the cave were the crackling of the fire, and the sounds of everyone eating. Liam had even brought a flask of whisky, which helped to ease the tension.

Aileen sat propped next to Stephen, a tartan wrapped around her. Her eyelids started to droop until another clap of thunder rumbled outside their shelter.

"Do you really believe Duncan is doing this?" asked Aileen, yawning.

"I don't think he is," Liam interrupted.

"Now why would ye think so?" Stephen questioned. "Urquhart is but a few days ride from here, so it would appear possible."

"Your brother is much changed, Stephen. I can tell you no more."

"Ye Fenian Warriors are all alike. Tossing out your crumbs of wisdom, leaving more questions on the path," he said in disgust. "I'll take the first watch." Brushing a soft kiss on Aileen's mouth, he left to stand guard at the entrance.

"He is worried about enemies?" her dad asked.

"You don't know, do you?" she whispered, her hand against her breast.

"The cleansing has begun?" Liam asked quietly.

Both heads snapped in unison at Liam.

"What *cleansing*?"

Aileen gave Liam a disgusted look. "He means the one where the bishops from Rome, at least that's what they claim, are here in Arbroath to *cleanse* the village of the pagan heathens."

"Bloody hell." Her dad's tone was angry. "Now it all makes sense why *Liam* forced himself to come back with me to find—"

"It's much worse," interrupted Aileen.

Her dad grimaced. "Isn't it always?"

"There is another, an evil druid by the name of Lachlan, who is working with the bishop. He was following us, but we managed to evade him." Aileen clutched the plaid more tightly around her, sensing a deep chill. "Stephen says it's only a matter of time before he and his men find us."

"God's teeth! How does this play out, Liam?"

A shadow of annoyance passed over Liam's face. "You know I am bound by a blood oath—one you took also."

"You bastard!"

Aileen felt the blood leave her face. Her father never used that language in front of her. Swallowing, she recognized their situation was probably far worse.

His voice took on a deadly calm when he spoke again. "Tell me this, have we screwed with the timeline?"

"No."

"Good. Then at dawn's first light, you will take Aileen and I back through the veil. I will not endanger my daughter's life with a raving lunatic menacing the Highlands."

"Obviously, you haven't heard a word I've said, *Dad*," she uttered with cold sarcasm. "I'm staying here with *my* people and marrying Stephen. If need be, I will fight along with him." She stood slowly, glaring down at him. "This raving lunatic, as you so aptly called him, must be stopped."

Walking over toward Stephen, she grasped his hand as he leaned against the entrance.

Stephen kept his gaze fixed out at the trees when he spoke. "Ye should at least consider his offer."

"Never," she avowed, lacing her fingers in his. Her courage and determination were like a rock grounding her.

She met his eyes, seeing the love that shone in their depths.

Bringing their joined hands to his lips, he brushed a kiss along her knuckles. "If anything were to happen to ye—" Stephen broke off in midsentence, wrapping his other arm around her.

"Nothing will happen to either of us," she said, breathing in his scent.

If only he could feel assured by her words, as she

did. However, something else was prickling at his senses. *Danger and death*. Their destinies were intertwined, sealed by the Fates. His heart lurched knowing that when the time came, he would do anything to see her safe.

Instantly, Stephen realized what had to be done.

Chapter Thirty-Three

"The cloak of truth can be a heavy burden to keep hidden."

Breathing in the fresh, brisk air, Stephen felt renewed. He had slept soundly for a few hours with Aileen snuggled against him. Rising early, he gathered the horses, content to let her rest a while longer.

They were greeted with sun, breaking through white billowy clouds. It was as if the storm had ceased to exist when morning arrived.

Each broke their fast in silence, happy to be on the road again. Losing almost a full day of riding worried Stephen. Their journey would take another two days. Again, fear crept through him warning him something was on the horizon.

Aidan had relented on his request from the night before. Instead of taking Aileen back with him, he decided he and Liam would accompany them to Grenlee. Now Stephen had to deal with the reactions from the people, who would probably drop to the ground, or run for the hills when they saw the great Aidan Kerrigan riding with them.

The man would surely wallow in their presence.

He gave a passing glance to Aileen, and she rewarded him with a smile. In just a few short days, much had changed between them. The Great Dragon spoke of a destiny with Aileen, making him wonder if forever was truly possible. Could he really find redemption?

For the first time in many moons, hope flared.

Flashes of memories swirled in his mind. Whispers of the night Meggie died. The Guardian had appeared, and her anger infused the words she spoke to them. She had seared them into his mind, but somehow he had forgotten.

Destiny...Love...Gate...

"By the hounds!" he gritted out through clenched teeth, slowly shifting his pace with Grian.

Stephen couldn't control the onslaught of not only the memories, but the vision that was taking hold. He heard Aileen call out his name, her voice a faint whisper in the back of his mind.

This vision was entirely different. There weren't any traces of the burning pain, which always accompanied them. He moved through the image, as if floating through water.

Stephen heard the conversation clearly.

"Ye can either take her place at the stake, or watch her burn. It is your choice." The man slithered past in an attempt to remove his stone. His breath reeked of the poison that was in him.

"I will not relinquish my relic, and ye will release her, this instant!"

Sadistic laughter greeted his response. "But that is not my bargain."

"Then I shall burn with my relic, and take ye with me!"

"So be it," the man hissed out. "Burn the woman!"

Violent screams ripped at him, the vision closing in

on Stephen.

"Stephen, please talk to me. What is it?" asked Aileen, her voice laced with fear.

"What's wrong with him?" questioned Aidan. "Why won't he answer you?"

Liam stood close to them, his head tilted to the side, studying Stephen. "Don't touch him, Aileen."

Her head snapped around to Liam. "Why?"

"He's having a vision. Your touch will hinder it."

"Now just a moment, Liam, I have helped him before—"

He cut her off with a wave of his hand. "This is different. You are now joined by your stones. I fear if you touch him, you will either stop the vision, or taint the outcome."

Aileen reached for her pendant.

"The vision is gone," muttered Stephen, still keeping his eyes closed. Letting his body become aware of its surroundings, he gradually opened them. Sunlight hit him squarely, and he waited for the shards of pain to follow.

Yet, nothing—*no pain.*

Stephen didn't wait a moment longer, for he jumped off his horse. Quickly going to Aileen, he drew her down to him.

"Are you okay?" Taking her hand across his forehead, he gave her a smile.

"Och, aye." Holding her close to his chest breathing in her scent. "Not only are my visions as they were before I was cursed, but now they are stronger in the telling." He cupped her face with his hands, brushing a light kiss on her nose. "I ken our stones are indeed linked, and I am stronger for it."

Seeing her tears, he brushed a thumb across one that had fallen, and she took a hold of his hand. "No longer will you have to suffer in blinding pain. Your visions can be revealed without the trauma it would inflict." She reached up, kissing him squarely on the lips.

Aidan cleared his throat, but made no attempt at some caustic remark.

"What did you see, Stephen?" inquired Liam.

"This man, Lachlan, is not after the villagers. He wants me and my stone. This hasn't been a journey on behalf of the bishop."

"It hasn't?" Aileen asked, seemingly stunned.

"Nae. He wants the power of the Dragon Knights, and will do anything to possess it, including"—Stephen captured her eyes with his—"taking what would mean certain death to me."

"And what would that be?" interjected Aidan.

Stephen met Aidan's look directly. "Aileen."

****

He waited patiently for the men to catch up, giving a firm pat to his horse. They would not be at the coast for another few weeks, unless he pushed them harder.

Though the sun was shining, the bite of the north wind blew past him, almost as if the *Cailleach* refused to release her hold on winter. Staring ahead at Caedons Pass, his nerves were taut with anticipation. Cathal had brought the news of Lachlan near Arbroath Abbey. The same abbey where untruths circulated that his brother had settled.

He wanted Lachlan dead more than anyone.

It was the druid's blade, which almost killed his beloved wife. Now the bloody bastard was near his brother. His hands clenched on the reins. There was only one possible explanation. Lachlan was after Stephen for his stone. Yet, Stephen no longer possessed it. *Unless...*

Someone shouted his name, and Duncan MacKay turned.

Gavin McTeague galloped forward with restless energy. They didn't have any enemies in these parts, but one never knew. He relied on Gavin to have their back, and to be their lookout on the road ahead. He and a small group of soldiers were all that remained at Urquhart Castle when Duncan returned after being gone for a year.

"What troubles ye, Gavin?"

"We are traveling the same path as four others." Gavin uttered, shifting uneasily.

"And why is that a concern?" asked Duncan, adding, "There are often travelers along these paths."

"The exact same path, Duncan? They used the cave up by the loch, as well."

"It cannot be," he replied mystified. "There are only a few from Urquhart who ken it exists."

"Including your brothers," stated Gavin.

Duncan reeled from Gavin's words. "Why would they not seek their home?"

Gavin arched a brow. "Ye ask such a question?"

Duncan blew out a curse.

"Shall I ride ahead?"

"Aye," said Duncan, slowly. "Here comes the MacFhearguis and his men."

Gavin sneered. "Do ye trust him?"

Duncan almost laughed, until he remembered Alex and Patrick MacFhearguis had been witnesses to

Lachlan's evil plan with him that night.

He rubbed a hand over the knot in his neck, longing to be back at Urquhart. "For the moment, Gavin, we all must trust each other."

Gavin nodded. However, before he started to leave, Duncan added, "Do not say a word about what ye have told me. I think it wise not to let Patrick ken another MacKay is within a day's ride."

"Agreed," answered Gavin.

Chapter Thirty-Four

"When the Knight drank the mead from the cup, he realized too late that it was tainted with magic—sealing his fate in the land of the faery."

The waning moon hung low in the evening sky greeting the night travelers.

What Aileen wouldn't give for a warm bed, instead of the rough trunk of the tree she was resting against. Feeling utterly drained from staying up most of the night talking with her father didn't help either. Her eyes weighed heavy, and at one point on the journey, she actually drifted off.

Now she cast her sight to the two men speaking in almost whispers.

Stephen was listening to something Liam was saying. The light of the fire cast shadows across his face lined with worry. He had come to her rescue when she almost spilled off of Buttertwill, letting her ride with him for a while. Watching him nod every so often at Liam, she noticed his hands were clenched.

Aileen wanted to abandon her tree trunk for his arms to soothe away his worry. The past twenty-four hours had brought changes to the three men. A bonding had occurred. Even her father had paid Stephen a compliment over their meal last night. She didn't understand what happened, but welcomed it all the same.

"Eager to be back at Grenlee tomorrow?" asked her father, stepping forth from the trees.

Aileen smiled. "Yes, for if anything there will be softer beds."

"What? You don't like the ground for support?" he chided.

"No, not at the moment."

He crouched down next to her, placing his arm around her shoulders. "Try to get some rest. You'll feel better in the morning."

"That's what Stephen said last night, and he was wrong."

Her dad gave a small chuckle.

"Dad?"

"Yes, Aileen."

"Are you staying?" It was the one question she feared to ask her father. Her heart ached at the thought of him returning. When he didn't answer her, a lump formed in her throat.

He sighed deeply. "No. I cannot."

"But why?" she blurted out.

He released his hold of her so he could look at her directly. "If I don't return by the full moon, Liam's life will be forfeit."

Aileen's eyes went wide. "They would do that? The fae would take his *life*?"

"Yes. He broke a sacred vow by bringing me through the veil."

"Why would you let him do it?"

"He knew the risk and was the one to make the suggestion. Though, I believe he feared me more than the fae."

"Oh Dad, you should not have come." Tears stung her weary eyes.

Crushing her back against him, he replied, "I would ask the fae myself, just to make sure you were all right. You forget, Aileen, I have lived in this century."

"I'm stronger than you think, Dad, and you already defied them once. You were fortunate they didn't take your life."

He smiled wistfully, and she touched his face. "The blood of the fae is strong within ye."

"Your brogue is slipping again," laughed Aileen.

"'Tis easy to slip back into when I'm around your Knight. Is there no way I can convince you to come back with me?"

"I love you, Dad, but my life is here with Stephen." She squeezed his arm, adding, "At least we have over a month until the full moon. I plan on not wasting any of that time."

He settled more firmly against the solid oak, pulling the tartan securely around them both. "It was a question I had to ask, though I knew your answer. Now then, perhaps I'll share another story of my life with you before you drift off."

"I would like that," she said quietly.

"Let's see...the year was 974, a few years before the great Brian Boru became king of Ireland."

"I love the story of Brian Boru," she uttered softly.

"Aye, but you've never heard how I saved his life, so he could become king." He scratched his day-old beard. "As I was saying, I met Brian Boru one fine summer morn, coming upon him and his brother, Mahon, in a display of swordsmanship. Their love for the other was fierce. But on this day, their anger sliced the air with each swing of their blades..."

Aileen tried so hard to listen, yet, the lure of the story and her father's voice soon had her drifting off into dreams of Ireland and King Brian Boru.

****

"Awake, *leannan*," murmured Stephen. "I wish I could wake ye properly, but we best be on our way."

Aileen sighed against his arms. "Even if we have the time, there is still the problem of our *company*." She yawned, stretching out her legs.

Stephen placed a gentle kiss on her lips before helping her to stand. "Go break your fast with your father. I'll ready the horses."

She smiled, giving him another long kiss.

Breaking from the kiss, Stephen smiled mischievously. "Ye are a verra lusty woman in the morning."

"Uh huh," she replied, grazing her lips across his smooth chin. "You shaved this morning."

Smacking her bottom, he sent her toward her father.

Stephen didn't turn when he heard Liam approach. He kept his eyes on Aileen, who was doing her best to walk ever so slowly, showing him just what he was missing.

"Remember your vow, Fenian. I will hold ye to it," Stephen uttered low.

"You have my word, Dragon Knight," replied Liam, tersely. He proceeded to shuffle past Stephen, and then paused. "You love her that much?"

"I would give my life for hers."

Liam shook his head in understanding as he made his way to his horse.

Stephen directed his gaze once more to Aileen. She was devouring her meal, yet managed to tease him mercilessly with each blackberry she placed on her tongue. She was thrilled to come upon them yesterday, telling him she longed to make something special when they returned to Grenlee.

He chuckled softly and whistled for Grian.

"No more, Dad." Aileen smacked his hand away. "I want to bake something for Stephen, and at the rate you keep popping them into your mouth there won't be any left."

"There's plenty."

"Humph!" she retorted. Gathering the rest of the food, she went over to Buttertwill placing them in her satchel.

A cool breeze drifted past her face, causing her hand to still on the horse. Something was utterly wrong. Cautiously moving away, Aileen staggered to the edge of the clearing.

Her vision blurred, their voices straining to reach her.

Stephen was the first to notice, rushing after her. Moments before he reached her, Liam blocked his path.

"Don't!" he demanded. Stephen's hand went for his throat, but Liam was faster. "Trust *me*. She will be fine."

Stephen watched in horror. "What is happening?"

Aidan froze in his steps. "What do you hear, Aileen." His voice calm.

Aileen thought she heard her father, but there was no time to answer him. Giving all her attention and energy to the voices, she clasped her pendant.

The air grew thick. A child was crying. Men yelled

at one another. The thread of evil permeated the air and ground. One voice called out to her.

"Hurry, Aileen. They are here," pleaded Betha.

The voices ceased, closing the door soundly. Aileen blinked rapidly for several seconds. Biting back the bile that rose, she turned toward them.

"We must ride hard and fast. Lachlan and his men have found them at Grenlee." Her voice barely a whisper.

Stephen all but shoved Liam out of the way to take her in his arms. "Are ye all right?"

She nodded.

"Your mother had the gift of *hearing*," spoke Aidan. "Your powers have increased, since your contact with the dragon."

Aileen looked up at Stephen. "I don't understand what the dragon did to my pendant, because I didn't experience any pain with their emotions." She clutched at his arms, adding, "I heard Betha *speak* to me in my mind."

He drew her more closely. "When we get there, I want ye to stay with Liam and your father." He tilted her head to meet his gaze. "Will ye do this for me, Aileen?"

She frowned. "Yes, but I don't..."

"Shhh, *leannan*." He placed his finger softly on her lips. "For me. I will ken ye are safe."

"For you," she whispered.

"Aileen, I need you to do something before we leave," interjected Liam.

Stephen flashed him a look of warning.

"What is it?" she asked, placing a comforting hand on Stephen's chest.

"I need you to send a message to Betha. Do you think you can do that?"

"Honestly? I don't know, Liam."

"Try, please."

"I'll try." Reaching up, she gave Stephen one last kiss before giving her full attention to Liam.

"What do you want me to tell her?"

Liam seemed to stand taller all of a sudden, as if drawing on his powers. "Tell her they will have the help of two Fenian Warriors." He glanced back at Aidan for approval.

Aidan stepped forward, placing his hand on Liam's shoulder. "Aye, tell her so."

Taking a hold of her pendant, Aileen took a few steps back and closed her eyes. Within moments, the wave of sight flooded her vision, carrying her words to Betha.

Chapter Thirty-Five

"Hold fast, my bonny lass, for if you fall into the water, the fae will sweep you away to the stars."

The moment Aileen could no longer see Stephen and her father in the distance, her inner sight took over. Sensing his need to push hard through the hills, he wasted no time, making it difficult for Buttertwill to keep the pace. And for that reason, Liam rode with her.

With the thud of hoofs pounding the ground, mixed with heavy breathing, her nerves were coiled tight. After she had sent out the message to Betha, it was as if a black cloak descended. Try as she might, there were no more visions or sounds. Aileen didn't want to panic. The only option was to remain positive, and it didn't hurt to toss out prayers along the way, too.

They were heading for a dense part of the hills where she knew it would slow them considerably. Again, she reached out to Stephen, sensing his fury and determination. Their connection became stronger by the hour, and she wrapped thoughts of love around his.

Pine boughs smacked against her legs and arms before murky water splashed against them. She dodged one at her face, coaxing Buttertwill onward.

Courage and strength infused her spirit.

The people needed them. *Her people*. In just a short time, they had become her family. A bond had formed, sealed with her destiny. As much as she loved her aunt and the others in her other time, this century had seared its mark into her very soul.

She was home...in this century.

A familiar caw could be heard above them. Sorcha circled through the trees as a beacon of light. They were near the crest that would take them down into Grenlee.

Aileen slowed her mount, taking a position behind some heavy pines.

Liam rode up beside her and cast a quick glance in all directions. "We are a few miles out." He narrowed his eyes upward. "Friend or foe?"

"Definitely friend. She belongs to the druid Cathal."

"Good, one can never be too sure..." Liam blanched. "Cathal is here?"

A look of surprise passed over her face. "You know him?"

He arched a brow. "Oh yes, and I can say that we have strength on our side. Cathal is a verra powerful druid. If there is anyone who can take out Lachlan, he can do it. There is only one problem."

"And what would that be?" asked Aileen, frowning.

"Is it possible for Cathal to kill his own brother?"

"Great Goddess!" she gasped. "They're brothers?"

Liam nodded solemnly. "I'm afraid to say they are."

Aileen continued to watch Sorcha fly overhead; wondering how one brother could kill his own family. "Do you know this Lachlan?"

"No. Lachlan was never known to favor the fae. In fact, he spent most of his life degrading our kind. He believed we had too much power and should share it with the druids."

"In the end, it always comes down to power," she said sadly, glancing back up at Sorcha.

"It always has, since the dawn of your mankind—the battle for higher power," Liam responded.

"Now what?" she asked.

"We wait. Stephen and your father will survey the situation. When the time comes, he will place you in protection with the others."

Aileen gritted her teeth. Being patient was not on her agenda today. Slipping free from Buttertwill, she sat down on the ground.

Dismounting from his horse, Liam removed his sword. He stood before her, sword arm crossed over the other.

"Liam, my father told me you risked your life by bringing him back in time. Why did you do this?" she asked plucking at the leaves scattered about her.

Liam gritted his teeth. "Is it always thus?"

"Excuse me?"

He raked a hand through his hair. "Humans and your questions. Always striving for the answers before they can be shown."

She shook her head. "We are a curious sort, I suppose. Yet, I am only half human."

He smirked, shifting his stance. "To answer your question, it had to be done. Your father would have had my head."

"So I wasn't supposed to go through the veil?"

He gave her a quick glance over his shoulder. "Aye, you were destined to go back."

"Do you know how this will all end?"

He gave a deep sigh, "Not anymore, and before you ask any more questions, I am still a Fenian Warrior, bound by an oath as ancient as your sun. Even if I knew, I could not share future events with you."

Aileen flinched. "But you went against your own people by bringing him back."

He cursed softly. "He is *still* my brother. I would die for him."

"Brother as in *fae*, right?"

He gave her a curt nod, resuming his watch.

"Thank you, Liam," she whispered.

Hours slipped past in silence. Birds chirped around them, and several deer ambled along, mindless of their position. Aileen had dozed off briefly, only to be awakened by a squirrel scampering over her feet.

Rubbing her eyes, she observed Liam still standing in the same position as before. Standing, she brushed out the dirt and leaves from her gown.

"It will be dark soon. We may have to seek better shelter," Liam said quietly.

"Shouldn't they be back by now?" Concern filled her voice. She cupped a hand over her eyes to filter out the sun as it started to make its descent in the west.

Liam didn't answer. Instead he asked, "Have you tried to contact Betha again?"

Aileen's shoulders slumped. "Yes, but I'm getting nothing. I can't even sense Stephen anymore."

"Just as I feared. Dark magic has sealed everything. We shall wait until dusk, and then we'll depart for higher ground."

"But how will they find us?" she blurted out.

Liam placed a gentle hand on her shoulder. "That's where your help and power will be necessary." He gave

271

her a reassuring smile and went to get the horses.

Dusk came too quickly for Aileen. With a heavy heart, she followed Liam to higher ground. They stopped within an hour, for the trail was too narrow to go further on horseback.

Finally, when she thought she would scream at him to stop, he led them to a thick group of pines. Ducking underneath, she emerged against the side of the hill. Water trickled down the rocks on the far edge.

Liam went directly over, splashing the water onto his face. "Get the water skins, and fill them. Then I'll let the horses have their fill. I'm going to climb on the rock's ledge to get a better view. It has the perfect vantage point, and I'll be able to easily scan the horizon."

Aileen numbly did as she was told, but not before taking huge gulps of the crisp, cool water. After splashing the water on her face, she filled all of their water skins.

"Aileen, try and reach out to Stephen. If you can, visualize the path we just took to get here."

Hope flared at his words. "Do you sense them? Can you see them?"

"No, Aileen. For now, we'll use your gifts," he answered.

Aileen took the water skin and poured some of the liquid onto her hands. Letting it soothe her, she thought only of Stephen, as she grounded herself.

Water. Stephen. Their love. It became her mantra in her mind. Over and over the words flowed. Seconds passed. Minutes passed. And she sensed...*nothing*.

Taking a hold of her pendant, she tried again

searching for anything.

A faint whisper touched her mind.

Her eyes flew open. "They're coming!"

"Show them the way, Aileen," commanded Liam.

Breathing deeply, she let her mind drift back to the path they took. She almost choked on a sob, when a ribbon of love wrapped around her thoughts.

Collapsing onto the ground, she rasped out, "He sees the way."

Liam jumped down, taking Aileen into his arms. Brushing his fingers along her forehead, he spoke in words she couldn't understand. Instantly, a surge of energy slammed into her, wiping out the draining effects she had previously encountered.

Her eyes sought his, which flashed with such brilliance Aileen had to blink several times. "What did you do to me?"

"Just a bit of healing, lass," he answered. "Come, let's get you standing before your beloved arrives. We don't want him to get any ideas."

Aileen snickered. "No. I don't think that's wise. He might put a blade through you."

"As if he could," he scoffed. "Let's go greet them, shall we?"

Making their way on foot part way down, Liam halted her from going any further.

Within moments, Stephen was stomping through the trees. Aileen almost threw herself into his arms from sheer relief.

"It's about time," she cried out as he crushed her against him.

"I'm happy to see ye, too, *leannan*," he chuckled softly, before kissing her deeply.

When Stephen broke from the kiss, he eyed Liam. "Thank ye, for taking her to safety. It is worse than we feared." He looked back down at Aileen. "Lachlan and his men have the entire village surrounded."

Aileen saw her father emerge from the trees and went over to embrace him. Seeing the weary look on his face, she said, "You both need to rest. We have some water, too."

After they were settled, Stephen went into detail on where everyone in the village was positioned. "They have the women and children separated from the men. It is as if they are searching for someone, or something."

"Did you locate Cathal?" Liam asked.

"No. He is not among them," her dad replied.

"What do you mean?"

"He and several of the other druids are not with the men, nor are they anywhere else."

Aileen frowned. "Could they have left?"

"Can't say."

"Or they could have been killed," interrupted Stephen.

A chill crept down Aileen's spine. "No, it can't be."

"Lachlan is a sadistic and evil man. I wouldn't put it past him," uttered Liam.

"So what do we do?"

All eyes bored into hers.

"*Ye* will do naught, but remain here," responded Stephen with a scowl.

Aileen looked aghast. "Bullshit!"

Stephen's eyebrows rose a fraction.

Liam coughed a remark into his hand.

Her dad loomed large over her.

"You can all stop trying to protect me," she clipped out. "I could be mauled by some animal, or taken prisoner just staying here all alone. I can help by getting the women and children to safety."

Stephen's jaw clenched as he looked at the others. "Her words ring true. However"—his gaze now directed at her—"if ye do this, ye will heed my words at all times."

She narrowed her eyes at him. "I'm not a fool, Stephen. I will be careful, and *heed* your words."

"I don't like it," interjected her father.

Aileen grabbed her father's hand. "Please have faith, Dad. You need my help, too." She waved her hand out at all of them. "There are only three of you, against how many? Until you can free the men, I'm afraid you'll require my strength, too. Let me do this."

Reluctantly, he relented.

"I hate to add more bad news to this scenario, but if you haven't noticed we're up against something else," uttered Liam.

"What?" they all asked in unison.

"Lachlan has resorted to using dark magic. He has become so powerful he can block out any powers or gifts that others may have. Aileen can no longer contact Betha. Lachlan has sealed them all inside his cloak of power."

Stephen stood slowly, unsheathing his sword. The hiss of steel filled the air. "I've always preferred bodily strength over magic any day."

Chapter Thirty-Six

"And the cry of the Celts rang out across the land, awakening those who were lost."

Stars twinkled in the early morning sky as Stephen stood gazing out over the land, his keen warrior senses on alert. They'd spent most of the night going over their final plans and what each one would be doing, including Aileen.

His stomach clenched at the thought of her going anywhere near Lachlan, but he had to squelch those feelings. It would do him no good if he went into battle not fully prepared. She was brave and strong. Perhaps, more so now than ever.

Words from the Guardian—words he had just recently remembered drifted into his mind...

Across the sea their destiny awaits...A love will meet through time and space...To right a wrong within this place...Beneath the gate to test your fate.

His destiny. His love. His fate. All linked to one. *Aileen.*

He was fully prepared to do anything to keep her safe. Some part of him was relieved that he had her father and Liam at his side. They were her protectors, too.

An owl hooted in the distance as the last glimmer of stars faded quickly. An omen of ill will? He would not dwell on its meaning.

Bending down on one knee, Stephen placed his sword on the ground. Removing his water skin, he poured the cool water over his head and across his sword. "Water, the mark of my life—the mark of my power. Bless me on this day, Gods and Goddess. St. Michael, give me your sword arm. Cuchulainn, your courage and cunning. And if I may include in my prayer, send those that would watch over the people in Grenlee. Great Goddess Danu, let my love act as a shield over Aileen to keep her safe."

His eyes shone brightly as his words floated across the early morning sky.

Picking up his sword, Stephen made his way back to the group. He wasn't surprised when Aileen was the first to greet him. Her smile stole the morning chill from his bones, and he gathered her into his arms. Tipping her head up to stare into those eyes he loved so much, Stephen let his lips brush over hers. His kiss was not one of goodbye, but a promise of more to follow.

"Braid my hair, tightly," she said huskily against his face.

Stephen placed his hands on her shoulders and turned her away from him. Taking the long strands, he braided them as tight as she could stand. He took the end and kissed the silken strand.

Twirling her back around, he slipped his hand under her gown up along her thigh. A slow wicked smile curved his features, when he found what he was searching for.

"Did I place the *sgian dubh* high enough?"

"Aye, verra well. Now show me the other leg."

Aileen moved to a log, and placed her leg on it.

Lifting her gown so that she gave Stephen a full view of her entire leg, she smiled wickedly. "See for yourself."

In two strides, he was in front of her, checking the placement of her dirk on the outside of her leg. He would have preferred to have her belt it around her waist, but she insisted on doing it her way. Pleased with it, he took his hand and stroked her inner thigh. His blood was hot. His need for her fierce.

"When this is over..." he rasped low into her ear, raking his tongue down her neck.

"I will find you, Stephen."

After sealing their bargain with a crushing kiss, Stephen led her over to Buttertwill. "Ride close to Liam."

She placed a hand against his cheek. "I will. Be safe, my love."

Liam walked over to his horse, giving a nod to them. Quickly mounting his horse, Stephen watched as he kept his sight on the valley below. They would ride south of the village where the women and children were kept. Once they were freed, Liam would join Aidan and him.

"Keep her safe," said Aidan, emerging from the trees. Taking a hold of his daughter's hand, he pressed a kiss on it. "Keep trying to reach Betha."

"I will, Dad, and you be safe, too."

Aidan snorted. "I may be human, but I still have a few fae tricks up my sleeve." Taking his leave, he mounted his horse and they were off.

****

Hours passed with the sun now peeking out through clouds, the air warm. Each rider on alert as they passed through the valley. Stephen held up his hand to signal they were coming near the crossroad where Liam and Aileen would part. His eyes sought hers and waited until she had ridden next to him.

Fear swamped her thoughts, but before she could utter a word, Stephen grasped her and silenced her worry with his lips.

"Courage, my love." His voice thick with emotion.

Gathering the reins on Grian, he nodded toward her dad. Glancing at Liam, he held his gaze. Finally, he spoke, "If all goes well, we shall meet at the old oak come nightfall."

"May you walk with the fae," Liam uttered softly.

Aileen waited until her father and the man she loved were no longer in sight. She squelched the uneasiness flaring inside. Time was their enemy, and they had to move quickly.

"I'm ready."

They rode silently through the trees, crossing a small stream. Instead of clearing the water, they rode along its bank. Nearing the end of town, both dismounted.

"Can you see anything, Liam?" She scanned the area, but couldn't make out anything. Huge oaks blocked most of her vision, so she stepped away from Liam. Bending down near the water, she let it trickle through her fingers and closed her eyes. *Talk to me, Betha...*

Silence greeted her.

Standing, Aileen shook the water out of her hand in frustration. "Nothing," she stated when she saw the look on Liam's face.

"We'll leave the horses here. See the oak on the far left?"

She nodded.

"Go forth to that one. Stay there and wait for my signal."

"Two short bursts of a falcon's cry," she replied.

"Aye."

As Aileen stepped forward, Liam grabbed her hand. "Remember, you have the blood of the fae in you. Call out to them if you need to."

Aileen frowned, but just nodded.

They crept forward cautiously, parting ways halfway to the trees. When Aileen made it to her destination, she crouched down against the old oak. Bile rose instantly in her throat at the scene in front of her.

Woman and children were tied together in groups of five and six spread out in the open. Some of the children were weeping quietly, or their eyes were wide open in fear. What fueled her fury more was apparently no fires had been lit to keep them warm at night.

A baby's sharp cry shook her out of her contemplation.

Inspecting the area, she noted only three guards. One was sitting on a log and the other two were deep in conversation. There was no way she could get to the group without being seen. They would have to wait until night before they could attempt a rescue, unless Liam could take out the guards.

Now focusing her gaze on the hostages, Aileen tried searching for Betha. Instantly, she spotted Ian. He was sitting with a group of other young boys, rocking back and forth with a odd look on his face. Was he meditating?

Aileen had to get his attention.

Closing her eyes, she reached out to him in her mind, but the first image that came to her was one of a red fox. Keeping her eyes shut, Aileen smiled and concentrated with all her might.

The voice was but a whisper on the breeze. *Shhh, Aileen. He will hear ye.*

Aileen's eyes snapped open to find Ian smiling at her. He took a finger to his lips in silence, and then tapped them on his temple.

Understanding flared in her and she swallowed. Settling back against the oak, Aileen waited.

****

Their plan had been simple. Take out as many guards as possible. However, a group of them stood near one man—*Lachlan*. It was as if he was conducting a meeting, waving his hands about. Stephen couldn't hear his words, but a response from one of the guards was greeted with a backhanded slap across his face. One of the other guards hesitated, his hand instinctively going for his sword.

Stephen glanced at Aidan, who also witnessed the interaction between the men. Making a sign to Aidan to move back within the trees, they crept away.

When they were a safe distance away, Stephen spoke low. "There might be discord among the guards."

Aidan grunted. "Aye, and that can be an advantage."

"I need ye to stay and find out more. I will check on Liam and Aileen. If we can free some of the others, we can worry about the rest come nightfall."

"Agreed," responded Aidan.

Quickly scrambling through the foliage, Stephen made his way out of anyone's vision. Snaking his way carefully, he spotted the horses, and proceeded on foot. Taking his time, he went out as far as possible. If he was seen, the element of surprise would be lost.

Aileen nearly bolted when a hand clamped over her mouth.

"'Tis me, Aileen." Stephen's voice low against her ear. Pulling her back, against him, he added, "Let's move away for a moment."

She nodded and followed his lead.

As soon as they were discreetly behind a group of oaks, Aileen lunged into Stephen's arms.

"Och, *mo gradh*." He placed a kiss along her brow. "What have ye observed?"

"They have the women and children clumped together in groups of five and six, scattered some feet apart. There are only three guards. I won't be able to help any of them without being seen." Her gaze snapped back to Stephen. "How many when you and my father scouted the area earlier?"

"We saw only one guard, believing ye would be able to free them while Liam took out the guard." Stephen backed away from her. "Bloody hell," he snapped.

She stepped in front of him. "There's another problem."

He rolled his eyes. "And that would be?"

"I recognized Ian in the group and attempted to make contact with him."

Stephen grasped her arms firmly. "It is a good sign."

Aileen shook her head slowly. "No. He quickly told me *he* can hear and to be quiet."

Stephen uttered a curse, nodding to Aidan as he

stepped through the trees.

Liam had silently made his way to them. "The druids are not among the others. From what I can gather, they are dead, *or* they have left for the hills to convene."

"Did you see Betha?" asked Aileen.

"Yes. She and a few of the others are being kept near Lachlan."

Stephen grimaced. "For what purpose?"

"If we are to save any of them, we must act as soon as the sun descends over the horizon," Liam answered with deadly calm.

Stephen arched a questioning brow.

"Lachlan plans on lighting the night sky with the burning of their bodies."

Aileen gasped, "*No.*"

"Not if I can stop his vile plan," said Duncan MacKay, stepping forth from the trees.

Chapter Thirty-Seven

"Have no fear, for there is more than one door that will lead you to your destiny."

The two brothers faced each other with wary expressions on their faces.

"So ye were the first," stated Stephen, still stunned at the man before him.

"Aye. In truth, it had to start with the most grievous of sins." Duncan's stance shifted ever so slightly.

Stephen nodded slowly. "True."

"I see ye travel with Fenian Warriors and a fae," Duncan remarked, his eyes never leaving Stephen's.

Aileen's mouth fell open, and she glared at Duncan.

Stephen cocked a brow. "Liam, Aidan, this is my brother, Duncan."

Liam stepped forward to greet Duncan, but Duncan remained unmoving.

"Still angry at Conn?" Liam inquired.

Duncan's eyes narrowed briefly. "Nae. All debts have been paid." He shifted his gaze to Aidan. "Would ye be the great Aidan Kerrigan?"

"Aye," replied Aidan.

"Clarify on how ye can be in this time if ye are no longer part of the royal guard?"

"It is thorny, brother," Stephen interjected.

It was Duncan's turn to arch a brow.

Aileen coughed loudly and moved forward. "It's really simple, Duncan. Liam brought *my father* back through the veil to find me. And just to set the record straight, I'm only *half* fae."

"Truth?" whispered Duncan, his question aimed at Stephen.

Reaching for Aileen's hand, Stephen replied, "Duncan, this is Aileen Kerrigan, daughter of Aidan." Placing a kiss along her fingers, he added the last, peering into her eyes. "And the woman I love."

Duncan gawked at his brother. "Clearly, your fate was the daughter of a Fenian Warrior. I would expect nothing else."

He made a slight bow before her. "I am honored, *Lady* Aileen."

"Please, call me Aileen." Stepping away from Stephen, she embraced Duncan, who was caught off guard. "It's good you are here to help us, and to reunite with your brother."

Duncan glanced at Stephen when he spoke. "It is just the beginning, *brother*."

It was Aidan who interrupted the trio. "It would be wise if we took shelter back within the trees until night."

"Agreed," replied Liam.

They approached the trees and instantly Stephen drew forth his sword. His blade held against the throat of Patrick MacFhearguis with a look of fury.

"Lugh's balls!" Stephen growled. "Do ye ride with these bastards, Duncan?"

The hiss of steel could be heard everywhere as all

the men, save Duncan, unsheathed their swords.

Patrick glowered. "Duncan, I believe ye had better explain to your brother that we are *now* on the same side."

Duncan clasped a firm hand on Stephen's sword arm. "Aye. We work together."

"Since when?" spat out Stephen, his eyes never deviating from Patrick.

"The night when Lachlan took my beloved. They helped to free her and stand with me *against* him."

His brother's words were not making sense. "*Beloved*?" he croaked.

Duncan slowly turned to face him. "Lachlan took the woman I love, Brigid, in order to attain this." He brought forth his sword.

Stephen lowered his blade. "The Dragon Knight sword," he uttered low. "Your quest? *Brigid*?"

Duncan smirked. "Aye. We are now married, and it would seem ye have found your *stone*. Good God brother, what has happened to it?" His eyes went round when he noticed its color had changed.

Stephen rubbed a hand over his forehead. Uneasiness quelled in him. He realized Aileen was part of his quest, but how would it all end?

Glancing back at his brother, Stephen said, "We have much to discuss. Yet, my question to ye"—pointing his blade at Patrick—"why are ye involved?"

"I can answer that," interjected Duncan.

Patrick held up his hand. "Nae, let me. It would appear Lachlan has betrayed all of us. His evil has twisted the two clans for some time. In truth, I have never trusted the druid, but Alex has just found this insight. Yet, our Laird still heeds his counsel."

"His magic grows," grumbled Liam. "It is good we have more to help in the fight."

Stephen remained silent. Suddenly, he felt Aileen's hand slip into his. A sense of calm washed through him. Bringing her hand to his lips, he kissed her palm. Gazing back at Patrick, he said, "Come, we have much to discuss before nightfall."

Hours later, they had formulated renewed plans. Patrick went to stand guard and sent Sean to keep a watch on Lachlan. It would be a long night, but one that had a renewed sense of energy.

Stephen eyed his brother. He detected a sense of peace within him. Did redemption bring that to him? How was he able to forgive himself? He dismissed the uneasiness of never finding peace.

"Have you no news regarding Angus and Alastair?" asked Stephen, taking a rock and flinging it out in the distance.

"Aye. Angus is on tourney and Alastair...well, our little brother has taken up with the Northmen."

Stephen gaped at Duncan. "Bloody hell! He *loathes* the water. Why?" He shook his head in frustration. Peering over his shoulder as he leaned against the tree, he noticed Aileen watching them.

"For the same reason ye went to a monastery. To run from the very part of ye that ye scorn," replied Duncan.

Stephen ran a hand over his face. He realized Duncan's words held truth—a truth he was still trying to fathom. "Did ye run?"

"Nae." Duncan strode over to Stephen, motioning to the dark clouds on the horizon. He took a deep breath in and let it out slowly. "I battled with myself and the

287

elements. At times, even daring them to destroy me."

"How did ye endure?" Stephen's voice barely a whisper when he asked.

"I was almost consumed by darkness..." Duncan paused. "...and then Brigid walked into my life." He closed his eyes, smiling.

Stephen nodded in understanding. "And the sword?"

Duncan chuckled. "She brought it with her."

"It would appear the Guardian has sent all of our relics through the veil," grumbled Stephen.

Duncan's eyes narrowed. "Your stone..." He glanced at Aileen. "The fae brought it with her?"

"Aye," smirked Stephen. "Should I daresay that Brigid traveled the veil, too?"

"In truth, eight hundred years."

"Sweet Danu!" exclaimed Stephen. "Aileen as well, though, she did not ken she was part fae until a short time ago. Her father kept much from her."

"Do not all Fenian Warriors?" scoffed Duncan.

"But not all challenge the Tuatha De Danann and marry a mortal. Aidan was the only one. He and her mother shielded her from her identity, fearing for her safety."

"From the *fae?*"

Stephen waved his hand in the air. "Nae. From a vision her mother, Rose Kerrigan had before her birth. She saw her life ending in Scotland. 'Tis complicated."

Duncan pointed to his relic. "And this?"

"Courtesy of the Great Dragon. She joined both my stone and the one Aileen wears."

"Cleansed, brother. Part of your quest."

Thunder rumbled in the distance, and Stephen

arched a brow at his brother.

Duncan's smile turned wicked. "Only if needed. A warning to Lachlan. This time we will fight as one, Stephen."

"To avenge our sister," he declared.

"Not only Meggie, but for Brigid, and the others, too." Duncan's look was positively sinister.

The last rays of sunlight quickly faded in the west and both brothers knelt. Heads bent, they uttered their prayers for courage and strength. And in his final prayer, Stephen reached out with his inner sight, seeking those he had banished from his being. When the light of the fae entered his mind, Stephen MacKay asked for forgiveness.

In that moment, the words whispered to him were as gentle as the breeze.

"*We are with you, Dragon Knight.*"

Chapter Thirty-Eight

"It is said that when the fae shed tears the rivers will overflow."

Lachlan watched and waited as the men finished setting the wooden logs into the ground. His lip almost curled in glee anticipating the first to catch fire. Their burning flesh would fill the night sky.

Giving the signal to one of the guards, he brought forth his sickle. Cries uttered forth from one of the women, and he smiled. She tried to break free from the guard's hold, but was greeted with a smack against her face.

"Tie her to the stake," ordered Lachlan.

"Should we not question them further?" asked one of the guards.

It was always the same with this one—a litany of questions and disregard for his authority. Twice, he wanted to speak to Manus and have him remove the difficult guard. However, that would present another host of problems from the others.

Lachlan tapped a finger to his lips in thought. "Hmmm…but what do ye think the bishop would counsel? Did he not tell me to do all that was deemed necessary? Would ye rather I torment them until their flesh falls off?"

The guard blanched at his words. "No."

"As I thought," snapped Lachlan. No sooner did his words leave his mouth than he frowned at the sight in the distance.

"What is it, Lachlan?" asked the guard, shifting uneasily.

Lachlan's jaw clenched. "Storm's brewing."

The guard looked in the direction of the horizon and saw the ominous clouds heading their way.

"Gather the rest and tie them to the wooden poles. I will make final preparations," demanded Lachlan.

Instantly, Manus strode over to him.

"We have another problem. Duncan MacKay is near," grumbled Lachlan.

"Will he pose a threat?" asked Manus.

"It is hard to say, though, his powers will be empty once he steps inside. I am more worried with the men he may bring." Peering over his shoulder to check on the progress, he glanced back at Manus. "Ye deal with Duncan and warn me the instant ye sight Stephen MacKay."

Manus gave a slight bow and as he was leaving, Lachlan stopped him. "When ye have killed Duncan, bring me his sword."

"Done," he replied.

****

As new plans were finalized, Aileen stood alone staring out ahead to where the battle would take place. Squelching the uneasiness knotting her stomach, she tried to maintain her focus. Her job was simple. Free the women and children and get them to safety. Yet, that wasn't why her insides were twisted. It was fear for the men she loved, and those they held dear.

Grasping her pendant, she gazed up into the sky.

"Oh Great Mother, watch over us all. Help us to fight this evil."

"Are ye ready, *leannan*?"

Taking a deep breath, Aileen reached out for Stephen. His arms came around her and she reveled in the warmth and security, unsure of when she would be within them again. "Let's get this over."

Stephen tilted her chin up, so he could look into her eyes. "Always believe in my love for ye, Aileen. Do ye hear my words?"

Her eyes misted, and she swallowed. "I will hold your love in my heart." She gave him a weak smile, adding, "But you can show me just how much *after* this is over with…*my love*."

Stephen captured her lips in savage intensity. She responded with equal fervor, grasping a hold of his head to deepen the kiss, fearing it would be their last.

Finally breaking free, he took her hands in his. "Forever, Aileen, *evermore*."

She placed a finger on his lips. "Say the words to me, when we wed."

Grasping her firmly against him, Stephen spoke softly in her ear, "Och, what ye do to my heart…"

"It is time, brother," whispered Duncan, standing a few paces back.

Giving her one more passionate kiss, Stephen turned to Liam. "Guard her with your life, Warrior."

Liam cocked a brow. "You forget, her father would slay me first before you." Then in a more serious tone, added, "You have my word and vow, Dragon Knight."

Duncan's brow furrowed.

Stephen glanced at his brother. "Is it not always wise to have a second plot?"

"Aye," replied Duncan slowly. "One that Angus taught us all. But with a Fenian Warrior?"

Stephen glanced over his shoulder at Aileen. "My quest, my plan."

Rubbing the back of his neck, Duncan nodded. "I sure hope ye understand the consequences of dealing with their kind."

"Always," replied Stephen.

When they were out of sight, Aileen and Liam ventured forward. The sun disappeared quickly, leaving just enough light for them to proceed. She had removed her *sgian dubh* and followed in Liam's wake.

Crouching down behind the oak she had been at earlier, she waited until Liam gave the signal. Then she would advance to the first group. The minutes ticked by, and her palms became sweaty. Sounds of the nocturnal creatures scurried past her, almost causing her to jump out of her skin.

Immediately, her thoughts went to Stephen and the others. What would they encounter? They were extremely fortunate to have Duncan and the extra men. For if this druid, Lachlan, was as powerful as they claimed he was then they would need any and all help. Even from the men they rescued.

An owl's screech pierced her thoughts. She waited. Another few minutes passed before she heard it again. Liam's signal. They had changed from a falcon's cry to one of an owl for night.

Squashing her fear back down, Aileen took a deep calming breath, and moved forward. Each step made with quiet stealth. Instantly, seeing the outline of the first group, she cautiously crept forward.

"Hello." Her voice barely a whisper.

"'Tis ye, lady?" asked one of the women quietly.

"Yes." Aileen inched closer until she could feel the woman's bonds. "Sit still," she murmured.

Afraid she would slit the woman's hand, it took longer than she anticipated. Finally, the ropes came free. The woman practically threw herself into Aileen's arms.

"Thank ye, lady," she sobbed.

Moving quickly to the next, she had more luck in removing the bonds and shifted to the next person, a child. After freeing her, she swiftly moved on.

"It is I, Lady Aileen," said Ian, softly.

After releasing him from his bonds, she embraced him. "Where are the druids, Ian?" Fearing his answer, she held her breath.

"They went to the hills to thwart the black magic from the evil druid."

Exhaling deeply, she wanted to jump for joy. "We feared they were dead," she whispered as she freed another child.

"Nae. They understood ye and Sir Stephen would return, and that ye would need their help."

Liam approached with a group of women and children. "We must move quickly, Aileen. I fear the other guards will return soon." He turned toward the group. "I want you to make for the cluster of oaks in that direction. Follow through until you find our horses. They are near a copse. Stay there until either myself, or Aileen comes for you. When all are freed, she will lead you away from here."

Silently, the small group took off, but not before Ian grasped Liam's hand. "What ye have done will not go unpunished, that I ken. But ye will always be our champion and your name honored." Releasing his hand, Ian sprinted off into the night.

Liam stood in shocked silence watching as the lad made it safely out of sight.

"Master druid in the making...ponder his words later," whispered Aileen. "Come, let us finish."

"Aye, later." Snatching his dirk, he moved to the next group.

****

Stooping low over a large boulder, Stephen and Duncan surveyed the area. Aidan, Patrick, and the rest of the men kept hidden among the pines. At Stephen's signal, they would descend on the guards, waiting until they spotted Lachlan.

Seeing Betha on the ground with two other women, they also noticed the men were face down, hands and feet bound. If they could just free some of the men, it would be to their advantage and strength.

As if sensing his thoughts, Aidan tilted his head to a group of men furthest from the guards. Stephen gave him a quick nod, letting him know to proceed. Aidan slipped silently toward the men.

Instantly, a shrill scream pierced the night. Stephen grasped his sword firmly, scanning the darkness. It was not long before light blazed forth in the night sky.

"Will ye lay down your heathen ways?" he demanded.

There could only be one person who the voice belonged to...*Lachlan!* Stephen gave the signal, lunging forth. Rushing forward, he thrust his sword into one of the guards. Caught unaware, the man didn't have time to even raise his weapon.

Stephen heard the others approaching and energy

surged forth.

Keeping his focus on the man in the center, Stephen and the others continued to battle those that would keep them from him. What bothered Stephen was Lachlan stood there smiling. He countered a blow and swiftly moved to the next. A prickling sensation of unease started at the base of his spine. Why wasn't the druid afraid? They were taking the guards down, inching closer to him.

Ducking to avoid a blow, he took his sword to the side of the guard, eventually standing before Lachlan.

"Ahh…here is the *Dragon Knight*," mocked Lachlan. "Pray tell me, ye have brought your brother, too?" Glaring at Stephen, he took the torch he was holding and moved to his first victim, Betha.

Stephen charged forth. Lachlan waved his hand in the air, and instantly Stephen was thrown backwards, landing on the ground. Duncan gave out a war cry as he approached Lachlan from the other side. After only a few steps, he, too, fell to the ground.

Lachlan's evil laughter filled the air. "Fools, all of ye! But first, I must thank ye for taking out the bishop's guards. Rome will be outraged to hear that the great Dragon Knights have stooped so low they are now attacking the church."

Standing, Duncan gathered his power. Lightning split the sky and thunder shook the ground.

Lachlan spread out his arms. "Take aim...*anywhere*."

Duncan drew forth his sword and unleashed his power. Nothing happened.

"I am still *waiting*," he snarled.

"What have ye done?" demanded Duncan.

"Your power is of no use inside here," interjected Betha, her voice raw.

"Silence!" Lachlan snapped.

Whipping his head back to Duncan, he motioned toward Stephen. "If ye would be so kind, drop your sword and stand over by your brother."

Resting his sword on the ground, Duncan walked over to Stephen, who was now standing. "What now?" he asked.

"Stephen, remove your stone and toss it over by the sword," ordered Lachlan.

"Ye are insane," Stephen hissed, his fists clenched by his sides. Slowly, he removed his medallion and threw it to the ground.

"*Insane?*" roared Lachlan. "By dawn, ye will see the full wrath of my power. Ye and your kind are under the assumption that power is for the few chosen. Well, I am here to prove everyone wrong." Turning back to Betha, he raised the torch at her. "If ye will not become one of my followers, then ye will all burn with a full blessing from the church."

"Stop!" Aidan had guardedly moved forward. "Ye have the relics. Take them and leave the people."

Lachlan narrowed his eyes at him. "The dark magic demands a sacrifice, and they refuse to follow me."

"Then I shall take their place," said Aidan.

"No!" cried out Stephen and Duncan in unison.

"Enough! Why would I want one, when there are many?" questioned Lachlan.

Aidan moved passed Stephen and Duncan. Both men glaring at him. Standing a few feet in front of the druid, he replied, "Would not the dark magic be grateful for the body of an elite Fenian Warrior?"

Silence descended. Sparks snapped from the torch as Lachlan considered this new piece of information. He cocked his head to the side, studying Aidan.

"Done." Snapping his fingers, two men came forth and took a hold of Aidan. "Nevertheless, this one is far too powerful to let live. Therefore, *she* will be the first."

Shouts erupted everywhere, and with a wave of his hand, the power smacked against them.

"Place him next to her," ordered Lachlan. Pointing a finger at the group, he yelled, "If there is another outburst, I will burn all of the children."

"Ye are a monster, Lachlan, and ye will sorely pay," growled Duncan.

"No! Let him go!" yelled Aileen, stumbling forward. Her hands were bound and on her face, a bruise started to emerge from where she had been hit.

Oblivious to the others, she ran toward her father. Whipping her head around to face Lachlan, she looked directly into the face of evil. "You will *not* take *my father*!"

Chapter Thirty-Nine

"When the knight emerged forth from the battle, he did not fear losing his soul, but his heart."

Stephen tried in vain to control the fear that seeped into his veins the moment Aileen stepped into view. *Where are ye, Liam?*

Dread filled him when Lachlan strode over to her. *Don't touch her*, his mind screamed. His hands flexed to be around the monster's throat. He wasn't the only one who was throwing daggers at Lachlan. Aidan tensed under the control of the two guards.

"Well, well, the Fenian Warrior has a...*daughter?*" Reaching out, he grabbed her chin.

"Take your hands off her," growled Stephen.

Slowly twisting his head around to glance at Stephen, Lachlan gripped her more firmly. "Would ye like me to snap her jaw?"

"I will not tell ye again." Stephen's tone had turned deadly.

"Brother," Duncan said quietly.

Lachlan released her. "This is a most unforeseen day. Not only do I have two Dragon Knights and a Fenian Warrior, but also his daughter, who is also *your beloved*, Stephen." He threw back his head and roared.

They were helpless, thought Stephen. This evil man's magic would kill them all. Their only hope would be a miracle.

"Tie him to the pole," ordered Lachlan, moving away.

Aileen held back a scream. Immediately, Liam's words rushed through. *Remember, you have the blood of the fae in you. Call out to them if you need to.*

Could it be so simple?

Aileen bent her head. *Blood of my blood...hear your daughter. I call out to you for help. Help us to fight this evil. I know of no other words...*

Immediately warmth infused her. She heard a tinkling of bells, and then a breeze touched her face.

Link your magic with that of the Dragon Knight.

Aileen kept her focus on Duncan and Stephen until she noticed they had sensed the shift in magic. Stephen gave his brother a quick nod, freed Aileen from her bonds, and swiftly took out the guard on his right. Lachlan threw another blast of magic, yet, it was not as powerful as the first.

"I warned ye, Dragon Knight," hissed Lachlan. Turning, he lowered his arm and set the pole on fire.

All hell broke loose, as Betha screamed in terror.

Instantly, Stephen and Aidan attempted to disarm the other guards. Duncan slammed his fist into one as they tried desperately to weaken Lachlan's power.

"Stop!" Lachlan howled. "Do ye all want to die?" Flinging out his arms, the power barely touched on the men fighting. Blind fury took over, and he charged for the sword.

Picking it up, he moved toward Aileen. "I will tear out your heart and watch ye die," he snarled, making long strides to her.

The other guards were now fighting some of the men that Aidan had freed, which left Aileen having to defend herself against the maniac approaching her. Fearing that her knife was no match against his sword, she turned to flee.

Hearing a thud behind her, Aileen peered over her shoulder. Another man was doing battle with the druid. Relief spread through her, but Betha's screams tore her vision to the pole.

"*Oh no*," she gasped. She would not let her friend die.

Instinct took over and scanning the area, she spotted Stephen. Running toward him, she yelled out, "We need water, quickly."

"Hold my sword. I need to call forth the water." He tipped her head up to meet his eyes. "Ye will have to defend me, *leannan*."

Swallowing the lump in her throat, Aileen nodded.

Stephen took a step back and closed his eyes. She watched as he breathed deeply, attuning his energy, and trying to draw forth the water from the nearby stream. Relaxing his hands, he tried to push through the barrier of magic, which still maintained partial energy.

The battle raged around them, and Aileen bit her lower lip in frustration. Watching the flames inch closer seized at her. In moments, they would engulf Betha. Something flickered past her right side and without thought, she plunged not only Stephen's sword, but also her dirk into the man. Registering a look of total shock, the man collapsed on the ground. She quickly drew them free from his body.

Feeling dizzy, she snapped her gaze back at Stephen. Beads of sweat broke out along his brow. *Why wasn't this working*? Smoke and terror filled the sky.

The ping of bells reminded Aileen of the message she heard earlier.

Tossing aside the sword, she faced Stephen and reached for his hand. He started to jerk free, but she held firm. Concentrating with all her being, she focused on the water. Flashes of light danced before her eyes.

The energy pulsed as she called, reached, pulled...

Heat flared into her body, and the ground rumbled. She heard it before it touched her. They both opened their eyes to see the water gushing forth from the stream. With their combined strength, they brought the direction of the water to them.

When Aileen looked into Stephen's eyes, they were so pale she could no longer see his irises. With no time to lose, he released her hand and guided the water toward Betha, letting it swirl and consume the flames.

Somehow, Donal had managed to get free and was helping Stephen cut through Betha's bonds. She collapsed into his arms, her legs only slightly singed. "I thank ye, Sir Stephen," said Donal, choking back emotion.

Her voice raspy from the smoke, Betha touched Stephen's arm. "The druids have weakened Lachlan's magic. Ye ken what must be done."

"Aye." He watched until they had safely parted. Taking a glance around, Stephen noted that Duncan was doing battle with two guards. The rest of their men were freed, but many had been injured. Most of them were no match against Lachlan's men. The best they could do would be to retreat. Another blaze had been set, but thankfully, no one was bound to it.

"Where the hell are ye, Lachlan," he muttered.

Fear seized his heart when he glanced to his left. "Sweet Danu—*nae!*" Lachlan held a blade at Aileen's throat, glaring at him.

Fury blinded him as he jumped down in rage to attack. Blocking his path, Manus landed a blow to his jaw, sending him back to the ground. Shaking his head, he spat out blood. It only infuriated him further.

Lachlan's laughter filled his ears. "I think I will let your woman watch ye die at the hands of Manus."

Stephen lunged forward only to be greeted with a kick to the face. Manus took his time with each blow, landing several onto his back. Then he took a slice out of his arm, blood gushing forth.

Lachlan sneered. "Do not think of calling forth your powers, either, or I will place the blade deeper into her neck."

"You bastard," Aileen muttered.

"Release her, *now*," growled Aidan, behind Lachlan. He had a blade leveled against the side of his neck.

His lip curled in disgust as he let go of Aileen.

Aidan took Aileen into his arms, never taking his eyes off Lachlan. "As much as I want to take your life, I made a promise to one of the Dragon Knights that you were his."

Lachlan laughed. "Well, if ye mean *that* Dragon Knight over there, I believe his life is about to end."

Both Aidan and Aileen looked to where Stephen lay bloodied. Manus had continued to beat him, and blood pooled all around him.

Aidan's brief glance away was all Lachlan required. Taking his dirk, he deftly stepped around Aidan, plunging it into his side. Removing it, he walked over to Stephen. As he raised his hands high, he shouted, "I have killed the great Fenian Warrior and now watch as your Dragon Knight dies, too!"

"*Nooo,*" screamed Aileen, clutching her father as he fell to the ground.

Out of the shadows, emerged Liam. He was bloodied and without his plaid, but immediately went to Aidan. "God's teeth!" he hissed.

"Aileen," blurted out Aidan. "You must...*leave.*"

Liam started tearing at Aileen's gown, pressing the pieces into his side to stanch the flow of blood. "Don't talk, Aidan. Aileen, hold these to his side and use your healing to stop the flow. I'll go help Stephen."

She nodded, but no sooner did she press her hand against the wound than blood gushed out. Summoning all of her will, she pulled forth her healing powers, letting the energy move from her body into her fathers.

Her father groaned. "Wound...too severe. Stop, Aileen."

"Liam," she pleaded, the blood soaking her hands and ground. "I can't heal him."

"Shit!" Liam halted mid-stride and turned back. Glancing back at Stephen, he saw that he was gazing directly at him.

"Your...vow," croaked Stephen.

Liam bent down. "Aidan, we must go. Do you understand, my brother? We don't have much time."

His eyes were closed, but he opened them when he heard Liam's words.

Confusion filled Aileen. "How can we *go*?" she demanded. "Go help Stephen. I will find someone to help me." Looking back at her father, she swallowed. "Stay with me, Dad." She tore more material from her dress and pressed it against his side.

Slowly, Liam stood. "I am sorry, Aileen." He stretched out his arms, chanting words of an ancient language beyond time.

Aileen snapped her head up. Understanding flared within her. "No, no, Liam. We can't go," she sobbed. Casting her gaze back at Stephen, she watched in horror as the man continued to beat him, Lachlan's laughter filling her ears.

Tears streamed down her face.

It was beginning. Trapped in a void, Aileen saw the lights spiraling around them with Liam's voice becoming louder, calling forth the power. Panic seized her. "*Stephen*." Her voice raw, her fingers reaching out to him.

When her vision started to blur, Aileen noticed Stephen was watching her. As her mind started to fade, and the world became black, she thought she heard him say...*Forever, leannan*.

Chapter Forty

"When you have crossed several life paths within the veil, your reality will be skewed."

A gentle breeze brushed across Aileen's face and with it the salty tang of the ocean. The sounds of seagulls filtered through her hearing, making her long for oblivion. Yet, it was the moan of someone near that jolted her fully awake. Blinking several times, she tried sitting up. Dizziness flooded her, and she took several deep breaths. A warm hand touched her shoulder.

"Aileen, I need your help," said Liam, his voice low but urgent.

"Dad," she muttered. Opening her eyes, she quickly shielded them from the sun with her hand. "Where is he?"

"To your left. Try to keep him from passing out. I'm going for help." She closed her eyes again, and he put another hand on her shoulder, shaking her. "Do you hear me?"

Smacking his hand away, she opened her eyes and gritted her teeth as she made her way over to her father. "Go," she snapped.

Liam immediately took off running down the hill toward the abbey.

"*Please, Dad,* open your eyes for me," she pleaded, stroking the hair from his face. Looking down she noticed the blood continued to flow but not as much as before. Tearing more fabric from her gown, she placed it against his wound.

He groaned instantly, his face ashen. His eyes fluttered open, and he gave Aileen a weak smile. "Home?" he whispered.

How could she possibly tell him this was not her home? "Yes, Dad, you're home. I need you to stay with me." She swallowed, watching his features twist in agony.

"Aye, daughter. What shall...we talk about? How I met your mother?"

"Yes. Tell me the story again," she said softly.

"Well, your mother was a bonny lass when my eyes..." Her dad wheezed, choking now on blood.

"Here, let me wipe your mouth." She tried to keep her voice steady. Realizing her father was near death, Aileen cradled his head in her lap.

"Have I told you how much I love you for the sacrifice you made? You gave up everything for her."

He opened his eyes, smiling up at her. "*For love.*" His eyes gave a far off look, remembering.

She only nodded, letting her tears drop onto his face. "Hold on, Dad. Liam is bringing help, and then when you are better, you can tell me more stories of Mom."

With great effort, he brought his hand up to Aileen's face. "Find a way to go back...to Stephen." He coughed again.

"We can talk about that later. Besides, I thought you didn't like him." She glanced down again. This time her legs were stained with her father's life blood. *Hurry, Liam!*

"Aileen"—his voice barely a whisper—"I gi...*give* my blessing."

Fear gripped her heart. "Shhh, Dad. It's my turn to talk about how I first met Stephen." She trembled as she put her arm around him. "He was in pain and wouldn't let me touch him, thinking I was a fae healer. Imagine, me not knowing I was part fae." She glanced down and noticed his eyes were closed. "Dad, are you *listening*?"

Then the smell of honeysuckle floated past Aileen.

"*Dad*?" she choked out, instantly realizing her father was no longer breathing.

Her mother had come for him.

"*Nooo!*" she screamed. "You can't leave me!" Great sobs racked her body as she rocked back and forth holding his lifeless body.

****

When Liam approached, he dropped down to the ground on his knees, staring in disbelief.

The great Fenian Warrior, Aidan Kerrigan, was dead.

Aileen's grief tore at him. He had failed not only his brother, but her, too. Reaching out, he placed a hand on hers. "I'm sorry," he uttered softly.

Eyes that blazed with fury, glared up at him. Snatching her hand back from his, she hissed, "This is all *your* fault. He would still be alive if you had not brought him back through the veil."

Liam held his tongue. She was partially correct. However, now was not the time to tell her.

"Let us take him down off the hill," he said.

"Don't touch him," she shrieked. "You are not worthy."

Clenching his jaw, he only nodded. Then turning to two men, Liam motioned for them to take Aidan.

Watching as they gently lifted her father from her lap, he spoke quietly to the men, instructing them to take the body to Balleycove. He would see to all the arrangements. Glancing back at Aileen, she kept staring at her hands, now covered in blood.

When Liam went to reach for her, she scooted away. Pushing herself off the ground, she knotted her fists at her sides. "Take me back," she demanded.

Liam frowned. "Back? To Stephen?"

"Yes!"

He closed his eyes, inhaling deeply. "I can't."

"You can't or you *won't*? He needs our help. We can't just leave him." She pounded her fist against her chest. "My *life* is back with him, and I won't let him die!"

Liam moved closer to her. "Aileen, if I could, I would send you back. But I *can't*."

She slapped Liam hard across the face.

Staring at her, he knew his eyes had shifted colors by her indrawn breath. Taking a step back, he started down the hill.

"*Why*?" she asked as tears streamed down her face.

Liam half turned toward her, his jaw clenched. "The truth? Because the moment we stepped back through the veil, the fae stripped me of all my powers." Spreading out his hands wide, he looked fully at her. "I am now earthbound. The same as your father."

Walking over to him, she shook her head sadly. "You are *nothing* like my father."

****

End this. It was his only thought as Stephen tried in

vain to block out the pain. Each time he tried to fight back, the man would beat him back to the ground. Trying to swipe the blood from his eyes, he tried to roll from the next blow.

He was going to die.

In truth, it did not matter anymore. His soul died the moment Aileen passed through the veil. All that was left was his body.

Just take a sword through my heart, for it is already gone.

Stephen closed his eyes and waited for the final strike. Dirt and blood filled his mouth, and he dug his hands into the ground. His mind drifted, letting the memories of Aileen flood his senses. He could not tell if it was blood or tears that streaked his face. In his last conscious moment, Stephen thanked the fae for sending him Aileen.

Then his world went black.

Chapter Forty-One

"A human heart can stand only so much pain, but a fae heart can only hold a drop."

The voices called out to him, but he kept on moving. He did not want to return. There was nothing there, and this other place beckoned to him with its dazzling lights and sounds. Hearing the chime of bells, he smiled. Then again, the other voice yelled at him. It was familiar, but he could not summon up whom it belonged to. Half-turning, he tried to remember.

The warmth of the lights lured him and turning to go through, he was instantly thrown into a cold, dark abyss.

"Wake, by God, Stephen! Do ye hear me!" roared Duncan, dousing him with a bucket of water.

Sputtering and choking on the water, Stephen groaned, heaving to the side.

Another bucket of water assaulted him, and Stephen waved his hand weakly at him. "Enough," he coughed hoarsely.

"By the Gods, I thought ye dead, brother," rasped Duncan, bending over him.

"Almost," Stephen whispered.

A great cry burst forth, and Duncan went to reach for his sword, only to find it some distance away in the back of Manus.

Lachlan was charging forth, sword extended with a crazed look on his face.

Fearing for his brother's safety, Duncan stood directly over Stephen ready to defend him to the death with only his bare hands.

Lachlan never had a chance. The blow to his head knocked him to the ground. A burning torch had felled him, splinters of the wood burning into the side of his face.

"What the bloody hell? Can someone account for this battle?" roared the man, eyes blazing with anger.

Duncan's mouth dropped open. Scotland's king stood before them. He knelt. "Greetings, Sire."

Stephen tried to raise his head, one eye already swollen shut. "*King William?*" he gasped.

"Who are ye and explain this madness?" His tone had an edge of steel.

"Sire, I am Duncan MacKay, and this is my brother, Stephen, who requires..."

King William held up his hand to silence Duncan. "For the love of God, Stephen?" He brushed past Duncan and stooped down next to Stephen.

"Bring me the healer," he bellowed.

"Sire…"

"Do not try to speak." Looking over his shoulder, he roared, "Healer!"

"Coming, Sire." A short, stout man pushed through the others, gasping for breath. "There are many wounded."

The king stood, directing his other men to bring forth a litter. Waving a hand to motion Duncan toward him, he asked, "Before ye tell what has befallen, who is this devil?"

Duncan glanced at Lachlan, afraid he would somehow disappear again. "This is the druid, Lachlan."

His eyes narrowed. "A druid burning his own people? For what reason would this serve?"

"His cause has been unclear until recently." Duncan paused, waiting. How much could he divulge to his king?

"Continue," demanded King William.

"He claimed to be obeying orders from Bishop Augustus. Stephen told me Rome sent the bishop and his men to rid Arbroath of the heathens. The villagers feared for their lives, and fled the town. Lachlan pursued them with his men."

King William ran a hand through his thick beard in thought. "Has this druid found the one God? What is his involvement with this bishop?"

"Nae. His intent was to use the bishop and his guards to further his own shrewd plans."

"Pray tell me."

Duncan reached down and retrieved Stephen's relic. Wiping the mud from it, he rubbed his thumb over the stone. Raising his head, he said, "To take the Dragon Knight relics to seize their power."

"By the rood! Monsters, all of them! Whoever this bishop is, I ken he has no orders from Rome. They are his alone, and I vow to send him back for the Pope to deal with his treachery." King William barked out orders to take Lachlan into custody, regardless of his injury.

"Sire, this druid has become verra powerful. I would suggest…" Duncan hesitated.

"Do not fear, he will not live much longer," the king sneered.

William glanced at the stone in Duncan's hand. "So the Dragon Knights have returned?"

"Aye," interjected Stephen. "In truth, we serve ye, Sire, too." He wheezed, spitting out blood.

King William roared with laughter. "Stephen, ye should have become a counselor." Taking a more serious tone, he added, "I could use ye at Arbroath Abbey to help rebuild."

Duncan held his breath, fearing he would lose his brother again.

Shaking his head slowly, Stephen winced from the pain. "Nae. Duncan and I must locate our other two brothers and restore Urquhart." Coughing again, he fought to find his breath. "It would be a boon, Sire."

"Agreed," replied the king.

"Please sir, ye must remain still," demanded the healer, attempting to cleanse Stephen's wounds.

Duncan's chest swelled. Striding over to the water, he dipped the stone into the water, removing the last traces of mud. Standing, he went and placed it over his brother's head. Gently placing his hand on his shoulder, he whispered, "It is good to have ye back."

Keeping his eyes closed, Stephen grunted.

Brother Osgar shuffled forward. "Sweet Brigid," he muttered when he saw Stephen. Noticing the king, he bowed his head. "Sire, it is good ye have found us."

"Indeed. Brother Osgar, let us convene elsewhere. Where are the others?"

"The women and children are safe beyond the trees. They are tending to the injured."

"Good," he said solemnly.

Before leaving, King William turned and looked at Stephen. "There is a belief among the druids and monks that both can work together. For this reason, I set the founding stone for Arbroath Abbey in a pagan village, so the two would become one—as our *one* God. This"—he waved his hand about—"was not my intention. I give ye my word, I will set this right."

The king then held out his arm, and Duncan understanding his meaning, grasped his forearm. "See that your brother mends, Duncan. When all the Dragon Knights return to Urquhart, I will pay a visit."

Duncan smiled. "On that day, we will be honored to welcome our king."

Giving him a quick nod, the king motioned for Osgar and his men, departing for the trees.

"Where do ye want us to take him?" asked the healer.

"With the others, and then we will proceed into the main village at dawn. The less we move him, the better."

Duncan watched as they carefully placed Stephen on the litter, concerned not for his physical wounds, for those would heal in time. However, the ones which could not be seen would never heal.

Quickly scanning the ground, he spotted the one last item he needed to recover before departing. Rolling over the dead body of Manus, he retrieved his sword. Taking it to the water, he washed off the blood. When the last remnants of the battle had been removed, Duncan said a silent plea to the fae to help heal his brother.

****

The new dawn brought renewed energy to everyone. For the first time in days, laughter rang out and children played. Many had been injured, but for the most part, all was well. Duncan's concern was for Stephen. He sustained major injuries, and he dreaded his brother would never be the same.

King William had departed before dawn, taking Lachlan with him. The druid had awoken, screaming foul curses at them until the king ordered him gagged. Again, Duncan warned the king this man was capable of dark magic and to be on guard. Heeding Duncan's warning, he placed a crucifix around the druid's neck as if to would ward off the evil. If it were only that simple, he thought.

The druids returned during the early hours before dawn. However, on hearing the news regarding Lachlan they were hesitant to rejoice. They reckoned this would not be the last they heard of Lachlan. His power may have been diminished with their help, yet they feared he could regain it at anytime.

Ian skidded to a halt before Duncan. "It is good to have ye here for Sir Stephen. I ken he will need ye for the rest of his quest."

He grimaced. "His quest is over, Ian."

Ian tilted his head to the side, frowning. "Just because ye cannot see the way does not mean the path is closed."

Duncan reeled back unable to comprehend the lad's words. Ian gave him a wide smile and ran off.

"I see ye have met the next Master Druid," stated Cathal, moving toward Duncan.

Duncan rubbed a hand over his weary face. "Truth?"

"Aye. Did ye ken his mother is my niece?"

"Stephen told me. So why am I not surprised the lad is meant for greatness." Duncan smirked. Though he may be kin to Cathal, he believed young Ian would go beyond his great-uncle in wisdom and power.

"I've just seen Stephen," said Cathal. "He is in great pain, though his wounds will heal in time. I would advise waiting for a week or two, until ye depart for Urquhart.

"I agree, though I fear some of his injuries will never heal," replied Duncan keeping his gaze on the children playing.

Cathal frowned. "Why did he send her back? Have ye asked him?"

"Nae. All he told me was he ordered Liam to take her and Aidan back. It appears Aidan was severely injured."

Cathal stiffened. "Ordered? Could he have feared for their lives?"

Shrugging, Duncan said, "Cannae say."

Remembering the night Brigid died in his arms, he glanced at Cathal. "I would have done the same."

"True, but the Guardian did bring her back."

"Sweet Danu," muttered Duncan. "Do ye think *she* would do the same for Stephen?"

Lowering his head, Cathal closed his eyes. When he finally opened them, he leaned onto his staff. "Nae, for Aileen did not pass into the realm near *Tir na Og*. She was taken back to her own time."

Duncan's eyes narrowed. "How do ye ken this?"

"Because the Fenian Warrior broke the fae law by bringing her father through the veil. He was not under his protection, his daughter was," interrupted Betha.

"Och, child, why are ye up?" Cathal went and placed an arm around her shoulder. "Ye should be resting."

317

"I am fine," Betha said curtly.

Cathal took a step back. "If what ye say is true, then this warrior will be swiftly dealt with by the fae."

"In truth, Stephen understood the risk," she snapped, walking away.

Duncan crossed his arms over his chest. "Is her mood always thus?"

Cathal stroked his beard in thought. "Nae."

"I think I will check on my brother. Coming?"

The druid nodded his head in agreement and the two wandered over to where Stephen lay. The litter had been placed away from the rest of the group, fearing he required peace after losing Aileen.

Word spread throughout the people that Lady Aileen and her father were taken away by the fae. Her loss affected everyone she touched. Some of the children started gathering flowers to mark the spot where she left.

He looked like hell, thought Duncan, approaching his brother. His face mirrored the battle he fought. One eye still swollen shut, and bruises marred his entire face. His nose definitely had been broken, and a few ribs, as well. The healer had stitched the gaping wound in his leg and arm, noting his concern for his inner injuries, wanting to bleed Stephen, but Duncan forbade it.

What troubled Duncan the most was Stephen's eyes carried a hollow emptiness—void of all emotion, except one. Grief.

He saw Cathal leaning back against the tree, giving them some time alone.

Taking a cup off the stump of a tree, Duncan poured some water into it. It would not have been his first choice, but his brother favored it. "Here, drink."

Stephen took a few sips before shoving it away.

Placing the cup back down, Duncan sat down next to him. "Why did ye send back Aileen, Stephen?" he asked softly.

Moments passed in silence, and Duncan feared he would never answer.

Swallowing, Stephen replied, "If her life was in danger and there was no chance. Liam would return her to her time. Aidan was dying, that I ken, and Lachlan would have surely killed her. There is more, but 'tis a long story."

"Short account, then."

Stephen sighed. "Aileen's mother had a vision before she was born seeing her death here in Scotland. That is why her parents kept her heritage from her. To keep her safe. She came through the veil on her own, not understanding she was part fae."

Duncan placed a hand gently on his shoulder. "Ye do grasp Liam will pay a price for taking them back."

Stephen snorted, then winced at the movement. "His life was forfeit when he brought her father through the veil."

Duncan's shoulders slumped. He had no great love for the Fenian Warriors, but Liam's actions might have earned him a death sentence. The fae laws were strict, especially between the warriors who were also travelers within the veil.

Betha strolled over, bringing some broth. Shoving it at Duncan, she stated, "Try to get him to drink some of this. It will help in the healing."

Before leaving, she glared at Stephen. "What troubles me about all of this is ye did not ask her how she felt about your choice. Ye have been planning this all along without her knowledge and for that, Stephen MacKay, I will be angry at ye *for Aileen*."

"At least she's safe," he muttered.

"Aye, that she may be, but her heart will not be the same. Did ye ever take that into account when ye made your fine plans with Liam?"

He did not answer her.

"I thought not." She snorted and walked away.

No, he didn't think of her heart *or* his. Only what had to be done. If his pain was this harsh, what could she be going through?

Och, my leannan, forgive me.

Chapter Forty-Two

"There is always a choice, always a light, always another way to find the correct path. But will it truly be the best?"

Aileen pushed open the massive front doors to Balleycove. Memories of the last time she fled this place caused her to place her hand over her chest, trying to ease the heavy ache. She remained as long as possible at the abbey, dreading to return. Instead, she stayed at the inn near the abbey until she felt strong enough to pass through these doors. This world had become a blur of noises and smells that were unfamiliar to her.

Liam had seen to the arrangements for her father's remains and within hours, her aunt came, bringing everyone else. Her shields came crashing down the moment she returned to this time. She couldn't bring herself to cry in front of them, her grief too overwhelming. She had lost the only two men she would ever love all in one day.

The not knowing if Stephen lived or died ate at her insides every day. Did he, didn't he? It was her constant question. After the fifth day, she made the decision to come back here in hopes of going through her father's books to find out anything on the Dragon Knights, especially Stephen.

Breathing deeply, she stepped inside. Flower arrangements were displayed everywhere with notes from those who sent their condolences.

Hugging her arms around herself, she vowed not to cry today. Her throat was raw and glancing in the entry mirror, she noticed how swollen and red her eyes were. Looking at herself, she did not recognize the person staring back at her. Gone was the tattered gown. In its place was a long dress with her jacket over it. For the rest of her life, she would never put on a pair of jeans.

Emptiness resided in the place that once held her heart.

Slowly walking to the great hall, Aileen paused at the entrance. "Oh Stephen, there you are." Her steps quickened as she made her way toward the tapestry.

With a trembling hand, she reached out and glided her hand over the depiction of *her Dragon Knight*. "It hurts *so* much." Leaning her head against the tapestry, the tears leaked out, falling freely down her face.

"What can I do?"

"Nothing, Aunt Lily." She choked on the word. "Did Liam explain it all?"

"Yes. Not only did you lose your father, but Stephen, too. And that great magic was involved."

Aileen didn't even bother to look up at her aunt. "I'm sure he left out that this is *his* fault."

"After hearing everything, I don't believe it is. Surely in time you will see the same."

"See? What I *see* is two men I loved dearly are now dead." Her tone sarcastic.

Her aunt didn't respond. She quietly left, leaving Aileen in tears.

****

Several weeks passed, and Aileen refused to eat, sleeping very little, and spending most of her days at the ocean.

"Did she eat her breakfast," asked Lily, watching Gwen pull out another batch of cranberry and orange scones from the oven.

Gwen tossed down her mitt, and shook her head. "If you consider a nibble, then yes. She did drink all of her tea, and then said she was going to her dad's workroom for the day. I'm worried, Lily."

"As am I," sighed Lily. "We all understand that grief affects us all differently. Not only did she watch her father die in her arms, she lost the man she loved— all while fighting a horrific battle."

"Has she spoken of that night?" Gwen asked, taking a sip of her tea.

"No," she answered, picking up a mug and pouring some coffee into it. "I don't want to press her, but I fear if she doesn't..." Lily couldn't finish. "She roams the castle at night and the ocean by day, as silent as a ghost."

"She's just a shell of herself." Concern filled Gwen's voice. "What can we do?"

Lily shrugged. "Watch, wait, and perhaps one day when she is ready, she will talk to one of us."

The front doors opened, and then Aileen strolled by the kitchen. "Would you like me to fix you something?" Gwen asked.

"No." Seeing the crestfallen look on her friend's face, Aileen tried to give her a weak smile. "Thank you. I'll let you know if I do. Do you know where I can find Liam?" She was hesitant to ask, since she had been avoiding him since her return.

"He's in the library with the attorney. Remember, today's the day he's bringing the documents of your father's will."

Aunt Lily emerged from the kitchen and stood next to Aileen. "I believe it would be best if you were present."

Aileen closed her eyes. "I had forgotten." Opening them, she asked, "Does it matter? I already know what it states. He left everything to me."

"Then I'll tell Liam you wish not to be present." Her aunt started to move down the hall, but Aileen grasped her hand.

"You're right. I should be there, not Liam. I need to talk to him anyway about the abbey." Releasing her hand, she started for the library.

"Aileen." Her aunt's tone held a warning.

She paused, realizing her aunt understood what she meant about the abbey. Glancing back over her shoulder, she replied, "I have to check again for the door. It can't have disappeared. I've got to find a way."

"Did it ever occur to you that you were only supposed to see it on that particular day?"

Aileen was desperate to try again—even to ask Liam to assist in her search. She had to return. Nothing *felt* right in this time. She did not answer her aunt, but continued down the hall to the library.

When she got there, she placed her hand on the handle. This was her father's library, a room he loved. Taking a deep breath, she opened it and stepped in. Both men stood as she entered.

"Good afternoon, Mr. Kenny."

"Miss Kerrigan, I am so sorry for your loss. Your father was a dear friend."

"Thank you."

Liam gave her a small smile, but she turned away from him taking a seat next to Mr. Kenny. "Please, I want to conclude our business quickly. My father had spoken to me about his will, so you don't have to go into any great details."

"Yes, of course." Mr. Kenny shuffled through his briefcase and pulled out the documents. "This is his will, in which you understand he has left his entire estate, including property in Ireland, to you."

Aileen frowned. "Ireland? I had no idea."

Mr. Kenney blanched. "Oh, I'm sorry. I thought he told you. Well, it's located in the Cuilcagh Mountains, near the River Shannon."

Aileen kept her hands folded on her lap, trying hard not to scream. What more didn't she know about her father?

Liam sat down across from her and placed his hands on his knees. "Your father was from Ireland, but chose to reside here with your mother when they got married."

She glared at him.

"Please continue, Mr. Kenny," said Aileen, trying to keep her voice steady.

"There is a clause he had me draft over a month ago. In the event you were unable to take control of his estates, he bequeathed all to the Society of the Thistle with a provision that Liam MacGregor would remain at Balleycove as the estate manager."

Aileen was confused. Did her father think she wouldn't return, for fear of her death? Or was there more? Did it really matter now? She was stuck here *forever*.

She had not realized Mr. Kenny was silent, waiting for her to respond. "Well, since I'm here"—she glanced briefly at Liam—"I will be taking full control and don't require Mr. MacGregor's assistance."

Mr. Kenny coughed. "I'm afraid Miss Kerrigan that part of the additional clause does include Mr. MacGregor as estate manager, regardless if you are in charge or not."

Aileen's eyes went wide. "You're kidding?"

"I don't jest, Miss Kerrigan," he replied.

"Is there anything else?"

Digging in his briefcase, Mr. Kenny pulled out an envelope. "This is for you."

She stared at the envelope. Reaching out tentatively, she took it from him. "Thank you. Is that all?"

"Yes. Your father's last request was his ashes be taken to the Great Glen and released into Loch Ness along with your mother's ashes."

Aileen swallowed. So, he didn't want to return to Ireland. Clenching the envelope, she stood. "If that is all, I'm sure Liam can show you out."

He stood abruptly. "Again, Miss Kerrigan, I am truly sorry for your loss."

She bit her lower lip and only nodded. Without glancing at Liam, Aileen walked out of the library. Even her father's final instructions had been made without her knowledge. Her entire life was one where her paths were chosen not by her, but by others.

She wanted to scream at them. Hysterical laughter bubbled forth, and she ran out the front door.

Clearing the estate, she roamed up the hill to get a view of the ocean. Breathing hard, she paused. "What good would yelling do, when you're all dead!"

Slumping down on the ground, the melancholy returned cloaking her and seeping into her veins. It was Aileen's constant companion.

With hands that shook, she opened the envelope and withdrew the letter.

My dearest Aileen...

I know you can never forgive us—your mother and I, for the life we kept from you and that is as it should be. Would we do the same? Perhaps...We loved you fiercely and the moment your mother had her vision, plans were formulated for your protection.

There will come a time in your life, and I pray it will be so, that you will have children. On that day, you will empathize.

I do not know where your path may lead, but if you are reading this then I can only assume it was necessary for you to return to your own time.

If it is not what you want, recall Aileen that you have the power of the fae in your blood. Seek your own path and follow your destiny. There is a reason why I put Liam in charge of running the estate.

Live the life you want, Aileen.

With love,

Your father

Her eyes clouded with unshed tears. Brushing her hands over the words, she wanted to somehow absorb something from the man who wrote them. "I wish...what do I really wish?" It was a question for which Aileen already knew the answer.

"How can I seek my own path when I can't return there? Answer me that, Dad."

Chapter Forty-Three

"Once love is given freely and lost, death may soon follow." ~Stephen MacKay, as told to the Guardian

The breeze was warm on the first day of June. Birdsong filled the air and flowers blanketed the ground. A young doe skittered past its mother with a playfulness that was full of innocence.

Yet, Stephen took no joy from the day or the scene in the distance. His wounds were healing, and they would soon depart for Urquhart. He had wanted to leave days ago, but Cathal insisted a few more days would serve him best. The druid had no idea his other wound would never heal. There was an emptiness within his soul he tried to seal, but it opened each day with just a simple thought. *Aileen.*

Her loss consumed him.

"Are ye ready, brother?" Duncan wandered forth, bringing their horses.

"Aye." Heaving himself up onto his horse, he was relieved to depart. This place contained far too many memories. By chance, some distance and home would ease the ache.

"We're ready," bellowed Duncan in the direction of a group of druids.

Frowning and shielding his eyes, Stephen asked, "Druids?"

Duncan kept his gaze forward. "Yes, Cathal is joining us."

Stephen saw Osgar standing apart, speaking with Ian. "If ye do not mind, I would like to say my farewells to Osgar."

His brother nodded.

Riding over to Osgar, he saw the man look up in surprise. Dismounting carefully, he smiled at him.

"So, ye take your leave to return to Urquhart?" Osgar asked, then added, "Ye will be missed, Stephen."

"As I shall miss ye, too, my friend. Ye gave me a home when I had none."

"And it will always remain a place if ye should ever decide to return. I am departing with Betha and Donal to Arbroath."

"I thought perhaps ye might."

Osgar frowned slightly. "I fear I must now."

"Why is that?"

"King William has put me in charge of the abbey. I cannot deny my king, especially one who helped us here."

Stephen smirked. "Ye could have said *no*."

"In truth, I ken it is my path. To help others find the light in both worlds—pagan and the new religion. The world is changing, Stephen. If I am used as a tool to forge a life for someone, then so be it." Osgar glanced down at Ian and placed a hand on his shoulder. "Both paths are joined by the one true light. *Love*."

"Peace be with ye, Brother Osgar," said Stephen, embracing him.

"And *peace* be with ye, Stephen."

Then Stephen knelt before Ian. "Ye ken ye are welcome at Urquhart anytime."

Ian flung himself into Stephen's arms. "I will miss ye the most, Sir Stephen. Promise ye will come for a visit?"

Stephen held him tight. "I promise." Releasing him, he asked, "When will the druids come for ye?"

"On my twelfth summer," Ian stated proudly.

"Then if I may ask, let me escort ye to them."

"I would be honored, Sir Stephen," beamed Ian.

Stephen stood and mounted Grian. "Be safe my friends."

He had only gone a few paces before he heard Ian shouting at him. Halting Grian, he waited until the lad ran forth.

"What is it Ian?"

"The light ye seek is at the gate."

Gazing into eyes that held an old soul, he frowned. "*What*?"

Ian shrugged, then scampered off.

Rubbing a hand across his bearded face, he shook his head. "Druids and their riddles. Let's leave this place, Grian." Giving the horse a nudge, they took off in search of Duncan.

Stephen saw him near a copse with Cathal and the look on his face was deadly. They had not even departed and trouble was brewing? Stephen clenched his jaw in frustration.

Reining his horse near the group, he blurted out, "Is there a problem, Duncan?"

Obviously there was, because Patrick MacFhearguis was on the other side, placing items on his horse. Duncan may have made peace with this one, but he still had his doubts.

"Would ye care to tell my brother what ye just told

me," growled Duncan.

Patrick sighed. "As I've stated before, though we have all come to an agreement regarding Lachlan, Michael is still intent on either getting a hold of the relics, Urquhart, *or both*."

Duncan crossed his arms across his chest and glared at Patrick. "Oh, but ye have saved the best for last, and why ye did not tell me before is a question I would like answered."

Instinctively, Stephen placed his hand on his sword. "Finish, MacFhearguis."

Patrick held Stephen's gaze. "My loyalty will always be with my laird, no matter how I may disagree."

"Out with it!" snapped Stephen.

"Michael took a group of men several days after I left with Duncan. They were headed to Urquhart."

"Bloody hell!" roared Stephen, lunging at Patrick.

Duncan interceded, blocking his path and holding him back. His eyes, which just moments before held fury, now held mirth. Stephen bit back a retort.

"No more violence, for now," said Duncan quietly.

His brother was not telling him everything.

Duncan turned and faced Patrick. "Should we take ye hostage until we arrive at Urquhart?"

Patrick stared angrily at him. "If that is what it will take to prove my loyalty to ye, then here." Thrusting out his hands at Duncan, he added, "I am yours."

Silence ensued.

"I think it best ye return to your home, Patrick. I do not fear your brother, since I would never leave my wife and Urquhart unguarded."

Patrick's eyes narrowed. "Ye knew?"

Shaking his head, Duncan answered, "Nae. Yet, I would not leave them alone—undefended." Grasping his shoulder, he looked into his eyes. "Go home. I ken Michael is your laird and brother, but watch him closely. Evil still lurks in his heart, and I do not know how far Lachlan's grasp extends."

"In truth, he had Alex with him. I made him vow to watch our brother and make sure no harm came to anyone at Urquhart." He rubbed a hand across the back of his neck. "Michael is seeking knowledge about Adam."

"He still believes we might have been involved." Duncan looked at Stephen. "I ken the feeling, so I will let the matter pass. Tell him that, for if I find he is on our land without a summons, I will not be to blame for what happens to him."

Patrick nodded in understanding. "Will ye help us find Adam?"

"Aye. I will ask Cormac Murray and the others to start spreading the word. Yet, my first interest is finding *my* brothers."

"As it should be," stated Patrick. Giving a brief glance at Stephen, he turned to leave.

"Safe journey, Patrick," spoke Cathal, and then added, "I will ask the other druids if they can lend a hand in your search of Adam. That is, if ye will allow us."

"Any help would do. Thank ye."

Stephen eyed him skeptically as he walked away. "Adam did not die that night?"

Duncan tensed. "Nae. His injuries were severe. Six moons after he healed, he left without a word. They feared he had sought vengeance with one of us and

333

died."

"'Tis madness," spat Stephen.

"'Tis Lachlan's doing," muttered Cathal.

Stephen's gut twisted at the mention of the druid. Memories of that night sliced through his mind. "Let us leave this place."

"Aye, brother."

****

It took them a day longer to reach Urquhart due to Stephen's injuries. Of all the brothers, he healed the quickest, but not this time. Cathal had mentioned to Duncan that perhaps he was prolonging the pain in order not to feel the one in his heart. Duncan assured him that once he was back at Urquhart, he would regain his strength.

However, his heart was another matter.

Passing through and over the ridge, he waited until Stephen caught up. By the Gods, his brother looked like he had aged a decade. He had refused to shave, as was his normal custom, and let his hair grow. Dark hollows were under his eyes, and he had hardly eaten on their journey. Duncan did not recognize the man in front of him.

"We are home, brother," said Duncan, giving him a smile.

"It is good," whispered Stephen.

As soon as they passed through the portcullis, Nell came screaming forth, followed by her faithful companion, Cuchulainn. The dog never left her side.

Duncan spotted Finn trudging along. He had only been gone a month, but he swore the lad had grown another foot. Dismounting, he gathered Nell into his arms.

"Och, Father, we missed ye," gushed Nell.

Duncan smiled. "As I did with ye, little lady." Placing her down, he hugged Finn, ruffling his hair.

Stephen sat on Grian his mouth gaped open.

Observing the shocked expression on his brother's face, he placed a hand on each child's shoulder, saying, "Stephen, this is Finn and Nell. My children."

"This is your brother, *Sir Stephen*?" exclaimed Nell.

Duncan's smile grew wide. "Aye."

Finn's eyes went round. "Truth?"

The laughter that burst forth from Duncan startled Stephen. He could not remember the last time he had seen his brother laugh, or even *embrace* a child.

"*Children*?" Stephen croaked.

"Duncan!"

Duncan turned and the sight that greeted him was one he would never forget. The woman had the most untamed mass of reddish curls he had ever seen. And eyes for only him. He glanced at Stephen, whose mouth gaped open in shock. Chuckling, he said, "We have much to discuss brother," barely getting the words out before Brigid ran into his arms.

"Damn, I've missed ye," she murmured right before Duncan gave her a searing kiss.

Breaking from the kiss, Duncan caught Stephen's gaze and noticed his brother was still on his horse. "Would ye care to dismount from that beast and greet my wife?"

Now it was Brigid's turn to gape at Stephen. "Which one?"

Remembering some sense of dignity, Stephen got off his horse. "I am Stephen, my lady."

Brigid's smile warmed him. "Please, call me Brigid. Welcome home, Stephen." She stepped forward and embraced him.

It was as if she cast a spell over him. Without realizing it, Stephen was smiling. "Thank ye. It is good to be back."

"Finn will take care of Grian. Shall we?" Duncan waved for Stephen to go forth sensing his unease. His first visit back was filled with the last time they had left the place. Anger and fear had seeped into each of them ending in a night which changed their lives forever.

Several children ran past Stephen, and he glanced their way. "There are some who are familiar and new faces. Ye have been busy, brother."

"Would ye like to see my family, Sir Stephen?"

He looked down at the lass. "Nell, is it?"

She beamed a smile. "Aye."

"Call me Stephen, Nell. Your *family*?" he asked in confusion.

"Nell..." Brigid stood with her hands on her hips, her head angled. "Remember what we told you about Stephen. Let him bathe and eat, then you can take him to meet your family."

Her shoulders slumped. "Aye, I will wait. But he has not given me an answer." She pivoted her head up to look at him. "Will ye?"

Stephen nodded his head in agreement, though a frown marred his features.

Giving his hand a firm squeeze, she ran off.

"Family?" he replied mystified.

Brigid smiled. "Her family consists of many misfit and injured animals. She has a gift when it comes to animals, and they adore her. Duncan actually built a special enclosure for them when we returned early in the spring."

"Ye were away?" he asked.

"We stayed with Cormac Murray at Castle Creag during the winter months. I was recovering from injuries and could not travel far."

"Lachlan." His voice strained.

She only nodded. Walking over to him, her frown was replaced with a smile. "I asked that the tub be brought into your room, and they're filling it as we speak."

Holding up his hand, he responded, "Nae, it will not be required. I will go down to the loch."

"But it's no trouble, since we keep it in our room..." Her words trailed off, followed by a blush staining her cheeks.

"In truth, I have never required a tub for bathing."

Duncan coughed, and Brigid turned around. Gathering her around his waist, he brought her close to him. "Stephen has the gift of water. He can have heated water anytime," he smirked.

Her eyes grew wide. "You can control the temperature of the water, as Duncan can do with the wind. *Fascinating*."

"I will gather some clothing before going down to the loch." Making his way past them, Stephen paused. Taking a step back toward Brigid, he grasped her hand and placed a kiss along her fingers. "I thank ye for the love ye have brought to my brother's heart," he said softly.

When he finally walked away, Duncan and Brigid stood in silence. Brigid moved and laid her head against his chest. "He is not the brother I ken." His tone was one filled with sorrow.

She hugged him fiercely, "Is this how you were...in the beginning?"

"Aye," he whispered.

Looking up into his face, she brushed a lock of hair from his eyes. "Oh Duncan, do you think there is a chance?"

He glanced back to where his brother had disappeared. "Cathal has informed me that his road is clouded. Aileen slipped through the veil under odd circumstances. Laws were broken by her Fenian Warrior."

"That was her name?"

"Aileen Kerrigan was the daughter of one of the most honored Fenian Warriors."

Brigid pushed away from him. "How is that possible? After everything you've told me?"

Duncan chuckled softly. "Have I not told ye about the story of the Fenian Warrior who defied the fae to marry a human?"

She playfully smacked at his chest. "No, you have not."

Scooping her up into his arms, Duncan silenced her pout with his lips, taking her gasp into his mouth. Slowly breaking from the kiss, he said, "I shall tell ye over a verra long bath."

"We can't."

Duncan arched a brow as he started to ascend the steps to their chambers. "And why not," he growled.

She snorted. "Because the tub is in Stephen's chambers, and they're filling it."

"Ye think a tub of water can stop *me*?"

When Duncan reached their chambers, he placed

Brigid down. "Make ready, wife. For I mean to take ye several times before my meal."

Giving her a swat on her bottom, he stormed down the corridor, bellowing loudly for two of the men. Apparently, Duncan was bringing the tub *and* the water to their chambers, whatever it took.

Chapter Forty-Four

"I cannot eat, I cannot sleep, I cannot breathe. I am a ghost wandering the hills out of sync with this time."
~Aileen Kerrigan, as told to the Guardian

Aileen grimaced glancing down at the bowl of oatmeal and fruit. Her mind rebelled at the food, but her body screamed. A battle of wills they fought daily. There was no escaping it now. She needed to keep up her strength. It was important. *Necessary*.

She sensed her aunt's footsteps approaching. Taking her spoon, she dipped it into her meal. Upon returning, her gifts had taken on more power. Clutching her pendant, she rubbed her finger over the stone, remembering.

"Good morning, Aileen," said Aunt Lily, stopping to place a kiss on her head. "It's good to see you eating."

Aileen nodded, taking a spoonful into her mouth.

"Coffee?" asked her aunt, pouring some into a mug.

"No, thanks. I've got some tea."

Giving Aileen a shocked look, she rested a hand on her forehead. "Are you feeling ill? Coffee has been a staple in your life since you were a young teen." Stifling a laugh, she added, "You used to sneak your mother's as I recall."

"I got used to not having it when I took my *trip*."

"Ahhh, but I don't think you ever mentioned that you wanted to give it up? You used to drink coffee as much as your father..." She paused. "I'm sorry. I should not have mentioned him."

Seeing the crestfallen look on her aunt's face, Aileen reached out to grasp her hand. "It's okay to talk about him. It's a good memory."

Aunt Lily squeezed her hand back. "And Stephen? Are you ready to talk about him?"

"My love for Stephen will never die. He would want me to live. But for as long as I live, there will not be another," Aileen stated.

Her aunt took a sip of her coffee. "Gwen and I will be staying on to help you and Liam."

"I know. Gwen spoke to me last evening. I agree with the decision to let Maeve take control of the Society in Boston. That is, until you return."

"I will stay as long as you need me. Have you spoken to Liam on when you'll depart for Loch Ness?"

Aileen pursed her lips at the mention of Liam's name. Shoving another spoonful into her mouth, she shook her head no.

"Will it always be this way between you both?" Her gaze grew troubled.

Sighing, Aileen stood and took her bowl over to the sink. She was tired of always being angry. All it took was for Liam to walk into a room and her fury would ignite. She was still embarrassed at the way she yelled at him the other day in front of everyone. He didn't even say a word—he just let her vent.

Her shoulders sagged, as she leaned against the sink. "I honestly don't know," she muttered. Turning around, she pounded her fist against her chest, saying, "My father and Liam were wrong in what they did. Hell, even *Stephen* was wrong in what he did!"

Aunt Lily sighed. "Was it so *wrong* for them to protect the woman they loved?"

"You can't count Liam with that group," she scoffed.

"Aileen, this isn't like you to shield yourself in anger."

Her eyes blazed with fury. "Well, perhaps it's the new me. They had no right...none of them, even you!" The words flew out before she could stop them.

Her aunt winced. Placing her cup down, she started for the door.

"Wait." Aileen rushed forward. Hugging her arms around herself, she whispered, "I'm sorry, Aunt Lily. Will the hurt ever go away?"

Taking a step toward her, she cupped her hand to Aileen's cheek. "The pain will always be there, though in time, it will fade."

"I fear it will never fade for Stephen," she sobbed, collapsing into her aunt's arms.

****

The last few days were spent in preparation for their journey to Loch Ness and Urquhart. Aileen requested a side trip to visit the ruins. She needed to walk the grounds where Stephen had lived. It did not matter to her that the place no longer resembled his home, only that some part existed.

She had made strides in being cordial to Liam, too. When she said good morning to him yesterday, he actually stumbled in shock causing her to laugh.

Loading the last bag into the car, she turned back to

the gathered group. Aileen had said her good-byes to Maeve, Teresa, Sally, and Cara yesterday before they left to return home. It seemed strange to her, thinking Boston was no longer her home. Now, Scotland would be the only place she would call *home*.

Her aunt and Gwen were laughing over something Liam said. Aileen blinked. Did he just wink at Gwen? He'd best remember that he was on the fae's black list. His fate still undetermined, and one she prayed did not mean his death.

Aileen embraced Gwen first. "Be careful with that one. I don't want you to lose your heart over him."

Gwen actually giggled, catching Aileen off guard. "Whatever, my friend. Love you."

"Love you, too, Aileen," whispered Gwen.

"Love you, Aunt Lily," she said, giving her a hug.

"Love you so very much, Aileen. Safe journey."

Getting into the car, she realized her aunt was crying. "Stop. I'll be back in a week."

Her aunt nodded and blew her a kiss.

"Ready?" asked Liam.

"Yes, and I meant what I said this morning. I want to learn how to drive in this country. If I'm staying here, I can't get around on a horse." Pausing in thought, she continued, "Well, not all of the time, right?"

"You've been to the stables?"

Aileen glanced out the window when she answered. "Yes. I can't imagine not seeing a horse every day." Angling her head back around at Liam, she added, "Besides, my father's horses are quite beautiful."

"Yes, your father did love his horses," responded Liam.

The next few hours passed in relative silence. Occasionally, Liam would point out a landmark to her, giving her a brief bit of its history. Aileen tried to take it all in, but as they drove higher into the highlands she ached to see the Scotland of old.

The scenery passed by her in a blur.

Sheep dotted the hills, and she longed to get out and walk alongside them. Feeling cramped in the vehicle, she rolled down the window. Summer was in a few weeks, and though the air held a chill, the sun warmed her face.

"Would you like to stop for lunch? I know a great little pub outside of Pitlochry."

"Is it that obvious?" she grumbled.

"Yes, you're frustrated."

She let out a sigh, wiping a loose strand out of her eyes. "Sure. I could use a walk, too. How much further to Newtonmore?"

"Only a few hours. We'll stay at Larken House for the night." Pointing his hand to the right, he added, "Blair Castle is just beyond those trees."

She gave him a small smile. The higher they went, the melancholy clawed a deeper furrow. Didn't she just travel these roads a few weeks ago? *Oh Stephen...*

It wasn't much longer until they drove up to a small pub, nestled amid some pine and birch trees. Aileen almost laughed, for it reminded her of an inn. Sure, there were cars, but overall it screamed medieval.

"The Red Branch Tavern? Any symbolism to the mythological Red Branch of Ireland?" she asked.

Shrugging, he hid behind a look that held many secrets.

Getting out of the car, she stretched to ease the

kinks. She followed Liam as they trekked through the dirt path, passing a sheep dog sitting off to the right.

The moment Aileen entered the pub the warmth and aromas assaulted her. Boisterous laughter shot out from one end as a group played darts in the corner. Liam directed her to a table near the window. No sooner did he pull out a chair than someone shouted his name.

"By the hounds!" roared the man, marching over toward them.

Aileen cringed, as a manic Highlander stormed their way. However, there was something about his eyes that reminded her of someone.

The man jabbed a finger into Liam's chest. "What makes you think you can stroll into my pub and not even greet your brother?"

Blinking, Aileen instantly recognized the similarities. "Brother, as in *Fenian Warrior*," she croaked.

"Aileen, this is my blood brother *and* Fenian Warrior, Rory. And Rory this is—"

"She is Aileen Kerrigan, daughter of Aidan Kerrigan," he interjected, staring at her in shock. "Sweet Mother Danu." Grasping her hands, he searched her face. "I am sorry to hear about the loss of your father. We all *felt* his passing."

Aileen could not move. Finally, after a few moments, Rory gently led her to her chair. "Welcome, daughter of Aidan."

Then turning around to his brother, he firmly grabbed him in a hug. "Sakes, Liam, do you ken what you've done? I feared you dead," he hissed.

"Can we discuss this later? We could do with a

couple of your best ales and some food."

"Excuse me," Aileen interrupted. "I'll just take a glass of water."

Rory frowned, yet shook his head in agreement. "Any preference on the food?"

"What's the special for today?" she asked.

Rory bent his head. "Guinness stew and dill bread."

Aileen let out a small gasp. "That was my dad's favorite."

Rory beamed a smile at her. "It is now a regular on the menu, too."

"Thank you," she said softly.

"Of course. Later, brother." He nodded to Liam as he walked away.

Scanning the room, Aileen would have bet all of her money there were more than several Fenian Warriors in the pub.

As if sensing her thoughts, Liam said, "Yes, they are all warriors. It is a gathering place and out of the way. A haven for them to rest and stay for a time."

"How could I *not* tell," she drawled. "And before you take this as some sort of compliment, are all warriors so gorgeous?"

Rory returned, bringing them their drinks and food. Hearing Aileen's comment, he interjected, "Yes, we are. But Liam is the ugliest of us."

"You wound me, brother," said Liam reaching for a drink.

Aileen disagreed. Liam was by far the most handsome of them all. Furthermore, she would never divulge that little secret to anyone, *ever*.

Dipping her spoon into the stew, she inhaled its

rich aroma. The first bite sent her taste buds spinning. Taking a sip of water, she then took another bite, closing her eyes in the sheer pleasure of eating.

"So it agrees with you, Aileen?" Rory asked.

"Oh yes," she uttered between mouthfuls.

Rory pulled up a chair and sat down next to Liam. "Where are you staying the night?"

"Up at Larken House," replied Liam, taking a swallow of ale.

"Why are you here, Liam? Have you heard from the Elders?"

"We are taking Aidan and Rose's ashes to Loch Ness. It was his request to have them scattered in the loch. And I have had no news regarding my fate."

Aileen slowly put down her spoon. "Would they truly take your life, Liam?"

"Yes," interrupted Rory. "It is the only law where if broken, death is the punishment."

Flinging out her hand in frustration, she blurted out, "But how could a loving people do such a horrible thing?"

Liam's tone was solemn when he spoke. "If we did not have this law, then I believe the warriors would have meddled with the timeline many times over. It is there for a purpose, and to answer your question again, I fully understood the risk I was taking when I brought your father back in time. So did he."

"You must have had your reasons, brother." Rory clenched his fist on the table. "But I'll be damned if I lose you without a fight."

"It is not your fight, Rory. Do not involve yourself."

Rory barked. Then pointing a finger at Liam, said,

"Isn't that what Aidan said? But it didn't stop us from trying."

Liam shook his head slowly. "This is not the same."

"Humph! We shall see." Glancing at Aileen, he asked, "When will you release your parent's ashes?"

"Dawn, the day after tomorrow."

He grasped her hand firmly and gazed into her eyes. "Then we shall be there with you."

"Why...thank you," Aileen stuttered. "Liam can give you directions."

His smile was sad. "I know the location. It was one of your father's special places for contemplation."

Tears pricked her eyes. Squeezing Rory's hand, she simply nodded.

Standing, Rory removed their bowls and glasses. "See me before you leave, Liam."

Liam rolled his eyes. "Yes, brother."

Crossing his arms across his chest, he looked out the window. "He may think he is going to stand and fight alongside me, but I will not let him. I will not involve anyone else in my fate."

"If you want to go and talk to him, I'll be outside. I want to take a short walk before we head back on the road," said Aileen.

Liam snapped his attention back to her. "Yes. I'll only be a few moments."

"Take your time." Standing, Aileen went around to Liam and hesitated briefly before placing her hand gently on his shoulder. "I may not agree with what you did, but I don't want your death, either."

"Go take your walk, Aileen," he said softly.

Chapter Forty-Five

"Solitude can bring forth the light, or call out the beast."

He could not stay here another day. There was too much happiness being tossed around, and he didn't want to be a part of it. Even the weather was warm, where he longed for storms and peace and quiet.

Stephen heard Nell screech with laughter, and he grimaced. She had sought him out daily, chattering non-stop and wanting him to visit her family before each meal. Last night she had thrown her arms around him and thanked him for coming with her. It was then Stephen made the decision to leave.

He did not want their love—any of it.

Shoving away from the wall, he went to seek out his brother. He had packed early in the morn, taking only a few items. After breaking his fast, he sought out Finn, telling him to prepare his horse. Yes, a few weeks alone would do him good. Away from the noise and especially the constant reminder of what he could never have each time he cast his eyes on Duncan and Brigid.

Stephen did not have to go far, when he saw him talking to the Murray. He had forgotten that their friend was leaving for his home.

Waving a hand in greeting, he stepped on over. "Taking your leave, Cormac?"

"Aye. I've stayed far too long."

"Safe journey."

Cormac mounted his horse, gathering the reins. "Be well, Stephen. Ye are welcome at Castle Creag anytime."

"I may take ye up on your offer."

With a wave of his hand to his men, they rode off.

Duncan eyed his brother skeptically. "What troubles ye?"

"I would like ye to take me to the island."

Duncan stiffened. "Why?"

A shard of anguish flashed through his heart. "I cannot stay here another day. 'Tis *killing* me."

Duncan placed a hand on his shoulder. "I shall have Finn ready the horses."

"Nae. My horse is already ready. I had Finn prepare him early."

"Food?"

"I have enough for a few weeks."

"I will take ye over there in the boat." Duncan moved to leave, but Stephen stopped him.

"Nae. I would like to return on my own time. I require only your help with supplies."

Duncan's jaw clenched. "Let me tell Brigid, and find Finn to fetch my horse."

Stephen let out a sigh. "Thank ye, Duncan." He did not want to fight with his brother and prayed he would understand.

Duncan grabbed both of his shoulders and looked into his eyes. "I want ye back here at Urquhart, do not forget that. I will not lose ye again. Dinnae forget I understand your grief."

"Aye, but 'tis too soon." His tone gruff.

****

Within an hour, they set out. The island was north of Urquhart, and the perfect place for some solitude. Their father had built a small cottage on the island in the early part of his marriage to their mother. It was their special retreat, and after they had lost them both, the brothers would often take a boat out to the island. Days would pass until Angus would herd them back into the boat and return to Urquhart.

A magical place, Stephen had once proclaimed.

Journeying around the bend in the road, he spotted it instantly. Inhaling deeply, a sense of calm descended over him. He had made the right decision in coming here.

Leading his horse down to where the two boats were tied together against a tree, Stephen dismounted. "I won't be gone long, my friend," he said while patting Grian.

Scanning the area, he had forgotten how beautiful the area was. Duncan had taken the boats to the water's edge and loaded his bundle into one of the boats. Striding over, Stephen dumped his supplies into his.

There was a twinkle in Duncan's eyes when he announced, "Race ye, brother?"

Never one to refuse a challenge, he didn't even wait to acknowledge his brother and took off.

In no time, Stephen was across the loch and at the island. Catching his breath, he waited for his brother who arrived shortly.

"I will let ye have it this time," Duncan mocked.

Hands on his hips, he waited for Duncan to toss out the rest of the supplies.

Rubbing a hand over his face, his brother made

ready to leave. In two strides, he was at Stephen's side. Hugging him fiercely, he growled, "If ye are not back by midsummer, I will come fetch ye myself."

Stephen grunted. He watched Duncan take his leave in the boat. Of course, his brother did have to issue one last order.

"By the Gods, shave and cut your hair, too. Ye are beginning to look like a hermit," he barked.

Stephen glared at him with his arms crossed over his chest. He kept his gaze on his brother until he reached land, then taking a deep sigh, picked up his belongings and trudged into the trees.

****

The first few days brought some solace. However, with each new dawn, he slipped further into the abyss of darkness. Dreams of Aileen haunted him, and he would awake feeling tormented by the loss. His soul was empty, void of any feeling but pain. The joy he had recently experienced with Aileen was now overshadowed by the events of the past month. All Stephen had left were the memories of the woman he loved. No tangible proof did he have that she existed, except in his heart.

"Is this my punishment, my cross to carry?" he yelled out one evening.

The sounds of the loch did not give him any answers, so he responded in his own way. Reaching down, he picked up a large stone and threw it out into the loch. A flock of geese startled by the noise flew off from their haven by the shore.

Storming off toward the cottage, he picked up his plaid. When he arrived, Stephen could only think of one thing. If he could not have Aileen in the flesh, he would draw her from his memories. Yet, each time he attempted to start, his hand shook. After several times of faltering, Stephen started with something simple.

Her pendant.

Soon the light faded and as he gathered his items, he prayed that tonight he would sleep without any dreams.

Chapter Forty-Six

"I am the light of all lights, the song of all songs, and there will never be another."

Aileen stood by the water's edge, gazing out at Loch Ness with the water gently lapping at her feet. She clutched the boxes that held the remains of her parents and waited. They would always be with her, but the thought of emptying them seemed so final. It was as if she was saying good-bye all over again.

A hawk caught her attention, making lazy circles high in the sky. Higher and higher it flew, until it disappeared over the treetops. "This place is perfect," she whispered.

Liam quietly stepped forward. "Your father loved this place, more for its remoteness. He often said it was a place where time stood still." He moved closer to the edge, his hands behind his back. "A place where one would never be able to distinguish what century they would be in."

Aileen gave a nervous laugh. "It is hard for me to fathom how old my father was. To live that long…" She paused trying to comprehend.

Liam angled his head and smiled. "You see your father in terms of *human*. I see him as *fae*."

"Of course," she said softly, fingering the boxes' clasps. Inhaling deeply, she placed both of them on a large stone slab. "Did he often sit here?"

"Aye, that he did."

Inhaling and exhaling deeply, Aileen opened her mother's box first. Next, came her father's and she gasped. "Great Goddess." Her father's ashes resembled fine crystals. She cupped a hand over her mouth to stifle a cry. They were so beautiful.

When she looked up at Liam, his eyes flashed with the light of many colors. "*Fae* ashes are different from your own."

As her eyes misted with tears, Aileen walked barefoot a few feet into the loch carrying the boxes. Carefully, she emptied them both at the same time into the water. Immediately, a great gust of wind blew by, swirling the ashes together in a brilliant display of colors.

"Mother Danu, bring home your warrior and his woman," sang out Liam.

Aileen whipped her head around at the sound of bells, their chimes muted in the distance. Mists instantly descended around the loch. Stumbling back onto the land, her mouth gaped open at the sight before her. Men had started to emerge from the trees and were lining the loch as far as her vision could see. They were chanting in low tones, their right fist held over their heart.

"Liam, what's happening?" demanded Aileen watching, as even he stood motionless.

"The Fenian Warriors are singing your mother and father home to *Tir na Og,* and paying their respects to you," he responded, his voice but a whisper on the wind.

Aileen was in awe. There were so many, dressed from so many time periods, her head swam. "A tribute to them," she murmured.

"It has never been done," stated Liam.

"Thank you," she mouthed, sending it out mentally as well. Warmth instantly cloaked her as they responded in kind. For the rest of her life, Aileen would never forget this day.

Time hung suspended and as they had come forth, they silently slipped back into the trees. As each one departed, the mists would lessen. When the last warrior left, the chanting ceased.

Looking out at the water, Aileen noticed all traces of her parent's ashes had vanished. They were gone— forever into a land where one day she would join with them. Her heart may ache; however, her parents were together. Unlike herself...

A wave of dizziness passed through her, and she stumbled. Liam flew to her side, helping her to sit down on the slab.

"You're suffering from the energy of so many," said Liam, walking over and pulling out a bottle of water. "Here, drink some."

Taking a few sips, she nodded. "I guess you're right. I could use some food, though."

Liam removed some sandwiches out of his backpack, offering one to Aileen, which she immediately took. Her hands shook, but she managed to take a few bites without dropping the entire meal.

Sitting in relative peace, she reflected on the past few months. Her life had twisted a number of times and it wasn't any wonder she didn't go crazy. She had learned magic had no boundaries. Her father was a warrior for the fae. She had stepped through a door to the past, and fell in love only to lose it all. Deep in the night when sleep eluded her, her mind tormented her with its questions. Did Stephen die? If he survived, did he find peace? Was there another woman in his life? It was becoming a familiar pattern each night.

Aileen stared out at the loch. "Liam?" She brushed the remnants of her sandwich onto the ground. "How far is the place where Margaret died?"

He eyed her skeptically. "Not far, closer than Urquhart. Why?"

"I want to see where it all began. It's something I have to do."

"It's a sad place. The ghosts of the battle still echo there."

She reached for his hand. "Please. It's important."

He flinched slightly from her touch. "We won't reach Urquhart until after dark."

Aileen shrugged. "Does it matter? Call it part of my healing process, or whatever, but I want to go there."

"Are you ready, then?" he asked.

Standing, she smiled. "Yes. I'm feeling much better."

Gathering her parent's empty boxes, she took one last look out at the loch. "Goodbye, Dad and Mom," she whispered.

It only took an hour before Liam veered the car off the main road and proceeded through a narrow dirt path, which dead ended at a large oak tree.

"We walk from here," he stated.

As Aileen stepped out of the car, a chill breeze swept past her. Hugging her arms, she tried to warm herself. Walking around the tree, Liam held out his hand to help her up over the ridge. The trees were so dense they partially blocked out the sun. An eerie silence permeated the place almost as a warning to man and beast not to enter as they made their way to a place of death.

Liam stopped at the clearing, and she quietly stood next to him. Great sorrow filled her when she cast her gaze on the ring of stones. They stood as a testament to that horrific night, reminding her of ancient guardians.

Without thought, Aileen reached for her pendant and moved out a few feet into the clearing. Almost immediately, the dizziness returned. Her vision blurred and colors danced before her eyes. Rubbing her eyes, she glanced over her shoulder at Liam.

He was as still as the stones, his eyes filled with an emotion she could not detect.

"Don't panic, Aileen. Keep moving toward the stones," he said calmly.

The reality of his words burned in her mind and heart. "I can return?"

"I was not sure until this moment."

"Oh Liam, but..." Panic seized her at the thought of traveling through time. Instinctively, she placed her hands over her abdomen.

He gave her a reassuring smile. "Your *child* will be protected. Now take hold of your pendant and keep your thoughts on Stephen. Trust me this one last time...*all* will be well."

Aileen didn't have time to be shocked at his knowledge of her child. Taking a firm hold of her pendant, she slowly walked forward.

"Give my regards to your husband," she heard Liam say as the colors of light swept her away to oblivion.

Chapter Forty-Seven

"As surely as the sun will dawn and set each day, I will forever love you—evermore."

~Stephen's vow to Aileen

"Breathe, Aileen, breathe..."

A strong arm held her around the waist, and she leaned against him. Within moments, her body jerked and turning away, Aileen heaved the entire contents of her stomach onto the ground.

Again, strong arms lifted her away from the mess she had created. He carried her for several minutes and gently placed her down. When she peeked open her eyes, she stared into the blazing ones of Rory MacGregor, dressed as a Highlander.

"Sweet Mother," she whispered, wiping her mouth with the back of her hand.

Rory crouched down in front of her and held out a flask. "Here, drink. 'Tis only water."

"You remembered," she mumbled.

He chuckled softly.

Closing her eyes, she sipped the cool water. After a few moments, she reopened them. "How did you know I would be here?"

He angled his head at her. "Liam."

Her eyes went wide. "I thought he had lost all of his powers?"

"We are blood brothers, Aileen. Liam may have lost all of his powers, but we will always have a bond. He notified me the moment ye passed through the stones."

Aileen shivered when she looked out passed Rory. Had she just traveled through time again?

"Would ye care to rest before our journey? Liam has told me of your condition."

Snapping her eyes back to his, she responded with a firm, "No." She looked up into the sky to determine the time. "How far to Urquhart?"

"If we ride steady, we shall be there late afternoon."

Aileen frowned. "I'm confused. When I left it was already *late afternoon*."

Rory stood. "Time has no fixed schedule, especially when one travels the veil. 'Tis only early morning."

Nodding, she reached for his outstretched hand and stood up.

"Our horses are this way," he said.

Aileen took a deep breath in and let it out slowly. Following Rory, she stopped suddenly when she saw one of her father's horses. "How is it possible that *Pegasus* is here?"

"Och, Aileen, anything is *possible* with fae magic."

As she walked over to the white mare, Aileen nuzzled her face against her mane. "I'm so glad you're here," she murmured.

Rory's smile was dazzling when Aileen looked up.

"I realized ye would need a gentle spirit while ye are traveling in your condition, and I have proper clothing for ye, too."

"Thank you, Rory." Goodness, he went from twenty-first-century man to thirteenth overnight, including his speech.

After helping her onto to her horse, Rory directed her out of the clearing and up along a path.

"I'm home," she whispered. Then abruptly her thoughts reached out to Stephen. *I'm here, my love.* Pain stabbed at her temples and she lurched forward.

"Rory," she gasped.

He was immediately at her side. "Aileen?"

"Head hurts," she muttered, taking a hand to shield the sun.

Rory grabbed the reins of her horse. "I'm sorry. It is my fault for not telling ye. Until your energy has a chance to settle, ye will not be able to use your powers for awhile."

Aileen's shoulders sagged. "Do you know how long?"

"Each one is different. Ye are part human, so it may take longer."

"Let's get going, then," she replied.

Rory raised a finger at her in warning. "Do not hesitate to let me know if ye need to rest. I can understand your need to see Sir Stephen, but he would have my heart if I endanger ye or your babe. Understand?"

Aileen gave him a salute. "Yes, my captain."

Rory snorted. "Be careful in these parts of using that word. They may mistake me for a spy."

Aileen laughed and ruffled Pegasus's mane.

****

The heat in the kitchen was stifling. "If only I had a fan," grumbled Brigid, wiping the flour from her hands.

She was helping the cook, Delia, with making the breads and being inside a medieval kitchen in June was proving to be a challenge for her. For a brief moment, she considered transforming her long gown into a mini skirt.

You'd like that, Duncan.

Wiping the perspiration from her forehead, Brigid walked outside. It was definitely going to be a warm day. However, with midsummer approaching next week, there was much preparation and no time for rest. Duncan had given her a list of the items he wanted along with Nell, Finn, and everyone else.

She waved at Henry, tending to one of the lambs, which had broken free, as she meandered over to Nell's home for her wayward critters. Cuchulainn greeted her instantly with licks on her hand. Brigid responded in kind with a scratch behind the ear.

"Where is your mistress today, Cuchulainn?"

He gave a short bark and trotted off around the back of the structure. Following, she found Nell crouched on the ground, trying to coax a squirrel into her outstretched hand. Brigid stood still, waiting to see how this would play out.

Several moments passed, and the squirrel ventured forth, scooping out the nuts in Nell's hand. Soon, she had the tiny one sitting next to her, looking like long lost friends. Not wanting to disturb the scene, Brigid crept silently away.

Hearing shouting at the gate, she picked up her pace, and frowned when she saw one of the guards positioning an arrow at whoever was at the entrance.

"Henry, put down the lamb and go get Duncan," she said in passing.

His shoulders sagged. "Do ye ken how long it took to find this one?"

"We'll worry about it later. I'll get Nell to help. We need Duncan, now!"

Nodding, he reluctantly put the animal down and scowled when it scampered off.

Brigid rushed to the entrance, pushing aside one of the guards. "Who is it?"

"He claims to be a MacGregor, but I do not recognize his plaid. And what business would a MacGregor be doing here?"

Brigid stepped forward and froze. "*Oh my*," she gasped. "Let me pass, Blaine."

"My lady, it would be wise to wait for Duncan," he replied, blocking her path.

Brigid placed her hands on her hips and glared at him. "I believe I may know who they are, and *they* are most welcome." However, she had doubts about the Fenian Warrior.

Grumbling something incoherent, Blaine let her pass.

Walking over to the woman on the white horse, Brigid smiled. "Welcome to Urquhart, Aileen. I'm Brigid, Duncan's wife." Turning to the man, she asked, "And you must be a Fenian Warrior, correct?"

Rory smirked. "Aye, Lady Brigid. And may I say, it is a pleasure to finally meet *ye*."

Aileen's mouth fell open. How could Brigid possibly know, unless she also had gifts? The woman was beautiful. Her dark red hair was having trouble staying in its braid, the curls escaping wildly around her face. Aileen could not help but smile and got down off her horse.

Brigid held out her arms. "I can't tell you how happy I am to see you, Aileen."

She went into Brigid's arms, engulfed in the smell of bread and warmth. Angling her head, she asked, "How did you know?"

Brigid laughed. "My husband, Duncan, went into great detail explaining your looks. If I didn't believe how much he loved me, I would have been jealous."

"I must thank him, for if you had not recognized us, I fear they would have let loose one of those arrows."

"Humph!" snorted Brigid. "Let's get you inside and away from all the gawkers."

Aileen frowned when Rory remained seated on his horse.

Brigid half-turned, saying, "I can offer you some food and drink before you depart."

"He is not welcome," growled Duncan, striding quickly toward them.

Aileen's knees went weak, but Brigid rolled her eyes.

Duncan placed himself between them and Rory.

"Oh for the love of...I thought your issues were with Conn," snapped Brigid.

He stood there with his arms crossed over his chest. "*None* of them are welcome at Urquhart."

When Brigid started to offer another retort, Rory held up his hand to stay her words. "My lady, it is true. I thank ye for your offer, but I must be on my way. It is a long journey where I am heading."

Sweeping past Duncan, Brigid held out her hand to him. He eyed Duncan warily, and then took her hand. "Perhaps another day," she said giving him a broad smile.

"Until that day, my lady."

Aileen moved past Duncan. "I would like to say something before Rory leaves."

"Of course." Grabbing Duncan's arm, Brigid said quietly, "Let's give them some privacy." Duncan let out a soft curse, but complied with her.

Rory dismounted from his horse. No sooner did his feet hit the ground than Aileen immediately took his hands in hers. Her eyes held sadness. "What is it, Aileen," he whispered.

She bowed her head slightly. "Please tell Liam I'm sorry for the way I've treated him these past few weeks. Some of it was warranted, yet, for the most part, I was cruel in my behavior. I never had a chance to tell him."

Rory took his finger and tilted her chin up. "Ye were filled with grief, and as a Fenian Warrior, we are owed no apologies. It is what we do, be it right or wrong in your eyes. Ye may not understand the decisions we make, and we don't expect ye to."

"I understand, but I was wrong." Concern filled her voice.

He nodded in understanding. "I will pass along your message, considering his fate is still undecided."

Aileen wrapped her arms around his neck. "Thank you, Rory."

He kissed her on the forehead, proceeding to get another curse from Duncan, which only made Rory smile broadly. Releasing her, he quickly got back on his horse. Chuckling softly, he shook his head. "I do not want the Dragon Knight unleashing his sword on me."

Giving her one last look, he said, "Be happy, *Lady* Aileen."

"I will."

Watching as he departed, she waited until he was out of sight before walking over to Duncan and Brigid. Her stomach was in knots. "Where is Stephen?" she blurted out, fearing the answer.

It was Brigid who spoke first, "Aileen, won't you come inside. I'm sure you must be tired."

Aileen gaped at her. "Honestly, Brigid, can you tell me that you would want to eat *first* before finding the man you thought you would never see again?"

Duncan stifled a cough. "She has a point, *wife*."

Brigid narrowed her eyes at her husband.

"He is not here," Duncan said quietly.

Aileen clutched a hand to her chest. "Is...is he *dead*?"

"Nae!" exclaimed Duncan. "He lives, though his injuries were harsh."

Taking a hold of his arm, she looked into his eyes. "Where is he?"

Duncan placed a hand over hers. "He is on an island out on the loch. He wanted some time to be alone."

"Take me to him," she demanded.

Backing away, she gathered the reins on Pegasus preparing to leave, when she sensed Brigid near her. "You would do the same, Brigid, so don't try and stop me."

"I wasn't, Aileen. Only, let me put together some more food and drink. I believe he doesn't have much left."

Aileen nodded. "I'll give you fifteen minutes, and then I'm gone."

"Hell, I would have said five," snickered Brigid as

she swept past Duncan and ran for the kitchens.

"Have Finn bring me my horse," shouted Duncan.

He glanced back at Aileen, a frown marring his features. "I must prepare ye, though, Stephen is much changed. Your loss has distressed him greatly."

"And that is why I can't prolong seeing him another minute."

True to her word, Brigid returned within fifteen minutes with food, and Finn followed with Duncan's horse. Duncan kissed his wife hard before they left, commenting on the taste of cinnamon on her lips, forcing Aileen to look away.

Nell came running forth and halted before Duncan, though she looked up at Aileen. "Before ye return with Stephen, will ye have him bring some of the water from the well?"

"I will ask him," replied Aileen, glancing at Duncan for an explanation.

"'Tis a magical well that Stephen created. Nell believes it helps to heal her wounded animals and birds."

"Thank ye, Lady Aileen," smiled Nell. She went and stood next to Brigid, waving.

"Shall we?" Duncan gave a nudge to his horse.

It did not take long for them to reach the bank across from the island. If Aileen had to guess, she would have said under an hour. Just looking at it, she sensed an unusual energy around it. Loch Ness was full of surprises, and this was another one to add to her list.

After dismounting from Pegasus, she helped Duncan gather the supplies, placing them in the boat. Her nerves were taut with anticipation. Breathing deeply, she closed her eyes and reached out in her mind toward Stephen. Several moments passed and when she finally opened her eyes, she let out a sigh.

Why won't you answer me, Stephen?

Duncan was quiet as they settled into the boat. He kept his gaze out beyond her. After some time, he spoke. "Is your father well?"

For a man who despised the Fenian Warriors, Aileen was shocked at his question. She swallowed the lump in her throat. "No. He died shortly after we returned."

Duncan stopped rowing and heaved a heavy sigh. "I am sorry for your loss. He was a great warrior."

"Yes, he was," she whispered. Dipping her fingers in the water, she marveled at the thought that earlier in the day, in the future, she had placed her parent's ashes in this very loch.

Duncan resumed rowing and Aileen was grateful he had no more questions. Her strength was fading, and she only had enough for one purpose. *Stephen.*

Upon reaching the shore of the island, Duncan jumped out and helped Aileen. Giving her hand a squeeze, he said, "Keep to the path, and it will lead ye to the cottage. In truth, he favors the area near the well under a tree. It is not far from the cottage. There is a stone path which can take ye there."

Seeing the worry in his face, she squeezed his hand back in reassurance. "We'll be fine."

"I believe your love will help to heal my brother."

Her eyes were wet with tears when she replied, "Don't worry, Duncan. I will bring back our Stephen." Placing a kiss on his cheek, Aileen stepped onto the path.

For better or worse, her destiny was with Stephen.

Now to make him realize that together their love would heal both their souls.

Chapter Forty-Eight

"True love's kiss will surely break the spell. But only if the warrior wants to be released."

Stephen, I'm here...where are you?

With each step, Aileen's stomach clenched. There was no sign of Stephen anywhere, and he still was not answering her. She couldn't determine if her frazzled nerves were from fear, or anticipation of seeing him.

"Why won't you answer me?" she shouted. Her only response was a sparrow, frightened by her outburst.

She stopped to catch her breath before the small stone cottage nestled against a cluster of birch and rowan trees. Dotted along the front were patches of bluebells, foxgloves, and roses. A woman planted these. Stephen's mother?

The thatched roof needed some tending, but overall it was a beacon of light on this island. She moved cautiously forward, pushing open the door. Musty smells greeted her, and she swiped at the cobwebs draped at the top. A table and two chairs sat in the center. Glancing to her left, was the hearth, two chairs framing its sides.

Carefully putting down her pack, Aileen eyes went wide at the massive bed on the right with furs covering it. This place had not been occupied for a long time. So, if Stephen was not sleeping here, where was he?

Wiping her palms down her gown, she placed them on either side of her temple, reaching out to him, again. When she got no response, she stomped her foot. "Damn it, Stephen! *I need you.*"

Storming out the door, she looked for the stone path Duncan had told her about. The path jutted out to the left of the cottage, and Aileen started out. As she made her way through thick foliage, she stumbled over a log and broke her fall against a pine tree. Wincing from the pain in her arm, she rubbed at it only to stop abruptly.

There, some thirty feet away crouched on the ground was Stephen.

Aileen's heart broke at the sight.

Duncan was correct. He was changed and barely recognizable. His matted and wild hair hung down past his chin. A face that always required shaving, now wore a full beard. The only item that covered him was his plaid, which looked filthy. She noticed fresh scars, determining these were from the battle last month. He continued to rock back and forth, clutching his head, reminding Aileen of a wounded animal.

Cautiously, she approached until she stood only a few feet from him. This was not how she expected their first meeting. It should be one of joy, but her knight, the man she loved, was *dying* right before her eyes.

Remembering the words she told Duncan, telling him she would bring back *their* Stephen, Aileen clutched at the folds of her gown and swallowed back the lump in her throat.

"Stephen, my love, *please* look at me," she pleaded.

371

He pounded his head. "'Tis cruel to hear such voices. Over and over, you weave through my mind, teasing and tormenting me. Your words are malicious, telling me *she* is here. If ye persist in your torture, I will slay ye."

"I'm here, my love. Just open your eyes." Aileen tried to keep her voice calm as panic seized her. He wasn't dying. Stephen was losing his mind.

"Leave me," he growled, his voice unrecognizable to Aileen.

Gathering what little strength she possessed, she bit out, "No, Stephen MacKay. I will stay right here until you open your eyes."

"Begone, vile demon!" Grabbing the dirk laying to his right, he got up slowly and opened his eyes.

Smiling weakly, Aileen held out her hand. "I'm *here*."

"The demon has taken *her* form." Lunging at Aileen, he held the dirk poised at her throat. "Ye die now," he hissed.

Aileen trembled, and she fought for control. "Then you will not only kill me, but our child, too."

His breathing ragged, Stephen blinked, trying to focus. Aileen gradually reached her hand up and cupped his face. He jerked from her touch.

"*Aileen*," he rasped in astonishment as if waking from a nightmare. His gaze saw the dirk at her throat, and he quickly dropped it. "By the Gods! What have I done?" He snapped his eyes back to hers, which were filled with tears.

Taking her other hand, she clasped his, firmly. "I came back, Stephen. I've been the one calling you. No others."

Crushing her in his arms, he muttered, "*Leannan, leannan*, please forgive me." Weak in body and spirit, Stephen collapsed onto the ground, bringing Aileen down with him. Great sobs racked his body. After several moments, he took her face in his hands. "I am not worthy—"

Aileen placed a finger on his lips to halt his words. Her voice thick with emotion, she said, "I did not endure all of this to have you walk away from me, Stephen MacKay."

The sun was making its descent and a cool breeze floated by.

"Do you think we could go to the cottage?" she whispered with a smile.

Stephen nodded, but when they got up, he immediately scooped her into his arms. Aileen let out a gasp, placing her arms around his neck. Though he had lost a great deal of weight, he was still toned. They were silent as he carried her all the way back to the cottage.

Stepping inside he gently placed her down. "Would ye care for something to eat?"

"No." Taking his hand, she pulled him over to the bed. Watching, she waited for any reaction. He remained unmoving. So Aileen removed her boots and then turned around. "Will you undo my laces?" She glanced over her shoulder, noticing his eyes had flashed.

Good, she thought.

She could feel his fingers fumbling with the laces. When she felt the last one slip free, she slipped it down past her shoulders and let it fall to the ground. Slowly turning around, Aileen noticed his fist clenched by his sides as if trying to control his desire.

Good, she thought, again.

With a sweep of her hand, she brought her braid around to the front and started to free it from its confines. Running her fingers through the mass, she shook it free. Her gaze gravitated down to see that he was fully erect.

Very good.

When she reached out to remove his plaid, he captured her hand. "Nae. Get in the bed."

She arched a brow at him, but complied.

Swiftly, he removed his plaid and moved onto the bed next to her. Turning her over, so her back faced him, Stephen brought the furs up and over them. He placed his arm around her, pulling her tight against him.

Aileen snuggled against his erection.

"Sleep, *leannan.* For on the morrow, I will take all of your body."

Letting out a deep sigh, Aileen smiled. *Yes, you will Stephen MacKay, and so will I.*

Within moments, Aileen and Stephen had fallen fast asleep.

****

As the first rays of light slipped through the shutters, Stephen awoke. He had slept fully, since exhaustion had devastated his mind and body. Aileen tucked against him was snoring softly. His heart soared knowing she had returned and was carrying his child. Making a vow then and there, he silently pledged to always keep her safe. They would never be parted again.

He touched her blond tendrils, taking them between his fingers, so soft and beautiful, and then stopped abruptly.

"Sweet Danu," he uttered quietly. Raising his hand up to his face, Stephen stared at the dirt caked on his hand. Closing his eyes, he let out a soft groan. It was a wonder Aileen did not flee the moment she saw him.

Moving slowly out from the covers, so as not to wake her, he edged out of the bed. Placing them back around her, he bent to retrieve his plaid from the ground. As he silently made his way out of cottage, Stephen took one last look at her.

"I will never lose ye again, Aileen."

After dousing himself in the loch, he proceeded to build a small fire. The Goddess was kind to provide the fish for their morning meal, and he gave thanks as he tended the blaze.

Smiling inwardly when the door of the cottage opened, he had hoped the lure of smoke and food would rouse his love from her bed. He could hear her stomach protesting loudly from where he sat.

"Good morning," she uttered softly.

Stephen stood and turned around smiling. "Good morning, my love." The sight she presented him caused his groin to tighten. All she had around her was a fur, casually draped over one shoulder. He could just make out the slight swell of one breast.

"Stephen!" she exclaimed. "You've shaved."

Her statement snapped him out of his lustful thoughts, and he rubbed a hand over his face. "Aye, as much as I could. I will have to wait until we return to Urquhart to cut my hair."

She frowned. "Where did you bathe? If there is was water nearby, I want some."

"The loch. Where else?"

"My Stephen has returned." Her voice soft.

He arched a brow. "Hungry? It is fish."

"For you." She let the fur slip further off her shoulder.

By the Gods, he wanted her. The fur only covered a small portion of her body, and he could see those long legs. He wanted to run his mouth and fingers over every inch of her body. Yet, she needed food to help nourish their child. "Ye have not eaten," he said gruffly. Stooping back down to turn the fish over, his hands shook.

"I want *you*—not food. We can eat later."

"Stubborn fae," he muttered, trying not to look at her.

Aileen rolled her eyes. Dropping the fur, she placed her hands on her hips and angled her head at him. "You can either make love to me, Stephen MacKay, or I'll take matters into my own hands."

He couldn't help himself and looked up. His mouth fell open at the sight before him. Turning around, she gave him a glorious view, sauntering away. "I'm going back to bed."

Lust roared instantly in him, and he dropped the trencher to the ground. Storming through the door, his chest heaving, Stephen's eyes roamed over her body sprawled out on the furs.

"Are *you* hungry, Stephen?" Her voice heavy with need, she stroked the bed in invitation.

Stephen's only response was a growl before he descended on her. Their lips met with savage harmony—hot with need. Cupping her breasts, he pinched her nipples as she groaned into his mouth. He could feel it resonating deep into him. Could not get enough of her. Could not taste enough. Could not feel enough.

He was drowning in Aileen.

Taking his fingers, he stroked between her womanly folds. She was wet, and her desire sent his mind spinning. He tried to be gentle, nipping, and trailing kisses down her neck.

Aileen dug her nails into his back matching her need with his. She grabbed his head, kissing him hard. Teasing and pulling at his bottom lip, she took his cock and stroked it near her opening.

Stephen plunged deep into her, and Aileen cried out with pleasure, arching up high. "*More*," she demanded.

He slid out slowly, and then slammed back into her watching her eyes glaze over. Gritting his teeth, he fought the wave that was ready to crash over him. His control shattered when she screamed out his name. A guttural cry of release tore forth from him, and he shook violently.

Moments passed before either could move.

When Stephen opened his eyes, he stared into Aileen's, which were shining with unshed tears. "Don't you *ever* send me away again. To live a life without knowing if you lived or died is not a life. I will stand by your side until I take my last breath."

"Aye," he murmured, taking his thumb and wiping away a tear that slipped down the side of her face. Stephen rolled over onto his back, crushing her against him. His voice was low when he spoke. "I ken it was not the right decision, but I feared for your life weeks before. When ye went through the veil, my life ended that night."

Aileen let the tears of joy and sorrow fall. "My father died shortly after I returned. I lost two men I loved that day. I *wanted* to die myself."

He let out a heavy sigh. "Och, *leannan*, I am sorry for your loss. Your father was a great warrior." Tilting her head to look into her eyes, he added, "There will be no talk of dying, hear me?"

She gave him a weak smile. Taking his hand, she placed it over her abdomen. "Our child was the only light that kept me going. I fear that if the baby had never reached out—" She swallowed back the lump in her throat, and he realized she was unable to continue.

"Whist, do not say such things." His eyes scanned her face in confusion. "In truth, Aileen, how can this be? How can ye tell so soon?"

Aileen shrugged and hiccupped. "Stephen, I conceived on Beltaine that I'm sure of. You forget our child has a heavy dose of fae blood. I believe this child will be vastly powerful."

Gathering her close, he kissed her softly. "I have wanted ye more than life itself. Willing to cross the veil in search of ye, defying the wrath of the fae." Cupping her face in his hands, his eyes bore into hers. "I *love ye*, Aileen."

"Oh Stephen, I love you, too," she whispered.

He silenced her with another kiss, this one more drawn out, leisurely. When he parted from her lips, her eyes were heavy with lust.

"Now, I will take my pleasure of ye unhurried."

His smile was wicked, and Aileen melted into his arms, letting the tide of bliss sweep them up and away.

Chapter Forty-Nine

"When the thread of love is woven around two hearts, two souls, they shall become one."

Aileen's body was sated from the past few days thanks to Stephen. Smiling, she looked down at him, sleeping softly. She had lost count of the many times he made love to her. Her heart sang each morning when she woke to find him staring at her, and she would never tire of being in his arms. A part of his life, forever. Happiness was a treasure, and she intended to enjoy every moment.

The sun was warm on her body as she continued to gaze at her future husband. His wounds were healing rapidly and color had returned to his face. She let her eyes travel over his body.

"Ready for me again, *leannan*?" he drawled keeping his eyes closed.

She smacked him playfully. "How long have you been awake?"

"Never went to sleep," he replied, opening one eye.

"Really? Hmmm..." She bent and placed a kiss along his jaw.

"I was figuring out how we were going to travel back to Urquhart."

Aileen put her hand on his chest and smiled. "It's all been arranged."

Giving her a questioning look, she took a finger to his lips to silent him. "I told Duncan to bring the horses on the third day."

Angling his head slightly, Stephen drew her hand down to his fully erect cock. "Ye are verra clever." His voice was tinged with a seductive husky quality.

"Yes, I am," she stated. Standing, she stretched and made to head back to the cottage.

"Just where do ye think ye are going?" he demanded.

"It's the third day, and Midsummer's Eve is next week. There is much to do, since I would like to get married on that day." She tossed the words over her shoulder, continuing to walk down the path.

Stephen's eyes narrowed. "So ye are going to leave me in this condition?" he barked.

All he got was her lovely backside and a wave of her hand.

"I'll show ye what happens when ye tease me, fae," he shouted.

When Aileen peeked over her shoulder, she could see Stephen stalking her at a steady pace. Intent on getting back and preparing to leave, she took off running.

Instantly, he was upon her, and a burst of laughter echoed throughout the trees.

****

No sooner did Brigid settle one problem than another presented itself. "Well, I can't blame it on the full moon. That was a few weeks ago." She narrowed her eyes studying the large tapestry. It had been tucked away in an empty chamber. She literally stumbled upon it one morning when inspecting one of the rooms. How in the heck was she going to place it on the wall in the great hall?

"What did ye say, Mistress?" asked Delia.

"Just talking out a problem." She swiped at a cobweb, which caught in her hair. You wouldn't know where I can find Henry or Joseph?"

"Och, I ken they are with Duncan."

"Is *everyone* with Duncan this morning?" she asked in exasperation.

Delia chuckled softly, nodding her head.

Instantly, both women jumped at the sound of someone shrieking. "Bloody hell," hissed Brigid. "What *now*?"

Dusting her hands off, she made her way down the corridor and ran smack into Nell. "What the..." Grabbing Nell to steady her, she could at least determine that whatever it was had to be good news. Nell was beaming.

"They've returned," exclaimed Nell.

Could it be, she thought. "*Stephen and Aileen*?"

"Aye! Let's go greet them."

"Wait, Nell. Go fetch Duncan. I'll meet you at the gate."

"No need. I am on my way," said Duncan, walking toward them.

They quickly descended the corridor and made their way to the front. Passing through the doors, Stephen and Aileen were entering through the portcullis.

"Blessed Danu," muttered Duncan. "It looks like my brother has healed."

Brigid wandered over to him taking his hand and squeezing it. "He's like a new man compared to the one

I remember," she said, gazing up at her husband.

"Aye."

Stephen dismounted and went to help Aileen off her horse. Stepping over to his brother, he took a deep breath in and released it. "Thank ye."

"For what, Stephen?"

"Sending Aileen."

"She was rather adamant."

The two brothers stared at each other as several moments passed.

Duncan was the first to speak. "It is good to have ye back." His voice low.

Reaching out, Stephen grasped Duncan. "As am I, brother."

When he released him, he grabbed Aileen's hand bringing her forth. Taking his hand, he cupped her face and gazed into her eyes. "I would like to marry Aileen on Midsummer's Eve."

Aileen grasped his hand and placed a kiss in his palm.

Stephen turned around. "Do ye ken if there will be a problem seeking out Cathal?"

Duncan smirked and rolled his eyes.

"Wonderful! I would be honored to join ye both," interrupted Cathal, walking between everyone.

Stephen blanched. "When did ye arrive?"

"The day I took Aileen out to ye," replied Duncan.

Cathal placed his hand on Stephen's arm. "I had a guest by the name of Rory MacGregor," he said, winking at Aileen.

"Liam's brother?" asked Stephen.

Cathal just shrugged.

"Yes," answered Aileen turning toward Stephen.

"Also, I forgot to tell you Liam sends his regards."

"Humph!" grunted Stephen, taking Aileen's hand in his. "Ye only shared that Liam had lost all of his powers and was awaiting a judgment from the fae regarding his life."

Brigid stepped toward them. "I am so happy for you both. It will only be a matter of time before all the brothers are reunited."

"Aye," smiled Duncan, embracing his wife.

They ambled along, chatting furiously.

Nell had taken Stephen's hand and was telling him the latest addition to her family. He peered back at Aileen who was deep in conversation with Brigid about the plans for their ceremony. Laughter rang out from behind him, and Stephen smiled.

It was good to be home.

However, until Alastair and Angus returned their home would not be whole. He and Duncan had much to discuss on the whereabouts of their brothers. Yet for now, he would enjoy the moment—*the happiness*.

"Are ye not hearing what I told ye, Stephen?"

Stephen stopped and bent down to Nell's level. "Forgive me, Nell. My mind is full of so many happy thoughts."

She smiled at him. Then hugging him, she muttered into his ear, "'Tis all right."

He gave her a kiss on the cheek and stood. "Go fetch your latest. I will be in the great hall."

Shrieking with delight, Nell scampered off.

Watching the young girl, Stephen pondered what his child would be, and his heart swelled. It truly did not matter, for the babe was already a blessing.

Stepping into the hall, shouts erupted as Duncan

handed him a mug.

"Welcome home, Stephen."

Epilogue

Loch Ness—Midsummer's Eve

As the sun slowly sank in the west, Aileen made her way down the flowered path toward Stephen. The air was warm against her face. A dragonfly flitted past her and birds chirped nearby.

In a few moments, she would be reunited with Stephen.

For the past few days, they had spent little or no time in each other's company. It was as if everyone had conspired to keep them apart. There was the endless lists that Brigid prepared, plus all the baking, and cleaning. And Duncan saw to it Stephen was busy, too. Showing him all the repairs he had done to Urquhart and keeping him in the lists every morning also.

All they had time for was a few ardent kisses in the corridors and alcoves. Somehow, Nell had convinced her she should sleep in her chambers, and Duncan had agreed. She stifled a giggle remembering how Stephen had wanted to take a fist to his brother in objection.

Making her way around the bend in the path, she held up her gown. It was beautiful—lavender lined in silver on the edges of her sleeves and hem. One of the women wove a crown of flowers for her hair, reminding her of the first time she made love to Stephen on Beltaine.

Placing her hand over her abdomen, her heart soared for the life growing within.

When she turned the last corner, Aileen stopped. Her lips trembled at the sight before her. There on the shore stood the man she loved. *Stephen.* He was magnificent in a royal blue tunic and leather trews, and he'd cut his hair short.

She stood still.

His eyes blazed when they met hers, and their world stopped.

Stephen inhaled sharply at the vision coming forth. "My Goddess."

Cathal gently placed his hand on his shoulder. "Breathe, Stephen."

Duncan emerged and took her hand, escorting Aileen the rest of the way. She had opted to go barefoot and carefully made her way along the path. Everyone had gathered on the grassy knoll—some holding flowers and others waving brightly colored ribbons.

Guiding her along, they finally made their way to Stephen and Cathal. Duncan placed a kiss on her hand before giving it to his brother. He then took his place beside Brigid, gathering her close to his side.

Aileen eyes misted with unshed tears as Stephen's smile sparkled to the depths in his eyes transforming his face with joy.

Cathal stepped forward. "Greetings, Stephen and Aileen." He raised his hands outward. "Welcome to all who have come together in this joyous occasion."

"May I have your hand, Stephen?" As Stephen held out his hand, Cathal took the *sgian dubh* of Stephen's and made a small incision in the palm.

Turning to Aileen, he asked, "May I have your

hand, lady?" She nodded, holding it out for him. After Cathal made the cut, he joined it with Stephen's hand.

"As your blood runs together, let each bond with the other become one.

Cathal then wove a crimson cord around their hands, saying,

"By the element of air, bless this union."

"By the element of fire, bless this union."

"By the element of water, bless this union."

"By the element of the Mother, bless this union."

Stephen drew Aileen close. "My blood to your blood, my heart to your heart. I take your hand by my own free will, as my wife, my lover, and my friend."

Looking into his eyes, Aileen repeated the same. "My blood to your blood, my heart to your heart. I take your hand by my own free will, as my husband, my lover, and my friend."

Cathal placed his hand across theirs. "With the binding of your hands, so, too, I bind the bonds of your love on this day, and eternally more." Carefully he undid the cord and stepped back.

Stephen took her hand and held it against his heart. "Ye are the water that quenches my thirst, Aileen."

"And you are the river that nourishes my soul, Stephen."

His voice husky with emotion, he added, "I will love ye forever, *evermore*."

"Oh, Stephen, I will love you even when we pass through the gates of *Tir na Og*."

His lips descended onto hers kissing her so passionately she was lost in only the two of them. The sound of boisterous laughter and remarks brought them out of their kiss. Stephen crushed her to his chest, whispering all the lovely things he was going to do to her later. A shiver of delight ran through Aileen.

With the last rays of light ebbing away, they waited. Within moments, darkness enveloped them. Casting their sight up onto the knoll, the first bonfire was lit, illuminating the sky. A joyous cry came forth from the crowd.

"Are ye ready for the feasting, my love?" whispered Stephen into her ear.

Taking a finger, Aileen ran it across his lips. "Can we eat quickly? I'd much rather have *my feast* in our chambers."

Stephen took one of her fingers in his mouth, stroking it with his tongue. "Aye, most surely."

****

In the early hours of dawn, Aileen slipped from their bed. Grabbing one of Stephen's plaids, she walked over the window arch and stared out at the new day. Glancing back over her shoulder, Stephen was lying sprawled on his stomach, arms flung out.

A glorious sight to behold.

Their attempt at trying to flee early proved impossible, as Duncan would always seem to manage to place another cup of ale in Stephen's hand for a toast. Aileen lost count of the many toasts not only from Duncan, but from the others, too.

She could not fault Duncan. This was a celebration not only of their wedding, but also of Stephen's return. Saying a silent prayer, Aileen asked that one day soon all the brothers would be reunited.

Smiling, she also stared at the tapestry she demanded be removed from the great hall and put in their chambers. She was speechless when she saw it days ago, depicting all the brothers and their sister—the exact one that hung in her father's castle in the future. How did he come into possession of it? A question which would never be answered.

After explaining to Brigid about her first encounter with the tapestry, the woman gathered Duncan and a few other men to place it in their chambers, understanding completely.

"Come back to bed, *leannan*," muttered Stephen.

Turning away from the window, Aileen walked back to the bed only to stop suddenly. Lying on a desk tucked against the wall was a journal. The very journal her father had shown her *and* lost.

"Great Goddess," she whispered, hastily walking over to it. She brushed her fingers lightly over its leather covering. Knowing exactly what she was looking for, Aileen opened it and flipped it to the back pages. Sure enough, there was the drawing of her pendant with her name nearby.

"So ye have found my drawings," yawned Stephen. He was looking at her propped up on one elbow. Seeing the look of panic on her face, he sat up. "What's wrong?"

Holding the book against her chest, she stumbled back to the bed. Placing the book opened to the page where he had drawn her pendant, she said slowly, "My father found your journal in one of his digs. He knew I was destined to come back in time and gave it to me." Hysterical laughter bubbled forth as she watched Stephen's eyes go wide. "I lost the journal when I passed through the veil. The only item I kept on me was *your* medallion."

Stephen uttered a soft curse.

"Oh my gosh!" Finally realizing what this meant made her go numb. "*Stephen*, we have to return to Arbroath."

"Why?"

"Don't you see? If we don't return it to Arbroath, my father will never find it. And if he doesn't find the journal, how can I come back?"

"Blessed Danu." He shook his head in understanding. Placing a warm hand over her womb, he looked into her eyes. "We will make the journey as soon as our child is born."

She smacked at his hand. "No. I want to leave in a few days. I would rather go now than wait months later." She cupped his face in her hands. "I won't be able to rest until I know it's safe."

His hands fisted on either side of her and she understood his concern. "Our baby will be fine, Stephen. If she or he could survive passing through the veil, I believe a journey to Arbroath will not cause any harm."

Stephen kissed her hard. When he broke from the kiss, he nodded in agreement. "He is already a warrior."

"Or *she*," smirked Aileen.

Glancing back down at the journal, his voice was low as he spoke. "Do ye ken when I drew this? The first day I left Urquhart. I thought if I could draw ye it would help keep ye alive with me."

Aileen grasped his hand.

"After I drew the pendant, I could go no further. Capturing your spirit would not bring ye back."

"I will never leave you—*ever*," she stated firmly. Crawling onto his lap, Aileen wrapped her arms around him.

Stephen inhaled her scent, cradling her close. "*My leannan, my fae.*"

Tipping her face up, his lips devoured hers, sealing their love for all eternity.

A word from the author...

I am a constant daydreamer, and I have been told often to remove my head from the clouds. Yet this is where I find the magic to write my stories. Not only do I love to weave a good tale, but I have a voracious appetite for reading. I worked for Borders Books for almost fourteen years. Imagine my delight to be surrounded by so many books and getting paid to talk about them—Bliss!

I have traveled to England, Scotland, Ireland, and France. There are those who know me well when I say, "My heart is in the Highlands." I believe I have left it there, or perhaps in Ireland.

When I'm not writing, I enjoy playing in my garden—another place where magic grows. Of course, there is time spent with my family. They are the ones that keep me grounded.

http://www.marymorganauthor.com

Other titles by Mary Morgan
DRAGON KNIGHT'S SWORD
Book 1 of the Order of the Dragon Knights Series